English-Chinese
Illustrated Dictionary for Students

商務小學生
彩圖英漢詞典

商務印書館

English-Chinese Illustrated Dictionary for Students

商務小學生彩圖英漢詞典

編　　著：霍慶文

審　　訂：陳國華　　Wendy Fillipich

繪　　圖：劉向衞　　劉　倩　　劉燕紅等

責任編輯：傅　伊

出　　版：商務印書館（香港）有限公司
　　　　　香港筲箕灣耀興道 3 號東滙廣場 8 樓
　　　　　http://www.commercialpress.com.hk

發　　行：香港聯合書刊物流有限公司
　　　　　香港新界大埔汀麗路 36 號中華商務印刷大廈 3 字樓

印　　刷：中華商務彩色印刷有限公司
　　　　　香港新界大埔汀麗路 36 號中華商務印刷大廈

版　　次：2011 年 8 月第 5 次印刷
　　　　　© 商務印書館（香港）有限公司
　　　　　ISBN 13 - 978 962 07 0266 2
　　　　　ISBN 10 - 962 07 0266 2
　　　　　Printed in Hong Kong

Notes for parents and teachers　寫給家長和老師

　　興趣是啟動學習動機的最大原動力之一。如何喚起孩子學習英語的興趣，相信是家長在家庭輔導中常常碰到的難題，也是老師在教學上經常要面對的課題。本詞典即是從這樣的角度入手，以激發孩子學習英語的興趣為中心宗旨，設計編寫內容，書中塑造了 Henry、Peter、Paul、Alice、Helen 等五個可愛的卡通人物，以眾人之間的關係和發生的事貫穿整本詞典，使孩子查詞典就好像翻閱一本有趣的故事書，寓學於樂。

　　幫助孩子克服學習英語的難點，也是保持學習興趣的一個關鍵。學生學習英語的難點在於詞的用法，主要表現在語法、搭配、語用等幾方面。本詞典提供大量的語法知識和用法說明，以幫助解決正確使用英語以及得體使用英語的問題，如 deer，語法知識為 "複數 deer"，表示 deer 單複數相同；如 teacher，用法說明為："teacher 指教師職業，不能用於稱呼。"除了語法及用法說明之外，本詞典更提供典型地道的例句，便於小學生在語境中掌握用法，有助提高口語能力。如 here you are "給你"，例句為：Can I borrow your pen? Yes, here you are.

　　本詞典專為學習英語的小學生編寫，收錄單詞及短語 3,000 條，選詞包括小學生英語課本及課外讀物內的基本詞彙，也包括生活裏關於家庭、季節氣候、顏色形狀、交通工具、嗜好活動等常用詞彙。從課堂學習到生活應用，本詞典都照顧周到，而且詞目釋義準確可靠，每條都力求清晰，比如把 sister 解釋為："姐；妹"，而非 "姐妹"，因為 "姐妹" 指 "姐姐和妹妹"，只有 sister 作複數時才有 "姐妹" 之意。

　　好的插圖，可以充分表達單純文字不易表達清楚的地方，比如抽象的空間概念，圖像可以比較直觀地表達出來，像介詞 above、under，書中都用插圖表達得一清二楚。此外，一些生活中常見的物品，也設計成動物類、水果類、食物類等主題圖，家長可借此引導孩子進行聯想記憶，從而擴充詞彙。

　　詞典是孩子學習英語的必備工具，使用本詞典不但可以引起學英語的興趣，也可以達到擴大詞彙、提高英語水平的目的。我們期待本詞典幫助學生，在小學就打好英語根基，奠定學習更上一層樓的良好基礎。

商務印書館編輯部

Contents 目錄

Notes for parents and teachers 寫給家長和老師   iii

How to Use the Dictionary 詞典使用説明   vi

English Pronunciation Table 英語發音表   ix

Characters 卡通人物   xi

The Dictionary 詞典正文   1-264

Appendices 附錄   265-275

  1. Numbers 數字   266

  2. Time 時間   267

  3. Common English names 常見英語人名   268

  4. Irregular verbs 不規則動詞   270

  5. English alphabet and phonics 英語字母表及讀音法   274

How to Use the Dictionary　詞典使用説明

● 詞目

詞目按字母順序排列，可以
是基本詞、複合詞、派生詞
及同形異性詞。

● 音標

用國際音標（**IPA**）標注英美
兩種不同發音，以英美使用
頻率最高的發音為標準，英
美發音相同者則只標注一種
發音。

● 釋義

釋義即漢語對應詞或對應詞
加限制性説明。
限制性説明作為釋義的一部
分，目的在於使詞義更加清
晰明確。

ache¹ /eɪk/ [名詞] 疼痛 I have an ache in my
back. 我背痛。☞ 參見 **pain** "疼痛"。

ache² /eɪk/ [動詞] （持續地）痛，疼痛 I'm aching
all over. 我渾身疼痛。

alarm clock /əˈlɑːm klɒk; 美 əˈlɑːrm klɑːk/ [又作
alarm] [名詞] 鬧鐘 I've set the alarm clock for six.
我把鬧鐘撥到了6點。

carefully /ˈkeəfəli; 美 ˈker-/ [副詞] 小心地；仔細
地 Drive carefully. 開車要小心。◇ Please listen
carefully. 請仔細聽。

ballet /ˈbæleɪ; 美 bæˈleɪ/ [名詞] [無複數] 芭蕾舞 Alice
is learning ballet. 艾麗斯在學芭蕾舞。

asleep /əˈsliːp/ [形容詞] [不用於名詞前] 睡着的
Dad was asleep in his chair. 爸爸在椅子上睡着了。
☞ [反] **awake** 醒着的

borrow /ˈbɒrəʊ; 美 ˈbɔːroʊ/ [動詞] （向別人）借，借
用 Can I borrow your pen? I left mine at home. 我
可以借用一下你的鋼筆嗎？我把我的忘在家裏了。
☞ 參見 **lend** "借出，借給"。

lend
借給

Henry is lending a
pen to Paul. 亨利正
在把鋼筆借給保羅。

borrow
借用

Paul is borrowing a
pen from Henry. 保羅正
在向亨利借鋼筆。

Christmas /'krɪsməs/ [又作**Christmas Day**] [名詞]
聖誕節 *Christmas is on 25 December.* 聖誕節是在
12月25日。◇ *Happy Christmas!* 聖誕快樂！
◇ *Merry Christmas!* 聖誕快樂！

eat /iːt/ [動詞] [過去式**ate** /et; 美 eɪt/，過去分詞**eaten**
/'iːtn/] 吃 *Do you want something to eat?* 你想吃東
西嗎？◇ *I don't eat meat.* 我不吃肉。

favourite /'feɪvrət/ [形容詞] [只用於名詞前] 最喜
愛的 *What's your favourite subject?* 你最喜歡甚麼
科目？☞ 美國英語拼寫為 **favorite**。

excuse² /ɪk'skjuːz/ [動詞] 原諒 *Please excuse me
for being so late.* 請原諒我這麼晚才到。
excuse me [用於引起別人的注意、打斷別人談話等]
勞駕，對不起 *Excuse me, can you tell me the way
to the station?* 勞駕，請問去車站的路怎麼走？

care¹ /keə; 美 ker/ [名詞] 小心，謹慎，注意 *Cross
the road with care.* 過馬路時要小心。
take care 小心，注意；[分別時或信末用語] 保重
When you are crossing the road, take care! 你過
馬路時要小心！
take care of 照顧 *Take care of your brother while
I am away.* 我不在時要照顧你弟弟。

care² /keə; 美 ker/ [動詞] 關心，在乎 *I really don't
care if he comes or not.* 我真的不在乎他來還是不
來。
care for 看護，照顧 *Who cared for her while she
was ill?* 她生病時是誰照顧她的？

● 例 句
每個詞條或義項給出至少一
個例句，有的給出多個例
句，例句與例句之間用空心
菱形塊隔開。

● 語 法 信 息
本詞典提供了適當語法信
息，如詞性以及動詞、名
詞、形容詞的不規則變化形
式和用法，旨在提高學生準
確運用英語的能力。

● 語 用 信 息
本詞典提供了適當語用信
息，旨在培養學生得體使用
英語的能力。

● 短 語
短語置於關鍵詞詞條之中。

● 短 語 動 詞
短語動詞置於該動詞義項之
後，按字母順序排列。

● **語體**

用於正式英語或非正式英語的詞標出"正式"或"非正式"。

● **口語**

主要用於口語的詞或短語標出"口語"。

● **用法説明**

講解詞語之間的區別及用法，兼備英美用法及拼法之別。

● ☞

指用法説明、同義詞、反義詞及參見另一個相關的詞。

● **卡通插圖**

卡通插圖給予詞義充分的形象展示，便於理解和記憶。

dad /dæd/ [名詞] [非正式] 爸爸，爹爹 *Is that your dad?* 那是你爸爸嗎？◇ *Come on, dad!* 快點，爸！

afraid /əˈfreɪd/ [形容詞] [不用於名詞前] 害怕的 'Are you afraid of dogs?' 'No, I'm not.' "你怕狗嗎？" "不，我不怕。"

I'm afraid [口語] 恐怕 [用於表示歉意的禮貌説法] *I'm afraid I can't come on Sunday.* 恐怕我星期天不能來。

between /bɪˈtwiːn/ [介詞] 在…之間 'Where's Peter?' 'He's standing between Henry and Paul.' "彼得在哪裏？" "他正站在亨利和保羅中間。" ☞ **between** 表示兩者之間；**among** 表示三者或更多者之間。

cinema /ˈsɪnəmə/ [名詞] 電影院 *What's on at the cinema?* 電影院在上映甚麼影片？◇ *Let's go to the cinema tonight.* 咱們今晚去看電影吧。 ☞ 英國英語用 **cinema**，美國英語用 **movies**。

big /bɪɡ/ [形容詞] 大的 [比較級 **bigger**，最高級 **biggest**] *These shoes are too big for me.* 這雙鞋對我來説太大了。 ☞ ① [同] **large** 大的 ② [反] **small** 小的

English Pronunciation Table 英語發音表

Vowels 元音

IPA 國際音標	Example 示例	IPA 國際音標	Example 示例
iː	see /siː/	ʌ	cup /kʌp/
i	happy /ˈhæpi/	ɜː	bird /bɜːd; 美 bɜːrd/
ɪ	sit /sɪt/	ə	about /əˈbaʊt/
e	bed /bed/	eɪ	make /meɪk/
æ	cat /kæt/	əʊ	nose /nəʊz; 美 noʊz/
ɑː	car /kɑː; 美 kɑːr/	aɪ	bike /baɪk/
ɒ	dog /dɒg; 美 dɔːg/	ɔɪ	boy /bɔɪ/
ɔː	horse /hɔːs; 美 hɔːrs/	aʊ	house /haʊs/
ʊ	foot /fʊt/	ɪə	here /hɪə; 美 hɪr/
u	influence /ˈɪnfluəns/	eə	hair /heə; 美 her/
uː	too /tuː/	ʊə	pure /pjʊə; 美 pjʊr/

Consonants 輔音

IPA 國際音標	Example 示例	IPA 國際音標	Example 示例
p	pen /pen/	s	sister /ˈsɪstə; 美 -ər/
b	bad /bæd/	z	zoo /zuː/
t	tea /tiː/	ʃ	ship /ʃɪp/
d	day /deɪ/	ʒ	measure /ˈmeʒə; 美 -ər/
k	key /kiː/	h	hot /hɒt; 美 hɑːt/
g	glass /glɑːs; 美 glæs/	m	man /mæn/
tʃ	church /tʃɜːtʃ; 美 tʃɜːrtʃ/	n	nice /naɪs/
dʒ	jam /dʒæm/	ŋ	ring /rɪŋ/
f	face /feɪs/	l	light /laɪt/
v	very /ˈveri/	r	red /red/
θ	thing /θɪŋ/	j	yes /jes/
ð	this /ðɪs/	w	wet /wet/

說明：

1. /ˈ/ 表示主重音，如 about /əˈbaʊt/ 。

2. /ˌ/ 表示次重音，如 afternoon /ˌɑːftəˈnuːn; 美 ˌæftər-/ 。

3. 英式發音與美式發音不同者，美式發音前有 "美" 的標示語，如 sister / ˈsɪstə; 美 -ər / 。

4. 連字符 /-/ 表示不變的讀音部分。

5. /r/ 表示在英式發音中後接元音開頭的詞，如 far away：在美式發音中所有的 /r/ 音都應讀出。

6. /i/ 既可以讀成 /iː/ ，也可以讀成 /ɪ/ ，也可以讀成兩者之間的音，如 happy /ˈhæpi/ 。

7. /ɒ/ 是英式發音，美式發音用 /ɑː/ 或 /ɔː/ ，如 box/bɒks; 美 bɑːks/ ，dog /dɒg; 美 dɔːg/ 。

8. /ɪə eə ʊə/ 是英式發音，美式發音用 /ɪr er ʊr/ ，如 here /hɪə; 美 hɪr/ ，hair /heə; 美 her/ ，pure /pjʊə; 美 pjʊr/ 。

Characters 卡通人物

Peter
彼得

Henry
亨利

Alice
艾麗斯

Paul
保羅

Helen
海倫

Aa

A /eɪ/ [名詞] (學業成績的)甲，優 *She got an A in maths.* 她數學得了個優。

a / 強 eɪ; 弱 ə/ [不定冠詞] **1** 一（個） *There's a concert on Sunday night.* 星期日晚上有一場音樂會。**2** 每，每一 *Brush your teeth three times a day.* 每天要刷三次牙。**3** （一類事物中的）任何一個 *An owl has very big eyes.* 貓頭鷹的眼睛很大。☞ **a** 用於以輔音音素開始的詞前，**an** 用於以元音音素開始的詞前。

ability /ə'bɪləti/ [名詞] [複數**abilities**] 能力 *Henry has the ability to pass his examinations.* 亨利有能力及格。

able /'eɪbl/ [形容詞] **be able to** [用作情態動詞] 能，會 *Henry is able to ride a bicycle.* 亨利會騎自行車。☞ 表示"能，會"，也可以用 **can**。

about¹ /ə'baʊt/ [介詞] 關於 *I'm reading a book about space travel.* 我正在讀一本關於太空旅行的書。☞ [同] **on²** 關於

about² /ə'baʊt/ [副詞] 大約；差不多 *It's about three o'clock.* 現在大約 3 點鐘。

above /ə'bʌv/ [介詞] 在…上面 *The plane was flying above the clouds.* 飛機正在雲層上面飛。☞ [反] **below** 在…下面

abroad /ə'brɔːd/ [副詞] 到國外；在國外 *He wants to go abroad.* 他想出國。◇ *My brother is studying abroad.* 我哥哥正在國外學習。

absent /'æbsənt/ [形容詞] 不在的，缺席的 *Two students are absent from class today.* 今天兩名學生缺課。☞ [反] **present¹** 在場的，出席的

accept /ək'sept/ [動詞] 接受 *I accept your invitation.* 我接受你的邀請。

accident /'æksɪdənt/ [名詞] 事故，意外 *Henry has had an accident — he has been hit by a car.* 亨利出事了，他被車撞了。

ache¹ /eɪk/ [名詞] 疼痛 *I have an ache in my back.* 我背痛。☞ 參見 **pain** "疼痛"。

ache² /eɪk/ [動詞] (持續地) 痛，疼痛 *I'm aching all over.* 我渾身疼痛。

across /əˈkrɒs; 美 əˈkrɔːs/ [介詞] 橫過，穿過 *Peter walked across the road.* 彼得步行穿過馬路。

act /ækt/ [動詞] **1** 行動 *Think carefully before you act.* 你行動前必須仔細想一想。 **2** 表演，演戲 *He acts very well.* 他很會演戲。

activity /ækˈtɪvəti/ [名詞] [複數 **activities**] 活動 *Swimming is my favourite activity.* 游泳是我最喜愛的活動。

actor /ˈæktə; 美 -ər/ [名詞] 演員 *He's a successful film actor.* 他是一位成功的電影演員。☞ **actor** 多指男演員。

actress /ˈæktrəs/ [名詞] [複數 **actresses**] (女) 演員 *She's a famous actress.* 她是一位著名演員。

add /æd/ [動詞] **1** 加，添加 *Do you want to add your name to the list?* 你想在名單上加上你的名字嗎? **2** 把…加起來 *If you add 2 and 3, you get 5.* 2 加 3 等於 5。

address /əˈdres; 美 ˈædres/ [名詞] [複數 **addresses**] 地址 *What's your address?* 你的地址是甚麼?

admire /ədˈmaɪə; 美 -ˈmaɪr/ [動詞] 欽佩，讚賞，羨慕 *We admire your courage.* 我們欽佩你的勇氣。

admit /ədˈmɪt/ [動詞] [現在分詞 **admitting**, 過去式和過去分詞 **admitted**] 承認 *You should admit your mistake.* 你應該承認錯誤。

adopt /ə'dɒpt; 美 ə'dɑːpt / [動詞] 收養 *They're hoping to adopt a child.* 他們希望收養一個孩子。

adult /'ædʌlt; 美 ə'dʌlt / [名詞] 成人 *The tickets are £3 for adults and £1.5 for children.* 成人票價是3英鎊，兒童票價是1.5英鎊。

adventure /əd'ventʃə; 美 -ər / [名詞] 冒險活動(經歷) *Our teacher told us about her adventures in Africa.* 老師給我們講述了她在非洲的冒險經歷。

aeroplane /'eərəpleɪn; 美 'er- / [又作 **plane**] [名詞] 飛機 *We watched the aeroplane take off.* 我們看着飛機起飛。☞ 英國英語用 **aeroplane**，美國英語用 **airplane**。

afford /ə'fɔːd; 美 ə'fɔːrd / [動詞] [通常與 **can**，**could** 或 **be able to** 連用] 買得起 *We can't afford a new car.* 我們買不起新車。

afraid /ə'freɪd / [形容詞] [不用於名詞前]害怕的 *'Are you afraid of dogs?' 'No, I'm not.'* "你怕狗嗎？" "不，我不怕。"

I'm afraid [口語] 恐怕 [用於表示歉意的禮貌説法] *I'm afraid I can't come on Sunday.* 恐怕我星期天不能來。

Africa /'æfrɪkə / [名詞] 非洲 *There are more than 50 countries in Africa.* 非洲有50多個國家。

African¹ /'æfrɪkən / [形容詞] 非洲(人)的 *There were several African students in the class.* 班裏有幾個非洲學生。

African² /'æfrɪkən / [名詞] 非洲人 *There were three Africans in the team.* 隊裏有3個非洲人。

after¹ /'ɑːftə; 美 'æftər / [介詞] 在⋯以後 *We went for a walk after supper.* 晚飯後，我們去散步。☞ [反] **before¹** 在⋯以前

after² /'ɑːftə; 美 'æftər / [連詞] 在⋯以後 *After we had lunch, we all went into the garden.* 吃過午飯後，我們都進了花園。☞ [反] **before²** 在⋯以前

afternoon /ˌɑːftə'nuːn; 美 ˌæftər- / [名詞] 下午 *I'll see you tomorrow afternoon.* 我們明天下午見。
good afternoon 下午好 *'Good afternoon, Mr Brown.' 'Afternoon, Henry.'* "下午好，布朗先生。" "下午好，亨利。" ☞ 在非正式場合説 "下午好"，也可以只用 **Afternoon**。

again /ə'gen / [副詞] 再 *Can you say that again? I didn't hear you.* 你能再説一遍嗎？我沒聽見你説的話。

against /ə'genst / [介詞] **1** 反對 *Are you for or against the plan?* 你是贊成還是反對這個計劃？ **2** 倚着，靠着 *Henry leaned his bicycle against the*

A

wall. 亨利把自行車倚在牆上。

age /eɪdʒ/ [名詞] 年齡，年歲，年紀 *He's six years of age.* 他6歲。◇ *What age is he?* 他多大年紀？

ago /ə'gəʊ; 美 ə'goʊ/ [副詞] 以前 *He died two years ago.* 他兩年前去世了。

agree /ə'griː/ [動詞] 同意 *I thought it was a good idea, but she didn't agree.* 我覺得這是個好主意，可她不同意。

ahead /ə'hed/ [副詞] 在前面，往前面 *Paul ran ahead.* 保羅跑在前面。◇ *Look straight ahead and don't turn around!* 一直往前看，別轉身！

air /eə; 美 er/ [名詞][無複數] 空氣 *Open the window — I need some fresh air.* 打開窗戶，我需要呼吸新鮮空氣。

aircraft /'eəkrɑːft; 美 'erkræft/ [名詞][複數**aircraft**] 飛行器 *Jets, planes and helicopters are all aircraft.* 噴氣式飛機、飛機和直升機都是飛行器。

aircraft 飛行器

plane 飛機

jet 噴氣式飛機

helicopter 直升機

airplane /'eəpleɪn; 美 'er-/ [名詞] [美國英語] = **aeroplane**

airport /'eəpɔːt; 美 'erpɔːrt/ [名詞] 機場 *Is the airport far from the town centre?* 機場離市中心遠嗎？

alarm clock /ə'lɑːm klɒk; 美 ə'lɑːrm klɑːk/ [又作 **alarm**] [名詞] 鬧鐘 *I've set the alarm clock for six.* 我把鬧鐘撥到了6點。

album /'ælbəm/ [名詞] 粘貼簿（指相冊、集郵簿等）*Alice has two photo albums.* 艾麗斯有兩本相冊。

alike /ə'laɪk/ [形容詞] [不用於名詞前] 相同的，相似的 *John and Jim are very alike.* 約翰和吉姆很相像。

alive /ə'laɪv/ [形容詞] [不用於名詞

前] 活着的 *Is your grandfather still alive?* 你祖父還活着嗎？

all /ɔːl/ [形容詞] 全部的，所有的 *All horses are animals, but not all animals are horses.* 所有的馬都是動物，但並非所有的動物都是馬。

allow /əˈlaʊ/ [動詞] 允許，准許 *No ball playing is allowed here.* 這裏不準玩球。◇ *She only allows the children to watch television at the weekends.* 她只允許孩子們週末看電視。

all right[1] /ɔːl ˈraɪt/ [形容詞] **1** 令人滿意的，可以的 *Is the coffee all right?* 咖啡好喝嗎？ **2** 安全的，健康的 *Do you feel all right?* 你覺得還好吧？

all right[2] /ɔːl ˈraɪt/ [感歎詞] 好，行 *'Shall we go to town?' 'All right. Let's go now.'* "我們去城裏好嗎？""好，咱們現在走吧。"

almost /ˈɔːlməʊst; 美 -moʊst/ [副詞] 幾乎，差不多 *There's almost nothing left.* 幾乎甚麼東西也沒剩下。◇ *It's almost nine o'clock.* 差不多9點了。

alone[1] /əˈləʊn; 美 əˈloʊn/ [形容詞] [不用於名詞前] 單獨的；獨自的 *Are you alone? Can I speak to you for a moment?* 你獨自一個人嗎？我能同你說一下話嗎？

alone[2] /əˈləʊn; 美 əˈloʊn/ [副詞] 單獨地；獨自地 *I don't like going out alone at night.* 我不喜歡晚上獨自外出。

along[1] /əˈlɒŋ; 美 əˈlɔːŋ/ [副詞] 一起 *Can I come along?* 我可以一起來嗎？

along[2] /əˈlɒŋ; 美 əˈlɔːŋ/ [介詞] 沿着，順着 *They walked along the road.* 他們沿着馬路散步。

aloud /əˈlaʊd/ [副詞] 出聲地，大聲地 *Alice is reading a poem aloud.* 艾麗斯正在朗讀一首詩。

alphabet /ˈælfəbet/ [名詞] 字母表 *There are 26 letters in the English alphabet.* 英語字母表中有26個字母。

already /ɔːlˈredi/ [副詞] 已經 *'Would you like some lunch?' 'No, I've already eaten, thanks.'* "你吃點午飯好嗎？""不用了，我已經吃過了，謝謝。"

also /ˈɔːlsəʊ; 美 ˈɔːlsoʊ/ [副詞] 也，還 *I enjoy football, and I also like tennis.* 我喜歡足球，也喜歡網球。☞ 參見 **too** "也"。

altogether /ˌɔːltəˈɡeðə; 美 -ər/ [副詞] 總共 *There were twenty people there altogether.* 那裏總共有20人。

always /ˈɔːlweɪz/ [副詞] **1** 總是 *I always get up at 6:30.* 我總是在6:30起牀。 **2** 永遠 *You'll always be my friend.* 你將永遠是我的朋友。

am /強 æm; 弱 əm/ *'How old are you?' 'I am six.'* "你幾歲？""我6歲。"☞ 參見 **be**[1]。

amazing /əˈmeɪzɪŋ/ [形容詞] 令人驚奇的 *Henry told me an amazing* *story.* 亨利給我講了一個令人驚奇的故事。

ambulance /'æmbjələns/ [名詞]
救護車 *I asked a neighbour to call an ambulance.* 我請鄰居叫了一輛救護車。

America /ə'merɪkə/ [名詞] **1** 美國
Have you been to America? 你去過美國嗎？ ☞ 參見 **the United States (of America)** "美利堅合眾國，美國"。

2 美洲 *Who discovered America?* 誰發現了美洲？

American¹ /ə'merɪkən/ [形容詞]
1 美國(人)的 *Henry enjoyed watching American films.* 亨利喜歡看美國電影。**2** 美洲(人)的 *Canada is a North American country.* 加拿大是一個北美洲國家。

American² /ə'merɪkən/ [名詞] **1** 美國人 *The prize was won by two Americans.* 這個獎被兩個美國人獲得

了。**2** 美洲人 *Canadians are North Americans.* 加拿大人是北美洲人。

among /ə'mʌŋ/ [介詞] 在…中間
`Where's Peter?' `He's standing among his friends.' "彼得在哪裏？"
"他正站在朋友們中間。" ☞ **among** 表示三者或更多者之間；**between** 表示兩者之間。

amount /ə'maʊnt/ [名詞] 量，數量
There is only a small amount of food left. 只剩下少量的食物。

an / 強 æn; 弱 ən/ [不定冠詞] ☞ 參見 **a**。

anchor /'æŋkə; 美 -ər/ [名詞] 錨 *In the morning they raised the anchor and sailed on.* 清晨他們起錨繼續航行。

and / 強 ænd; 弱 ənd; ən/ [連詞] **1** 和，及，並 *Henry and I are good friends.* 我和亨利是好朋友。**2** [用來連接數詞] 加 *Six and four is ten.* 6加4等於10。

angry /'æŋgri/ [形容詞] [比較級

A

angrier，最高級 **angriest**] 生氣的 *My parents will be angry if I get home late.* 如果我回家晚了，我父母會生氣的。

animal /ˈænɪml/ [名詞] 動物 *Horses,*

fish, birds and insects are all animals. 馬、魚、鳥和昆蟲都是動物。

ankle /ˈæŋkl/ [名詞] 腳踝 *Peter twisted his ankle when he was*

animals 動物

ant 螞蟻

bee 蜜蜂

beetle 甲蟲

bird 鳥

butterfly 蝴蝶

caterpillar 毛蟲

chickens 雞

chimpanzee 黑猩猩

crab 螃蟹

crocodile 鱷魚

deer 鹿

dolphin 海豚

duck 鴨

elephant 大象

fish 魚

frog 青蛙

giraffe 長頸鹿

kangaroo 袋鼠

fly 蒼蠅

goose 鵝

A

horse
馬

lion
獅子

lizard
蜥蜴

monkey
猴子

mosquito
蚊子

moth
蛾

octopus
章魚

owl
貓頭鷹

rhinoceros
犀牛

seagull
海鷗

shark
鯊魚

snail
蝸牛

snake
蛇

spider
蜘蛛

squirrel
松鼠

swan
天鵝

tiger
老虎

tortoise
烏龜

turkey
火雞

wasp
黃蜂

whale
鯨魚

wolf
狼

zebra
斑馬

running. 彼得跑步時扭傷了腳踝。

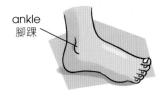

ankle
腳踝

annoy /əˈnɔɪ/ [動詞] 使生氣 *Henry was really annoying me.* 亨利真的使我很生氣。

another /əˈnʌðə; 美 -ər/ [形容詞] 又一個的，再一個的 *'Would you like another drink?' 'No, thanks.'* "再喝杯飲料好嗎？" "不，謝謝。"

answer¹ /ˈɑːnsə; 美 ˈænsər/ [動詞] 回答 *I've asked you a question, now please answer me.* 我問了你一個問題，現在請回答我。

answer² /ˈɑːnsə; 美 ˈænsər/ [名詞] 答案 *Do you know the answer?* 你知道答案嗎？

ant /ænt/ [名詞] 螞蟻 *An ant is an insect.* 螞蟻是昆蟲。

any /ˈeni/ [形容詞] **1** [通常用於疑問句或否定句] 一些 *Is there any coffee?* 有咖啡嗎？◇ *He doesn't have any money.* 他沒有錢。**2** 任何一個的 *Take any book you like.* 你喜歡哪本書就拿哪本吧。☞ 參見 **some¹** "一些"。

anybody /ˈenibɒdi; 美 -bɑːdi/ [代詞] = **anyone**

anyone /ˈeniwʌn/ [又作 **anybody**] [代詞] **1** [通常用於疑問句或否定句] 任何人，有人 *Is there anyone at home?* 家裏有人嗎？◇ *I don't want to see anyone right now.* 我現在不想見人。**2** [用於肯定句] 任何人 *Anyone can learn to swim.* 任何人都能學會游泳。

anything /ˈeniθɪŋ/ [代詞] **1** [通常用於疑問句或否定句] 任何東西，一些（事物）*Can you see anything?* 你能看見甚麼嗎？◇ *There isn't anything in that box.* 那個盒子裏沒有任何東西。**2** [用於肯定句] 無論甚麼東西，隨便甚麼事情 *I'm so hungry—I'll eat anything.* 我很餓，吃甚麼都可以。

anywhere /ˈeniweə; 美 -wer/ [副詞] **1** [通常用於疑問句或否定句] 任何地方，甚麼地方 *'Where did you go?' 'I didn't go anywhere.'* "你去哪裏啦？" "我哪裏也沒去。"**2** 任何地方，無論何處 *You can sit anywhere you like.* 你喜歡坐哪裏，就可以坐哪裏。

apart /əˈpɑːt; 美 -ɑːrt/ [副詞] 分開，相距 *Stand with your feet apart.* 兩腳分開站立。

take sth apart 把某物拆開 *Henry is taking his bicycle apart.* 亨利在拆自行車。

apartment /əˈpɑːtmənt; 美 -ɑːr-/ [名詞] [美國英語] = **flat²**

ape /eɪp/ [名詞] 猿 *Chimpanzees and gorillas are apes.* 黑猩猩和大猩猩都屬於猿類。

gorilla
大猩猩

chimpanzee
黑猩猩

apologize /əˈpɒlədʒaɪz; 美 əˈpɑ-/ [動詞] 道歉 *Peter apologized for breaking the chair.* 彼得為弄壞椅子而道歉。

appear /əˈpɪə; 美 əˈpɪr/ [動詞] 出現 *He suddenly appeared from round the corner.* 他突然從拐角附近冒了出來。 ☞ [反] **disappear** 不見，失蹤；消失

apple /ˈæpl/ [名詞] 蘋果 *An apple a day keeps the doctor away.* 每天吃一個蘋果，醫生遠離我。

apricot /ˈeɪprɪkɒt; 美 -kɑːt/ [名詞] 杏 *Do you like apricot juice?* 你喜歡喝杏汁嗎？

April /ˈeɪprəl/ [名詞] 四月 *Her birthday is in April.* 她的生日是在4月。 ☞ ① 參見 **August** 的示例。② **Apr** 是 **April** 的縮寫。

apron /ˈeɪprən/ [名詞] 圍裙 *He always wears an apron when he's cooking.* 他做飯時總是繫着圍裙。

aquarium /əˈkweəriəm; 美 əˈkwer-/ [名詞] [複數 **aquariums** 或 **aquaria** /əˈkweəriə; 美 əˈkwer-/] 水族箱，養魚缸 *Dad keeps some fish in an aquarium.* 爸爸在養魚缸裏養了幾條魚。

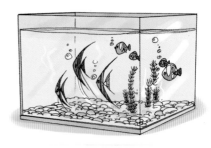

are / 強 ɑː; 美 ɑːr; 弱 ə; 美 ər/ *Why are you late?* 你為甚麼遲到？ ☞ 參見 **be¹**。

area /ˈeəriə; 美 ˈer-/ [名詞] 地區 *Do you live in this area?* 你住在這一地區嗎？

aren't /ɑːnt; 美 ɑːrnt/ **are not** 的縮

寫 *These strawberries aren't ripe yet.* 這些草莓還沒熟。

argue /'ɑːgjuː; 美 'ɑːr-/ [動詞] 爭論，爭辯 *Don't argue with your mother.* 不要跟你母親爭論。

arm /ɑːm; 美 ɑːrm/ [名詞] 手臂，胳膊 *Henry fell and broke his arm.* 亨利跌了一跤，摔斷了胳膊。

armchair /'ɑːmtʃeə; 美 'ɑːrmtʃer/ [名詞] 扶手椅，單人沙發 *Dad is sitting in an armchair.* 爸爸正坐在單人沙發上。

army /'ɑːmi; 美 'ɑːr-/ [名詞] [複數 **armies**] 軍隊 *My brother joined the army last year.* 我哥哥去年參軍了。

around /ə'raʊnd/ [介詞] **1** 在…周圍；環繞 *There was a fence around the house.* 房子周圍圍着一道籬笆。◇ *The earth moves around the sun.* 地球繞着太陽轉。

2 在…附近 *Is there a bank around here?* 這附近有銀行嗎？

arrange /ə'reɪndʒ/ [動詞] **1** 安排，準備 *Mum is arranging a party for Peter's birthday.* 媽媽正在為彼得的生日準備一個聚會。**2** 整理，排列 *The books are arranged in alphabetical order.* 這些書是按字母順序排列的。

arrive /ə'raɪv/ [動詞] 到達 *The bus has just arrived.* 公共汽車剛到。◇ *We've just arrived at the park.* 我們剛到公園。☞ [同] **get，reach** 到達

arrow /'ærəʊ; 美 -oʊ/ [名詞] **1** 箭 *Henry is learning to shoot an arrow.* 亨利正在學射箭。**2**（指示方向的）箭頭 *Let's follow the arrows.* 我們跟着箭頭走吧。

arrow 箭   arrow 箭頭

art /ɑːt; 美 ɑːrt/ [名詞] [無複數] 藝術；美術 *Helen is good at art.* 海倫擅長美術。

artist /'ɑːtɪst; 美 -əst/ [名詞] 藝術家；美術家（尤指畫家） *Helen wants to be an artist when she grows up.* 海倫長大後想當畫家。

as / 強 æz; 弱 əz / [連詞] **1** 正當…的時候 *The phone rang just as I was leaving the house.* 就在我要離開家的時候，電話響了。**2 as...as** [表示比較] 和…一樣 *He's as tall as his father.* 他現在和他父親一樣高。

Asia /ˈeɪʒə/ [名詞] 亞洲 *Asia is the largest continent in the world.* 亞洲是世界上最大的洲。

Asian¹ /ˈeɪʒən/ [形容詞] 亞洲（人）的 *China is an Asian country.* 中國是一個亞洲國家。

Asian² /ˈeɪʒən/ [名詞] 亞洲人 *Two Asians were killed in the plane crash.* 兩名亞洲人在飛機失事中遇難。

ask /ɑːsk; 美 æsk / [動詞] **1** 問 *Can I ask a question?* 我能問個問題嗎？ **2** 要求，請求 *He asked me to go to the cinema with him.* 他請我同他一起去看電影。

asleep /əˈsliːp/ [形容詞] [不用於名詞前] 睡着的 *Dad was asleep in his chair.* 爸爸在椅子上睡着了。☞ [反] **awake** 醒着的

assembly /əˈsembli/ [名詞] [複數 **assemblies**]（學校師生的）集會 *Assembly begins at 9: 30.* 集會9:30開始。

astonish /əˈstɒnɪʃ; 美 əˈstɑː-/ [動詞] 使驚訝 *His words astonished me.* 他的話使我感到驚訝。

astronaut /ˈæstrənɔːt/ [名詞] 宇航員，太空人 *Peter wants to become an astronaut.* 彼得想成為一名宇航員。

at / 強 æt; 弱 ət / [介詞] **1** [表示地點] 在 *I left my bag at the station.* 我把包忘在車站了。**2** [表示時間] 在 *OK, I'll see you at 6.* 好，我們6點見。**3** [表示方向] 對着，朝着 *Don't shout at me!* 別對着我大喊大叫！ **4** [表示某人在某方面的能力] 在…方面 *I'm good at maths.* 我擅長數學。

ate /et; 美 eɪt/ **eat** 的過去式 *Yesterday we ate at the restaurant.* 昨天我們在餐館吃的飯。

attach /əˈtætʃ/ [動詞] 繫；貼；連接 *I attached a label to each suitcase.* 我把每個衣箱都繫上了標籤。

attack /əˈtæk/ [動詞] 攻擊，襲擊 *The enemy attacked the town.* 敵人襲擊了那個城鎮。

attention /əˈtenʃn/ [名詞] [無複數] 注意，專心 *Can I have your attention* please, class? 同學們，請注意聽我講好嗎？◇ *You must pay attention to the teacher.* 你必須專心聽老師講課。

attract /ə'trækt/ [動詞] 吸引 *The castle attracts many visitors each year.* 這座城堡每年都吸引着許多遊客。

audience /'ɔːdiəns/ [名詞] 觀眾；聽眾 *The audience stood up and cheered at the end of the performance.* 觀眾們在演出結束時站起來歡呼。

August /'ɔːgəst/ [名詞] 八月 *She was born in August.* 她是8月出生的。◇ [英國英語] *She was born on the eighth of August/August the eighth.* 她是8月8日出生的。◇ [美國英語] *She was born on August eighth.* 她是8月8日出生的。◇ *We went to France last August.* 去年8月我們去了法國。 ☞ **Aug** 是 **August** 的縮寫。

aunt /ɑːnt; 美 ænt/ [名詞] 姑母；姨母；嬸母；伯母；舅母 *Henry has two aunts.* 亨利有兩個姑姑。

Australia /ɒ'streɪliə; 美 ɔː-/ [名詞] 澳大利亞 *He lives in Australia.* 他居住在澳大利亞。

Australian[1] /ɒ'streɪliən; 美 ɔː-/ [形容詞] 澳大利亞（人）的 *Australian people like to travel a lot.* 澳大利亞人非常喜歡旅遊。

Australian[2] /ɒ'streɪliən; 美 ɔː-/ [名詞] 澳大利亞人 *He is an Australian.* 他是澳大利亞人。

autumn /'ɔːtəm/ [名詞] 秋天，秋季 *Autumn comes between summer and winter.* 秋天在夏天和冬天之間。

awake /ə'weɪk/ [形容詞] [不用於名詞前] 醒着的 *Peter is still awake.* 彼得還醒着呢。 ☞ [反] **asleep** 睡着的

away /ə'weɪ/ [副詞] **1** （離）開 *Go away! I'm busy!* 走開！我忙着呢！◇ *He turned round and walked away.* 他轉身走開了。**2** [用於名詞後] 離…多遠 *The lake is two miles away.* 湖離這兒有兩英里遠。

awful /'ɔːfl/ [形容詞] 糟糕的 *The weather is awful today.* 今天天氣很糟糕。

awkward /'ɔːkwəd; 美 -wərd/ [形容詞] **1** 難處理的 *That's an awkward question.* 這是一個很難回答的問題。**2** 笨拙的，不熟練的 *He's very awkward—he keeps dropping* things. 他真笨，老是掉東西。　　　　棵樹。

axe /æks/ [名詞] 斧頭 *He cut down a tree with an axe.* 他用斧頭砍倒一

A

B b

baby /'beɪbi/ [名詞] [複數**babies**] 嬰兒，寶寶 *The baby is playing with toys.* 寶寶正在玩玩具。

back¹ /bæk/ [名詞] **1** 背(部) *Helen says that her back aches.* 海倫說她的背痛。**2** 後面 *Henry is sitting at the back of the bus.* 亨利坐在公共汽車的後面。☞ [反] **front** 前面

back² /bæk/ [副詞] **1** 回原處 *Go back to sleep.* 回去睡覺。◇ *Please give me my ball back.* 請把球還給我。**2** 往後 *Stand back!* 往後站！

backwards /'bækwədz; 美 -wərdz/ [又作**backward**] [副詞] **1** 向後 *He fell over backwards.* 他向後跌了一跤。☞ [反] **forwards** 向前 **2** 倒，逆 *Can you say the alphabet backwards?* 你能倒着背字母表嗎？

bad /bæd/ [形容詞] [比較級 **worse** /wɜːs; 美 wɜːrs/，最高級 **worst** /wɜːst; 美 wɜːrst/] **1** 壞的，不好的 *This drawing is bad.* 這幅畫畫得不好。☞ [反] **good** 好的 **2** (指能力)差的 *He's bad at sport.* 他運動能力差。**3** (指食物)腐爛的，腐壞的 *The milk has gone bad.* 牛奶已經壞了。

badly /'bædli/ [副詞] **1** 差 *She sang very badly.* 她唱得很差。**2** 很，非常；嚴重地 *They badly needed help.* 他們非常需要幫助。◇ *He was badly hurt in the accident.* 他在那次事故中傷得很重。

badminton /'bædmɪntən/ [名詞] [無複數] 羽毛球(運動) *They often play badminton after school.* 他們經常在放學後打羽毛球。

racket 球拍

shuttlecock 羽毛球

bag /bæg/ [名詞] 包，袋 *She brought some sandwiches in a plastic bag.* 她用塑料袋帶來一些三明治。

B

bake /beɪk/ [動詞] 烤 *Mum baked a cake.* 媽媽烤了蛋糕。

balance /'bæləns/ [動詞] (使)保持平衡 *The dog balanced a ball on its nose.* 狗用鼻子頂着球，使其保持平衡。

balcony /'bælkəni/ [名詞] [複數 **balconies**] 陽台 *Our flat has a large balcony.* 我們住的公寓有一個大陽台。

bald /bɔːld/ [形容詞] (指人)禿頭的 *Grandpa is going bald.* 爺爺快禿頂了。

ball /bɔːl/ [名詞] 球 *Throw me the ball.* 把球扔給我。

balls 球

basketball 籃球
tennis ball 網球
ping-pong ball 乒乓球
rugby ball 橄欖球
volleyball 排球
football 足球

ballet /'bæleɪ; 美 bæ'leɪ/ [名詞] [無複數] 芭蕾舞 *Alice is learning ballet.* 艾麗斯在學芭蕾舞。

balloon /bə'luːn/ [名詞] 氣球 *Could you help me to blow up some balloons?* 你能幫我吹幾個氣球嗎？

bamboo /ˌbæm'buː/ [名詞] [無複數] 竹子 *This chair is made of bamboo.* 這把椅子是用竹子做成的。

banana /bə'nɑːnə; 美 -'næ-/ [名詞] 香蕉 Mum bought some bananas at the market. 媽媽在市場上買了一些香蕉。

band /bænd/ [名詞] 1 樂隊 She's a singer with a band. 她是樂隊的歌手。 2 箍；帶子 Alice is wearing a hair band. 艾麗斯頭上戴着一個髮箍。

bandage¹ /'bændɪdʒ/ [名詞] 繃帶 The doctor wrapped a bandage round his arm. 醫生用繃帶把他的手臂包紮起來。

bandage² /'bændɪdʒ/ [動詞] 用繃帶包紮 The doctor bandaged his arm. 醫生用繃帶把他的手臂包紮起來。

bang¹ /bæŋ/ [動詞] 砰的一聲關上 Don't bang the door. 不要把門砰的一聲關上。

bang² /bæŋ/ [名詞] 砰的一聲 The door shut with a bang. 門砰的一聲關上了。

bank /bæŋk/ [名詞] 1 銀行 Is there a bank near here? 這兒附近有銀行嗎？ 2 河岸 He jumped in and swam to the opposite bank. 他跳進水裏，游向河對岸。

bar /bɑː; 美 bɑːr/ [名詞] 棒，條，塊 Some of the houses have iron bars on the windows. 有些人家的窗户上有鐵條。

barbecue /'bɑːbɪkjuː; 美 'bɑːr-/ [名詞] (户外)燒烤 We had a barbecue on the beach. 我們在海灘上燒烤。

bare /beə; 美 ber/ [形容詞] 1 (指身體的某部位)赤裸的 Henry ran out into the street in bare feet. 亨利赤腳跑到大街上。 2 空的 It was a bare room with no furniture. 那是一個空房間，一件傢

具也沒有。

bare feet
赤腳

bark /baːk; 美 baːrk / [動詞] (狗)吠，
叫 *The dog always barks at strangers.*
那條狗總是對着陌生人叫。

barn /baːn; 美 baːrn / [名詞] 穀倉；
牲口棚 *The farmer keeps his cows in
the barn.* 那個農民在牲口棚裏養奶牛。

barn
牲口棚

barn
穀倉

barrel /'bærəl/ [名詞] 桶 *This barrel
is made of wood.* 這隻桶是木製的。

baseball /'beɪsbɔːl/ [名詞] [無複數]
棒球(運動) *Who's your favourite
baseball player?* 你最喜愛的棒球運動
員是誰？

basin /'beɪsn/ [名詞] 盆；水盆；洗
臉盆 *Pour the hot water into a basin.*
把熱水倒進盆裏。

basket /'baːskɪt; 美 'bæskət / [名詞]
籃子 *This basket is full of apples.* 這隻
籃子裏裝滿了蘋果。

basketball /'baːskɪtbɔːl; 美
'bæskətbɔːl/ [名詞] 1 [無複數] 籃球(運

動) *Do you like playing basketball?* 你喜歡打籃球嗎？**2** 籃球 *A basketball is larger than a football.* 籃球比足球大。

bat /bæt/ [名詞] **1** 球棒 *Henry has a baseball bat.* 亨利有一個棒球球棒。**2** 蝙蝠 *A bat flies at night.* 蝙蝠在夜裏飛行。

bat
球棒

bat
蝙蝠

bath /bɑːθ; 美 bæθ/ [名詞] **1** 浴缸 *We have a green bath.* 我們有一個綠色的浴缸。**2** 洗澡，沐浴 *I have a bath every day.* 我每天都洗澡。☞ 英國英語通常用 **have a bath**，美國英語通常用 **take a bath**。

bath
浴缸

bathroom /ˈbɑːθruːm; 美 ˈbæθ-/ [名詞] 浴室，盥洗室，洗手間 *Can you tell me where the bathroom is?* 你能告訴我浴室在哪裏嗎？

battery /ˈbætri/ [名詞] [複數 **batteries**] 電池 *I need new batteries for my radio.* 我的收音機該換新電池了。

be¹ /強 biː; 弱 bi/ [動詞] [現在分詞 **being** /ˈbiːɪŋ/，過去分詞 **been** /biːn; 美 bɪn/] **1** 是 *What's that?* 那是甚麼？◇ *I'm Helen.* 我是海倫。**2** [表示時間、年齡、日期、價值等] *It's 9 o'clock.* 現在9點鐘。◇ `How old are you?' `I'm 8.' "你幾歲啦？""我8歲。"**3 there is/are** [表示存在] 有 *There isn't any milk in the fridge.* 冰箱裏沒有牛奶。◇ *There are a lot of trees in our garden.* 我們的花園裏有許多樹。☞ **be** 的兩種時態及其單複數見下表：

時態	人稱	單數	複數
現在式	第一人稱	I am (I'm)	We are (We're)
	第二人稱	You are (You're)	You are (You're)
	第三人稱	He/She/It is (He's/She's/It's)	They are (They're)
過去式	第一人稱	I was	We were
	第二人稱	You were	You were
	第三人稱	He/She/It was	They were

be² /強 biː; 弱 bi/ [助動詞] **1** [用以構成動詞的進行時] `What are you doing?' `I'm painting a picture.' "你在做甚麼？""我在畫畫。"**2** [用以構成被動語態] *The thief was caught.* 小偷被抓住了。

beach /biːtʃ/ [名詞] [複數 **beaches**] 海灘 *The children were playing on the beach.* 孩子們正在海灘上玩。

bead /biːd/ [名詞] (有孔的)珠子 *She wore a string of beads round her neck.* 她脖子上戴着一串珠子。

beak /biːk/ [名詞] 鳥嘴，喙 *A bird has a hard beak.* 鳥有一張堅硬的嘴。

bean /biːn/ [名詞] 豆子；豆莢 *Mum is cooking green beans.* 媽媽在炒青豆莢。

bear /beə; 美 ber/ [名詞] 熊 *Some bears catch fish to eat.* 有些熊捕魚吃。

beard /bɪəd; 美 bɪrd/ [名詞] (下巴上的)鬍鬚 *My father has a beard.* 我爸爸留着鬍鬚。

beard 鬍鬚　　moustache 小鬍子

beat /biːt/ [動詞] [過去式**beat**，過去分詞**beaten** /ˈbiːtn/] 1 打敗，戰勝，贏 *He always beats me at tennis.* 他打網球總是贏我。2 (連續地)打，擊 *She beat the dog with a stick.* 她用棍子打狗。◇ *Who's beating the drum?* 誰在敲鼓？

beautiful /ˈbjuːtəfl/ [形容詞] 美麗的；美好的 *Their mother was a beautiful woman.* 他們的媽媽是個美麗的女人。◇ *What a beautiful day—the weather's perfect!* 多麼美麗的一天，天氣好極了！

became /bɪˈkeɪm/ **become**的過去式 *The two boys soon became good friends.* 那兩個男孩不久成了好朋友。

because /bɪˈkɒz; 美 -ˈkʌz/ [連詞] 因為 *The baby is crying because he is hungry.* 寶寶在哭，因為他餓了。

become /bɪˈkʌm/ [動詞] [過去式 **became** /bɪˈkeɪm/，過去分詞 **become**] 成為，變成，變得 *They became good friends.* 他們成了好朋友。◇ *The weather became warmer.*

天氣漸漸暖和了。

bed /bed/ [名詞] 牀 *What time do you usually go to bed?* 你通常幾點上牀睡覺？

pillow 枕頭
blanket 毛毯
bed 牀
sheet 牀單

bedroom /'bedru:m/ [名詞] 臥室 *There are two beds in the bedroom.* 臥室裏有兩張牀。

bee /bi:/ [名詞] 蜜蜂 *Bees make honey.* 蜜蜂釀蜜。

beef /bi:f/ [名詞] [無複數] 牛肉 *Do you want beef or chicken?* 你想吃牛肉還是雞肉？

beer /bɪə; 美 bɪr/ [名詞] [無複數] 啤酒 *Dad doesn't drink beer, only wine.* 爸爸不喝啤酒，只喝葡萄酒。

beetle /'bi:tl/ [名詞] 甲蟲 *There are many different types of beetle.* 甲蟲有許多不同的種類。

before[1] /bɪ'fɔ:; 美 -'fɔ:r/ [介詞] 在…以前 *You must leave before 8 o'clock.* 你必須在8點以前離開。☞ [反] **after**[1] 在…以後

before[2] /bɪ'fɔ:; 美 -'fɔ:r/ [連詞] 在…以前 *Say goodbye before you go.* 你走以前要説再見。☞ [反] **after**[2] 在…以後

begin /bɪ'gɪn/ [動詞] [現在分詞 **beginning**，過去式 **began** /bɪ'gæn/，過去分詞 **begun** /bɪ'gʌn/] 開始 *The exam begins at 9: 00.* 考試9點開始。◇ *It's beginning to rain.* 開始下雨了。☞ [反] **end**[2] 結束

behave /bɪ'heɪv/ [動詞] **1** 表現 *How does Peter behave at school?* 彼得在學校表現怎麼樣？◇ *The children behaved very badly.* 孩子們表現很差。**2** 守規矩 *Mum's always telling me to behave when we go out.* 我們出去時，媽媽總是告訴我要守規矩。

behind /bɪ'haɪnd/ [介詞] 在…後面 *Look! There's someone behind the tree.* 瞧！樹後有人。

believe /bɪ'li:v/ [動詞] 相信 *Do you believe him?* 你相信他嗎？◇ *I'll* *believe it when I see it.* 我要親眼見到才能相信。

bell /bel/ [名詞] 鐘;鈴 *The bell's ringing.* 鈴響了。

belong /bɪˈlɒŋ; 美 -ˈlɔːŋ/ [動詞] **1** 屬於 *This book belongs to Helen.* 這本書是海倫的。 **2** 是…的一員 *Henry belongs to the school football club.* 亨利是學校足球俱樂部的成員。

below /bɪˈləʊ; 美 -ˈloʊ/ [介詞] 在…下面 *Fish swim below the surface of the water.* 魚在水下游。 [反] **above** 在…上面

belt /belt/ [名詞] 皮帶 *Henry has a new belt.* 亨利有一條新皮帶。

bench /bentʃ/ [名詞] [複數 **benches**] 長椅,長凳 *Alice was sitting on a bench in the park.* 艾麗斯坐在公園的長椅上。

bend /bend/ [動詞] [過去式和過去分詞 **bent** /bent/] **1** (使)彎曲 *It's hard to bend an iron bar.* 把鐵棒弄彎很難。 **2** 彎身 *Helen bent down to pick up a book from the floor.* 海倫彎下身從地板上撿起一本書。

bend
使彎曲

bend
彎身

beneath /bɪˈniːθ/ [介詞] 在…下面 *They sat beneath the tree.* 他們坐在樹下。

bent /bent/ **bend**的過去式和過去分詞 *That naughty boy bent the fork.* 那個頑皮的孩子把叉子弄彎了。

berry /ˈberi/ [名詞] [複數 **berries**] 漿果 *Some berries taste good.* 有些漿

果很好吃。

berries
漿果

beside /bɪ'saɪd/ [介詞] 在…旁邊 Helen sits beside Paul at school. 海倫在學校坐在保羅旁邊。

best¹ /best/ [形容詞] [**good**的最高級] 最好的 It was the best film I've ever seen. 這是我看過的最棒的電影。

best² /best/ [副詞] [**well**的最高級] 最 Which one do you like best? 你最喜歡哪一個？

best³ /best/ [名詞] [用作單數] 最好的人（或事物）We are the best of friends. 我們是最好的朋友。
do/try one's best 盡力而為 Don't worry about the exam—just do your best. 別擔心考試，盡力而為就行。

better¹ /'betə; 美 -ər/ [形容詞] **1** [**good**的比較級] 更好的 We need a better computer. 我們需要一台更好的電腦。**2** [**well**的比較級] (病況) 好轉的 Are you feeling a bit better today? 你今天覺得好點了嗎？

better² /'betə; 美 -ər/ [副詞] [**well**的比較級] 更好 He speaks English better than I do. 他英語說得比我好。

between /bɪ'twiːn/ [介詞] 在…之間 'Where's Peter?' 'He's standing between Henry and Paul.' "彼得在哪裏？""他正站在亨利和保羅中間。"
☞ **between** 表示兩者之間；**among** 表示三者或更多者之間。

bicycle /'baɪsɪkl/ [又作 **bike**] [名詞] 自行車 Did you come by bicycle? 你騎自行車來的嗎？

bicycle 自行車

brake 車閘　handlebars 把手
saddle 車座
pedal 踏板
wheel 車輪
chain 鏈子

big /bɪg/ [形容詞] 大的 [比較級

bigger，最高級**biggest**] *These shoes are too big for me.* 這雙鞋對我來說太大了。☞ ①[同] **large** 大的 ②[反] **small** 小的

bike /baɪk/ [名詞] [非正式] 自行車 *He fell off his bike.* 他從自行車上摔了下來。◇ *Helen's just learnt to ride a bike.* 海倫剛學會騎自行車。

bill /bɪl/ [名詞] 賬單 *Have you paid the bill?* 你付賬了嗎？

bin /bɪn/ [名詞] 垃圾箱 *He threw the letter in the bin.* 他把信扔進了垃圾箱。☞ 參見**dustbin** "(放在室外的)垃圾箱"。

dustbin
(放在室外的)垃圾箱

bin
垃圾箱

bird /bɜːd; 美 bɜːrd/ [名詞] 鳥 *Most birds can fly.* 大多數鳥會飛。

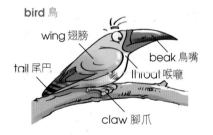

bird 鳥
wing 翅膀
beak 鳥嘴
tail 尾巴
throat 喉嚨
claw 腳爪

birthday /ˈbɜːθdeɪ; 美 ˈbɜːrθ-/ [名詞] 生日 '*When is your birthday?*' '*My birthday is on August the eighth.*' "你的生日是甚麼時候？" "我的生日是8月8

日。" ◇ *Happy birthday!* 生日快樂！

biscuit /ˈbɪskɪt/ [名詞] 餅乾 *Who wants a chocolate biscuit?* 誰要巧克力餅乾？

bit /bɪt/ [名詞] **1 a bit** [用作副詞] 有點兒；稍微 *I'm a bit tired.* 我有點兒累了。**2 a bit of sth** 一小塊；一點點 *I have only finished a bit of my homework.* 我只做了一點點作業。

bite /baɪt/ [動詞] [過去式**bit** /bɪt/，過去分詞**bitten** /ˈbɪtn/] 咬 *Don't worry about the dog—she never bites.* 別擔心那條狗，它從不咬人。◇ *Sophie was bitten by a dog.* 索菲被狗咬傷了。

bitter /ˈbɪtə; 美 ər/ [形容詞] 苦(味)的 *I need some sugar in my coffee—it's too bitter.* 我需要在咖啡裏加點糖，太苦了。☞ [反] **sweet**[1] 甜(味)的

black[1] /blæk/ [形容詞] 黑色的 *She had short black hair.* 她留一頭黑短髮。

black[2] /blæk/ [名詞] 黑色 *She*

always dresses in black. 她總是穿黑色衣服。

blackboard /'blækbɔːd; 美 -bɔːrd/ [名詞] 黑板 The teacher wrote ABC on the blackboard. 老師在黑板上寫上ABC。

blade /bleɪd/ [名詞] 刀刃 The blade of this knife is blunt. 這把刀的刀刃鈍了。

blade
刀刃

blame /bleɪm/ [動詞] 責備 It's your idea—don't blame me if it doesn't work. 這是你的主意，如果不靈可別怪我。

blank /blæŋk/ [形容詞] 空白的 Do you have a blank tape? 你有空白磁帶嗎？

blanket /'blæŋkɪt; 美 -ət/ [名詞] 毯子 When it is cold I put a blanket on my bed. 天冷時我在牀上鋪條毯子。

bleed /bliːd/ [動詞] [過去式和過去分詞**bled** /bled/] 流血 Henry's nose bled when he bumped into the door. 亨利撞在門上，鼻子流血了。

blew /bluː/ **blow**的過去式 The wind blew a tree down. 風把一棵樹颳倒了。

blind /blaɪnd/ [形容詞] 瞎的，盲的，失明的 Some children were born blind. 有些孩子生下來就是瞎的。

blink /blɪŋk/ [動詞] 眨眼 Henry blinked in the bright sunlight. 亨利在燦爛陽光的照射下眨着眼睛。

block¹ /blɒk; 美 blɑːk/ [名詞] 一大塊 The baby was playing with building blocks. 寶寶正在玩積木。

block² /blɒk; 美 blɑːk/ [動詞] 阻塞，堵塞 A truck is blocking the road. 一輛卡車阻塞了道路。

blood /blʌd/ [名詞] [無複數] 血，血液 He lost a lot of blood in the accident. 他在事故中失了很多血。

blouse /blaʊz; 美 blaʊs/ [名詞] （女

式) 襯衫 *Helen was wearing a white blouse.* 海倫穿着一件白襯衫。

blow /bləʊ; 美 bloʊ/ [動詞] [過去式 **blew** /bluː/，過去分詞 **blown** /bləʊn; 美 bloʊn/] (風)吹，颳 *Alice blew out all the candles on her cake.* 艾麗斯吹滅了蛋糕上所有的蠟燭。◇ *The wind blew the fence down.* 風把籬笆颳倒了。

blue[1] /bluː/ [形容詞] 藍色的 *She has blue eyes.* 她有一雙藍眼睛。◇ *The sky is blue.* 天空是藍色的。

blue[2] /bluː/ [名詞] 藍色 *Blue is my favourite colour.* 藍色是我最喜歡的顏色。

blunt /blʌnt/ [形容詞] (指鉛筆、刀等)鈍的 *This knife's blunt!* 這把刀鈍了！ ☞ [反] **sharp** 鋒利的，銳利的

board /bɔːd; 美 bɔːrd/ [名詞] **1** 木板 *There's a loose board in the bedroom.* 臥室裏有塊木(地)板鬆了。**2** 棋盤 *I want to play chess but I can't find the board.* 我想下棋，但找不到棋盤。

boast /bəʊst; 美 boʊst/ [動詞] 吹噓，誇耀 *He boasted that he could run very fast.* 他吹噓說他跑得很快。

boat /bəʊt; 美 boʊt/ [名詞] 小船 *We're going by boat.* 我們打算坐船去。

body /'bɒdi; 美 'bɑːdi/ [名詞] [複數 **bodies**] 身體 *Our bodies need vitamins to stay healthy.* 我們的身體需要維生素保持健康。

body 身體

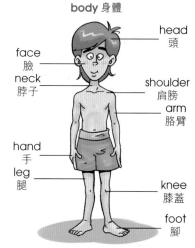

boil /bɔɪl/ [動詞] **1** (液體)沸騰；(水)開 *Water boils at 100℃.* 水在攝氏100度時沸騰。◇ *The kettle's boiling.* 水開了。**2** 煮(食物) *Boil the eggs for five minutes.* 把雞蛋煮5分鐘。

bomb /bɒm; 美 bɑːm/ [名詞] *A bomb exploded outside the hotel.* 旅館外面有顆炸彈爆炸了。

bone /bəʊn; 美 boʊn/ [名詞] 骨，骨頭 *The dog was chewing a bone.* 狗在啃一根骨頭。

bonfire /ˈbɒnˌfaɪə; 美 ˈbɑːnˌfaɪr/ [名詞] 篝火 *The children made a bonfire at the seaside.* 孩子們在海邊生起篝火。

book¹ /bʊk/ [名詞] 書 *What book are you reading?* 你在看甚麼書?

book² /bʊk/ [動詞] 預訂 *You can phone up and book tickets.* 你可以打電話訂票。

bookcase /ˈbʊkkeɪs/ [名詞] 書櫥,書櫃 *There's a small bookcase in his room.* 他的房間裏有一個小書櫃。

bookshop /ˈbʊkʃɒp; 美 -ʃɑːp/ [名詞] 書店 *You can buy books at a bookshop.* 你可以在書店裏買書。 ☞ 美國英語用**bookstore** /ˈbʊkstɔː; 美 -stɔːr/。

boot /buːt/ [名詞] [通常用作複數] 靴子 *She was wearing a new pair of boots.* 她穿着一雙新靴子。

born /bɔːn; 美 bɔːrn/ [動詞] **be born** 出生 *'Where were you born?' 'I was born in London.'* "你在哪裏出生的?" "我在倫敦出生的。"

borrow /ˈbɒrəʊ; 美 ˈbɔːroʊ/ [動詞] (向別人)借,借用 *Can I borrow your pen? I left mine at home.* 我可以借用一下你的鋼筆嗎?我把我的忘在家裏了。 ☞ 參見**lend** "借出,借給"。

lend 借給
borrow 借用

Henry is lending a pen to Paul. 亨利正在把鋼筆借給保羅。
Paul is borrowing a pen from Henry. 保羅正在向亨利借鋼筆。

both¹ /bəʊθ; 美 boʊθ/ [形容詞] 兩,雙 *Hold the dish with both hands.* 用雙手端盤子。

both² /bəυθ; 美 boυθ/ [代詞] 兩者, 倆 I have two sisters. Both of them live in London. 我有兩個妹妹,她們倆都住在倫敦。

bother /'bɒðə; 美 'ba:ðər/ [動詞] 打擾 Don't bother your father now—he's very busy. 現在不要打擾你父親,他很忙。

bottle /'bɒtl; 美 'ba:tl/ [名詞] 瓶 These bottles are made of glass. 這些瓶子是玻璃的。 ◇ They opened another bottle of wine. 他們又打開了一瓶葡萄酒。

bottom /'bɒtəm; 美 'ba:-/ [名詞] **1** [通常用作單數] 底部 Helen found the keys at the bottom of her bag. 海倫在書包底部找到了鑰匙。 **2** 屁股 Henry fell on his bottom. 亨利一屁股摔倒在地。

bought /bɔ:t/ **buy**的過去式和過去分詞 Mum bought two bars of chocolate. 媽媽買了兩塊巧克力。

bounce /baυns/ [動詞] **1** (球)彈起 The ball bounced twice before he caught it. 球彈了兩次他才接住。

bounce
(球)彈起

2 (人)跳起 The child was bouncing on the bed. 孩子在牀上蹦蹦跳跳。

bow /bəυ; 美 boυ/ [名詞] **1** 蝴蝶結 She had a beautiful bow in her hair. 她頭上戴了一個漂亮的蝴蝶結。 **2** 弓 They shot birds with bows and arrows. 他們用弓箭射鳥。

bow
蝴蝶結

bow
弓

bowl /bəυl; 美 boυl/ [名詞] 碗 Henry ate two bowls of rice. 亨利吃了兩碗飯。

box /bɒks; 美 ba:ks/ [名詞] [複數 **boxes**]箱子,盒子 Helen kept all the letters in a box. 海倫把所有的信都存放在一個盒子裏。

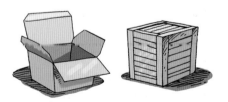

boxing /'bɒksɪŋ; 美 'ba:ks-/ [名詞] [無複數] 拳擊(運動) Boxing is a dangerous sport. 拳擊是一項危險的運動。

B

boy /bɔɪ/ [名詞] 男孩 *They have five children: three boys and two girls.* 他們有五個孩子：三個男孩兩個女孩。

bracelet /'breɪslət/ [名詞] 手鐲 *She wore a beautiful bracelet.* 她戴着一隻漂亮的手鐲。

brain /breɪn/ [名詞] **1** 腦 *Boxing can damage the brain.* 拳擊運動有可能損傷大腦。**2** 頭腦，智力 *He has a very quick brain and learns fast.* 他腦子靈，學得快。

brake¹ /breɪk/ [名詞] 剎車，閘 *There's something wrong with the brakes.* 剎車出毛病了。

brake² /breɪk/ [動詞] 剎車 *The driver braked quickly to avoid an accident.* 為了避免事故，司機迅速剎車。

branch /brɑːntʃ; 美 bræntʃ/ [名詞] [複數 **branches**] 樹枝 *Henry climbed the tree and hid in the branches.* 亨利爬上樹，藏在樹枝上。

branch
樹枝

brave /breɪv/ [形容詞] 勇敢的 *The brave boy saved the baby from the river.* 那個勇敢的男孩把嬰兒從河裏救了上來。

bread /bred/ [名詞] [無複數] 麵包 *Can you cut me a slice of bread, please?* 請你給我切一片麵包好嗎？

break /breɪk/ [動詞] [過去式 **broke** /brəʊk; 美 broʊk/，過去分詞 **broken** /'brəʊkən; 美 'broʊ-/] **1** 打破，打碎，打斷 *The ball hit the window and broke the glass.* 球擊中窗戶，打碎了玻璃。

2 (機器) 壞掉 *My watch has broken.* 我的手表壞了。

breakfast /'brekfəst/ [名詞] 早餐，早飯 *I haven't had breakfast yet.* 我

還沒有吃早飯。◇ *What would you like for breakfast?* 你早餐想吃甚麼？

breathe /briːð/ [動詞] 呼吸 *Fish cannot breathe out of water.* 魚離開水就無法呼吸。

breeze /briːz/ [名詞] 微風 *There's not much breeze today.* 今天沒甚麼風。

brick /brɪk/ [名詞] 磚 *The old house was made of red brick.* 那棟舊房子是用紅磚砌的。

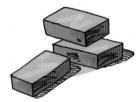

bridge /brɪdʒ/ [名詞] 橋 *They are building a new bridge over the river.* 他們正在河上建一座新橋。

bright /braɪt/ [形容詞] **1** 明亮的 *The room's small but bright.* 房間雖小卻很明亮。 ☞ [反] **dark¹** 黑暗的 **2** 聰明的，伶俐的 *He's a bright boy.* 他是個聰明的孩子。

brilliant /ˈbrɪljənt/ [形容詞] [非正式] 精彩的 *That was a brilliant film!* 那是一部精彩的電影！

bring /brɪŋ/ [動詞] [過去式和過去分詞 **brought** /brɔːt/] 帶來，拿來 *You can take that book home, but bring it back tomorrow, please.* 你可以把那本書帶回家，但明天請把它帶來回來。

Britain /ˈbrɪtn/ [名詞] 不列顛，英國 = **Great Britain** 大不列顛，英國 ☞ 參見 **United Kingdom** "聯合王國，英國"。

British¹ /ˈbrɪtɪʃ/ [形容詞] 不列顛(人)的；英國(人)的 *Everyone says that British weather is terrible.* 人人都說英國的天氣很糟糕。

British² /ˈbrɪtɪʃ/ [名詞] [與 **the** 連用，作複數] 英國人 *The British are very proud of their history.* 英國人對自己的歷史十分自豪。

broad /brɔːd/ [形容詞] 寬的，寬闊的 *This is a broad street.* 這條街很寬。 ☞ [反] **narrow** 窄的，狹窄的

broke /brəʊk; 美 broʊk/ **break** 的過去式 *Who broke this plate?* 誰把這個盤子打破了？

broken /ˈbrəʊkən; 美 ˈbroʊ-/ **break** 的過去分詞 *I'm sorry—I've broken a glass.* 對不起，我打破了一個玻璃杯。

broom /bruːm/ [名詞] 掃帚 *She was sweeping the floor with a broom.*

她正在用掃帚掃地板。

brother /ˈbrʌðə; 美 -ər/ [名詞] 兄；弟 *They're brothers.* 他們是親兄弟。◇ *Peter is my younger brother.* 彼得是我弟弟。

brought /brɔːt/ **bring** 的過去式和過去分詞 *Henry brought a friend to the party.* 亨利帶了一位朋友來參加聚會。

brown[1] /braʊn/ [形容詞] 褐色的，棕色的 'What colour are your shoes?' 'They are brown.' "你的鞋是甚麼顏色的？" "是棕色的。"

brown[2] /braʊn/ [名詞] 褐色，棕色 *Her favourite colour is brown.* 她最喜歡的顏色是褐色。

bruise /bruːz/ [名詞] (人體碰撞後產生的) 青腫，擦傷 *Henry had a bruise on his knee.* 亨利的膝上有一處擦傷。

brush[1] /brʌʃ/ [名詞] [複數 **brushes**] 刷子；畫筆；髮刷 *Alice is painting a picture with a brush.* 艾麗斯正在用畫筆畫畫。

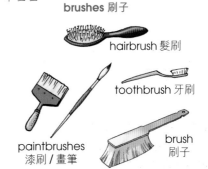

brushes 刷子

hairbrush 髮刷

toothbrush 牙刷

paintbrushes 漆刷 / 畫筆

brush 刷子

brush[2] /brʌʃ/ [動詞] 刷 (牙等)；梳理 (頭髮) *I brush my teeth twice a day.* 我一天刷兩次牙。◇ *Helen's brushing her hair in front of the mirror.* 海倫正在對着鏡子梳理頭髮。

brush 刷 (牙)

bubble /ˈbʌbl/ [名詞] 泡，氣泡 *Children love blowing bubbles.* 孩子們喜歡吹泡泡。

bucket /ˈbʌkɪt; 美 -ət/ [名詞] 水桶，提桶 *The bucket is full of water.* 水桶

裏盛滿了水。

build /bɪld/ [動詞] [過去式和過去分詞 **built** /bɪlt/] 建築，建造 *The house is built of wood.* 這棟房子是用木頭造的。

building /'bɪldɪŋ/ [名詞] 建築物 *There are a lot of very old buildings in this town.* 這個鎮上有許多古老的建築。

built /bɪlt/ **build**的過去式和過去分詞 *They've built a new bridge across the river.* 他們在河上建了一座新橋。

bulb /bʌlb/ [名詞] 燈泡 *Henry changed the bulb in the lamp.* 亨利把電燈的燈泡換了。

bull /bʊl/ [名詞] 公牛 *The bull was very fierce.* 那頭公牛非常兇猛。

bump /bʌmp/ [動詞] 碰撞 *Be careful not to bump your head.* 小心別碰着頭。

bunch /bʌntʃ/ [名詞] [複數 **bunches**] 串，束 *Mum bought a*

bunch of grapes. 媽媽買了一串葡萄。

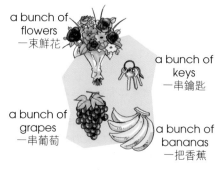

a bunch of flowers 一束鮮花

a bunch of keys 一串鑰匙

a bunch of grapes 一串葡萄

a bunch of bananas 一把香蕉

burn /bɜːn; 美 bɜːrn/ [動詞] [過去式和過去分詞 **burned** 或 **burnt** /bɜːnt; 美 bɜːrnt/] 1 燃燒 *Is the fire still burning?* 火還在燃燒嗎？

2 焚燒，燒毀 *They burned the garden rubbish on the bonfire.* 他們用篝火把花園裏的垃圾燒掉了。3 燒傷；燙傷 *Be careful not to burn your mouth.* 小心別燙着嘴。

burst /bɜːst; 美 bɜːrst/ [動詞] [過去式和過去分詞 **burst**] 爆裂，脹破 *A tyre burst with a bang.* 一隻輪胎砰的一聲爆了。◇ *The balloon burst when I kicked it.* 我一踢氣球破了。

bury /'berɪ/ [動詞] [過去式和過去分詞**buried**] **1** 埋葬(死者) *The boys buried the dead bird in the backyard.* 男孩子們把死鳥埋在了後院。**2** (尤指用土)埋藏,掩埋 *Our dog always buries its bones in the garden.* 我們家的狗總是把骨頭埋在花園裏。

bus /bʌs/ [名詞] [複數**buses**] 公共汽車 *The children go to school by bus.* 孩子們乘公共汽車上學。◇ *Where do you usually get on the bus?* 你通常在哪裏坐公共汽車?

bush /buʃ/ [名詞] [複數**bushes**] 灌木 *The house was surrounded by thick bushes.* 房子四周灌木叢生。

bus station /'bʌs ˌsteɪʃn/ [名詞] 公共汽車總站 *Is the bus station far from here?* 公共汽車總站離這裏遠嗎?

bus stop /'bʌs stɒp; 美 'bʌs sta:p/ [名詞] 公共汽車站 *I saw her waiting at the bus stop.* 我看見她在公共汽車站等車。

busy /'bɪzi/ [形容詞] [比較級**busier**,最高級**busiest**] 忙的,繁忙的 *Don't bother him. He's busy.* 不要打擾他,他很忙。◇ *Henry's busy with his homework.* 亨利在忙着做作業。◇ *She's busy writing a letter.* 她在忙着寫信。

but /強 bʌt; 弱 bət/ [連詞] 但是 *I like apples, but I don't want one now.* 我喜歡吃蘋果,但現在不想吃。

butcher /'butʃə; 美 -ər/ [名詞] 屠夫;肉商 *The butcher sold them the meat.* 肉商把肉賣給了他們。

butter /'bʌtə; 美 -ər/ [名詞] [無複數] 牛油,黃油 *She put some butter on her bread.* 她在麵包上塗了些黃油。

butterfly /'bʌtəflaɪ; 美 -ər-/ [名詞] [複數**butterflies**] 蝴蝶 *There's a butterfly on the flower.* 花上有一隻蝴蝶。

button /'bʌtn/ [名詞] **1** 鈕扣,扣子 *This blouse is too tight—I can't fasten the buttons.* 這件襯衣太緊,我扣不上扣子。

B

2 按鈕，鍵 *I pressed the button, and the bell rang.* 我按了一下按鈕，鈴響了。

buy /baɪ/ [動詞] [過去式和過去分詞 **bought** /bɔːt/] 買 *We always buy mum a birthday present. Last year we bought her some flowers.* 我們總會給媽媽買生日禮物，去年我們給她買了一些花。 ☞ [反] **sell** 賣

by /baɪ/ [介詞] **1** 靠近，在…旁邊 *Come and sit by me.* 過來坐在我身旁。**2** 在…之前 *Can you finish your homework by six o'clock.* 你能在6點以前做完作業嗎？**3** 被，由 *She was knocked down by a car.* 她被汽車撞倒了。**4** [表示方法、手段] 用，靠，乘，通過 *Are you going by car or by train?* 你是坐汽車去還是坐火車去？

bye /baɪ/ [感歎詞] [非正式] 再見 *Bye! See you next week.* 再見！下週見。☞ 也可以説 **bye-bye**。

C c

cabbage /'kæbɪdʒ/ [名詞] 洋白菜，捲心菜 *Do you like cabbage?* 你喜歡吃洋白菜嗎？

café /'kæfeɪ; 美 kæ'feɪ/ [名詞] 咖啡館；小餐館 *Henry had lunch in a café.* 亨利在一家小餐館吃了午餐。

cage /keɪdʒ/ [名詞] 籠子 *Is the parrot happy in its cage?* 鸚鵡在籠子裏快樂嗎？

cake /keɪk/ [名詞] 蛋糕 *It's your birthday—you must cut the cake.* 今天是你的生日，必須由你來切蛋糕。

calculator /'kælkjuleɪtə; 美 -jəleɪtər/ [名詞] 計算器 *Can I borrow your calculator?* 我能借用一下你的計算器嗎？

calendar /'kælɪndə; 美 -ər/ [名詞] 日曆 *Do you have next year's calendar?* 你有明年的日曆嗎？

call /kɔːl/ [動詞] **1** 喊，叫 *I heard someone calling my name.* 我聽見有人叫我的名字。**2** 給…打電話 *Alice calls her aunt every week.* 艾麗斯每週都給姨媽打電話。**3** 把…叫做，稱呼，給…取名叫 *My name's Susan, but you can call me Sue.* 我的名字叫蘇珊，但你可以叫我蘇。◇ *They called the baby Ben.* 他們給寶寶取名叫本。**4** 召喚 *Dad called us in for lunch.* 爸爸叫我們進來吃午飯。

calm /kɑːm/ [形容詞] 鎮靜的 *Try to keep calm—the doctor will be here* *soon.* 要保持鎮靜，醫生馬上就到。

came /keɪm/ **come**的過去式 *Paul came home late.* 保羅回家晚了。

camel /'kæml/ [名詞] 駱駝 *They call the camel 'the ship of the desert'.* 人們把駱駝稱為"沙漠之舟"。

camera /'kæmərə/ [名詞] (照)相機 *I've got a new camera.* 我有一架新相機。

camp /kæmp/ [名詞] 營地 *Let's return to camp.* 咱們回營地吧。◇ *At camp we have a fire each night.* 在營地，我們每晚都生火。

can¹ /強 kæn; 弱 kən/ [情態動詞] [過去式**could** /強 kʊd; 弱 kəd/] 1 [表示可能性或能力] 能，會 *I can run fast.* 我能跑快。◇ *Can you ride a bike?* 你會騎自行車嗎？ ☞ 參見**able**。2 [表示許可或請求，代替**may**] 可以，能 *Can I have a drink, please?* 我喝點飲料可以嗎？◇ *Can I read your*

newspaper? 我可以看看你的報紙嗎？

can² /kæn/ [名詞]罐頭，聽 *Dad bought a can of beer.* 爸爸買了一罐啤酒。☞ 美國英語通常用**can**，英國英語通常用**tin**。

candle /'kændl/ [名詞] 蠟燭 *He lit the candle.* 他點燃蠟燭。

candle 蠟燭

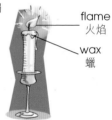
flame 火焰
wax 蠟

candy /'kændi/ [名詞] [複數 **candies**] 糖果 *You ate too much candy.* 你吃糖果吃得太多了。☞ 美國英語用**candy**，英國英語用**sweet** "糖果"。

cannot /'kænɒt; 美 -nɑːt/ **can¹**的否定詞 *I cannot speak Japanese.* 我不會説日語。

can't /kɑːnt; 美 kænt/ **cannot**的縮寫 *I can't swim.* 我不會游泳。

cap /kæp/ [名詞] (有舌無檐的)帽子 *Henry is wearing a baseball cap.* 亨利戴着一頂棒球帽。☞ 參見**hat** "(有

檐的)帽子"。

cap　　　　hat
(有舌無檐的)帽子　(有檐的)帽子

capital /ˈkæpɪtl/ [名詞] **1** 首都 *Beijing is the capital of China.* 北京是中國的首都。**2** [又作 **capital letter**] 大寫字母 *Write your name in capitals.* 用大寫字母寫你的名字。

car /kɑː; 美 kɑːr/ [名詞] 小汽車，轎車 *He's not old enough to drive a car.* 他還不到開車的年齡。

card /kɑːd; 美 kɑːrd/ [名詞] **1** 卡片 *Alice stuck the pictures on cards.* 艾麗斯把圖畫貼在卡片上。**2** 賀卡 *Henry received a Christmas card from his friend.* 亨利收到一張朋友寄來的聖誕賀卡。**3** 紙牌，撲克牌 *Let's play cards.* 咱們打牌吧。

cardigan /ˈkɑːdɪɡən; 美 ˈkɑːr-/ [名詞] (開襟)毛衣 *She wears a cardigan when it is cold.* 天冷時，她穿一件開襟毛衣。

care¹ /keə; 美 ker/ [名詞] 小心，謹慎，注意 *Cross the road with care.* 過馬路時要小心。

take care 小心，注意；[分別時或信末用語] 保重 *When you are crossing the road, take care!* 你過馬路時要小心！

take care of 照顧 *Take care of your brother while I am away.* 我不在時要照顧你弟弟。

care² /keə; 美 ker/ [動詞] 關心，在乎 *I really don't care if he comes or not.* 我真的不在乎他來還是不來。

care for 看護，照顧 *Who cared for her while she was ill?* 她生病時是誰照顧她的？

careful /ˈkeəfl; 美 ˈker-/ [形容詞] **1** 小心的 *Be careful!* 小心！◇ *Be careful with the glasses.* 小心玻璃杯。◇ *Be careful not to wake the baby.* 小心別吵醒寶寶。**2** 細心的，仔細的 *She's a careful student.* 她是一名細心的學生。

carefully /ˈkeəfəli; 美 ˈker-/ [副詞] 小心地；仔細地 *Drive carefully.* 開車要小心。◇ *Please listen carefully.* 請仔細聽。

careless /ˈkeələs; 美 ˈker-/ [形容詞] 粗心的，疏忽的 *He's very careless.* 他很粗心。

carpet /ˈkɑːpɪt; 美 ˈkɑːrpət/ [名詞] 地毯 Alice has a new carpet in her bedroom. 艾麗斯的卧室裏鋪了一條新地毯。

carpet
地毯

carrot /ˈkærət/ [名詞] 胡蘿蔔 Have some more carrots. 再吃點胡蘿蔔。

carry /ˈkæri/ [動詞] [過去式和過去分詞**carried**] 拿；提；抱；背；扛；搬 He was carrying a suitcase. 他提着衣箱。◇ She carried her baby in her arms. 她懷裏抱着嬰兒。

cartoon /kɑːˈtuːn; 美 kɑːr-/ [名詞] **1** 漫畫 Henry is learning to draw

cartoons. 亨利在學畫漫畫。**2** 卡通片，動畫片 Alice likes to watch cartoons on television. 艾麗斯喜歡看電視裏的動畫片。

case /keɪs/ [名詞] 盒，匣 Mum keeps her glasses in a case. 媽媽把眼鏡放在盒裏。

in case 以防萬一 Take an umbrella in case it rains. 帶上雨傘，以防下雨。

cash /kæʃ/ [名詞] [無複數] 現金 Do you have any cash? 你有現金嗎？

cassette /kəˈset/ [名詞] (盒式) 磁帶 Henry is listening to a music cassette. 亨利正在聽音樂磁帶。

castle /ˈkɑːsl; 美 ˈkæ-/ [名詞] 城堡 Most castles were built a long time

ago. 大多數城堡是很久以前建造的。

cat /kæt/ [名詞] 貓 *The cat is eating.* 貓在吃東西。

catch /kætʃ/ [動詞] [過去式和過去分詞**caught** /kɔːt/] **1** 接住 *I threw a ball to him and he caught it.* 我把球扔給他，他接住了。**2** 捉住，抓住，捕獲 *Cats catch mice.* 貓捉老鼠。◇ *How many fish did you catch?* 你捕了多少魚？**3** 趕上 *Henry caught the last bus home.* 亨利趕上最後一班公共汽車回家。

caterpillar /ˈkætəpɪlə; 美 -tərpɪlər/ [名詞] 毛蟲 *Caterpillars turn into butterflies.* 毛蟲變成蝴蝶。

cattle /ˈkætl/ [名詞] [複數] 牛 *We saw some cattle in the fields.* 我們看見田裏有幾頭牛。

cattle 牛

cow
母牛

bull
公牛

caught /kɔːt/ **catch**的過去式和過去分詞 *The cat caught another mouse.* 那隻貓又捉住一隻老鼠。

C

cauliflower /ˈkɒliˌflaʊə; 美 ˈkɑːliˌflaʊər/ [名詞] 花椰菜，菜花 *Helen cooked some cauliflower for lunch.* 海倫午飯煮了些菜花。

cave /keɪv/ [名詞] 山洞；地洞 *Bats live in the cave.* 蝙蝠居住在山洞裏。

CD /ˌsiː ˈdiː/ [**compact disc**的縮寫] [名詞] 鐳射唱片 *Helen is listening to her new CD.* 海倫正在聽自己的新鐳射唱片。

CD-ROM /ˌsiː diː 'rɒm; 美 -'rɑːm / [名詞] 唯讀光碟 *His computer can read CD-ROM.* 他的電腦能讀光碟。

ceiling /'siːlɪŋ / [名詞] 天花板 *She lay on her back staring up at the ceiling.* 她仰臥凝視着天花板。

celebrate /'seləbreɪt / [動詞] 慶祝 *Peter celebrated his birthday yesterday.* 彼得昨天慶祝生日。

cent /sent / [名詞] [貨幣單位] 分 *There are 100 cents in a dollar.* 1元等於100分錢。

centre /'sentə; 美 -ər / [名詞] 中心，中央 *The fruit is in the centre of the table.* 水果在桌子中央。 ☞美國英語拼寫為 **center**。

century /'sentʃəri / [名詞] [複數 **centuries**] 世紀 *There were two world wars in the twentieth century.* 20世紀發生了兩次世界大戰。

cereal /'sɪəriəl; 美 'sɪr- / [名詞] **1** [通常用作複數] 穀物，穀類植物 *Wheat and rice are cereals.* 小麥和水稻都是穀類植物。**2** [無複數] 穀類食品(如麥片等) *Peter ate a bowl of cereal.* 彼得吃了一碗麥片。

certain / 'sɜːtn; 美 'sɜːr- / [形容詞] [不用於名詞前] 肯定的，確信的 *I'm certain that she saw me.* 我肯定她看見我了。

certainly /'sɜːtnli; 美 'sɜːr- / [副詞] **1** 確實，無疑 *He certainly works very hard.* 他工作確實非常努力。**2** 當然 'Can I come along?' 'Certainly.' "我可以一起來嗎？""當然可以。" ☞[同] **sure²** 當然

certificate /sə'tɪfɪkeɪt; 美 sər- / [名詞] 證書 *My birth certificate shows where and when I was born.* 我的出生證上寫着我是何時何地出生的。

chain /tʃeɪn / [名詞] 鏈子，鏈條 *She always wears a gold chain round her neck.* 她的脖子上總是戴着一條金項鏈。◇ *My bicycle chain broke.* 我的自行車鏈條斷了。

gold chain
金項鏈

chair /tʃeə; 美 tʃer / [名詞] 椅子 *He got up from the chair.* 他從椅子上站了起來。

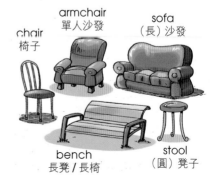

armchair
單人沙發

sofa
(長)沙發

chair
椅子

bench
長凳 / 長椅

stool
(圓)凳子

chalk /tʃɔːk/ [名詞] 粉筆 *The teacher was writing with a piece of chalk.* 老師在用粉筆寫字。☞ **chalk** 指 "粉筆" 是不可數名詞，説 "一枝粉筆" 要用 **a piece of chalk**；**chalk** 指 "彩色粉筆" 是可數名詞，説 "幾枝彩色粉筆" 要用 **some coloured chalks**。

champion /'tʃæmpjən/ [名詞] 冠軍 *He is the tennis champion of his school.* 他是學校裏的網球冠軍。

chance /tʃɑːns; 美 tʃæns/ [名詞] 機會 *I never miss a chance to play football.* 我從不錯過踢足球的機會。

change¹ /tʃeɪndʒ/ [動詞] **1** 改變；(使)變化 *Henry changed the date of his party.* 亨利把聚會日期改了。◇ *She's changed a lot since I last saw her.* 自從我上次看見她以後，她變了許多。 **2** [後跟複數賓語] 交換(座位、位置等) *Can we change seats?* 我們可以換換座位嗎？◇ *Can I change seats with you?* 我可以和你換一下座位嗎？ **3** 換衣服 *Helen changed before she went out.* 海倫出去前換了衣服。

change² /tʃeɪndʒ/ [名詞] [無複數] 零錢 *Henry has change in his pocket.* 亨利的口袋裏有零錢。

chapter /'tʃæptə; 美 -ər/ [名詞] (書的)章 *Turn to Chapter 1, please.* 請翻到第一章。

character /'kærəktə; 美 -ər/ [名詞] **1** 人物，角色 *He played a bad character in the film.* 他在電影裏演一個壞人。 **2** 性格，品質 *His character is very different from his wife's.* 他和妻子的性格迥然不同。

charge¹ /tʃɑːdʒ; 美 tʃɑːrdʒ/ [名詞] 負責，主管，掌管 *Paul is in charge of his baby brother while his mother is out.* 媽媽不在時，保羅負責照看小弟弟。◇ *The head teacher is in charge of the school.* 校長負責掌管學校。

charge² /tʃɑːdʒ; 美 tʃɑːrdʒ/ [動詞] 要價，收費 *How much do you charge for mending a pair of shoes?* 修一雙鞋要多少錢？

chase /tʃeɪs/ [動詞] 追趕 *The dog is chasing a cat.* 狗在追貓。

cheap /tʃiːp/ [形容詞] 便宜的 *Oranges are cheap at the moment.*

橙子現在便宜。[反]**expensive** 昂貴的

cheat /tʃi:t/ [動詞] 作弊 *He always cheats at cards.* 他玩牌時總是作弊。

check¹ /tʃek/ [名詞] 方格圖案 *Alice is wearing a check skirt.* 艾麗斯穿着一條方格裙。

check² /tʃek/ [動詞] 檢查；核對 *Check your work before you hand it in.* 交作業以前，要先檢查一下。

cheek /tʃi:k/ [名詞] 面頰 *The cold wind makes my cheeks red.* 寒風把我的面頰吹紅了。

cheer /tʃɪə; 美 tʃɪr/ [動詞] (向…) 歡呼，(為…) 喝彩 *The audience cheered the singer.* 聽眾們向歌手歡呼。

cheerful /'tʃɪəfl; 美 'tʃɪr-/ [形容詞] 高興的，快樂的 *You don't look very cheerful today. What's the matter?* 你今天看上去不大高興，怎麼啦？

cheers /tʃɪəz; 美 tʃɪrz/ [感歎詞] [用於祝酒時] 祝你健康；干杯 '*Cheers,' she said, raising her wine glass.* "干杯，"她舉起酒杯說。

cheese /tʃi:z/ [名詞] 乳酪，奶酪 *Peter does not like cheese.* 彼得不喜歡吃奶酪。

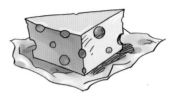

cherry /'tʃeri/ [名詞] [複數 **cherries**] 櫻桃 *Alice likes cherry pie.* 艾麗斯喜歡吃櫻桃餡餅。

chess /tʃes/ [名詞] [無複數] 國際象棋 *Can you play chess?* 你會下國際象棋嗎？

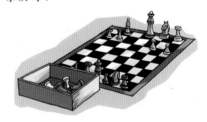

chest /tʃest/ [名詞] 胸部 *He was shot in the chest.* 他的胸部被射中了。

chew /tʃu:/ [動詞] 咀嚼 *Chew your food well before you swallow it.* 食物要先嚼爛再吞嚥。

chewing gum /'tʃu:ɪŋ gʌm/ [又作 **gum**] [名詞] [無複數] 口香糖 *You cannot take chewing gum to school.* 你不能帶口香糖上學。

chick /tʃɪk/ [名詞] 小雞 *The baby chick is soft and yellow.* 剛孵出的小

雞軟軟的、黃黃的。

chicken /'tʃɪkɪn/ [名詞] **1** 雞 *There are five chickens in the yard: a cock, a hen and three chicks.* 院子裏有5隻雞：1隻公雞、1隻母雞和3隻小雞。

2 [無複數] 雞肉 *Do you like chicken?* 你喜歡吃雞嗎？

child /tʃaɪld/ [名詞] [複數 **children** /'tʃɪldrən/] 孩子；兒童 *A group of children were playing in the park.* 一羣孩子正在公園裏玩。

chimney /'tʃɪmni/ [名詞] 煙囱，煙筒 *Smoke came out of the chimney.* 煙從烟筒裏冒出來。

chimpanzee /ˌtʃɪmpæn'ziː/ [又作 **chimp** /tʃɪmp/] [名詞] 黑猩猩 *The chimpanzee is an African animal.* 黑猩猩是一種產於非洲的動物。

chin /tʃɪn/ [名詞] 下巴 *Alice has chocolate on her chin.* 艾麗斯的下巴上沾有巧克力。

China /'tʃaɪnə/ [名詞] 中國 *China is a big country.* 中國是個大國。

Chinese¹ /ˌtʃaɪ'niːz/ [形容詞] 中國（人）的 *We went to a Chinese restaurant.* 我們去了一家中餐館。

Chinese² /ˌtʃaɪ'niːz/ [名詞] **1** [複數 **Chinese**] 中國人 *Many Chinese live abroad.* 很多中國人居住在國外。**2** 中國話，中文，漢語 *He can speak Chinese.* 他會說漢語。

chip /tʃɪp/ [名詞] [通常用作複數] （炸）薯條 *We had hamburger and chips for lunch.* 我們午餐吃了漢堡包和炸薯條。

chocolate /'tʃɒklət; 美 'tʃɔːk-/ [名詞] **1** [無複數] 巧克力 *Most children like* chocolate. 大部分孩子愛吃巧克力。

2 巧克力糖 *Mum bought a box of chocolates.* 媽媽買了一盒巧克力糖。

C **choose** /tʃuːz/ [動詞] [過去式 **chose** /tʃəʊz; 美 tʃoʊz/，過去分詞 **chosen** /'tʃəʊzn; 美 'tʃoʊ-/] 選擇，挑選 *Henry is choosing a toy.* 亨利在挑選玩具。

chop /tʃɒp; 美 tʃɑːp/ [動詞] [現在分詞**chopping**，過去式和過去分詞 **chopped**] 砍，劈 *Can you chop some firewood?* 你能不能劈些木柴？

chopsticks /'tʃɒpstɪks; 美 'tʃɑːp-/ [名詞] [複數] 筷子 *Most Chinese use bowls and chopsticks to eat.* 大多數中國人用碗筷吃飯。

chose /tʃəʊz; 美 tʃoʊz/ **choose**的過去式 *Who chose this book?* 誰挑

選的這本書？

chosen /'tʃəʊzn; 美 'tʃoʊ-/ **choose** 的過去分詞 *Dad has chosen a bicycle for my birthday present.* 爸爸選了一輛自行車作為我的生日禮物。

Christmas /'krɪsməs/ [又作 **Christmas Day**][名詞] 聖誕節 *Christmas is on 25 December.* 聖誕節是在12月25日。◇ *Happy Christmas!* 聖誕快樂！◇ *Merry Christmas!* 聖誕快樂！

church /tʃɜːtʃ; 美 tʃɜːrtʃ/ [名詞] [複數**churches**] 教堂 *The church is close to the school.* 教堂離學校很近。

cinema /'sɪnəmə/ [名詞] 電影院 *What's on at the cinema?* 電影院在上映甚麼影片？◇ *Let's go to the cinema tonight.* 咱們今晚去看電影吧。 ☞ 英國英語用**cinema**，美國英語用**movies**。

circle /'sɜːkl; 美 'sɜːr- / [名詞] 圓，圓圈 *They sat in a circle around the fire.* 他們圍成一圈坐在爐火旁邊。

circus /'sɜːkəs; 美 'sɜːr- / [名詞] [複數**circuses**] **1** 馬戲團 *This circus has a famous clown.* 這家馬戲團有個著名的小醜。**2** 馬戲 *Henry loves going to the circus.* 亨利喜歡看馬戲。

city /'sɪti / [名詞] [複數**cities**] 城市 *Which is the world's largest city?* 世界上最大的城市是哪個？

clap /klæp/ [動詞] [現在分詞 **clapping**，過去式和過去分詞 **clapped**] 鼓掌，拍手 *When the singer finished, we clapped.* 歌手唱完後，我們鼓了掌。

class /klɑːs; 美 klæs / [名詞] [複數 **classes**] **1** 班級 *Paul and Helen are in the same class at school.* 保羅和海倫在學校裏的同一個班。**2** 課 *I have a maths class at 9 o'clock.* 我9點上數學課。

classmate /'klɑːsmeɪt; 美 'klæs- / [名詞] 同班同學 *Paul and Helen are classmates.* 保羅和海倫是同班同學。

classroom /'klɑːsruːm; 美 'klæs- / [名詞] 教室 *Which classroom are you in?* 你在哪一個教室？

claw /klɔː / [名詞] （動物的）腳爪 *Cats have sharp claws.* 貓長着尖爪。

clay /kleɪ / [名詞] [無複數] 黏土 *The pots are made from clay.* 這些壺是用黏土製成的。

clean[1] /kliːn / [形容詞] 整潔的，乾淨的 *Are your hands clean?* 你的手乾淨嗎？ ◇ *Try to keep your room* clean and tidy. 盡量保持房間整潔乾淨。 ☞ [反] **dirty** 髒的

clean² /kliːn/ [動詞] 打掃，清理 It took half an hour to clean the kitchen. 打掃廚房用了半個小時。

clear /klɪə; 美 klɪr/ [形容詞] **1** 透明的 Glass is clear. 玻璃是透明的。**2** 清楚的，明白的 You must never do that again. Is that clear? 你千萬不要再那樣做了，明白嗎？

clever /'klevə; 美 -ər/ [形容詞] 聰明的 Helen is the cleverest girl in the class. 海倫是班上最聰明的女孩。

cliff /klɪf/ [名詞] (尤指海邊的) 懸崖，峭壁 They climbed down the cliff to the beach. 他們爬下懸崖來到了海灘。

climb /klaɪm/ [動詞] 攀，爬 'What's Henry doing?' 'He's climbing the tree.' "亨利在幹甚麼？" "他在爬樹。"

clinic /'klɪnɪk/ [名詞] 診所 I went to the clinic because I broke my arm. 我去了診所，因為我的胳膊摔斷了。

clock /klɒk; 美 klɑːk/ [名詞] 時鐘 The clock is fast. 時鐘快了。◇ The clock has stopped. 時鐘停了。

close¹ /kləʊz; 美 kloʊz/ [動詞] **1** 關上；閉上；合上 Please close the door. 請關上門。◇ Now close your book and see how much you can remember. 現在合上書看看你記住了多少。 ☞ ① [同] **shut** 關上；閉上；合上 ② [反] **open²** 開；打開；張開；睜開 **2** 關門；停止營業 What time do the shops close? 商店幾點鐘關門？ ☞ ① [同] **shut** 關門；停止營業 ② [反] **open²** 開門；營業

close² /kləʊs; 美 kloʊs/ [形容詞] (指時間、空間等) 近的，接近的 The church is close to the shops. 教堂離商店很近。

closed /kləʊzd; 美 kloʊzd/ [形容詞] **1** 關着的 Are all the windows closed? 所有的窗戶都關着嗎？ ☞ [反] **open¹** 開着的 **2** 關門的；停止營業的 The supermarket is closed. 超市關門了。

[反] **open**¹ 開門的；營業的

cloth /klɒθ; 美 klɔːθ/ [名詞] **1** [無複數] 布料 *How much cloth do you need to make the jacket?* 你做夾克需要多少布料？**2** 一塊布 *Cover the food with a cloth.* 用布把食品蓋起來。

clothes /kləʊðz; 美 kloʊz/ [名詞] [複數] 衣服，服裝 *Helen was wearing new clothes.* 海倫穿着新衣服。◇ *Put on your school clothes.* 穿上你的校服。

cloud /klaʊd/ [名詞] 雲 *There wasn't a cloud in the sky.* 天空無雲。

cloudy /ˈklaʊdi/ [形容詞] (指天空) 多雲的 *The sky was cloudy, so I took my umbrella.* 天空多雲，所以我帶了雨傘。

clown /klaʊn/ [名詞] 小丑 *The clown gave Alice a flower.* 小丑給

C

clothes 衣服

jacket 夾克／短上衣
tie 領帶
gloves 手套
blouse （女式）襯衫
scarf 圍巾
waistcoat 背心／馬甲
shorts 短褲
shirt 襯衫
belt 皮帶
sweater （套頭）毛衣
sweatshirt 運動衫
socks 短襪
dress 連衣裙
cardigan （開襟）毛衣
coat 外套
suit 套裝
trousers 褲子
tights 緊身褲
jeans 牛仔褲

了艾麗斯一朵花。

C

club /klʌb/ [名詞] 俱樂部 *Henry is a member of a computer club.* 亨利是一家計算機俱樂部的會員。

clue /kluː/ [名詞] 線索 *Police have found a vital clue.* 警方已經發現一條重大線索。

clumsy /'klʌmzi/ [形容詞] [比較級 **clumsier**，最高級**clumsiest**] (指人)笨拙的 *He's too clumsy to be a good dancer.* 他笨手笨腳的，當不了一名好的舞蹈演員。

clutch /klʌtʃ/ [動詞] 緊抓，緊握，緊抱 *I clutched the book in my arms.* 我把書緊緊抱在懷裏。

coach /kəutʃ; 美 koutʃ/ [名詞] [複數**coaches**] **1** 長途汽車 *They travelled by coach.* 他們乘長途汽車旅行。**2** 教練 *He's a famous football coach.* 他是一位著名的足球教練。

coal /kəul; 美 koul/ [名詞] [無複數] 煤 *Put some more coal on the fire.* 往火裏再加點煤。

coast /kəust; 美 koust/ [名詞] 海岸，海濱 *We live on the coast.* 我們住在海濱。

coat /kəut; 美 kout/ [名詞] 外衣，外套，大衣 *Put your coat on—it's cold outside.* 穿上外套，外面冷。

cobweb /'kɒbweb; 美 'kɑːb-/ [名詞] 蜘蛛網 *A spider makes a cobweb to catch insects.* 蜘蛛結網來捕食昆蟲。

Coca-Cola /ˌkəukə 'kəulə; 美 ˌkoukə 'koulə/ [又作**Coke**] [名詞] [商標] **1** [無複數] 可口可樂 **2** 一杯(一瓶、一聽)可口可樂 ☞ 參見**Coke**的示例。

cock /kɒk; 美 kɑːk/ [名詞] 公雞 *I heard a cock crow every morning.* 每天早晨我都聽見公雞啼叫。

coffee /'kɒfi; 美 'kɔ:fi/ [名詞] **1** [無複數] 咖啡 *I enjoy a cup of coffee after a meal.* 我喜歡在飯後喝杯咖啡。**2** 一杯咖啡 *Two coffees, please.* 請來兩杯咖啡。

coin /kɔɪn/ [名詞] 硬幣 *Peter has two coins in his hand.* 彼得手裏有兩枚硬幣。

Coke /kəʊk; 美 koʊk/ [名詞] [商標] [非正式] **1** [無複數] (可口) 可樂 *You can have some Coke.* 你可以喝點可樂。**2** 一杯 (一瓶、一聽) (可口) 可樂 *Can I have a Coke?* 我可以喝杯可樂嗎？

cold¹ /kəʊld; 美 koʊld/ [形容詞] 冷的，寒冷的 *Put your gloves on—it's cold outside today!* 戴上手套，今天外面冷！☞ [反] **hot** 熱的

cold² /kəʊld; 美 koʊld/ [名詞] 感冒，傷風 *Alice has a bad cold.* 艾麗斯得了重感冒。

collar /'kɒlə; 美 'kɑ:lər/ [名詞] 衣領 *I turned up my collar against the wind.* 我把衣領豎起來擋風。

collect /kə'lekt/ [動詞] **1** 收集 *Do you collect stamps?* 你集郵嗎？**2** 接走 *He collected the children from school.* 他把孩子們從學校接走了。

college /'kɒlɪdʒ; 美 'kɑ:-/ [名詞] 大學；學院 *My brother is going to college in the autumn.* 我哥哥秋天就要上大學了。

colour /'kʌlə; 美 -ər/ [名詞] 顏色 *'What colour is your pencil?' 'It's red.'* "你的鉛筆是甚麼顏色的？" "是紅色的。" ☞ 美國英語拼寫為 **color**。

colours 顏色

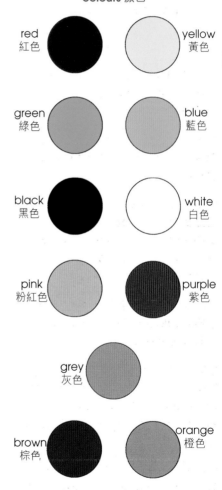

red 紅色
yellow 黃色
green 綠色
blue 藍色
black 黑色
white 白色
pink 粉紅色
purple 紫色
grey 灰色
brown 棕色
orange 橙色

comb¹ /kəʊm; 美 koʊm/ [名詞] 梳子 *Helen always takes a comb to school to keep her hair tidy.* 海倫總是帶着梳子上學，以便保持頭髮整齊。

comb² /kəʊm; 美 koʊm/ [動詞] 梳 *Your hair's a mess! It needs combing.* 你的頭髮一團糟！該梳一梳了。

come /kʌm/ [動詞] [過去式**came** /keɪm/，過去分詞**come**] 來 `Can you come?' 'I'm afraid I can't.'' "你能來嗎？" "恐怕不能來。"

come from 來自；出生於 `Where do you come from?' `I come from England.' "你是哪裏人？" "我是英格蘭人。"

come in 進來 *Come in and sit down.* 進來坐下。

come on 快點，趕快 *Come on, we'll be late!* 快點，我們要遲到了！

comfortable /ˈkʌmftəbl/ [形容詞] 舒適的，舒服的 *This is a very comfortable chair.* 這是一把很舒適的椅子。 [反] **uncomfortable** 不舒適的，不舒服的

common /ˈkɒmən; 美 ˈkɑː-/ [形容詞] 普通的；普遍的 *Computers are common in schools.* 計算機在學校很普遍。

compare /kəmˈpeə; 美 -ˈper/ [動詞] 比較，對照 *Compare your answers with those at the back of the book.* 把你的答案與書後的答案對一下。

compass /ˈkʌmpəs/ [名詞] [複數

compasses] 1 指南針 *Dad looked at his compass.* 爸爸看了看指南針。 2 [用作複數] 圓規 *Use your compasses to draw a circle.* 用你的圓規畫一個圓。

compasses 圓規　compass 指南針

competition /ˌkɒmpəˈtɪʃn; 美 ˌkɑːm-/ [名詞] 比賽 *I came first in the swimming competition.* 我獲得了游泳比賽的第一名。

complete¹ /kəmˈpliːt/ [形容詞] 完整的；全部的；完全的 *He read the complete works of Shakespeare.* 他讀了莎士比亞全集。

complete² /kəmˈpliːt/ [動詞] 完成 *Alice completed her homework and went out to play.* 艾麗斯做完作業就出去玩了。

computer /kəmˈpjuːtə; 美 -ər/ [名詞] 計算機，電腦 *Do you like playing computer games?* 你喜歡玩電腦遊戲嗎？

concentrate /ˈkɒnsntreɪt; 美 ˈkɑːn-/ [動詞] 集中(思想、精力、注意

力等）*I can't concentrate on my homework when I'm hungry.* 我餓了就沒法集中精力做作業。

concert /'kɒnsət; 美 'kɑːnsɜːrt/ [名詞] 音樂會 *They went to a concert last night.* 他們昨晚去聽了一場音樂會。

conductor /kən'dʌktə; 美 -ər/ [名詞]（公共汽車的）售票員 *Did the conductor check your ticket?* 售票員檢查你的票了嗎？

confuse /kən'fjuːz/ [動詞] 使糊塗 *Don't give me so much information—you're confusing me.* 別跟我說那麼多信息，你都把我搞糊塗了。

congratulations /kən-ˌgrætʃuˈleɪʃnz; 美 kənˌgrætʃə-/ [名詞] [複數，用作感歎詞] 恭喜，祝賀 *Congratulations on your 10th birthday!* 祝賀你10歲生日！

connect /kəˈnekt/ [動詞] 連接 *Connect the pipe to the tap.* 把管子接在水龍頭上。

consist /kənˈsɪst/ [動詞] consist of 由…組成，由…構成 *This book consists of two parts.* 這本書由兩部分組成。

consonant /'kɒnsənənt; 美 'kɑːn-/ [名詞] 輔音字母 *There are twenty-one consonants in the English alphabet.* 英語字母表中有21個輔音字母。

contain /kənˈteɪn/ [動詞] 包含，含有 *Sea water contains salt.* 海水含有鹽分。◇ *What does that box*

contain? 那個箱子裏裝的是甚麼？

container /kənˈteɪnə; 美 -ər/ [名詞] 容器 *Boxes, bags and baskets are all containers.* 箱子、袋子和籃子都是容器。

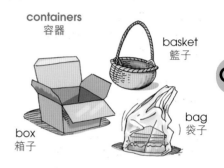

containers
容器

basket
籃子

bag
袋子

box
箱子

continent /'kɒntɪnənt; 美 'kɑːntə-/ [名詞]（大）洲；大陸 *There are seven continents in the world.* 世界上有七大洲。

continue /kənˈtɪnjuː; 美 -ju/ [動詞] 繼續 *We continued our lessons after lunch.* 午飯後我們繼續上課。

control /kənˈtrəʊl; 美 -ˈtroʊl/ [動詞] [現在分詞**controlling**，過去式和過去分詞**controlled**] 控制 *Henry controlled his bicycle very well.* 亨利騎自行車控制自如。

conversation /ˌkɒnvəˈseɪʃn; 美 ˌkɑːnvər-/ [名詞] 交談，會話 *Henry and Helen are having a conversation.* 亨利和海倫正在交談。

cook¹ /kʊk/ [動詞] 烹調，燒，煮，做（飯）'*What's Paul doing?*' '*He's learning to cook.*' "保羅在幹甚麼？" "他在學做飯。"

cook² /kʊk/ [名詞] 厨師 *My mother is a good cook.* 我媽媽飯菜做得很好。

cool /ku:l/ [形容詞] 涼的，涼爽的 *Cotton clothes are cool in summer.* 夏天穿棉布衣服涼快。☞[反] **warm** 温暖的，暖和的

copy¹ /'kɒpi; 美 'kɑːpi/ [名詞] [複數 **copies**] 副本；複製品 *The painting is only a copy.* 這幅畫只是一件複製品。

copy² /'kɒpi; 美 'kɑːpi/ [動詞] [過去式和過去分詞**copied**] **1** 抄寫 *She copied the phone number into her address book.* 她把電話號碼抄在她的地址簿上。**2** 複製，拷貝 *He copied the information into a notebook computer.* 他把信息複製到筆記本電腦裏。**3** 模仿 *Alice is copying Helen.* 艾麗斯在模仿海倫。**4** 抄襲 *She copied his answers.* 她抄襲了他的答案。

cord /kɔːd; 美 kɔːrd/ [名詞] (細)繩 *Tie the box with a piece of cord.* 用繩把箱子捆上。

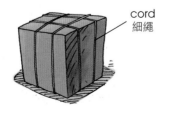

cord
細繩

corner /'kɔːnə; 美 'kɔːrnər/ [名詞] 角落；拐角處 *Put the lamp in the corner of the room.* 把燈放在房間的角落裏。

correct¹ /kə'rekt/ [形容詞] 正確的，對的 *Well done! All your answers were correct.* 做得好！你所有的答案都對了。☞① [同] **right¹** 正確的，對的 ② [反] **wrong** 錯誤的

correct² /kə'rekt/ [動詞] 改正，糾正 *Correct my pronunciation if it's wrong.* 如果我的發音錯了，就幫我糾正過來。

corridor /'kɒrɪdɔː; 美 'kɔːrədər/ [名詞] 走廊 *The children walked along the corridor to their classroom.* 孩子們沿着走廊走到教室。☞ [同] **passage** 通道；走廊

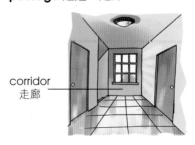

corridor
走廊

cost¹ /kɒst; 美 kɔːst/ [名詞] 價錢；費用 *What's the cost of the shirt?* 這

件襯衣要多少錢？

cost² /kɒst; 美 kɔːst/ [動詞] [過去式和過去分詞**cost**] 花費，值 `How much did the book cost?` `It cost six pounds!` "那本書要多少錢？" "6英鎊！"

costume /ˈkɒstjuːm; 美 ˈkɑːstuːm/ [名詞] (某地或某時期的) 服裝 They all wore national costume. 他們都穿着民族服裝。

cot /kɒt; 美 kɑːt/ [名詞] 嬰兒牀 A baby sleeps in a cot. 寶寶在嬰兒牀裏睡覺。

cottage /ˈkɒtɪdʒ; 美 ˈkɑː-/ [名詞] 村舍，小屋 He bought a cottage in a village. 他在鄉村買了一間小屋。

cotton /ˈkɒtn; 美 ˈkɑːtn/ [名詞] [無複數] **1** 棉布 This skirt is made of cotton. 這條裙子是用棉布做的。**2** 棉線 I need a needle and cotton. 我需要針線。

cough¹ /kɒf; 美 kɔːf/ [動詞] 咳嗽 The child was coughing all night. 孩子整夜都在咳嗽。

cough² /kɒf; 美 kɔːf/ [名詞] 咳嗽 I've got a bad cough. 我咳嗽得很厲害。

could /強 kʊd; 弱 kəd/ **can**的過去式 He said that he could run fast. 他說他能跑快。

couldn't /ˈkʊdnt/ **could not**的縮寫 I couldn't see because it was dark. 因為天黑，我看不見。

count /kaʊnt/ [動詞] 數 Close your eyes and count to 20. 閉上眼睛，從1數到20。

counter /ˈkaʊntə; 美 -ər/ [名詞] 櫃台 I put my money on the counter. 我把錢放在櫃台上。

country /ˈkʌntri/ [名詞] [複數 **countries**] 1 國家 China and Japan are Asian countries. 中國和日本是亞洲國家。2 鄉下，鄉村 He lives in the country. 他住在鄉下。

courage /ˈkʌrɪdʒ; 美 ˈkɜːr-/ [名詞] [無複數] 勇氣 I didn't have the courage to tell him. 我沒有勇氣告訴他。

cousin /ˈkʌzn/ [名詞] 堂兄；堂弟；堂姐；堂妹；表兄；表弟；表姐；表妹 Henry and I are cousins. 亨利和我是堂兄弟。

cover /ˈkʌvə; 美 -ər/ [動詞] 蓋；覆蓋；遮蓋 She covered her child with a blanket. 她給孩子蓋上毛毯。◇ Snow covered the ground. 白雪覆蓋着地面。

cow /kaʊ/ [名詞] 母牛；奶牛 The farmer milks his cows twice a day. 那個農民每天擠兩次牛奶。

crab /kræb/ [名詞] 螃蟹 Crabs have ten legs. 螃蟹有10條腿。

crack /kræk/ [名詞] 裂縫；裂紋 Don't go skating today—there are dangerous cracks in the ice. 今天別去滑冰了，冰上有裂縫，很危險。◇ This glass has a crack in it. 這個杯子上有一道裂紋。

crack
裂紋

crane /kreɪn/ [名詞] 起重機 A crane is a machine that lifts things. 起重機是一種能吊起東西的機器。

crash¹ /kræʃ/ [動詞] 猛撞；撞毀 The car crashed into a tree. 那輛小汽車撞在一棵樹上。

crash² /kræʃ/ [名詞] [複數 **crashes**] 1 (汽車)撞車事故；(飛機)失事 There was a serious car crash this morning. 今天早晨發生了一起嚴重的撞車事故。 **2** 碰撞聲 The tree fell with a great crash. 那棵樹嘩啦一聲倒了。

crawl /krɔːl/ [動詞] 爬,爬行 A baby crawls before it can walk. 嬰兒先會爬,後會走。

crayon /'kreɪɒn; 美 -ɑːn/ [名詞] 蠟筆 Some crayons are made from wax. 有些蠟筆是用蜂蠟做成的。

cream /kriːm/ [名詞] [無複數] 奶油 My dad likes to put cream in his coffee. 我爸爸喜歡在咖啡裏加奶油。

creature /'kriːtʃə; 美 -ər/ [名詞] 生物 Horses, lizards, fish, birds and insects are all creatures. 馬、蜥蜴、魚、鳥和昆蟲都是生物。

creep /kriːp/ [動詞] [過去式和過去分詞**crept** /krept/] 躡手躡腳地走 She crept into the room so as not to wake the baby. 為了不吵醒寶寶,她躡手躡腳地進了房間。

crew /kruː/ [名詞] 全體船員;(飛機等的)機組人員 The plane crashed, killing all the passengers and crew. 飛機失事了,所有乘客和機組人員都遇難了。

cricket /'krɪkɪt; 美 -ət/ [名詞] **1** 蟋蟀 You can often hear crickets during the summer. 夏天你能經常聽到蟋蟀的叫聲。**2** [無複數] 板球(運動) They played cricket all day. 他們打了一天板球。

cried /kraɪd/ **cry**的過去式和過去分詞 She cried for half an hour. 她哭了半個小時。

crocodile /'krɒkədaɪl; 美 'krɑː-/ [名詞] 鱷魚 A crocodile is a reptile. 鱷魚是爬行動物。

crop /krɒp; 美 krɑːp/ [名詞] 農作物，莊稼 *Wheat, potatoes and rice are crops.* 小麥、土豆和水稻都是農作物。

cross[1] /krɒs; 美 krɔːs/ [名詞] [複數 **crosses**] 叉號 *Put a cross if the answer is wrong.* 如果答案錯了，就打個叉。

cross[2] /krɒs; 美 krɔːs/ [動詞] 越過，穿過，渡過 *Peter is crossing the road.* 彼得正在過馬路。

crossword /ˈkrɒsw3ːd; 美 ˈkrɔːsw3ːrd/ [又作 **crossword puzzle**] [名詞] 縱橫填字遊戲 *Paul is doing the crossword in the newspaper.* 保羅正在做報紙上的縱橫填字遊戲。

crowd /kraʊd/ [名詞] [與單數或複數動詞連用] 人羣 *The crowd was/were very noisy.* 人羣很嘈雜。

crown /kraʊn/ [名詞] 王冠 *The queen's crown has jewels on it.* 女王的王冠上有寶石。

cruel /ˈkruːəl/ [形容詞] [比較級 **crueller**，最高級 **cruellest**] 殘忍的，殘酷的 *He is cruel to animals.* 他對動物很殘忍。

crush /krʌʃ/ [動詞] 壓碎，壓壞 *Don't crush the box — there are eggs inside!* 別壓這個箱子，裏面有雞蛋！

crust /krʌst/ [名詞] 麵包皮；糕餅皮 *Peter never eats his crusts.* 彼得從來不吃麵包皮。

cry /kraɪ/ [動詞] [過去式和過去分詞 **cried**] 哭，哭泣 *The child was crying for her mother.* 孩子在哭着要媽媽。

cube /kjuːb/ [名詞] 立方體 *A cube has eight corners.* 立方體有8個角兒。

cucumber /ˈkjuːkʌmbə; 美 -ər/ [名詞] 黃瓜 *Dad likes cucumber sandwiches.* 爸爸喜歡吃黃瓜三明治。

cup /kʌp/ [名詞] **1** (有柄的)杯子 *Would you like a cup of tea?* 你想不想喝杯茶？

2 一杯(飲料) *I'd like another cup.* 我想再喝一杯。

cupboard /ˈkʌbəd; 美 -ərd/ [名詞] 橱櫃 *Peter put his toys in the cupboard.* 彼得把他的玩具放在櫥櫃裏。

curious /ˈkjʊəriəs; 美 ˈkjʊr-/ [形容詞] 好奇的 *Henry was curious about the parcel.* 亨利對這個包裹很好奇。

curtain /ˈkɜːtn; 美 ˈkɜːrtn/ [名詞] 窗簾 *Could you draw the curtain, please?* 請把窗簾拉上好嗎？

curve /kɜːv; 美 kɜːrv/ [名詞] 曲線，彎曲 *The mountain road has many curves.* 這條山路有很多彎。

cushion /ˈkʊʃn/ [名詞] 坐墊，靠墊 *She put two cushions behind her and felt more comfortable.* 她在背後放了兩個靠墊，覺得舒服多了。

customer /ˈkʌstəmə; 美 -ər/ [名詞] 顧客 *The shop was full of customers.* 商店裏擠滿了顧客。

cut /kʌt/ [動詞] [過去式和過去分詞 **cut**] **1** 切，割，剪 *Henry cut the apple in half.* 亨利把蘋果切成兩半。

2 切下，割下，剪下 *Can you cut me a piece of cake, please?* 請給我切一塊蛋糕可以嗎？

cycle /ˈsaɪkl/ [動詞] 騎自行車 *I cycle to school every day.* 我每天騎自行車上學。

D d

dad /dæd/ [名詞] [非正式] 爸爸，爹爹 *Is that your dad?* 那是你爸爸嗎？ ◇ *Come on, dad!* 快點，爸！

daddy /'dædi/ [名詞] [複數 **daddies**] [非正式] 爸爸，爹爹 [多用於兒語] *I want my daddy.* 我要爸爸。

daily¹ /'deɪli/ [形容詞] 每日的，每天的 *Is this a daily newspaper?* 這是日報嗎？

daily² /'deɪli/ [副詞] 每日，每天 *Take the medicine twice daily.* 每天服藥兩次。

damage /'dæmɪdʒ/ [動詞] 損害，毀壞 *The house was badly damaged by the fire.* 這座房子被大火嚴重燒毀了。

damp /dæmp/ [形容詞] 潮濕的 *Use a damp cloth to clean the table.* 用濕布把桌子擦乾淨。

dance /dɑːns; 美 dæns/ [動詞] 跳舞 *Alice loves to dance.* 艾麗斯喜歡跳舞。

dancer /'dɑːnsə; 美 'dænsər/ [名詞] 跳舞者；舞蹈演員 *She's a good dancer.* 她跳舞跳得很好。

danger /'deɪndʒə; 美 -ər/ [名詞] [無複數] 危險 *Danger! Do not enter.* 危險！請勿入內。

dangerous /'deɪndʒərəs/ [形容詞] 危險的 *Some snakes are dangerous.* 有些蛇很危險。 ☞ [反] **safe** 安全的

dare /deə; 美 der/ [動詞] 敢 *I daren't ask her to lend me any more money.* 我不敢再問她借錢了。

dark¹ /dɑːk; 美 dɑːrk/ [形容詞] **1** 黑暗的 *It was so dark that I couldn't see anything.* 天這麼黑，我甚麼也看不見。 ☞ [反] **bright** 明亮的 **2** 深色的 *Alice wore a dark blue dress.* 艾麗斯穿了一件深藍色的連衣裙。 ☞ [反] **light²** 淺色的

dark² /dɑːk; 美 dɑːrk/ [名詞] 黑暗 *Cats can see in the dark.* 貓在黑暗中也能看見東西。 ◇ *Are you afraid of the dark?* 你怕黑嗎？

date /deɪt/ [名詞] 日期；日子 'What's the date today?' 'It's the first of May.' "今天幾號？" "5月1日。"

daughter /'dɔːtə; 美 -ər/ [名詞] 女兒 *They have two daughters and a son.* 他們有兩個女兒一個兒子。

day /deɪ/ [名詞] **1** 天，日 'What day is it today?' 'It's Thursday.' "今天星期幾？""星期四。" **2** 白天，白晝 Most people work during the day and sleep at night. 大多數人白天工作，晚上睡覺。

dead /ded/ [形容詞] 死的 I'm afraid he's dead. 恐怕他已經死了。◇ Police found a dead body under the bridge. 警察在橋下發現一具死屍。☞ [反] **alive** 活着的

deaf /def/ [形容詞] 聾的 He can't hear you — he's deaf. 他聽不見你說的話，他是聾子。

dear¹ /dɪə; 美 dɪr/ [形容詞] [用於書信的開頭，收信人稱呼之前] 親愛的 Dear Sir 親愛的先生 ◇ Dear Mr Brown 親愛的布朗先生

dear² /dɪə; 美 dɪr/ [感歎詞] [表示驚訝、惱火、失望等] 啊；哎呀 Oh dear! I've forgotten something. 哎呀！我忘了件事。

December /dɪ'sembə; 美 -ər/ [名詞] 十二月 Her birthday is in December. 她的生日是在12月。☞ ①參見 **August** 的示例。② **Dec** 是 **December** 的縮寫。

decide /dɪ'saɪd/ [動詞] 決定 We've decided to go to France for our holidays. 我們決定去法國度假。

deck /dek/ [名詞] （船的）甲板；（公共汽車的）一層 Let's go up on deck and sit in the sunshine. 我們到上面甲板上去，坐着曬太陽吧。

deck 甲板

decorate /'dekəreɪt/ [動詞] 裝飾 Paul and Henry are decorating a Christmas tree. 保羅和亨利正在裝飾一棵聖誕樹。

deep /diːp/ [形容詞] 深的 Be careful — the water is very deep. 小心，水很深。☞ [反] **shallow** 淺的

deer /dɪə; 美 dɪr/ [名詞] [複數 **deer**] 鹿 Are there deer in the forest? 森林裏有鹿嗎？

delicious /dɪ'lɪʃəs/ [形容詞] 美味的，可口的 This soup is delicious. 這湯很可口。

deliver /dɪ'lɪvə; 美 -ər/ [動詞] 遞送 He delivers newspapers every morning. 他每天早晨送報。

dentist /ˈdentɪst; 美 -əst / [名詞] 牙醫 *The dentist examined my teeth.* 牙醫檢查了我的牙齒。

department store /dɪˈpɑːtmənt stɔː; 美 dɪˈpɑːrtmənt stɔːr/ [名詞] 百貨商店 *This is a famous department store in London.* 這是倫敦一家著名的百貨商店。

depth /depθ/ [名詞] 深度 *What's the depth of the swimming pool?* 這個游泳池有多深？

describe /dɪˈskraɪb/ [動詞] 描述；敘述 *Can you describe the bag you lost?* 你能描述一下你丟的包嗎？

desert /ˈdezət; 美 -ərt/ [名詞] 沙漠 *In the desert it is very dry.* 沙漠裏很乾燥。

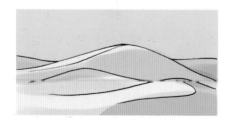

deserve /dɪˈzɜːv; 美 -ˈzɜːrv/ [動詞] 應受，應得，值得 *You've been working all morning— I think you deserve a rest.* 你整個上午都在忙，我覺得你應該休息一下。

desk /desk/ [名詞] 書桌 *Alice sits at the desk.* 艾麗斯坐在書桌旁。

dessert /dɪˈzɜːt; 美 -ˈzɜːrt/ [名詞] (飯後吃的) 甜食 *We had ice cream for dessert.* 我們甜食吃冰淇淋。

destroy /dɪˈstrɔɪ/ [動詞] 摧毀；毀壞；破壞 *The building was destroyed by fire.* 這座建築物被大火燒毀了。

diagram /ˈdaɪəgræm/ [名詞] 圖表，圖解 *The book uses simple diagrams to explain the rules of chess.* 這本書用簡圖來說明國際象棋的規則。

diamond /ˈdaɪəmənd/ [名詞] 鑽石 *The ring has a diamond.* 這枚戒指上有顆鑽石。

diary /ˈdaɪəri/ [名詞] [複數 **diaries**] 日記；日記簿 *Do you keep a diary?*

你寫日記嗎？◇ Can I read your diary? 我可以看一下你的日記嗎？

dictionary /ˈdɪkʃənri; 美 -neri/ [名詞] [複數 **dictionaries**] 字典；詞典 Look up the word in your dictionary. 在詞典裏查一查這個詞。

did /dɪd/ **do** 的過去式 Did you go to school yesterday? 你昨天去上學了嗎？

didn't /ˈdɪdnt/ **did not** 的縮寫 We didn't go to the beach. 我們沒有去海灘。

die /daɪ/ [動詞] [現在分詞 **dying** /ˈdaɪɪŋ/，過去式和過去分詞 **died**] 死 She's very ill and I'm afraid she's dying. 她病得很重，恐怕快要死了。

different /ˈdɪfrənt/ [形容詞] 不同的 The twins are wearing different colours. 這對雙胞胎穿着不同顏色的衣服。◇ Cricket is different from baseball. 板球與棒球不同。☞ [反] **same¹** 相同的，同一的

difficult /ˈdɪfɪkəlt/ [形容詞] 困難的 The exam questions were too difficult. 考題太難了。◇ I find it difficult to get up early in the morning. 我覺得早晨早起很難。☞ ① [同] **hard¹** 困難的 ② [反] **easy** 容易的

dig /dɪg/ [動詞] [現在分詞 **digging**，過去式和過去分詞 **dug** /dʌg/] 挖（洞），掘（地）Paul is busy digging in the sand. 保羅正忙着在沙地上挖洞。

spade
鐵鍬

dinner /ˈdɪnə; 美 -ər/ [名詞]（中午或晚上吃的）正餐 What's for dinner, mum? 晚飯吃甚麼，媽？◇ What time do you usually have dinner? 你通常幾點鐘吃飯？

dinosaur /ˈdaɪnəsɔː; 美 -sɔːr/ [名詞] 恐龍 Dinosaurs became extinct millions of years ago. 千百萬年以前恐龍就滅絕了。

direction /daɪˈrekʃn; 美 də-/ [名詞] **1** 方向 They got lost because they went in the wrong direction. 他們迷路了，因為他們走錯了方向。**2** [通常用作複數] 說明，提示 I didn't read the directions on the package before I made the cake. 我在做蛋糕前沒有看包裝上的說明。

dirty /ˈdɜːti; 美 ˈdɜːr-/ [形容詞] [比較級 **dirtier**，最高級 **dirtiest**] 髒的 Your hands are dirty—go and wash them! 你的手髒，去洗一洗！ ☞ [反] **clean**¹ 乾淨的

disagree /ˌdɪsəˈgriː/ [動詞] 意見不同，不同意 I disagree with you about this. 對於這件事我跟你意見不同。

disappear /ˌdɪsəˈpɪə; 美 -ˈpɪr/ [動詞] 不見，失蹤；消失 The dog has disappeared. 狗不見了。◇ The sun disappeared behind a cloud. 太陽在雲後消失了。 ☞ [反] **appear** 出現

disappointed /ˌdɪsəˈpɔɪntɪd; 美 -əd/ [形容詞] 失望的，沮喪的 My parents will be disappointed in me if I fail the exam. 如果我考試不及格，我父母會對我感到失望的。

disaster /dɪˈzɑːstə; 美 -ˈzæstər/ [名詞] 災難 Floods and earthquakes are disasters. 洪水和地震都是災難。

discover /dɪˈskʌvə; 美-ər/ [動詞] 發現 Columbus discovered America in 1492. 哥倫布於1492年發現了美洲。

discuss /dɪˈskʌs/ [動詞] 討論 I discussed the problem with my parents. 我和父母討論了這個問題。

disease /dɪˈziːz/ [名詞] 病；疾病

Rats and flies spread disease. 老鼠和蒼蠅都傳播疾病。

dish /dɪʃ/ [名詞] [複數 **dishes**] 碟子，盤子 Be careful with the dish! 小心盤子！

dishonest /dɪsˈɒnɪst; 美 -ˈɑ-/ [形容詞] 不誠實的 You can't trust him — he's dishonest. 你不能信任他，他不誠實。 ☞ [反] **honest** 誠實的

disk /dɪsk/ [名詞] 磁盤 Paul put the disk in his computer. 保羅把磁盤插進電腦裏。

dislike /dɪsˈlaɪk/ [動詞] 不喜歡，厭惡 I dislike getting up early. 我不喜歡早起。

disobey /ˌdɪsəˈbeɪ/ [動詞] 不服從，不聽 She disobeyed her mother and went to the party. 她沒有聽母親的話，去參加聚會了。 ☞ [反] **obey** 服從

display /dɪˈspleɪ/ [名詞] 陳列；展示 All kinds of toys were displayed in the shop window. 商店的櫥窗裏陳列着各種各樣的玩具。

dissolve /dɪˈzɒlv; 美 -ˈzɑːlv / [動詞] 溶解 *Sugar dissolves in water.* 糖在水裏溶解。

distance /ˈdɪstəns / [名詞] 距離 *It's a short distance from my house to the school.* 從我家到學校的距離很短。

disturb /dɪˈstɜːb; 美 -ˈstɜːrb / [動詞] 打擾 *I'm sorry to disturb you.* 對不起，打擾你了。

dive /daɪv / [動詞] 跳水 *Henry dived into the pool.* 亨利跳進游泳池裏。

divide /dɪˈvaɪd / [動詞] **1** 分，劃分 *The teacher divided the class into groups of three.* 老師把學生分成三人一組。**2** 除 *10 divided by 5 is 2.* 10除以5等於2。

do[1] / 強 duː; 弱 du / [助動詞] [與其他動詞連用構成疑問句或否定句，也用於簡短的回答或附加問句] *Do you drink coffee?* 你喝咖啡嗎？◇*I like football but I don't like tennis.* 我喜歡足球，但不喜歡網球。◇*You live in London, don't you?* 你住在倫敦，是嗎？

do[2] / 強 duː; 弱 du / [動詞] [過去式**did** /dɪd / ，過去分詞**done** /dʌn /] 做，幹 *'What are you doing?' 'I'm doing my homework.'* "你在做甚麼？""我在做作業。"

doctor /ˈdɒktə; 美 ˈdɑːktər / [名詞] 醫生 *'What does your father do?' 'He's a doctor.'* "你父親是做甚麼的？""他是醫生。"

does / 強 dʌz; 弱 dəz / **do** 的第三人稱單數形式 *Does she speak English?* 她說英語嗎？

doesn't /ˈdʌznt / **does not** 的縮寫 *Peter doesn't like maths.* 彼得不喜歡數學。

dog /dɒg; 美 dɔːg / [名詞] 狗 *Henry took the dog for a walk.* 亨利領着狗去散步了。◇ *I could hear a dog barking.* 我聽見狗在叫。

doll /dɒl; 美 dɑːl / [名詞] 玩偶，洋娃娃 *Alice bought a new doll.* 艾麗斯買了一個新的洋娃娃。

dollar /'dɒlə; 美 'dɑːlər/ [名詞] 元 [美國、加拿大、澳大利亞等國的貨幣單位,符號為$] *There are 100 cents in a dollar.* 1 元等於 100 分錢。

dolphin /'dɒlfɪn; 美 'dɑːl-/ [名詞] 海豚 *Dolphins are very intelligent.* 海豚很聰明。

donkey /'dɒŋki; 美 'dɑːŋki/ [名詞] 驢 *Donkeys are smaller than horses.* 驢比馬小。

don't /dəʊnt; 美 doʊnt/ **do not**的縮寫 *I don't know his address.* 我不知道他的地址。

door /dɔː; 美 dɔːr/ [名詞] 門 *Can you close the door, please?* 請你把門關上

好嗎? ◇ *I can hear someone knocking at the door.* 我聽見有人在敲門。

double /'dʌbl/ [形容詞] 兩倍的 *His weight is double hers.* 他的體重是她的兩倍。

doubt /daʊt/ [動詞] 1 懷疑 *I doubt his honesty.* 我對他的誠實表示懷疑。2 認為…不可能,不相信 *I doubt if he will come.* 我看他不一定會來。

down[1] /daʊn/ [副詞] 向下 *This arrow points down.* 這個箭頭指向下方。◇ *Put that box down on the floor.* 把那個箱子放在地板上。☞ [反] **up**[1] 向上

down[2] /daʊn/ [介詞] 向(低處)*We ran down the hill.* 我們跑下山。☞ [反]**up**[2] 向(高處)

downstairs /ˌdaʊn'steəz; 美 -'sterz/ [副詞] 樓下 *Come downstairs, Peter.* 到樓下來,彼得。◇ *Wait downstairs in the hall.* 在樓下大廳裏等。☞ [反] **upstairs** 樓上

dozen /'dʌzn/ [名詞] 一打,十二個 *A dozen eggs, please.* 請給我一打雞蛋。

drag /dræg/ [動詞] [現在分詞 **dragging** ,過去式和過去分詞 **dragged**] (用力)拖,拉 *Alice dragged the chair into the bedroom.*

艾麗斯把椅子拖進臥室。

drag
拖／拉

dragon /ˈdrægən/ [名詞] 龍 *Alice read a story about dragons.* 艾麗斯讀了一個關於龍的故事。 ☞ 西方人眼中的 **dragon** 是長有鷹爪鷹翅、獅頭獅腳、羚羊角和蛇尾、口中噴火的怪獸，基督教視之為惡魔的化身，與象徵善的中國龍（**Chinese dragon**）成對比。

dragon
（西方）龍

Chinese dragon
中國龍

drain /dreɪn/ [名詞] 排水管；下水道 *The drain was blocked.* 下水道堵了。

drama /ˈdrɑːmə/ [名詞] 戲劇 *She's studying drama.* 她在學習戲劇。

drank /dræŋk/ **drink**的過去式 *Who drank all the juice?* 誰把果汁都給喝了？

draw /drɔː/ [動詞] [過去式 **drew** /druː/，過去分詞 **drawn** /drɔːn/]（用鉛筆、鋼筆或蠟筆）畫 *Paul drew a car.* 保羅畫了一輛小汽車。◇ *Paul draws very well.* 保羅很會畫畫。

drawer /drɔː; 美 drɔːr/ [名詞] 抽屜 *The pen is in my desk drawer.* 鋼筆在我書桌的抽屜裏。

D

drawing /ˈdrɔːɪŋ/ [名詞] 素描 *She's good at drawing.* 她擅長素描。

drawn /drɔːn/ **draw** 的過去分詞 *I've drawn a picture of you.* 我給你畫了一幅畫。

dream¹ /driːm/ [名詞] 夢 *I had a strange dream last night.* 昨晚我做了一個怪夢。

dream² /driːm/ [動詞] [過去式和過去分詞 **dreamed** /dremt; 美 driːmd/ 或 **dreamt** /dremt/] 做夢；夢見 *Do you* *dream at night?* 你夜裏做夢嗎？◇ *I dreamed about you last night.* 我昨晚夢見你了。

dress¹ /dres/ [名詞] [複數 **dresses**] 連衣裙 *Alice is wearing a new dress.* 艾麗斯穿着一件新連衣裙。

dress² /dres/ [動詞] **1** 穿衣服 *Paul dressed quickly and went out.* 保羅匆匆穿上衣服出去了。

2 給…穿衣服 *Could you dress the baby for me?* 你替我給寶寶穿上衣服好嗎？

drew /druː/ **draw** 的過去式 *Helen drew a picture.* 海倫畫了一幅畫。

dried /draɪd/ **dry** 的過去式和過去分詞 *Henry dried his hands on the towel.* 亨利用毛巾把手擦乾。

drill /drɪl/ [名詞] 鑽 *Mr Smith made a hole in the wall with his drill.* 史密斯先生用鑽在牆上鑽了個洞。

drink¹ /drɪŋk/ [動詞] [過去式 **drank** /dræŋk/，過去分詞 **drunk** /drʌŋk/] 喝；飲 *Is there anything to drink?* 有甚麼喝的嗎？◇ *What do you want to drink?* 你要喝甚麼？

drink² /drɪŋk/ [名詞] 飲料 *Can I have a drink?* 我可以喝點飲料嗎？

drip /drɪp/ [動詞] [現在分詞 **dripping**，過去式和過去分詞 **dripped**] 滴下 *The tap is dripping.* 水龍頭在滴水。

drive /draɪv/ [動詞] [過去式 **drove** /drəʊv; 美 droʊv/，過去分詞 **driven** /ˈdrɪvn/] 駕駛（汽車），開車 *Can you*

drive? 你會開車嗎？◇ *Don't drive so fast.* 不要開這麼快。

driver /'draɪvə; 美 -ər/ [名詞] 駕駛員，司機 *He's a taxi driver.* 他是一名出租車司機。

drop¹ /drɒp; 美 drɑːp/ [動詞] [現在分詞 **dropping**，過去式和過去分詞 **dropped**] (使) 落下，掉下 *Be careful! Please don't drop the vase!* 小心！請別把花瓶摔了！◇ *The vase dropped and broke.* 花瓶掉下來摔碎了。

drop² /drɒp; 美 drɑːp/ [名詞] 滴 *Drops of rain ran down the window.* 雨滴順着窗戶往下流。

drove /drəʊv; 美 droʊv/ **drive**的過去式 *They drove to the station.* 他們開車去了車站。

drown /draʊn/ [動詞] (使)淹死 *The boy fell into the river and drowned.* 那個男孩掉進河裏淹死了。

drum /drʌm/ [名詞] 鼓 *He plays the drums in a band.* 他在樂隊裏打鼓。

drunk /drʌŋk/ **drink**的過去分詞 *All the juice has been drunk.* 所有的果汁都給喝了。

dry¹ /draɪ/ [形容詞] [比較級 **drier**，最高級**driest**] 乾的 *These clothes are dry.* 這些衣服乾了。 ☞ [反] **wet** 濕的

dry² /draɪ/ [動詞] [現在分詞 **drying**，過去式和過去分詞 **dried**] 弄乾 *You can use this towel to dry your hands.* 你可以用這條毛巾把手擦乾。

duck /dʌk/ [名詞] 鴨 *Every afternoon they went to the park to feed the ducks.* 他們每天下午都去公園餵鴨子。

dug /dʌg/ **dig** 的過去式和過去分詞 *We dug a big hole.* 我們挖了一個大洞。

dull /dʌl/ [形容詞] 乏味的，無聊的，沉悶的 *Life is never dull in the city.* 城市裏的生活從不沉悶。

during /'djʊərɪŋ; 美 'dɜːr-/ [介詞] 在…期間 *We go swimming every day during the summer.* 夏天我們每天都去游泳。

dust /dʌst/ [名詞] [無複數] 灰塵，塵土 *There is dust everywhere in our house.* 我們的房子裏到處都是灰塵。

dustbin /'dʌstbɪn/ [名詞] (放在室外的) 垃圾箱 *Throw the rubbish into the dustbin.* 把垃圾扔到垃圾箱裏。 ☞ 參見 **bin** "垃圾箱"。

D

E e

each¹ /iːtʃ/ [形容詞] 每；各 *Each student must take the examination.* 每個學生都必須參加考試。

each² /iːtʃ/ [代詞] 每一，每個；各自 *Each of the students must take the examination.* 每個學生都必須參加考試。◇ *Each has his own room.* 每個人都有自己的房間。

each other /iːtʃ ˈʌðə; 美 -ˈɪr/ [代詞] 彼此，相互 *Henry and Peter looked at each other.* 亨利和彼得相互看着對方。☞參見 **one another** "彼此，相互"。

eager /ˈiːgə; 美 -ər/ [形容詞] 熱切的，渴望的 *He is eager to meet you.* 他很想見你。◇ *He is eager for success.* 他渴望成功。

eagle /ˈiːgl/ [名詞] 鷹 *The eagle caught a rabbit.* 鷹抓住了一隻兔子。

ear /ɪə; 美 ɪr/ [名詞] 耳朵 *'What's the matter?' 'My ear hurts.'* "你怎麼啦？""我耳朵痛。"

early¹ /ˈɜːli; 美 ˈɜːrli/ [形容詞] [比較級 **earlier**，最高級 **earliest**] 早的；提早的 *I was early for the lesson.* 我上課早來了一會兒。◇ *The bus was ten minutes early.* 公共汽車早到10分鐘。☞[反] **late**¹ 遲的，晚的

early² /ˈɜːli; 美 ˈɜːrli/ [副詞] [比較級 **earlier**，最高級 **earliest**] 早；提早 *I have to get up early tomorrow.* 我明天得早起。☞[反] **late**² 遲，晚

earn /ɜːn; 美 ɜːrn/ [動詞] 掙(錢) *He earns £20 000 a year.* 他每年掙兩萬英鎊。

earth /ɜːθ; 美 ɜːrθ/ [名詞] [用作單數，與 **the** 連用] 地球 *The earth goes round the sun.* 地球繞着太陽轉。

earthquake /ˈɜːθkweɪk; 美 ˈɜːrθ-/ [名詞] 地震 *The earthquake destroyed many buildings.* 地震摧毀了許多建築物。

east /iːst/ [名詞] [用作單數，常與 **the** 連用] 東，東方 *Which way is east?* 哪個方向是東？◇ *The sun rises* *in the east.* 太陽從東方升起。

easy /ˈiːzi/ [形容詞] [比較級 **easier**，最高級 **easiest**] 容易的 *The exam was easy.* 考試很容易。 ☞ [反] **difficult**，**hard**[1] 困難的

eat /iːt/ [動詞] [過去式 **ate** /et; 美 eɪt/，過去分詞 **eaten** /ˈiːtn/] 吃 *Do you want something to eat?* 你想吃東西嗎？ ◇ *I don't eat meat.* 我不吃肉。

echo /ˈekəʊ; 美 -oʊ/ [名詞] [複數 **echoes**] 回聲，回音 *Henry shouted 'Hello' and listened for the echo.* 亨利大聲喊"喂"，然後傾聽回音。

edge /edʒ/ [名詞] 邊，邊緣 *The crayon is on the edge of the table.* 蠟筆在桌子的邊上。

effect /ɪˈfekt/ [名詞] 結果；影響 *Eating too many sweets has had a bad effect on his teeth.* 吃太多的糖讓他的牙齒不好了。

effort /ˈefət; 美 -ərt/ [名詞] 努力 *Please make an effort to get there on time.* 請盡力準時到達那裏。

egg /eg/ [名詞] 蛋 *Henry always has a boiled egg for breakfast.* 亨利早餐總要吃一個煮雞蛋。

eight /eɪt/ [數詞] 八 *Two times four is eight.* 2乘4得8。 ☞ 參見 **five** 的示例。

eighteen /ˌeɪˈtiːn/ [數詞] 十八 *Two times nine is eighteen.* 2乘9得18。 ☞ 參見 **five** 的示例。

eighth /eɪtθ/ [數詞] 第八 *Today is the eighth of August.* 今天是8月8日。 ☞ 參見 **fifth** 的示例。

eighty /ˈeɪti/ [數詞] 八十 *Eight times ten is eighty.* 8乘10得80。 ☞ 參見 **fifty** 的示例。

either[1] /ˈaɪðə; 美 ˈiːðər/ [形容詞] （兩者之中）任一的 *You can park on either side of the street.* 街道哪邊都可以停車。

either[2] /ˈaɪðə; 美 ˈiːðər/ [代詞] （兩者之中的）任何一個 *There's coffee and tea. You can have either.* 咖啡和茶都有，你喝哪一種都行。

either[3] /ˈaɪðə; 美 ˈiːðər/ [副詞] [用於否定句] 也（不…） *'I can't swim.' 'I can't either.'* "我不會游泳。""我也不會。"

either⁴ /'aɪðə; 美 'i:ðər / [連詞]
either...or... 不是…就是…，要麼…要
麼… It's either blue or green — I
can't remember. 不是藍的，就是綠
的，我記不清了。

elbow /'elbəʊ; 美 -boʊ / [名詞] 肘；
肘部 Paul hurt his elbow when playing
tennis. 保羅打網球時傷了胳膊肘。

elbow
肘部

electricity /ɪˌlek'trɪsəti / [名詞] [無
複數] 電 Don't waste electricity! 不
要浪費電！

elephant /'elɪfənt / [名詞] 大象 An
elephant has a long nose. 大象長着
個長鼻子。

elevator /'elɪveɪtə; 美 -ər / [名詞] [美
國英語] = **lift**²

eleven /ɪ'levn / [數詞] 十一 Ten and
one make eleven. 10加1等於11。
☞ 參見 **five** 的示例。

else /els / [副詞] [用於疑問詞或

anyone、**no one**、**someone** 等詞
之後]另外；其他 What else did he
say? 他還說了些甚麼？◇ Did you see
anyone else? 你見到其他人了嗎？

email¹ /'i:meɪl / [名詞] 電子郵件
Henry is sending an email to his
friend. 亨利正在給朋友發電子郵件。

email² /'i:meɪl / [動詞] 給…發電子郵
件 Paul emailed me yesterday. 保
羅昨天給我發了電子郵件。

empty /'empti / [形容詞] [比較級
emptier，最高級**emptiest**] 空的 Your
glass is empty — would you like
another drink? 你的杯子空了，要不要
再來杯飲料？

encyclopedia /ɪnˌsaɪklə'pi:diə /
[名詞] [複數**encyclopedias**] 百科全書
'Does anyone know when
Shakespeare was born?' 'Look it up
in the encyclopedia.' "有人知道莎
士比亞是甚麼時候出生的嗎？" "查一
查百科全書。"

end¹ /end / [名詞] 末端；盡頭 My
house is at the end of the street. 我
家就在這條街的盡頭。◇ We're going
on holiday at the end of July. 我們7
月底去度假。

end² /end / [動詞] 結束 The party

ended at midnight. 聚會半夜才結束。 ☞ [反] **begin** 開始

enemy /'enəmi/ [名詞] [複數 **enemies**] 敵人；仇人 *He's made a lot of enemies at school.* 他在學校樹敵很多。

energy /'enədʒi; 美 -ər-/ [名詞] [無複數] **1** 精力；活力 *Children are usually full of energy.* 孩子們一般都精力充沛。 **2** 能量；能源 *It is important to try to save energy.* 盡量節約能源很重要。

engine /'endʒɪn/ [名詞] 發動機，引擎 *This car has a new engine.* 這輛汽車的發動機是新的。

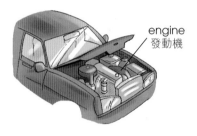

engine 發動機

England /'ɪŋglənd/ [名詞] **1** 英格蘭 *Mike lives in England.* 邁克住在英格蘭。 **2** 英國 *He's going to study in England next year.* 他明年去英國留學。

English[1] /'ɪŋglɪʃ/ [名詞] **1** 英語 *Do you speak English?* 你說英語嗎？ ◇ *I've been learning English for five years.* 我學英語5年了。 **2** [與 **the** 連用，作複數] 英國人 *What do you think of the English?* 你覺得英國人怎麼樣？

English[2] /'ɪŋglɪʃ/ [形容詞] **1** 英格蘭（人）的 *My mother is English and my father is Scottish.* 我母親是英格蘭人，

父親是蘇格蘭人。 **2** 英國（人）的 *Her mother is English and her father is American.* 她母親是英國人，父親是美國人。 **3** 英語的 *It's an English dictionary.* 這是一本英語詞典。

enjoy /ɪn'dʒɔɪ/ [動詞] 喜愛，喜歡 *Alice enjoys singing.* 艾麗斯喜歡唱歌。 ◇ *Did you enjoy the film?* 你喜歡那部影片嗎？

enjoy oneself 玩得開心，過得快活 *Enjoy yourself!* 好好玩吧！ ◇ *I always enjoy myself.* 我總是玩得很開心。

enormous /ɪ'nɔːməs; 美 -ɔːr-/ [形容詞] 巨大的，龐大的 *Mr and Mrs Smith have an enormous house.* 史密斯夫婦有一棟巨大的房子。

enough[1] /ɪ'nʌf/ [形容詞] 足夠的，充足的 *There isn't enough time.* 時間不夠了。

enough[2] /ɪ'nʌf/ [代詞] 足夠，充分 *'Would you like some more to eat?' 'No thanks, I've had enough.'* "再吃點好嗎？" "不，謝謝，我吃飽了。"

enough[3] /ɪ'nʌf/ [副詞] 足夠地，充分地 *The rope isn't long enough.* 這繩子不夠長。

enter /'entə; 美 -ər/ [動詞] 進入，進來 *Knock before you enter.* 進來前要敲門。 ◇ *They all stood up when he entered the room.* 他進入房間時，他們都站了起來。

entrance /'entrəns/ [名詞] 入口，進口，入口處，大門口 *Excuse me,*

E

where is the entrance to the cinema? 對不起，請問電影院的入口在哪裏？ ☞ [反] **exit** 出口

envelope /'envələup; 美 -loup/ [名詞] 信封 *Have you written his address on the envelope?* 你在信封上寫上他的地址了嗎？

environment /ɪn'vaɪrənmənt/ [名詞] **1** （指生活、工作、學習等）環境 *Students need a good learning environment.* 學生需要一個良好的學習環境。**2** [用作單數]（自然）環境 *We must do more to protect the environment.* 我們必須採取更多的辦法來保護環境。

equal /'iːkwəl/ [形容詞] 相等的，相同的，同樣的 *Cut the cake into six equal pieces.* 把蛋糕切成相等的6塊。

equator /ɪ'kweɪtə; 美 -ər/ [名詞] 赤道 *Countries on the equator are very hot.* 位於赤道上的國家很熱。

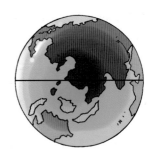

equipment /ɪ'kwɪpmənt/ [名詞] [無複數] 設備；器械；用具 *We bought some sports equipment.* 我們買了一些運動器械。

eraser /ɪ'reɪzə; 美 -ər/ [名詞] 橡皮；黑板擦 *Do you have an eraser?* 你有橡皮嗎？ ☞ **eraser** 尤用於美國英語，英國英語用 **rubber (2)**。

escape /ɪ'skeɪp/ [動詞] 逃跑，逃走 *The bird escaped from the cage.* 鳥從籠子裏飛走了。◇ *He escaped from prison.* 他從監獄裏逃走了。

especially /ɪ'speʃəli/ [副詞] 特別，格外，尤其 'Do you like chocolates?' 'Not especially.' "你喜歡吃巧克力嗎？" "不是特別喜歡。" ◇ *Helen loves animals, especially dogs.* 海倫喜歡動物，尤其是狗。

euro /'juərəu; 美 'jurou/ [名詞] [複數 **euros**] 歐元 [歐盟大多數國家使用的貨幣單位，符號為€] *This shirt cost 30 euros.* 這件襯衫賣 30 歐元。

Europe /ˈjʊərəp; 美 ˈjʊr-/ [名詞] 歐洲 *France is in Europe.* 法國位於歐洲。

European[1] /ˌjʊərəˈpiːən; 美 ˌjʊr-/ [形容詞] 歐洲（人）的 *France is a European country.* 法國是一個歐洲國家。

European[2] /ˌjʊərəˈpiːən; 美 ˌjʊr-/ [名詞] 歐洲人 *Europeans now live in all parts of the world.* 歐洲人現在生活在世界的各個角落。

even /ˈiːvn/ [形容詞] **1** 平的，平坦的，平滑的 *I fell over because the floor wasn't even.* 由于地面不平，我摔了一跤。 **2** 偶數的，雙數的 *2, 4, 6, 8, 10 are all even numbers.* 2，4，6，8，10 都是偶數。 ☞ [反] **odd** 奇數的，單數的

evening /ˈiːvnɪŋ/ [名詞] 傍晚；晚上 *The sun sets in the evening.* 太陽在傍晚落山。

good evening 晚上好 *'Good evening, Helen.' 'Evening, Henry.'* "晚上好，海倫。""晚上好，亨利。" ☞ 在非正式場合說"晚上好"，也可以只用 **Evening**。

ever /ˈevə; 美 -ər/ [副詞] [用於疑問句或否定句] 在任何時候 *'Have you ever been to London?' 'Yes, I have. Not long ago.'* "你去過倫敦嗎？""去過，不久前去的。"

every /ˈevri/ [形容詞] [與單數名詞連用] 每一，每個 *She knows every student in the school.* 她認識學校裏的每一個學生。

everybody /ˈevriˌbɒdi; 美 -ˌbɑːdi/ [代詞] [與單數動詞連用] 每個人；人人；大家 *Everybody wants to have lunch in the garden.* 大家都想在花園裏吃午飯。 ☞ = **everyone**

everyone /ˈevriwʌn/ [又作 **everybody**] [代詞] 每個人；人人；大家 *She likes everyone in her class.* 她喜歡班上的每一個人。

everything /ˈevriθɪŋ/ [代詞] [與單數動詞連用] 每樣東西，所有東西 *Everything is very expensive in this shop.* 這家商店裏每樣東西都很貴。

everywhere /ˈevriweə; 美 -wer/ [副詞] 到處，處處 *I looked for my pen everywhere, but I couldn't find it anywhere.* 我到處找我的鋼筆，但哪裏也找不到。

evil /ˈiːvl/ [形容詞] 壞的；邪惡的 *The police caught the evil men.* 警方把那些壞人抓住了。

exactly /ɪɡˈzæktli/ [副詞] **1** 確切地，精確地 *Tell me exactly where she lives.* 確切地告訴我，她住在甚麼地方。 **2** 恰好；正是 *This shirt is exactly what I wanted.* 這件襯衫正是我想要的。 **3** [用於表示同意某人] 確實如此，一點不錯 *'The boy is quite clever.' 'Exactly.'* "這個男孩很聰明。""一點不錯。"

exam /ɪɡˈzæm/ [又作 **examination**] [名詞] 考試 *'How was the exam, Henry?' 'Not too bad.'* "考試考得怎麼樣，亨利？""不算太壞。"

examination /ɪgˌzæmɪˈneɪʃn/ [名詞] [正式] 考試 Students will take an examination at the end of the year. 學生們年底要參加考試。  = **exam**

example /ɪgˈzɑːmpl; 美 -ˈzæm-/ [名詞] 例子 Can you give me an example? 你能給我舉個例子嗎？

excellent /ˈeksələnt/ [形容詞] 極好的；卓越的；出色的 She's Japanese, but her English is excellent. 她是日本人，但她的英語講得極好。

except /ɪkˈsept/ [介詞] 除…之外 Everyone was tired except Henry. 除亨利外，大家都累了。

excited /ɪkˈsaɪtɪd; 美 -əd/ [形容詞] 興奮的；激動的 I was so excited that I couldn't sleep. 我興奮得睡不着覺。

exciting /ɪkˈsaɪtɪŋ/ [形容詞] 令人興奮的；使人激動的 It was an exciting film. 那是一部令人興奮的電影。

excuse¹ /ɪkˈskjuːs/ [名詞] 借口；理由 Late again! What's your excuse this time? 又遲到了！這一次是甚麼理由？

excuse² /ɪkˈskjuːz/ [動詞] 原諒 Please excuse me for being so late. 請原諒我這麼晚才到。
excuse me [用於引起別人的注意、打斷別人談話等] 勞駕，對不起 Excuse me, can you tell me the way to the station? 勞駕，請問去車站的路怎麼走？

exercise /ˈeksəsaɪz; 美 -ər-/ [名詞]

1 [無複數] 運動，鍛煉 Running is good exercise. 跑步是很好的體育鍛煉。

2 練習，習題 Please do Exercise 3 on page 4. 請做第 4 頁上的練習 3。

exit /ˈeksɪt; 美 -ət/ [名詞] 出口 Where is the exit? 出口在哪裏？  [反] **entrance** 入口，進口

expect /ɪkˈspekt/ [動詞] 預計，預料 I expect she'll pass the exam. 我預計她會通過考試。

expensive /ɪkˈspensɪv/ [形容詞] 昂貴的 I can't afford it — it's too expensive. 我買不起，太貴了。  [反] **cheap** 便宜的

experiment /ɪkˈsperɪmənt/ [名詞] 實驗，試驗 The teacher is doing a scientific experiment for the class. 老師正在為全班同學做科學實驗。

explain /ɪkˈspleɪn/ [動詞] 解釋；說

明 *Mr Brown is explaining how to do these sums.* 布朗先生正在講解怎樣做這些算術題。

explode /ɪk'spləʊd; 美 -'sploʊd / [動詞] 爆炸 *A bomb exploded there last night.* 昨晚那裏有顆炸彈爆炸了。

explore /ɪk'splɔː; 美 -'splɔːr / [動詞] 探險，考察 *Columbus discovered America but did not explore the new continent.* 哥倫布發現了美洲，但沒有考察這塊新大陸。

extinct /ɪk'stɪŋkt / [形容詞] （指動物等）絕種的，滅絕的 *Tigers are nearly extinct in the wild.* 野生老虎快要絕種了。

extra /'ekstrə / [形容詞] 額外的 *I need some extra money.* 我需要一些額外的錢。

extraordinary /ɪk'strɔːdnri; 美 ɪk'strɔːrdəneri / [形容詞] **1** 非常奇怪的 *I had an extraordinary dream last night — I dreamt that I could fly.* 昨晚我做了一個非常奇怪的夢，我夢見自己會飛。**2** 特別的；非凡的 *He had an extraordinary musical talent.* 他具有非凡的音樂天賦。

E

eye /aɪ / [名詞] 眼睛 *Henry closed his eyes and went to sleep.* 亨利閉上眼睛睡着了。

F f

face¹ /feɪs/ [名詞] 臉 *Have you washed your face?* 你洗過臉了嗎？

face 臉
forehead 前額
eye 眼睛
nose 鼻子
cheek 臉頰
mouth 嘴
chin 下巴

face² /feɪs/ [動詞] 面朝，面向；面對 *The garden faces south.* 花園朝南。◇ *The two boys stood facing each other.* 兩個男孩面對面站着。

fact /fækt/ [名詞] 事實 *It is a fact that plants need water.* 植物需要水，這是事實。

factory /'fæktrɪ/ [名詞] [複數 **factories**] 製造廠，工廠 *He works in a car factory.* 他在汽車製造廠工作。

fade /feɪd/ [動詞] 褪色 *Jeans fade when you wash them.* 牛仔褲洗後會褪色。

fail /feɪl/ [動詞] **1** 失敗 *If you don't work hard, you may fail.* 不努力就可能會失敗。 ☞ [反] **succeed** 成功 **2** 沒有通過（考試）；不及格 *She failed all her tests.* 她所有的考試都不及格。◇ *How many students failed last term?* 上學期有多少學生不及格？ ☞ [反] **pass** 通過（考試）；及格

fair /feə; 美 fer/ [形容詞] **1** 公平的，公正的 *It's not fair! Why should she always have first choice?* 這不公平！為甚麼總是由她先挑選？ ☞ [反] **unfair** 不公平的，不公正的 **2** （頭髮）金色的 *He has fair hair.* 他有一頭金髮。

fairy /'feərɪ; 美 'ferɪ/ [名詞] [複數 **fairies**] 小仙子；小精靈 *Alice likes stories about fairies.* 艾麗斯喜歡小仙女的故事。

fairy tale /'feərɪ teɪl; 美 'fer-/ [又作 **fairy story**] [名詞] 神話；童話 *The teacher read a fairy tale to the children.* 老師給孩子們唸了一個童話故事。

fall /fɔːl/ [動詞] [過去式 **fell** /fel/，過去分詞 **fallen** /ˈfɔːlən/] **1** 落下；掉下；摔下 *Leaves fall in autumn.* 秋天樹落葉。◇ *I fell off my bicycle.* 我從自行車上摔了下來。**2** 跌倒，倒下 *Henry fell over and hurt his knee.* 亨利跌了一跤，摔傷了膝蓋。

false /fɔːls/ [形容詞] 錯誤的；不真實的 *A whale is a fish—true or false?* 鯨魚是一種魚，對還是錯？

family /ˈfæmli/ [名詞] [複數 **families**] 家庭 *How many people are there in your family?* 你們家有幾口人？

famous /ˈfeɪməs/ [形容詞] 著名的 *This town is famous for its beautiful buildings.* 這個城鎮以美麗的建築而聞名。◇ *She's a famous singer.* 她是一位著名歌手。

fan /fæn/ [名詞] 扇子；電扇 *I am hot —may I switch on the fan?* 我熱，打開電扇可以嗎？

far[1] /fɑː; 美 fɑːr/ [副詞] [比較級 **farther** /ˈfɑːðə; 美 ˈfɑːrðər/ 或 **further** /ˈfɜːðə; 美 ˈfɜːrðər/，最高級 **farthest** /ˈfɑːðɪst; 美 ˈfɑːr-/ 或 **furthest** /ˈfɜːðɪst; 美 ˈfɜːr-/] 遠 *How far is it to the supermarket?* 到超市有多遠？

far[2] /fɑː; 美 fɑːr/ [形容詞] [比較級 **farther** /ˈfɑːðə; 美 ˈfɑːrðər/ 或 **further** /ˈfɜːðə; 美 ˈfɜːrðər/，最高級 **farthest** /ˈfɑːðɪst; 美 ˈfɑːr-/ 或 **furthest** /ˈfɜːðɪst; 美 ˈfɜːr-/] 遠的 *Let's walk — it's not far.* 我們走着去吧，那兒並不遠。☞ [反] **near**[1] 近的

fare /feə; 美 fer/ [名詞]（公共汽車、火車、出租車等的）車費 *What's the fare to the park?* 去公園的車費是多少？

farm /fɑːm; 美 fɑːrm/ [名詞] 農場 *He keeps chickens on his farm.* 他在農場養雞。

farmer /ˈfɑːmə; 美 ˈfɑːrmər/ [名詞] 農民 He is a farmer. 他是農民。

fast¹ /fɑːst; 美 fæst/ [形容詞] **1** 快的 Henry is a fast runner. 亨利跑得很快。 ☞ [反] **slow** 慢的 **2** [用於名詞後] (鐘錶) 走得快的 My watch is five minutes fast. 我的錶快了5分鐘。 ☞ [反] **slow** (鐘錶) 走得慢的

fast² /fɑːst; 美 fæst/ [副詞] 快 Henry runs very fast. 亨利跑得很快。 ☞ [反] **slowly** 慢

fasten /ˈfɑːsn; 美 ˈfæ-/ [動詞] 繫牢, 扣住 Please fasten your seat belts. 請繫好安全帶。

fat /fæt/ [形容詞] [比較級 **fatter**, 最高級 **fattest**] 胖的 You'll get fat if you

eat too much. 吃得太多會發胖。 ☞ [反] **thin** 瘦的

father /ˈfɑːðə; 美 -ər/ [名詞] 父親, 爸爸 Where do your mother and father live? 你父母住在哪裏?

fault /fɔːlt/ [名詞] **1** 缺點, 毛病 One of my faults is that I'm always late. 我的缺點之一就是老遲到。 **2** 過錯 It will be your own fault if you don't pass your exams. 如果你考不及格, 那是你自己的錯。

favour /ˈfeɪvə; 美 -ər/ [名詞] 恩惠 Would you do me a favour and open the door? 請您幫個忙把門打開好嗎? ☞ 美國英語拼寫為 **favor**。

favourite /ˈfeɪvrət/ [形容詞] [只用於名詞前] 最喜愛的 What's your favourite subject? 你最喜歡甚麼科目? ☞ 美國英語拼寫為 **favorite**。

fear /fɪə; 美 fɪr/ [名詞] 害怕, 恐懼 I have a fear of snakes. 我怕蛇。

feast /fiːst/ [名詞] 盛宴, 宴會 We had a feast at the wedding. 我們吃了一頓豐盛的婚宴。

feather /ˈfeðə; 美 -ər/ [名詞] 羽毛 The hen had white feathers. 這隻母雞的羽毛是白色的。

February /ˈfebruəri; 美 ˈfebjueri/ [名詞] 二月 *His birthday is on the eighth of February.* 他的生日是 2 月 8 日。 ☞ ① 參見 **August** 的示例。 ② Feb 是 **February** 的縮寫。

feed /fiːd/ [動詞] [過去式和過去分詞 **fed** /fed/] 餵（養） *Don't forget to feed the dog.* 別忘了餵狗。

feel /fiːl/ [動詞] [過去式和過去分詞 **felt** /felt/] 感到，覺得 *How are you feeling today?* 你今天感覺怎麼樣? ◇ *Do you feel cold?* 你覺得冷嗎?

feeling /ˈfiːlɪŋ/ [名詞] 感覺 *I suddenly had a feeling of fear.* 我突然有一種恐懼感。◇ *I have a feeling that we've met before.* 我覺得我們以前見過面。

fell /fel/ **fall** 的過去式 *Something wet fell on my head.* 有個濕東西掉在了我頭上。

felt /felt/ **feel** 的過去式和過去分詞 *After taking the medicine, I felt a lot better.* 吃過藥後，我覺得好多了。

female /ˈfiːmeɪl/ [名詞] 女子 *This clinic is for females only.* 這是一家婦科診所。 ☞ [反] **male** 男子

fence /fens/ [名詞] 柵欄，籬笆 *There is a fence round the park.* 公園四周有一道柵欄。

ferry /ˈferi/ [名詞] [複數 **ferries**] 渡船，渡輪 *We travelled to France by ferry.* 我們乘渡輪到了法國。

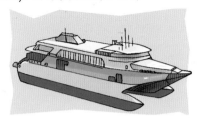

festival /ˈfestɪvl/ [名詞] 節日 *Christmas is one of the most important festivals in the West.* 聖誕節是西方最重要的節日之一。

fetch /fetʃ/ [動詞] [尤用於英國英語] （去）拿來 *Let me fetch you a chair (=Let me fetch a chair for you).* 我去給你拿一把椅子。

fever /ˈfiːvə; 美 -ər/ [名詞] 發燒，發熱 *Helen has a very high fever.* 海倫在發高燒。

few /fjuː/ [形容詞] [與複數可數名詞連用] 很少的 *Few people live to be 100.* 很少人活到 100 歲。 ☞ [反] **many** 許多的
a few 幾個 *Alice only has a few strawberries.* 艾麗斯只有幾個草莓。

field /fiːld/ [名詞] 田地 *The farmer grew vegetables in the field.* 那位農民在田裏種菜。

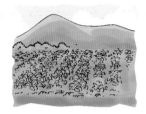

fierce /fɪəs; 美 fɪrs / [形容詞] 兇猛的，兇狠的 They have a fierce dog. 他們養了一條兇猛的狗。

fifteen /ˌfɪfˈtiːn / [數詞] 十五 Three times five is fifteen. 3 乘 5 得 15。☞ 參見 **five** 的示例。

fifth /fɪfθ / [數詞] 第五 I've had four cups of coffee already, so this is my fifth. 我已喝了 4 杯咖啡，所以這是我的第 5 杯。◇ Today is the fifth of May. 今天是 5 月 5 日。◇ His office is on the fifth floor. 他的辦公室在 5 層。

fifty /ˈfɪfti / [數詞] 五十 There are fifty pages in the book. 這本書有 50 頁。◇ Fifty students passed the examination. 50 名學生通過了考試。

fight /faɪt / [動詞] [過去式和過去分詞] **fought** /fɔːt /] 打架，搏鬥 The two children are always fighting. 這倆孩子總是打架。

fill /fɪl / [動詞] 裝滿 Can you fill the glass with water, please? 請你把玻璃杯倒滿水好嗎？

film /fɪlm / [名詞] **1** 影片，電影 Let's go to the cinema—there's a good film on this week. 我們去看電影吧，這個星期正在放映一部好影片。☞ 英國英語用 **film**，美國英語用 **movie**。**2** 膠卷 Henry put a new film in his camera. 亨利在相機裏裝了一個新膠卷。

find /faɪnd / [動詞] [過去式和過去分詞 **found** /faʊnd /] **1** 找到 Did you find the pen you lost? 你找到丟失的鋼筆了嗎？**2** 發現 I soon found that it was quicker to go by bus. 我不久發現坐公共汽車去更快。

fine /faɪn / [形容詞] **1** 身體好的 'How are you?' 'I'm fine, thanks. And you?' "你好嗎？" "很好，謝謝。你呢？" **2**（天氣）晴朗的 If it's fine, we could have a picnic. 如果天晴，我們就可以去野餐。

finger /ˈfɪŋgə; 美 -ər/ [名詞] 手指 *Children learn to count on their fingers.* 孩子們用手指學數數。

finish /ˈfɪnɪʃ/ [動詞] 結束；完成 *When I finish my homework, can I watch TV?* 我做完作業可以看電視嗎？

fire /ˈfaɪə; 美 ˈfaɪr/ [名詞] **1** 火 *Most animals are afraid of fire.* 大多數動物怕火。

2 火災，失火 *It took them two hours to put out the fire.* 他們花了兩個小時把火撲滅。**3** 爐火 *It's cold—don't let the fire go out!* 天冷，不要把火熄滅！

fire engine /ˈfaɪə ˌendʒɪn; 美 ˈfaɪr ˌen-/ [名詞] 消防車，救火車 *Three fire engines arrived at the fire.* 三輛消防車到達火災現場。

fire extinguisher /ˈfaɪə ɪkˌstɪŋgwɪʃə; 美 ˈfaɪr ɪkˌstɪŋgwɪʃər/ [名

詞] 滅火器 *There's a fire extinguisher on the wall.* 墻上掛着一個滅火器。

fireman /ˈfaɪəmən; 美 ˈfaɪr-/ [複數 **firemen** /ˈfaɪəmən; 美 ˈfaɪr-/] 消防隊員 *My uncle is a fireman.* 我叔叔是消防隊員。

firework /ˈfaɪəwɜːk; 美 ˈfaɪrwɜːrk/ [名詞] 煙火，煙花 *Be careful not to burn your fingers when you let off that firework.* 放那個煙花時要小心，別把手指燒傷。

firm /fɜːm; 美 fɜːrm/ [形容詞] 堅固的，堅硬的 *A firm bed is better for your back.* 硬牀對你的背更有益處。

first¹ /fɜːst; 美 fɜːrst/ [數詞] 第一 *Monday is the first day of the week.* 星期一是一個星期的第一天。

first² /fɜːst; 美 fɜːrst/ [副詞] **1** 首先，先 'Let's go.' 'I'll have to find my keys first.' "我們走吧。""我得先找到鑰匙。" **2** 第一次，首次 *When did you first meet him?* 你是甚麼時候第一次遇見他的？

first aid /ˌfɜːst ˈeɪd; 美 ˌfɜːrst ˈeɪd/ [名詞] [無複數] 急救 *Do you know anything about first aid?* 你知道急救是怎麼回事嗎？

fish /fɪʃ/ [名詞] [複數 **fish** 或 **fishes**] 魚

Fish live in water. 魚生活在水裏。◇ *Henry caught three different fishes.* 亨利捉到了三條不同的魚。

fist /fɪst/ [名詞] 拳頭 *He hit me with his fist.* 他用拳頭打我。

fit¹ /fɪt/ [動詞] [現在分詞 **fitting**，過去式和過去分詞 **fitted**] (使)適合，(使)合身 *Helen's sweater doesn't fit. It's too big for her.* 海倫的毛衣不合身，她穿太大了。◇ *These shoes don't fit me.* 這雙鞋不適合我穿。

fit² /fɪt/ [形容詞] [比較級 **fitter**，最高級 **fittest**] 健康的 *Paul plays tennis to keep fit.* 保羅通過打網球來保持身體健康。

five /faɪv/ [數詞] 五 *Do you have change for five dollars?* 你有 5 塊錢的零錢嗎？◇ *The answers are on page five.* 答案在第 5 頁。◇ *Five of the students are absent today.* 今天有5名學生缺課。◇ *They have five cats.* 他們養了 5 隻貓。◇ *Five and one are six.* 5 加 1 等於 6。

fix /fɪks/ [動詞] **1** 固定，安裝 *Alice is fixing her doll's hair.* 艾麗斯正在安裝洋娃娃的頭髮。**2** 修理 *Can you fix my bicycle?* 你能修一下我的自行車嗎？

flag /flæg/ [名詞] 旗 *The Chinese flag is called the Five-Star Red Flag.* 中國國旗叫做五星紅旗。

flame /fleɪm/ [名詞] 火焰 *Red flames came up from the burning leaves.* 燃燒的樹葉冒着紅色的火焰。◇ *The house was in flames.* 房子着火了。

flash /flæʃ/ [名詞] [複數 **flashes**] 閃光 *There was a flash of lightning.* 天空中出現了一道閃電。

flat¹ /flæt/ [形容詞] **1** 平坦的；平的 *A table has a flat top.* 桌子的面是平的。**2** (輪胎)癟的，氣不足的 *This tyre looks flat.* 這隻輪胎看起來癟了。

flat² /flæt/ [名詞] 公寓；單元住宅；

一套房間 Our flat is on the eighth floor. 我們的公寓在 8 層。☞ 英國英語通常用 **flat**，美國英語通常用 **apartment**。

flavour /ˈfleɪvə; 美 -ər/ [名詞] 味道 What flavour is your ice cream? 你的冰淇淋是甚麼味的？☞ 美國英語拼寫為 **flavor**。

flew /fluː/ **fly** 的過去式 My father flew to America last week. 我父親上週乘飛機去了美國。

float /fləʊt; 美 floʊt/ [動詞] 漂浮 Leaves floated on the water. 樹葉漂浮在水面上。

flock /flɒk; 美 flɑːk/ [名詞] 一羣(綿羊、山羊、鳥等) The farmer kept a flock of sheep. 那個農民養了一羣羊。

flood /flʌd/ [名詞] 洪水，水災 The town was destroyed by the floods. 這座小鎮被洪水沖毀了。

floor /flɔː; 美 flɔːr/ [名詞] 1 [通常用作單數] (室內的) 地面，地板 Don't come in — there is broken glass on the floor! 別進來，地板上有碎玻璃！ 2 (樓房的) 層 His office is on the second floor. 他的辦公室在二層。

flour /ˈflaʊə; 美 ˈflaʊr/ [名詞] [無複數] 麵粉 Bread is made from flour. 麵包是用麵粉做的。

flow /fləʊ; 美 floʊ/ [動詞] 流，流動 The river flows through the town. 這條河流過小鎮。

flower /ˈflaʊə; 美 -ər/ [名詞] 花 He gave me a bunch of flowers. 他送給我一束花。

flown /fləʊn; 美 floʊn/ **fly** 的過去分詞 The parrot has flown away. 那隻鸚鵡飛走了。

flu /fluː/ [名詞] [無複數] 流行性感冒；流感 You have flu so you must stay at home. 你患了流感，所以必須待在家裏。

fly¹ /flaɪ/ [動詞] [現在分詞 **flying**，過去式 **flew** /fluː/，過去分詞 **flown** /fləʊn; 美 floʊn/] 1 (指鳥、昆蟲、飛機等) 飛 The bird flew away. 那隻鳥飛走了。 2 放 (風箏等) Henry is flying a kite. 亨利正在放風箏。

fly² /flaɪ/ [名詞] [複數 **flies**] 蒼蠅 We should keep flies off our food. 我們應讓蒼蠅遠離我們的食物。

fog /fɒg; 美 fɑːg/ [名詞] [無複數] （濃）霧 Helen got lost in the fog. 海倫在霧中迷路了。

fold /fəʊld; 美 foʊld/ [動詞] 摺疊，對摺 Paul folded the letter and put it in the envelope. 保羅把信摺起來，然後放進信封裏。

folder /ˈfəʊldə; 美 ˈfoʊldər/ [名詞] 文件夾 Henry kept his test papers in a folder. 亨利把考試卷保存在文件夾裏。

follow /ˈfɒləʊ; 美 ˈfɑːloʊ/ [動詞] 跟隨，跟着 Follow me please. I'll show you the way. 請跟我來，我給你領路。

fond /fɒnd; 美 fɑːnd/ [形容詞] [不用於名詞前] 喜歡的，喜愛的 Henry is very fond of skiing. 亨利非常喜歡滑雪。

food /fuːd/ [名詞] [無複數] 食物 What's your favourite food? 你最喜歡甚麼食物？

food 食物

sandwich
三明治

ice cream
冰淇淋 / 雪糕

hamburger
漢堡包

pancakes
薄煎餅

bread
麵包

soup
湯

hot dog
熱狗

pizza
薄餅

fish
魚

butter
牛油 / 黃油

chicken
雞 (肉)

cake
蛋糕

biscuits
餅乾

sausages
香腸

salad
色拉 / 沙拉

yoghurt
酸乳酪

eggs
雞蛋

fool /fuːl/ [名詞] 蠢人；傻瓜 *I'm a fool—I did the wrong homework!* 我真傻，把作業做錯了！

foolish /'fuːlɪʃ/ [形容詞] 愚蠢的；傻的 *He's a foolish boy—he often does silly things.* 他是個愚蠢的男孩，經常做傻事。

foot /fʊt/ [名詞] 1 [複數**feet** /fiːt/] 腳 *My feet are aching.* 我的腳痛。 2 [複

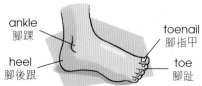

foot 腳

ankle
腳踝

toenail
腳指甲

heel
腳後跟

toe
腳趾

數 **feet** 或 **foot**] 英尺 *'How tall are you?' 'Five foot six (inches).'* "你有多高？""五英尺六 (英寸)。"

football /'fʊtbɔːl/ [名詞] 1 [無複數] 足球(運動) *Henry is playing football.* 亨利正在踢足球。 2 足球 *Whose football is this?* 這是誰的足球？

footprint /'fʊtprɪnt/ [名詞] 腳印*We left footprints in the snow.* 我們在雪地上留下了腳印。

for /強 fɔː; 美 fɔːr; 弱 fə; 美 fər/ [介詞] 1 [表示對象] 為，給 *There's a letter for you.* 有你的一封信。 2 [表示目的] 為了 *Let's go for a walk.* 我們去散步吧。 3 [表示一段時間] 達，計 *I'm going away for a few days.* 我要離開幾天。 ◇ *She has lived here for 20 years.* 她在這裏住了 20 年了。

forehead /'fɔːhed; 美 'fɔːrhed/ [名詞] 前額 *When you have a fever,*

forehead
前額

your forehead is hot. 你發燒時，前額會很熱。

foreign /'fɒrən; 美 'fɔːrən/ [形容詞] 外國的 *Can you speak a foreign language?* 你會說外語嗎？

foreigner /'fɒrənə; 美 'fɔːrənər/ [名詞] 外國人 *There are many foreigners in Beijing.* 北京有不少外國人。

forest /'fɒrɪst; 美 'fɔːrəst/ [名詞] 森林 *The children got lost in the forest.* 孩子們在森林裏迷路了。

forever /fər'evə; 美 -ər/ [副詞] 永遠 *They will remember her forever.* 他們會永遠記住她。

forgave /fə'geɪv; 美 fər-/ **forgive** 的過去式 *Mr Brown forgave Henry for breaking the window.* 亨利打破了窗玻璃，布朗先生原諒了他。

forget /fə'get; 美 fər-/ [動詞] [過去式 **forgot** /fə'gɒt; 美 fər'gɑːt/，過去分詞 **forgotten** /fə'gɒtn; 美 fər'gɑːtn/] 忘記 *I'm sorry, I've forgotten his name.* 對不起，我忘了他的名字。 ◇ *Don't forget to do your homework.* 別忘了做作業。 ☞ [反] **remember** 記得；記住

forgive /fə'gɪv; 美 fər-/ [動詞] [過

去式 **forgave** /fə'geɪv; 美 fər-/，過去分詞 **forgiven** /fə'gɪvn; 美 fər-/] 原諒，饒恕 *Please forgive me — I didn't mean to be rude.* 請原諒我，我並非有意無禮。

forgot /fə'gɒt; 美 fər'gɑːt/ **forget** 的過去式 *He had to walk to school because he forgot his wallet.* 他不得不走着去上學，因為他忘了帶錢包。

forgotten /fə'gɒtn; 美 fər'gɑːtn/ **forget** 的過去分詞 *I've forgotten your cousin's name.* 我忘了你表哥的名字。

fork /fɔːk; 美 fɔːrk/ [名詞] 叉子 *Peter picked up his knife and fork.* 彼得拿起刀叉。

fortnight /'fɔːtnaɪt; 美 'fɔːrt-/ [名詞] [通常用作單數] 兩個星期，兩週 *We're going on holiday for a fortnight.* 我們打算去度兩個星期的假。

forty /'fɔːti; 美 'fɔːrti/ [數詞] 四十 *Four times ten is forty.* 4 乘 10 得 40。 ☞ 參見 **fifty** 的示例。

forward /'fɔːwəd; 美 'fɔːrwərd/ [又作 **forwards**] [副詞] 向前 *Keep going forward and try not to look back.* 向前直走，不要往後看。 ☞ [反] **backwards** 向後

fought /fɔːt/ **fight** 的過去式和過去分詞 *The two brothers fought a lot when they were younger.* 這倆兄弟小時候經常打架。

found /faʊnd/ **find**的過去式和過去分詞 Look! I've found the pencil you lost! 瞧！我找到了你丟的鉛筆！

fountain /ˈfaʊntɪn; 美 ˈfaʊntn/ [名詞]（人造）噴泉；噴水池 There is a fountain in the park. 公園裏有個噴水池。

four /fɔː; 美 fɔːr/ [數詞] 四 Two and two are four. 2加2等於4。 ☞ 參見 **five** 的示例。

fourteen /ˌfɔːˈtiːn; 美 ˌfɔːr-/ [數詞] 十四 Ten and four make fourteen. 10加4等於14。 ☞ 參見 **five** 的示例。

fourth /fɔːθ; 美 fɔːrθ/ [數詞] 第四 Today is the fourth of May. 今天是5月4日。 ☞ 參見 **fifth** 的示例。

fox /fɒks; 美 fɑːks/ [名詞] [複數 **foxes**] 狐狸 A fox is a wild animal. 狐狸是野生動物。

fraction /ˈfrækʃn/ [名詞] 分數 ½ is a fraction. 二分之一是個分數。

frame /freɪm/ [名詞]（門、畫、窗等的）框 The window frames need painting. 窗框需要油漆了。

France /frɑːns; 美 fræns/ [名詞] 法國 He comes from France. 他是法國人。

free /friː/ [形容詞] **1** 自由的 You are free to leave at any time. 你可以隨時離開。 **2** 免費的 'Are the drinks free?' 'No, you have to pay for them.' "這些飲料免費嗎？" "不，你得花錢買。" **3** 有空的，閒着的 Are you free this afternoon? 你今天下午有空嗎？

freeze /friːz/ [動詞] [過去式 **froze** /frəʊz; 美 frouz/，過去分詞 **frozen** /ˈfrəʊzn; 美 ˈfrou-/] 結冰，冷凍 Water freezes at 0℃. 水在0℃時結冰。

freezer /ˈfriːzə; 美 -ər/ [名詞] 冰櫃 Put the ice cream in the freezer. 把冰淇淋放在冰櫃裏。 ☞ 參見 **fridge** "冰箱"。

French[1] /frentʃ/ [形容詞] 法國（人）的 His mother is French. 他媽媽是法

國人。

French² /frentʃ/ [名詞] 法語 Helen can speak a little French. 海倫會說一點法語。

fresh /freʃ/ [形容詞] (尤指食物) 新鮮的 Mum bought some fresh eggs. 媽媽買了些新鮮雞蛋。

Friday /'fraɪdeɪ/ [名詞] 星期五 It's Friday tomorrow. 明天是星期五。☞ ① 參見**Monday**的示例。② **Fri**是**Friday** 的縮寫。

fridge /frɪdʒ/ [又作 **refridgerator**] [名詞] 冰箱 Is there any milk in the fridge? 冰箱裏有牛奶嗎？

fried /fraɪd/ **fry** 的過去式和過去分詞 Dad fried the noodles with onions. 爸爸用洋蔥炒麵。

friend /frend/ [名詞] 朋友 He's my friend. 他是我的朋友。

friendly /'frendli/ [形容詞] [比較級 **friendlier**，最高級 **friendliest**] 友好的，友善的 My neighbours are very friendly. 我的鄰居很友好。

frightening /'fraɪtnɪŋ/ [形容詞] 令人恐怖的，駭人的 It was a frightening film. 那是一部恐怖片。

frog /frɒg; 美 frɑːg/ [名詞] 青蛙 Frogs usually live in wet places. 青蛙通常生活在潮濕的地方。

from / 強 frɒm; 美 frʌm; 弱 frəm / [介詞] **1** [表示起點] 自，從，由 The train goes from Paris to Rome. 這列火車由巴黎開往羅馬。**2** [表示來源] 來自 'Where are you from?' 'I'm from China.' "你是哪國人？" "我是中國人。"

front /frʌnt/ [名詞][通常用作單數，與 **the**連用] 前面 There is a small garden at the front of the house. 房子前面有個小花園。☞ [反]**back** 後面
in front of 在…前面 Alice was sitting in front of the television. 艾麗斯坐在電視機前。

frost /frɒst; 美 frɔːst/ [名詞] [無複數] 霜 The trees were white with frost. 樹上結滿了白霜。

frown /fraʊn/ [動詞] 皺眉 What's wrong? Why are you frowning? 出甚麼事了？你為甚麼皺着眉頭？

froze /frəʊz; 美 froʊz/ **freeze** 的過去式 *It was so cold that the pond froze.* 天氣非常冷，池塘都結冰了。

frozen /'frəʊzn; 美 'froʊ-/ **freeze** 的過去分詞 *The pond has frozen.* 池塘結冰了。

fruit /fruːt/ [名詞] [無複數] 水果 *What's your favourite fruit?* 你最喜歡甚麼水果？

fruit 水果

coconut 椰子

mango 芒果

dates 棗

peach 桃

watermelon 西瓜

seeds 籽

grapes 葡萄

apple 蘋果

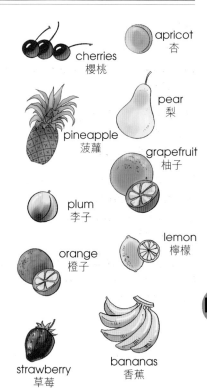

cherries 櫻桃

apricot 杏

pineapple 菠蘿

pear 梨

grapefruit 柚子

plum 李子

lemon 檸檬

orange 橙子

strawberry 草莓

bananas 香蕉

fry /fraɪ/ [動詞] [現在分詞 **frying**，過去式和過去分詞 **fried**] 煎，炸，炒 *Dad is frying some eggs.* 爸爸正在煎雞蛋。

full /fʊl/ [形容詞] 滿的，充滿的 *My*

F

cup is full. 我的杯子是滿的。◇ *The box is full of books.* 箱子裏裝滿了書。

fumes /fjuːmz/ [名詞] [複數] (難聞而有害的) 煙，氣 *Cars make fumes.* 汽車排放廢氣。

fun /fʌn/ [名詞] [無複數] 樂趣 *We had a lot of fun on holiday.* 我們假期玩得很開心。

funny /ˈfʌni/ [形容詞] [比較級 **funnier**，最高級 **funniest**] 滑稽的；有趣的；可笑的 *He's very funny.* 他很逗。◇ *Paul told a very funny joke.* 保羅講了一個很有趣的笑話。

fur /fɜː; 美 fɜːr/ [名詞] [無複數] (獸類的) 軟毛 *Cats and rabbits have fur.* 貓和兔子身上有軟毛。

fur
軟毛

furious /ˈfjʊəriəs; 美 ˈfjʊr-/ [形容詞] 狂怒的 *Dad will be furious if we're late.* 如果我們遲到了，爸爸會大發雷霆的。

furniture /ˈfɜːnɪtʃə; 美 ˈfɜːrnɪtʃər/ [名詞] [無複數] 傢具 *There were only three pieces of furniture in the room.* 房間裏只有三件傢具。

fuss /fʌs/ [動詞] 大驚小怪 *Don't fuss —we'll get there on time.* 不要大驚小怪，我們會準時到達那裏。

future /ˈfjuːtʃə; 美 -ər/ [名詞] [用作單數，與 **the** 連用] 將來，未來 *Who knows what will happen in the future?* 誰知道將來會怎麼樣？
in future 今後 *I'll be more careful in future.* 今後我會更加小心。

G g

gallop /ˈɡæləp/ [動詞] (馬) 飛奔，疾馳 *The horse galloped away.* 馬飛奔而去。

game /ɡeɪm/ [名詞] 遊戲；運動 *Shall we play a game?* 我們玩個遊戲好嗎？◇ *Let's have a game of tennis.* 咱們打一場網球吧。

gang /ɡæŋ/ [名詞] [非正式] 一幫，一伙 (朋友) *Do you want to go to the cinema with the gang tonight?* 你今晚想跟那幫朋友一起去看電影嗎？

gap /ɡæp/ [名詞] 裂縫，裂口，缺口，豁口 *There was a gap in the wall.* 牆上有個裂縫。

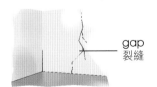

gap
裂縫

garage /ˈɡærɑːʒ; 美 ɡəˈrɑːʒ/ [名詞] 1 車庫 *The garage is big enough for two cars.* 車庫很大，可以停放兩輛汽車。 2 汽車修理廠；加油站 *The car's at the garage.* 那輛汽車在修理廠。

garden /ˈɡɑːdn; 美 ˈɡɑːr-/ [名詞] 花園；菜園 'Where's Sophie?' 'She's in the garden.' "索菲在哪裏？" "她在花園裏。"

gas /ɡæs/ [名詞] 1 [複數 **gases**] 氣體 *Air is a mixture of gases.* 空氣由多種氣體混合而成。 2 [無複數] 天然氣；煤氣 *We use gas for cooking.* 我們用煤氣做飯。

gate /ɡeɪt/ [名詞] 大門 *Henry pushed open the garden gate.* 亨利推開花園的門。

gave /ɡeɪv/ **give** 的過去式 *Dad gave me a bicycle as a birthday present.* 爸爸送我一輛自行車作為生日禮物。

geese /ɡiːs/ **goose** 的複數 *There were several white geese near the* *lake.* 湖邊有幾隻白鵝。

generous /'dʒenərəs/ [形容詞] 慷慨的，大方的 *My friends have always been very generous to me.* 我的朋友一直對我很慷慨。

gentle /'dʒentl/ [形容詞] (指人)溫和的；溫柔的 *Paul is a gentle boy.* 保羅性格溫和。

gentleman /'dʒentlmən/ [名詞] [複數 **gentlemen** /'dʒentlmən/]用於對男子的尊稱]先生 *There's a gentleman at the door.* 門外有位先生。

germ /dʒɜːm; 美 dʒɜːrm/ [名詞] 病菌；細菌 *Cover your mouth when you cough, so that you don't spread your germs.* 咳嗽時要捂住嘴，以免傳播細菌。

German¹ /'dʒɜːmən; 美 'dʒɜːr-/ [形容詞]德國(人)的 *The music you are listening to is German.* 你現在聽的這段音樂是德國的。

German² /'dʒɜːmən; 美 'dʒɜːr-/ [名詞] **1** 德國人 *Many Germans speak excellent English.* 很多德國人英語說得極好。**2** 德語 *Do you speak German?* 你說德語嗎？

Germany /'dʒɜːməni; 美 'dʒɜːr-/ [名詞] 德國 *When are you going to Germany?* 你甚麼時候去德國？

get /get/ [動詞] [現在分詞 **getting**，過去式和過去分詞 **got** /gɒt; 美 gɑːt/] **1** 收到 *I got a lot of presents for my birthday.* 我收到許多生日禮物。**2** 買到

Where did you get your bike? 你在哪裏買的自行車？**3** 有 *Have you got any money?* 你身上有錢嗎？◇ *I've got a lot to do today.* 我今天有許多事情要做。**4** (去)拿來 *Can I get you a drink?* 我給你拿杯飲料好嗎？**5** 變成 *The food's getting cold.* 飯菜涼了。◇ *Mum got angry.* 媽媽生氣了。**6** 到達 *When did you get here?* 你甚麼時候到這裏的？◇ *We got to London late in the evening.* 我們晚上很晚才到倫敦。

☞ [同] **arrive**，**reach** 到達

get off 下(公共汽車、火車等) *Where did you get off the bus?* 你在哪裏下的公共汽車？

get on 上(公共汽車、火車等) *I got on the wrong bus.* 我上錯了公共汽車。

get up 1 起牀 *What time do you usually get up?* 你通常幾點鐘起牀？**2** 起身，站起 *The class got up when the teacher came in.* 老師進來時，全班同學起立。

ghost /gəʊst; 美 goʊst/ [名詞] 鬼 *Do you believe in ghosts?* 你相信有鬼嗎？

giant¹ /'dʒaɪənt/ [名詞] (童話或神話故事中的)巨人 *In the story the giant was three metres tall.* 故事中，那個巨人有三米高。

giant² /'dʒaɪənt/ [形容詞] [只用於名詞前] 巨大的；巨型的 *The film was about giant insects.* 這是一部關於巨型昆蟲的電影。

gift /ɡɪft/ [名詞] 禮物 *Did you give your mother a gift?* 你給你母親送禮物了嗎？◇ *Thank you for your gift.* 謝謝你的禮物。 ☞ [同] **present²** 禮物

giggle /'ɡɪɡl/ [動詞] 格格地笑，傻笑 *The children couldn't stop giggling.* 孩子們不停地傻笑。

giraffe /dʒə'rɑːf; 美 -'ræf/ [名詞] 長頸鹿 *Giraffes have very long necks.* 長頸鹿的脖子很長。

girl /ɡɜːl; 美 ɡɜːrl/ [名詞] 女孩 *Is the baby a boy or a girl?* 那個寶寶是男孩還是女孩？

give /ɡɪv/ [動詞] [過去式 **gave** /ɡeɪv/，過去分詞 **given** /'ɡɪvn/] 給；送 *Give me the keys — I'll open the door.* 給我鑰匙，我要開門。◇ *Give the keys to me.* 給我鑰匙。

glad /ɡlæd/ [形容詞] [不用於名詞前] 高興的 *'I passed the test.' 'I'm so glad!'* "我考試及格了。""我真替你高興！"◇ *I'm glad to meet you. I've heard a lot about you.* 很高興認識你，我聽說了許多有關你的事。◇ *I'm glad that you're feeling better.* 很高興你身體好些了。

glass /ɡlɑːs; 美 ɡlæs/ [名詞] **1** [無複數] 玻璃 *Bottles are made of glass.* 瓶子是玻璃製的。**2** [複數 **glasses**] 玻璃杯 *Helen poured some juice into her glass.* 海倫往自己的杯子裏倒了些果汁。

glasses /'ɡlɑːsɪz; 美 'ɡlæsəz/ [名詞] [複數] 眼鏡 *Do you know where my glasses are?* 你知道我的眼鏡放在哪裏嗎？

glasses 眼鏡

frame 鏡框

lens 鏡片

globe /ɡləʊb; 美 ɡloʊb/ [名詞] 地球儀 *Show me Africa on the globe.* 請在地球儀上給我指出非洲的位置。

glove /glʌv/ [名詞] 手套 I need a new pair of gloves. 我需要一副新手套。

glue /gluː/ [名詞] [無複數] 膠；膠水 Put glue on the picture and stick it in the book. 在照片上塗上膠水，然後把它貼在書裏。

go /gəʊ; 美 goʊ/ [動詞] [現在分詞 **going**，過去式 **went** /went/，過去分詞 **gone** /gɒn; 美 gɔːn/] 去 Let's go home. 我們回家吧。◇ Peter goes to school by bus. 彼得坐公共汽車上學。
go away 走開；離開 Go away! I'm doing my homework. 走開！我正在做作業。
go back 返回 The children have to go back to school next week. 孩子們下週要返校了。
go on 1 發生 What's going on here? 這裏發生了甚麼事情？**2** 繼續 I wanted to go on learning French. 我想繼續學習法語。
go out 1 出去 Let's go out for a meal tonight. 咱們今晚出去吃飯吧。**2** (燈、火等) 熄滅 Suddenly all the lights went out. 突然所有的燈都滅了。

goat /gəʊt; 美 goʊt/ [名詞] 山羊 The goat is running down the hill. 那隻山羊正在往山坡下跑。

gold /gəʊld; 美 goʊld/ [名詞] [無複數] 金，黃金 Is your ring made of gold? 你的戒指是金的嗎？

goldfish /ˈgəʊldfɪʃ; 美 ˈgoʊld-/ [名詞] [複數 **goldfish**] 金魚 Henry has two goldfish in a glass bowl. 亨利在玻璃魚缸裏養了兩條金魚。

gone /gɒn; 美 gɔːn/ **go** 的過去分詞 Mum has gone out. 媽媽出去了。

good /gʊd/ [形容詞] [比較級 **better** /ˈbetə; 美 -ər/，最高級 **best** /best/] **1** 好的 That's a really good idea! 那真是個好主意！◇ Her English is very good. 她的英語很好。☞ [反] **bad** 壞的，不好的 **2 good at sth** 擅長某

事 *Helen is good at music.* 海倫擅長音樂。**3** 愉快的；高興的 *Did you have a good time in London?* 你在倫敦過得愉快嗎？◇ *It's good to see you again.* 很高興能再次見到你。**4 good for sb** 對某人的健康有益 *Apples are good for you.* 蘋果對你的健康有益。

goodbye /ˌɡʊdˈbaɪ/ [感歎詞] 再見 *Goodbye! See you tomorrow.* 再見！明天見。

goose /ɡuːs/ [名詞] [複數 **geese** /ɡiːs/] 鵝 *A goose is bigger than a duck.* 鵝比鴨大。

got /ɡɒt; 美 ɡɑːt/ **get** 的過去式和過去分詞 *I got full marks in the maths test.* 我數學測驗得了滿分。

grab /ɡræb/ [動詞] [現在分詞 **grabbing**，過去式和過去分詞 **grabbed**] 搶；攫取；抓取 *The thief grabbed my bag.* 小偷搶走了我的包。◇ *Don't grab — there's plenty for everyone.* 別搶，東西很多，人人都有份。

grade /ɡreɪd/ [名詞] (美國學校的) 年級 *Henry is in the third grade.* 亨利上小學三年級。

grain /ɡreɪn/ [名詞] **1** 穀物 *The US is a major producer of grain.* 美國是穀物生產大國。**2** 穀粒 *There are a few grains of rice on the table.* 桌子上有幾粒米。

grandchild /ˈɡræntʃaɪld/ [名詞] [複數 **grandchildren** /ˈɡrænˌtʃɪldrən/] 孫子；孫女；外孫子；外孫女 *Mrs Green has five grandchildren.* 格林太太有 5 個孫子孫女。

granddaughter /ˈɡrænˌdɔːtə; 美 -ər/ [名詞] 孫女；外孫女 *Mary is Mrs Green's granddaughter.* 瑪麗是格林太太的孫女。

grandfather /ˈɡrænˌfɑːðə; 美 -ər/ [名詞] 祖父，爺爺；外祖父，外公，姥爺 *Mr Green is Mary's grandfather.* 格林先生是瑪麗的祖父。

grandma /ˈɡrænmɑː/ [名詞] [非正式] 奶奶；外婆，姥姥 *My grandma is seventy years old.* 我奶奶 70 歲了。☞ 參見 **granny** "奶奶；外婆，姥姥"。

grandmother /ˈɡrænˌmʌðə; 美 -ər/ [名詞] 祖母，奶奶；外祖母，外婆，姥姥 *Mrs Green is Mary's grandmother.* 格林太太是瑪麗的祖母。

grandpa /ˈɡrænpɑː/ [名詞] [非正式] 爺爺；外公，姥爺 *My grandpa is seventy-two years old.* 我爺爺 72 歲了。

grandparent /ˈɡrænˌpeərənt; 美 -ˌper-/ [名詞] [通常用作複數] 祖父；祖母；外祖父；外祖母 *This is a picture of my grandparents.* 這是我祖父母的照片。

grandson /ˈɡrænsʌn/ [名詞] 孫子；

外孫子 *Mrs Green has two grandsons and three granddaughters.* 格林太太有兩個孫子三個孫女。

granny /ˈgræni/ [名詞] [複數 **grannies**] [非正式] 奶奶；外婆，姥姥 *Granny has to walk with a stick now.* 奶奶現在不得不拄着拐杖走路。☞ 參見 **grandma** "奶奶；外婆，姥姥"。

grape /greɪp/ [名詞] 葡萄 *Grapes are green or black.* 葡萄有綠色的和紫色的。

grapefruit /ˈgreɪpfruːt/ [名詞] [複數 **grapefruit**] 柚子，葡萄柚，西柚 *Do you like grapefruit juice?* 你喜歡喝西柚汁嗎？

grass /grɑːs; 美 græs/ [名詞] [無複數] (青) 草 *Don't walk on the grass.* 勿踏草地。

grateful /ˈgreɪtfl/ [形容詞] 感激的；感謝的 *I'm really grateful to you for your help.* 我真的感謝你的幫助。

graze /greɪz/ [動詞] 1 (牛、羊等) 吃草 *A sheep was grazing in the fields.* 一隻羊正在地裏吃草。

2 擦傷 *Helen fell and grazed her knee.* 海倫跌了一跤，擦傷了膝蓋。

great /greɪt/ [形容詞] 1 大的，巨大的 *The great ship sailed into the harbour.* 那艘巨輪駛進了海港。 2 偉大的 *Einstein was a great scientist.* 愛因斯坦是一位偉大的科學家。

Great Britain /ˌgreɪt ˈbrɪtn/ [又作 **Britain**] [名詞] 大不列顛 (含英格蘭、蘇格蘭和威爾士)，英國 *Henry was born in Great Britain.* 亨利出生在大不列顛 (或英國)。☞ 參見 **United Kingdom** "聯合王國，英國"。

greedy /ˈgriːdi/ [形容詞] [比較級 **greedier**，最高級 **greediest**] 貪婪的 *Don't be so greedy!* 不要這麼貪婪！

green¹ /griːn/ [形容詞] 綠色的 *Grass is green.* 草是綠色的。

green² /griːn/ [名詞] 綠色 *Alice was dressed in green.* 艾麗斯穿着綠衣服。

greenhouse /ˈgriːnhaʊs/ [名詞] 温室 *People grow plants in greenhouses.* 人們在温室裏種植植物。

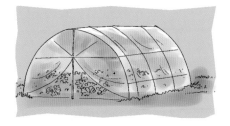

grew /gruː/ **grow** 的過去式 *The tree grew very tall.* 那棵樹長得很高。

grey[1] /greɪ/ [形容詞] 灰色的 *He wore grey trousers and a black coat.* 他穿着灰褲子和黑大衣。☞ 美國英語拼寫為 **gray**。

grey[2] /greɪ/ [名詞] 灰色 *Helen was dressed in grey.* 海倫穿着灰衣服。☞ 美國英語拼寫為 **gray**。

grin /grɪn/ [動詞] [現在分詞 **grinning**，過去式和過去分詞 **grinned**] 咧着嘴笑 *She grinned at me.* 她朝我咧着嘴笑。

grip /grɪp/ [動詞] [現在分詞 **gripping**，過去式和過去分詞 **gripped**] 抓住 *Henry gripped my hand.* 亨利緊緊抓住我的手。

ground /graʊnd/ [名詞] [用作單數，與 **the** 連用] 地面 *Henry lost his balance and fell to the ground.* 亨利失去平衡，摔在地上。

group /gruːp/ [名詞] 一羣；一組 *A group of people were standing outside the shop.* 商店外面站着一羣人。

grow /grəʊ; 美 groʊ/ [動詞] [過去式 **grew** /gruː/，過去分詞 **grown** /grəʊn; 美 groʊn/] 1 成長，長大 *Children grow very quickly.* 孩子們長得很快。2 (植物) 生長；種植 *Bananas grow in hot countries.* 香蕉生長在熱帶國家。◇ *They grow vegetables in their garden.* 他們在園子裏種蔬菜。

grown-up /ˈgrəʊn ʌp; 美 ˈgroʊn-/ [名詞] 成人 *If you're good you can eat with the grown-ups.* 如果你乖，你可以和大人一起吃飯。

guard /gɑːd; 美 gɑːrd/ [動詞] 保衞；看守 *The dog guarded the house.* 狗看守着那所房子。

guess /ges/ [動詞] 猜想，猜測 *Can you guess what's in the box?* 你能猜出盒子裏是甚麼嗎？

guest /gest/ [名詞] 客人 *We have guests coming to dinner tonight.* 我們今晚有客人來吃飯。

guitar /gɪˈtɑː; 美 -ˈtɑːr/ [名詞] 吉他

His son plays the guitar in a band.
他兒子在樂隊彈吉他。

gun /gʌn/ [名詞] 槍 *Guns are very dangerous.* 槍很危險。

gymnastics /dʒɪm'næstɪks/ [名詞] [無複數] 體操 *Look! Alice is doing gymnastics.* 瞧！艾麗斯正在表演體操。

G

H h

habit /ˈhæbɪt/ [名詞] 習慣 *Smoking is a bad habit.* 吸煙是一種壞習慣。

had / 強 hæd; 弱 həd / **have** 的過去式和過去分詞 *We had fish for dinner.* 我們晚飯吃的是魚。

hadn't /ˈhædnt/ **had not** 的縮寫 *They hadn't walked far when it started to rain.* 他們沒走多遠就下起了雨。

hair /heə; 美 her/ [名詞] [無複數] 頭髮 *She has long hair.* 她留着長髮。

hail /heɪl/ [動詞] 下冰雹 *Look! It's hailing!* 瞧！下冰雹了！

half /hɑːf; 美 hæf/ [名詞] [複數**halves** /hɑːvz; 美 hævz/] 一半 *Helen cut her apple into halves.* 海倫把蘋果切成兩半。◇ *The second half of the book is more exciting.* 書的後半部分更激動人心。

hall /hɔːl/ [名詞] **1** 門廳 *Leave your coat in the hall.* 把你的外套放在門廳裏。 **2** 大廳，禮堂 *The party will be held in the school hall.* 晚會將在學校禮堂舉行。

hamburger /ˈhæmˌbɜːgə; 美 -ˌbɜːrgər/ [名詞] 漢堡包 *A hamburger and chips, please.* 請來一份漢堡包和炸薯條。

hammer /ˈhæmə; 美 -ər/ [名詞] 錘子，榔頭 *Paul used a hammer to put a nail in the wall.* 保羅用錘子在牆上釘了個釘子。

hand¹ /hænd/ [名詞] 手 *I took the child by the hand.* 我拉着孩子的手。

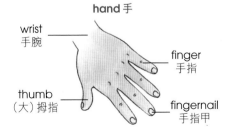

hand 手

wrist 手腕
finger 手指
thumb (大)拇指
fingernail 手指甲

hand² /hænd/ [動詞] 交給；遞給 *Please hand me that book.* 請把那本書遞給我。

handbag /'hændbæg/ [名詞]（女用的）手提包 *She left her handbag at the shop.* 她把手提包忘在商店了。

handkerchief /'hæŋkətʃɪf; 美 -ər-/ [名詞] [複數 **handkerchiefs**] 手帕 *Peter has a new handkerchief.* 彼得有塊新手帕。

handle /'hændl/ [名詞] 柄，把手 *Alice turned the door handle slowly.* 艾麗斯慢慢轉動門把手。

handsome /'hænsəm/ [形容詞]（指男人）漂亮的，英俊的 *Peter is a very handsome boy.* 彼得是個十分英俊的男孩。

handwriting /'hænd,raɪtɪŋ/ [名詞]

[無複數] 筆跡 *I can't read his handwriting.* 我看不懂他的筆跡。

hang /hæŋ/ [動詞] [過去式和過去分詞 **hung** /hʌŋ/] 懸掛 *Hang your coat up on the hook.* 把你的外套掛在衣鈎上。

hook
掛鈎

happen /'hæpən/ [動詞] 發生 *How did the accident happen?* 事故是怎樣發生的？

happy /'hæpi/ [形容詞] [比較級 **happier**，最高級 **happiest**] 1 高興的，快樂的 *I'm happy to see you again.* 很高興再次見到你。 [反] **unhappy** 不高興的，不快樂的；**sad** 悲哀的，傷心的，難過的 2 **Happy** [用於祝願對方快樂] ◇ *Happy Birthday!* 生日快樂！ ◇ *Happy Christmas!* 聖誕快樂！ ◇ *Happy New Year!* 新年快樂！

harbour /'hɑːbə; 美 'hɑːrbər/ [名詞] 港口，海港 *The harbour was full of ships.* 港口停滿了船。

H

hard¹ /haːd; 美 haːrd/ [形容詞] **1** 硬的，堅硬的 *I couldn't sleep because the bed was too hard.* 我睡不着，因為牀太硬了。 ☞ [反] **soft** 軟的，柔軟的 **2** 困難的 *The exam was very hard.* 這次考試很難。 ☞ ① [同] **difficult** 困難的 ② [反] **easy** 容易的

hard² /haːd; 美 haːrd/ [副詞] **1** 努力地 *You'll have to work harder if you want to pass this exam.* 如果你想通過這次考試，就必須更加用功。 **2** 猛烈地 *It's raining hard.* 雨下得很大。

harmful /'haːmfl; 美 'haːrm-/ [形容詞] 有害的 *Smoking is harmful to your health.* 吸煙有害健康。

harmonica /haːˈmɒnɪkə; 美 haːrˈmɑː-/ [名詞] 口琴 *Do you play the harmonica?* 你吹口琴嗎？

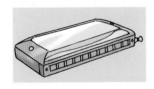

harvest /'haːvɪst; 美 'haːr-/ [名詞] **1** 收獲 *It's harvest time.* 現在是收獲季節。 **2** 收成 *The harvest was good this year.* 今年收成不錯。

has /強 hæz; 弱 həz/ **1** 動詞 **have** 的第三人稱單數現在式 *She has two brothers and a sister.* 她有兩個哥哥一個姐姐。 ☞ 參見 **have²**。 **2** 助動詞 **have** 的第三人稱單數 [用於構成完成時態] *Has anyone seen my pen?* 有人看見了我的鋼筆嗎？ ◇ *It's stopped raining now.* 現在雨停了。

☞ 參見 **have¹**。

hasn't /'hæznt/ **has not** 的縮寫 *Henry hasn't been abroad before.* 亨利以前沒出過國。

hat /hæt/ [名詞] （有檐的）帽子 *Helen was wearing a yellow hat.* 海倫戴着一頂黃帽子。 ☞ 參見 **cap** "（有舌無檐的）帽子"。

hatch /hætʃ/ [動詞] 孵出 *Ten chicks hatched this morning.* 今天上午孵出 10 隻小雞。

hate /heɪt/ [動詞] 討厭，不喜歡 *I hate snakes.* 我討厭蛇。 ◇ *He hates driving at night.* 他不喜歡晚上開車。

have¹ /強 hæv; 弱 həv/ [助動詞] [與過去分詞連用，構成完成時態] 已經 *I've finished my homework.* 我已經做完作業了。 ◇ *Have you seen Peter?* 你看見彼得了嗎？

have² /強 hæv; 弱 həv/ [動詞] [過去式和過去分詞 **had** /hæd/] **1** [英國英語又作 **have got**] 有 *Do you have a computer?* 你有電腦嗎？ ◇ *Have*

you got any brothers or sisters? 你有
兄弟姐妹嗎？**2** 吃；喝 What time do
you have breakfast? 你幾點鐘吃早餐？
3 發生；經歷 She had an accident.
她發生了意外。**4** [又作 **have got**] 患
（病）Henry has got a bad cold. 亨利
得了重感冒。 ☞ **have** 的兩種時態及
其單複數見下表：

時態	人稱	單數	複數
現在式	第一人稱	I have (I've)	We have (We've)
	第二人稱	You have (You've)	You have (You've)
	第三人稱	He/She/It has (He's/She's/It's)	They have (They've)
過去式	第一人稱	I had (I'd)	We had (We'd)
	第二人稱	You had (You'd)	You had (You'd)
	第三人稱	He/She/It had (He'd/She'd/It'd)	They had (They'd)

haven't /'hævnt/ **have not** 的縮寫
Haven't you done your homework
yet? 你還沒有做完作業嗎？

have to /'hæv tə/ [又作 **have got
to**][情態動詞] 必須，不得不 Sorry, I've
got to go. 對不起，我得走了。◇ Do
you have to go? 你必須走嗎？◇ You
don't have to answer all the
questions. 你不必回答所有的問題。

he / 強 hi:; 弱 hi / [代詞] [主格] 他
'When is Paul coming?' 'He'll be
here in a minute.' "保羅甚麼時候
到？""他馬上就到。"

head /hed/ [名詞] **1** 頭，頭部 The
ball hit him on the head. 球打在他的
頭上。**2** 頭腦，才智 Use your head!
動動腦筋！**3** [又作 **head teacher**] 校

長 Who is going to be the new
head? 誰將成為新任校長？

headache /'hedeɪk/ [名詞] 頭疼
I've got a headache. 我頭疼。

heal /hi:l/ [動詞] (傷口)癒合 The cut
on his leg healed quickly. 他腿上的
傷口很快癒合了。

health /helθ/ [名詞] [無複數] 健康
Exercise is good for your health. 運
動有益於健康。

healthy /'helθi/ [形容詞] [比較級
healthier，最高級 **healthiest**] **1** 健康的
Alice is a healthy child. 艾麗斯是個健
康的孩子。**2** 有益於健康的 It is healthy
to eat fruit. 吃水果有益於健康。

hear /hɪə; 美 hɪr/ [動詞] [過去式和過
去分詞 **heard** /hɜ:d; 美 hɜ:rd/] 聽見 I'm
sorry, I didn't quite hear what you
said. 對不起，我沒太聽清你說甚麼。

heart /hɑ:t; 美 hɑ:rt/ [名詞] 心；心
臟 Your heart beats faster when you
run. 跑步時心跳會加快。

heat /hi:t/ [動詞] 加熱 Heat the oil
and add onions. 先把油加熱，然後
再放洋蔥。

heavy /'hevi/ [形容詞] [比較級

heavier，最高級 **heaviest**] 重的 *The suitcase is too heavy for me to carry.* 衣箱太重，我提不動。 ☞ [反] **light²** 輕的

he'd / 強 hiːd; 弱 hid / **1 he had** 的 縮寫 *Henry said he'd never been abroad.* 亨利說他從未出過國。 **2 he would** 的縮寫 *Henry said he'd love to go to America some day.* 亨利說 有朝一日他要去美國。

heel /hiːl/ [名詞] 腳後跟 *I've got a sore heel.* 我的腳後跟疼。

height /haɪt/ [名詞] 高度；身高 *What is the height of this mountain?* 這座山有多高？ ◇ *She asked me my height, weight and age.* 她問我的身高、體重和年齡。

held /held/ **hold** 的過去式和過去分 詞 *We stood in a circle and held hands.* 我們站成一圈，手拉着手。

helicopter /'helɪkɒptə; 美 -əkɑːptər/ [名詞] 直升機 *Helicopters have no wings.* 直升機沒有機翼。

he'll / 強 hiːl; 弱 hil / **he will** 的縮寫 *I can't go to the cinema, but Peter said he'll go with you.* 我不能去看電 影了，但彼得說他跟你去。

hello /hə'ləʊ; 美 -'loʊ / [又作 **hallo** /hə'ləʊ; 美 -'loʊ /] [感歎詞] [問候語] 喂， 你好 *Hello, how are you?* 喂，你好 嗎？ ◇ *Hello, is there anybody there?* 喂，那裏有人嗎？

helmet /'helmɪt; 美 -ət / [名詞] 頭盔 *Henry wore a bicycle helmet.* 亨利 戴着一個自行車頭盔。

help¹ /help/ [動詞] 幫助 *Could you help me to answer this question?* 你 幫我回答這個問題好嗎？

help² /help/ [名詞] 幫助 *Thanks for your help.* 謝謝你的幫助。

helpful /'helpfl/ [形容詞] 給予幫助 的 *She's so kind and helpful.* 她既善 良又樂於助人。

hen /hen/ [名詞] 母雞 *The hen laid three eggs.* 那隻母雞下了三個蛋。

her¹ / 強 hɜː; 美 hɜːr; 弱 hə; 美 hər / [代詞] [**she** 的賓格] 她 *Give her the book.* 把書給她。

H

her² / 強 hɜː; 美 hɜːr; 弱 hə; 美 hər / [形容詞] [**she** 的所有格] 她的 *Her name is Alice.* 她的名字叫艾麗斯。

herd /hɜːd; 美 hɜːrd / [名詞] 一羣 (牛、鹿、大象等) *The farmer kept a herd of cattle.* 那個農民養了一羣牛。

here /hɪə; 美 hɪr / [副詞] 這裏,在這裏 *Come here!* 到這裏來! ◇ *I live here.* 我住在這裏。 ◇ *Put the box here.* 把箱子放在這裏。

here you are [口語] 給你 [用於給某人所要之物] *'Can I borrow your pen?' 'Yes, here you are.'* "我可以借用一下你的鋼筆嗎?""可以,給你。"

hero /ˈhɪərəʊ; 美 ˈhiːroʊ / [名詞] [複數 **heroes**] 英雄 *Abraham Lincoln is a national hero of the United States.* 亞伯拉罕·林肯是美國的一位民族英雄。

hers /hɜːz; 美 hɜːrz / [代詞] [**she** 的物主代詞] 她的(東西) *Are these keys hers?* 這些鑰匙是她的嗎?

herself / 強 hɜːˈself; 美 hɜːr-; 弱 həˈself; 美 hər- / [代詞] [**she**的反身代詞] 她自己 *Helen looked at herself in the mirror.* 海倫照了照鏡子。

he's / 強 hiːz; 弱 hiz / **1** he is 的縮寫 *He's a doctor.* 他是醫生。 **2** he has

的縮寫 *Henry can't come out to play — he's got a bad cold.* 亨利不能出來玩了,他得了重感冒。

hi /haɪ / [感歎詞] [非正式] [問候語] 喂,你好 *Hi Peter! How are you?* 喂,彼得!你好嗎?

hid /hɪd / **hide** 的過去式 *Alice hid behind a big tree.* 艾麗斯藏在一棵大樹後面。

hide /haɪd / [動詞] [過去式 **hid** /hɪd /,過去分詞 **hidden** /ˈhɪdn /] **1** 隱藏 *Where did you hide the money?* 你把錢藏在哪裏了? **2** 躲藏 *The child was hiding behind the door.* 那個孩子藏在門後。

hidden /ˈhɪdn / **hide** 的過去分詞 *The three bears' house was hidden deep in the forest.* 那三隻熊的房子藏在森林深處。

high /haɪ / [形容詞] **1** (指物)高的 *What's the highest mountain in the world?* 世界上哪座山最高? ☞ [反] **low** 矮的 **2** (指高於通常的水平或數量)高的 *She's got a high temperature.* 她發高燒。 ☞ [反] **low** 低的 **3** 高聲的 *She has a very high voice.* 她的嗓門很高。 ☞ [反] **low** 低聲的

hill /hɪl / [名詞] 小山 *The car slowly*

climbed the hill. 汽車緩慢地爬上山坡。

him /hɪm/ [代詞] [**he**的賓格] 他 *Give him the book.* 把書給他。 ◇ *What did you say to him?* 你對他說了甚麼？

himself /hɪm'self/ [代詞] [**he** 的反身代詞] 他自己 *Peter introduced himself.* 彼得作了自我介紹。

his¹ /hɪz/ [形容詞] [**he** 的所有格] 他的 *It's not his fault.* 這不是他的錯。

his² /hɪz/ [代詞] [**he** 的物主代詞] 他的（東西）*Are these books yours or his?* 這些書是你的還是他的？

history /'hɪstri/ [名詞] [無複數] 歷史 *History is my favourite subject.* 歷史是我最喜歡的科目。

hit /hɪt/ [動詞] [現在分詞**hitting**，過去式和過去分詞**hit**] **1** 打，擊 *He hit me on the head.* 他打我的頭。 ◇ *He hit me in the face.* 他打我的臉。 **2** 碰，撞 *The car hit a tree.* 小汽車撞在一棵樹上。

hobby /'hɒbi; 美 'hɑː-/ [名詞] [複數 **hobbies**] 愛好，嗜好 *'What hobbies do you have?' 'Swimming and stamp collecting.'* "你有甚麼愛好？" "游泳和集郵。"

hold /həʊld; 美 hoʊld/ [動詞] [過去式和過去分詞**held** /held/] **1** 拿着；握着；抱着 *Henry was holding an umbrella.* 亨利拿着一把雨傘。 ◇ *She was holding a baby in her arms.* 她懷裏抱着一個嬰兒。 **2** 舉行 *The Olympic Games are held every four years.* 奧林匹克運動會每4年舉行一次。 **3** 可容納；包含 *How much does this bottle hold?* 這個瓶子能裝多少？

hole /həʊl; 美 hoʊl/ [名詞] 洞 *There is a hole in the wall.* 牆上有個洞。

holiday /'hɒlədeɪ; 美 'hɑː-/ [名詞] 假日 *Where are you going for your holidays this year?* 你今年去哪裏度假？

hollow /'hɒləʊ; 美 'hɑːloʊ/ [形容詞] 空心的 *The tree trunk is hollow inside.* 樹幹裏面是空心的。

H

home /həʊm; 美 hoʊm / [名詞] 家 *We are going to stay at home today.* 我們今天打算待在家裏。◇ *He left home at sixteen.* 他 16 歲離開了家。

homework /ˈhəʊmwɜːk; 美 ˈhoʊmwɜːrk/ [名詞] [無複數]（家庭）作業 *I can't come out tonight because I have a lot of homework to do.* 我今晚不能出來，因為我有許多作業要做。

honest /ˈɒnɪst; 美 ˈɑːnəst / [形容詞]（指人）誠實的 *My father is an honest man.* 我父親為人誠實。 ☞ [反] **dishonest** 不誠實的

honey /ˈhʌni/ [名詞] [無複數] 蜂蜜 *Alice loves to eat honey on her bread.* 艾麗斯喜歡在面包上抹蜂蜜吃。

hoof /huːf/ [名詞] [複數 **hoofs** 或 **hooves** /huːvz/]（馬或其他動物的）蹄 *We heard the noise of a horse's hooves.* 我們聽到馬蹄聲。

hook /hʊk/ [名詞] 鈎，掛鈎 *Hang your towel on the hook.* 把你的毛巾掛在掛鈎上。

hope /həʊp; 美 hoʊp/ [動詞] 希望 *I hope that you feel better soon.* 希望你早日康復。◇ *I hope to see you tomorrow.* 我希望明天能見到你。◇ *'Is Henry coming to the party?' 'I hope so.'* "亨利來參加聚會嗎？""希望他能來。"

◇ *'Are we going to be late?' 'I hope not.'* "我們要遲到了嗎？""希望不會。"

horn /hɔːn; 美 hɔːrn/ [名詞] **1**（牛、羊等的）角 *Goats and bulls have horns.* 山羊和公牛頭上長角。

2（汽車等的）喇叭 *The taxi blew its horn.* 出租車鳴響了喇叭。**3**（樂器中的）號 *She plays the French horn in the school orchestra.* 她在校管弦樂隊吹法國號。

horrible /ˈhɒrəbl; 美 ˈhɔːr-/ [形容詞] [非正式] 糟糕的，討厭的 *This coffee tastes horrible!* 這咖啡真難喝！◇ *Don't be so horrible!* 別這麼討厭！

horse /hɔːs; 美 hɔːrs / [名詞] 馬 *I learnt to ride a horse when I was four.* 我 4 歲學騎馬。

horse 馬

tail 尾巴

hoof 蹄

hospital /ˈhɒspɪtl; 美 ˈhɑː-/ [名詞] 醫院 *His mother's in hospital.* 他母親住院了。◇ *The ambulance took her to hospital.* 救護車把她送進了醫院。

hot /hɒt; 美 hɑːt / [形容詞] [比較級 **hotter**，最高級 **hottest**] 熱的；燙的 *Do you like this hot weather?* 你喜歡這種炎熱的天氣嗎？◇ *This coffee is too hot to drink.* 這咖啡太燙，沒法喝。☞ [反] **cold¹** 冷的

hot dog /ˌhɒt 'dɒg; 美 ˌhɑːt 'dɔːg / [名詞] 熱狗 *The children ate hot dogs at their friend's birthday party.* 孩子們在朋友的生日聚會上吃了熱狗。

hotel /ˌhəʊ'tel; 美 ˌhoʊ- / [名詞] 旅館，飯店 *They stayed in a hotel.* 他們住在一家旅館裏。

hour /'aʊə; 美 'aʊr / [名詞] 小時 *There are 24 hours in a day.* 1 天有 24 個小時。

house /haʊs / [名詞] 房子；住宅 *Where is your house?* 你們家在哪裏？

how /haʊ / [副詞] **1** 怎樣，如何 *How do you spell your name?* 你的名字怎麼拼寫？◇ *I can't remember how* to get there. 我記不得怎樣去那裏了。 **2** [用以詢問程度、數量、年齡] 多少 *How tall are you?* 你多高？◇ *How old are you?* 你多大了？◇ *How much does this cost?* 這個多少錢？◇ *How many students are there in your class?* 你們班有多少學生？

How are you? 你好嗎？[見到熟人時用的問候語，常回答 **Fine**，**Good**，**Not so bad** 等] `How are you?' `Fine, thanks.' "你好嗎？" "很好，謝謝。"

How do you do? 你好！[初次見面時用的問候語，對方也用同樣的話回答]

hug /hʌg / [動詞] [現在分詞 **hugging**，過去式和過去分詞 **hugged**] 擁抱 *His daughter hugged him.* 女兒抱了一下他。

huge /hjuːdʒ / [形容詞] 巨大的，龐大的 *They have a huge house in the country.* 他們在鄉下有一棟大房子。

human /'hjuːmən / [又作 **human being**] [名詞] 人 *Dogs can hear much better than humans.* 狗的聽覺比人的好得多。

hundred /'hʌndrəd / [數詞] 百 *There were a hundred people in the room.* 房間裏有一百人。

hung /hʌŋ/ **hang** 的過去式和過去分詞 *Mum hung the clean clothes up in the wardrobe.* 媽媽把乾淨衣服掛在衣櫃裏。

hungry /ˈhʌŋgri/ [形容詞] [比較級 **hungrier**，最高級 **hungriest**] 飢餓的 *I'm hungry. What's for supper?* 我餓了，晚飯吃甚麼？

hunt /hʌnt/ [動詞] 追獵；獵取；獵食 *Lions sometimes hunt alone.* 獅子有時獨自獵食。

hurry /ˈhʌri; 美 'hɜːri/ [動詞] [現在分詞 **hurrying**，過去式和過去分詞 **hurried**] 趕快；急忙 *Don't hurry. There's plenty of time.* 別急，還有很多時間。
hurry up [非正式] 趕緊 *Hurry up! We're going to be late.* 快點！我們要遲到了。

hurt /hɜːt; 美 hɜːrt/ [動詞] [過去式和過去分詞 **hurt**] **1** 弄痛，使受傷 *She hurt her leg when she fell.* 她摔傷了腿。 **2** 痛 *My leg hurts.* 我的腿痛。

husband /ˈhʌzbənd/ [名詞] 丈夫 *Her husband is a doctor.* 她丈夫是醫生。

hut /hʌt/ [名詞] （簡陋的）小屋 *They live in huts in the forest.* 他們住在森林裏的小屋裏。

H

I i

I /aɪ/ [代詞] [主格] 我 *I want to go home.* 我想回家。◇ *I'm very glad to see you.* 很高興見到你。◇ *My friend and I went to the cinema.* 我和朋友去看電影了。

ice /aɪs/ [名詞] [無複數] 冰；冰塊 *Henry slipped on the ice.* 亨利在冰上滑了一跤。◇ *He put some ice in his drink.* 他在飲料裏加了些冰塊。

ice cream /ˌaɪs 'kriːm/ [名詞] 冰淇淋，雪糕 *I ate some chocolate ice cream.* 我吃了一些巧克力冰淇淋。◇ *Who wants an ice cream?* 誰要冰淇淋？

I'd /aɪd/ **1** I had 的縮寫 *I couldn't remember where I'd seen the film.* 我記不得在哪裏看過那部電影。 **2** I would 的縮寫 *I'd love a piece of cake.* 我想吃塊蛋糕。

idea /aɪˈdɪə; 美 -ˈdiːə/ [名詞] 主意，想法 *I have an idea.* 我有個主意。◇ *That's a good idea!* 那是個好主意！

identical /aɪˈdentɪkl/ [形容詞] 相同的，一樣的 *Your shoes are identical to mine.* 你的鞋和我的一模一樣。

if /ɪf/ [連詞] **1** 如果 *If it rains tomorrow, I'll take the umbrella.* 如果明天下雨，我就帶雨傘。 **2** 是否 *I don't know if I'll be able to come.* 我不知道是否能來。

ill /ɪl/ [形容詞] [不用於名詞前] 生病的 *Helen can't go to school because she's ill.* 海倫因病不能去上學了。

illness /ˈɪlnəs/ [名詞] 病；疾病 *Henry missed five days of school because of illness.* 亨利因病缺了 5 天課。

I'll /aɪl/ **I will** 的縮寫 *I'll see you later.* 一會兒見。

I'm /aɪm/ **I am** 的縮寫 *I'm ten today.* 我今天 10 歲了。

I

imagine /ɪ'mædʒɪn/ [動詞] 想像 *Close your eyes and imagine that you're in a forest.* 閉上眼睛，想像你在森林裏。

imitate /'ɪmɪteɪt/ [動詞] 模仿 *Alice imitated the way her teacher talked.* 艾麗斯模仿老師說話的樣子。

immediately /ɪ'miːdiətli/ [副詞] 立即，馬上 *Can you come home immediately?* 你能馬上回家嗎？ ☞ [同] **at once** 立刻，馬上

impatient /ɪm'peɪʃnt/ [形容詞] 不耐煩的 *Don't be so impatient! The bus will be here soon.* 別這麼不耐煩，公共汽車馬上就來。 ☞ [反] **patient** 耐心的

important /ɪm'pɔːtnt; 美 -ɔːr-/ [形容詞] 重要的 *It is important to clean your teeth every day.* 每天刷牙很重要。

impossible /ɪm'pɒsəbl; 美 -'pɑː-/ [形容詞] 不可能的 *That's impossible!* 那不可能！ ☞ [反] **possible** 可能的

improve /ɪm'pruːv/ [動詞] 改進；進步 *His English has improved.* 他的英語進步了。

in¹ /ɪn/ [副詞] **1** 進入 *Please come in.* 請進來。 ☞ [反] **out** 出去 **2** 在家 *Is Henry in?* 亨利在家嗎？ ☞ [反] **out** 不在家

in² /ɪn/ [介詞] **1** 在…裏面 *She put her keys in her pocket.* 她把鑰匙放在口袋裏。 **2** [表示地點] 在 *Henry lives in London.* 亨利住在倫敦。 **3** [表示時間] 在…期間 *My birthday is in August.* 我的生日是在 8 月。 ◇ *He was born in 1996.* 他是 1996 年出生的。 **4** [表示時間] 在…之後 *I'll be ready in a few minutes.* 我過幾分鐘就準備好。 **5** 穿着 *Mr Brown was dressed in a suit.* 布朗先生穿着一套西裝。 **6** [表示語言、材料等] 用 *Say it in English.* 用英語說。 ◇ *Please write in pen.* 請用鋼筆寫。

inch /ɪntʃ/ [名詞] [複數**inches**] 英寸 *There are 12 inches in a foot.* 1 英尺等於 12 英寸。

increase /ɪn'kriːs/ [動詞] 增加，增長 *The population of this town has increased.* 這個城鎮的人口增加了。

indoors /ˌɪn'dɔːz; 美 -'dɔːrz/ [副詞] 在室內，在屋裏 *It's raining — let's go indoors.* 下雨了，我們進屋吧。 ☞ [反] **outdoors** 在室外，在戶外

infant /'ɪnfənt/ [名詞] 嬰兒，幼兒 *She could see two infants in the room.* 她看見房間裏有兩個嬰兒。

infectious /ɪn'fekʃəs/ [形容詞]（指疾病等）傳染的 *Flu is very infectious.* 流感傳染性很強。

information /ˌɪnfə'meɪʃn; 美 -ər-/ [名詞] [無複數] 信息；資料；消息 *This book contains a lot of useful information.* 這本書裏含有許多有用的

資料。

ingredient /ɪnˈgriːdiənt/ [名詞]
(烹調用的) 配料,原料,成分 *Flour, milk, and eggs are the main ingredients of bread.* 麵粉、牛奶和雞蛋是麵包的主要原料。

initial /ɪˈnɪʃl/ [名詞] (姓名的) 首字母 *His name is John Smith, so his initials are J. S.* 他的姓名是約翰‧史密斯,所以英文首字母是J.S.。

injure /ˈɪndʒə; 美 -ər/ [動詞] 使受傷;傷害 *Two people were injured in the accident.* 有兩個人在這次事故中受傷。

ink /ɪŋk/ [名詞] [無複數] 墨水 *The letter was written in black ink.* 那封信是用黑墨水寫的。

insect /ˈɪnsekt/ [名詞] 昆蟲 *Ants, bees and beetles are all insects.* 螞蟻、蜜蜂和甲蟲都是昆蟲。

insects 昆蟲

butterfly
蝴蝶

bee
蜜蜂

ant
螞蟻

beetle
甲蟲

inside¹ /ˌɪnˈsaɪd/ [介詞] 在…裏面 *Is there anything inside the box?* 箱子裏面有東西嗎? [反] **outside²** 在…外面

inside² /ˌɪnˈsaɪd/ [副詞] 在裏面 `Where's Peter?' `He's inside.' "彼得在哪裏?""他在裏面。" [反] **outside¹** 在外面

instead /ɪnˈsted/ [副詞] 代替 *I didn't have a pen, so I used a pencil instead.* 我沒有鋼筆,所以才用鉛筆代替。

instead of /ɪnˈsted əv/ [介詞] 代替…,而不是… *Can you come on Saturday instead of Sunday?* 你別星期天來了,改在星期六行嗎?

instructions /ɪnˈstrʌkʃnz/ [名詞] [複數] 用法説明 *Read the instructions carefully.* 仔細看使用説明。

instrument /ˈɪnstrəmənt/ [名詞] **1** 器具;器械;儀器 *A telescope is a scientific instrument.* 望遠鏡是一種科學儀器。**2** 樂器 `What instrument do you play?' `The violin.' "你演奏甚麼樂器?""小提琴。"

intelligent /ɪnˈtelɪdʒənt/ [形容詞] 聰明的 *Peter is very intelligent.* 彼得非常聰明。

interested /ˈɪntrəstɪd/ [形容詞] 感興趣的 *Henry is very interested in maths.* 亨利對數學很感興趣。

interesting /ˈɪntrəstɪŋ/ [形容詞] 有趣的;引起興趣的 *This book is very interesting.* 這本書很有趣。

I

Internet /'ɪntənet; 美 -tər-/ [名詞] [用作單數，與 the 連用] 互聯網，因特網 *I get a lot of information from the Internet.* 我從互聯網上獲得很多信息。

interrupt /ˌɪntə'rʌpt/ [動詞] 打斷（某人）講話 *Please don't interrupt me when I'm speaking.* 請不要打斷我的話。

into /強 'ɪntuː; 弱 'ɪntə; 'ɪntu/ [介詞] 進，入 *Come into the house.* 到屋裏來。◇ *He fell into the water.* 他掉進水裏了。

invent /ɪn'vent/ [動詞] 發明 *They've invented a computer that can talk.* 他們發明了一台會說話的電腦。

invention /ɪn'venʃn/ [名詞] 發明 *The telephone is a very useful invention.* 電話是一項十分有用的發明。

invisible /ɪn'vɪzəbl/ [形容詞] 看不見的 *Air is invisible.* 空氣是看不見的。

invitation /ˌɪnvɪ'teɪʃn/ [名詞] 邀請；請柬 *Did you get an invitation to the party?* 你有沒有收到參加聚會的請柬？

invite /ɪn'vaɪt/ [動詞] 邀請 *Henry invited me to his party.* 亨利邀請我去參加他的聚會。

iron /'aɪən; 美 'aɪərn/ [名詞] 1 [無複數] 鐵 *The gates are made of iron.* 這些門是鐵的。 2 熨斗 *Be careful*

— *the iron is hot!* 小心，熨斗燙！

is /ɪz/ *My name is Henry.* 我的名字叫亨利。☞ 參見 **be¹**。

island /'aɪlənd/ [名詞] 島 *An island is surrounded by water.* 島四周環水。

isn't /'ɪznt/ **is not** 的縮寫 *Peter isn't at school today.* 彼得今天沒來上學。

it /ɪt/ [代詞] 1 它，這，那 [指已提到過的事物或動物] *'Whose coat is this?' 'It's mine.'* "這是誰的外套？" "是我的。" 2 [作先行代詞，引導後面的短語或從句] *It's nice to see you again.* 再次見到你真高興。◇ *It's a pity that you forgot.* 真可惜你忘了。3 [作主語，指時間、日期、距離、天氣等] *It's six o'clock.* 6點了。◇ *It's hot today.* 今天很熱。◇ *It's 100 kilometres to London.* 到倫敦有100公里。◇ *It's raining.* 下雨了。

its /ɪts/ [形容詞] [**it** 的所有格] 它的 *The dog hurt its leg.* 狗的腿受傷了。

it's /ɪts/ 1 **it is** 的縮寫 *It's me.* 是我。◇ *It's raining outside.* 外面下雨了。2 **it has** 的縮寫 *It's stopped raining.* 雨停了。

itself /ɪt'self/ [代詞] 1 [**it** 的反身代詞]

它自己 *The cat was washing itself.* 貓在給自己洗澡。**2** [用以加強語氣] 自身，本身 *The garden is enormous, but the house itself is very small.* 花園很大，但房子本身卻很小。

I've /aɪv/ **I have**的縮寫 *I've seen this film before.* 我以前看過這部電影。

J j

jacket /'dʒækɪt/ [名詞] 夾克，短上衣 Mum bought me a red jacket. 媽媽給我買了一件紅夾克。

jam /dʒæm/ [名詞] 果醬 Peter loves bread with jam. 彼得喜歡吃抹了果醬的麵包。

January /'dʒænjuəri; 美 -jueri/ [名詞] 一月 She was born in January. 她是1月出生的。☞ ① 參見 **August** 的示例。② **Jan** 是 **January** 的縮寫。

Japan /dʒə'pæn/ [名詞] 日本 Japan is a country made up of many islands. 日本是一個由許多島嶼組成的國家。

Japanese¹ /ˌdʒæpə'niːz/ [形容詞] 日本（人）的 Do you like Japanese food? 你喜歡吃日本餐嗎？

Japanese² /ˌdʒæpə'niːz/ [名詞] **1** [複數 **Japanese**] 日本人 Most Japanese live in cities. 大多數日本人住在城裏。 **2** 日語 Do you speak Japanese? 你說日語嗎？

jar /dʒɑː; 美 dʒɑːr/ [名詞]（通常指玻璃做成的）瓶；罐 I bought a jar of honey. 我買了一罐蜂蜜。

jaw /dʒɔː/ [名詞] 頜；顎 Our jaws move when we eat. 我們吃東西時，上下顎會動。

jealous /'dʒeləs/ [形容詞] 忌妒的 I'm very jealous of your new bicycle. 我很忌妒你的新自行車。

jeans /dʒiːnz/ [名詞] [複數] 牛仔褲 These jeans are a bit too tight. 這條牛仔褲太緊了點。

jeep /dʒiːp/ [名詞] 吉普車 My uncle

has a blue jeep. 我叔叔有一輛藍色吉普車。

jelly /'dʒeli / [名詞] [複數 **jellies**] 果凍 Henry likes jelly. 亨利愛吃果凍。

jet /dʒet / [名詞] 噴氣式飛機 Most planes are jets now. 現在大部分飛機是噴氣式飛機。

jewel /'dʒuːəl / [名詞] 寶石 She wore beautiful jewels round her neck. 她脖子上戴着漂亮的珠寶。

jewellery /'dʒuːəlri / [名詞] [無複數] [總稱] 珠寶；首飾 She wears a lot of jewellery. 她戴着許多珠寶首飾。

jewellery 珠寶

necklace 項鏈　　bracelets 手鐲　　ring 戒指

jigsaw /'dʒɪgsɔː / [又作 **jigsaw puzzle**] [名詞] 拼圖 Henry is doing a jigsaw. 亨利正在拼拼圖。

job /dʒɒb; 美 dʒɑːb / [名詞] 1 職業；工作 He's looking for a new job. 他在尋找新的工作。 2 職責 My mother does all the jobs around the house. 我媽媽做所有的家務。

join /dʒɔɪn / [動詞] 1 連接 This road joins the two villages. 這條路把兩個村莊連接起來。 2 加入 He joined the army. 他參軍了。

joke /dʒəʊk; 美 dʒoʊk / [名詞] 笑話 Our teacher told us a funny joke. 老師給我們講了一個滑稽的笑話。

journey /'dʒɜːni; 美 'dʒɜːrni / [名詞] 旅行，旅程 Did you have a good journey? 你旅行愉快嗎？

jug /dʒʌg / [名詞] （有柄的）壺 I'll fetch a jug of water. 我去拿一壺水。

juggle /'dʒʌgl / [動詞] 耍（球、盤等） How many balls is the clown juggling? 那個小醜在耍幾個球？

juice /dʒuːs / [名詞] [無複數] 果汁 Can I have a glass of orange juice?

J

我可以喝杯橙汁嗎？

July /dʒu'laɪ/ [名詞] 七月 *Last July we went to France.* 去年 7 月我們去了法國。☞ ① 參見 **August** 的示例。② **Jul** 是 **July** 的縮寫。

jump /dʒʌmp/ [動詞] 跳；跳躍 *How high can you jump?* 你能跳多高？

jumper /'dʒʌmpə; 美 -ər/ [名詞] (套頭)毛衣 *Alice is wearing a purple jumper.* 艾麗斯穿着一件紫毛衣。☞ **jumper** 用於英國英語，**sweater** 既可用於英國英語，也可用於美國英語。

June /dʒuːn/ [名詞] 六月 *My mother's birthday is in June.* 我母親的生日是在 6 月。☞ ① 參見 **August** 的示例。② **Jun** 是 **June** 的縮寫。

jungle /'dʒʌŋgl/ [名詞] (熱帶地區的)叢林，密林 *There were snakes in the jungle.* 叢林裏有蛇。

just /dʒʌst/ [副詞] **1** 剛剛，剛才 *I've just got home.* 我剛回到家裏。◇ *He has just arrived.* 他剛到。**2** 正好，恰好 *It's just eight o'clock.* 正好 8 點。◇ *That's just what I meant.* 那正是我的意思。**3** 僅僅，只是 *I play tennis just for fun.* 我打網球只是為了好玩。◇ *He's just a child.* 他只是個孩子。

J

K k

kangaroo /ˌkæŋɡəˈruː/ [名詞] [複數**kangaroos**] 袋鼠 *A kangaroo can jump very far.* 袋鼠能跳很遠。 ◇ *The kangaroo is an Australian animal.* 袋鼠是一種產於澳大利亞的動物。

keen /kiːn/ [形容詞] 熱切的；熱心的；渴望的 *Alice is a keen swimmer.* 艾麗斯非常喜歡游泳。
be keen on sth 非常喜歡某事 *Alice is keen on swimming.* 艾麗斯非常喜歡游泳。

keep /kiːp/ [動詞] [過去式和過去分詞 **kept** /kept/] **1** 保留；保存；保持 *You can keep that book — I don't need it any more.* 那本書你可以留着，我用不着了。 **2** 存放 *Where do you keep the keys?* 你把鑰匙放在哪裏了？ **3** （使）保持（某種狀態） *Paul kept his hands in his pockets.* 保羅把手揣在口袋裏。 ◇ *I'm sorry to keep you waiting.* 對不起，讓您久等了。 **4** 一直做某事 *I keep losing my keys.* 我老是丟鑰匙。 **5** 飼養，喂養 *What type of pet would you like to keep?* 你想養哪一類寵物？

kept /kept/ **keep**的過去式和過去分詞 *I didn't know that you kept rabbits.* 我不知道你養着兔子。

kettle /ˈketl/ [名詞] （燒水用的）水壺 *The kettle is boiling.* 壺裏的水燒開了。

key /kiː/ [名詞] **1** 鑰匙 *Henry turned the key and opened the door.* 亨利轉動鑰匙把門打開。 ◇ *Where's the key to the back door?* 後門的鑰匙在哪裏？ **2** （鋼琴、計算機等的）鍵 *Pianos have black and white keys.* 鋼琴上有黑鍵和白鍵。 ◇ *Where's the 'Enter' key on your computer?* 你電腦上的回車鍵在哪裏？

keyboard /ˈkiːbɔːd; 美 -bɔːrd/ [名詞] （鋼琴、計算機等的）鍵盤 *Computers have keyboards.* 計算機都有鍵盤。

kick /kɪk/ [動詞] 踢 *Henry kicked the ball.* 亨利踢球。

kid /kɪd/ [名詞] [非正式] 孩子 *He's just a kid.* 他只是個孩子。

kill /kɪl/ [動詞] 使喪生；殺死 *He was killed in a car crash.* 他在一次車禍中喪生。

kilo /ˈki:ləʊ; 美 -oʊ/ [名詞] [複數 **kilos**] 公斤，千克 *I'd like a kilo of apples, please.* 請給我稱一公斤蘋果。 ☞ **= kilogram** 或 **kilogramme**

kilogram /ˈkɪləgræm/ [又作 **kilo**] [名詞] 公斤，千克 *Mum bought two kilograms of potatoes.* 媽媽買了兩公斤土豆。 ☞ ① **kilogram**是美國英語拼法，英國英語拼寫為 **kilogramme**。② **kilogram** 的縮寫為 **kg**。

kilometre /ˈkɪləˌmi:tə; 美 kəˈlɑ:mətər/ [名詞] 公里，千米 *They live 100 km from London.* 他們住在離倫敦 100 公里遠的地方。 ☞ ① 美國英語拼寫為 **kilometer**。② **kilometre** 的縮寫為 **km**。

kind¹ /kaɪnd/ [名詞] 種類 *What kind of music do you like?* 你喜歡甚麼樣的音樂？ ◇ *A butterfly is a kind of insect.* 蝴蝶是一種昆蟲。

kind² /kaɪnd/ [形容詞] 仁慈的；和藹的 *Thank you. You're very kind.* 謝謝你，你真好。 ◇ *He was a very kind man.* 他是一個非常和藹可親的人。 ☞ [反] **unkind** 不仁慈的；刻薄的；殘忍的

king /kɪŋ/ [名詞] 國王 *The King of Spain is visiting England.* 西班牙國王正在訪問英國。

kiss /kɪs/ [動詞] 吻 *She kissed me on the cheek.* 她吻了一下我的面頰。 ◇ *They kissed each other goodbye.* 他們相互吻別。

kitchen /ˈkɪtʃən/ [名詞] 廚房 *She's in the kitchen.* 她在廚房裏。

kite /kaɪt/ [名詞] 風箏 *Children love flying kites.* 孩子們喜歡放風箏。

kitten /ˈkɪtn/ [名詞] 小貓 *This kitten is lovely.* 這隻小貓真可愛。

knee /niː/ [名詞] 膝;膝蓋 *Helen fell and hurt her knee.* 海倫跌了一跤，傷了膝蓋。 ◇ *Come and sit on my knee.* 過來坐在我的膝蓋上。

kneel /niːl/ [動詞] [過去式和過去分詞**knelt** /nelt/ 或 **kneeled**] 跪下，跪着 *She knelt down to pray.* 她跪下祈禱。

knelt /nelt/ **kneel**的過去式和過去分詞 *Henry knelt down and looked under the table.* 亨利跪下在桌子底下找。

knew /njuː; 美 nuː/ **know** 的過去式 *I knew I was right.* 我知道我是對的。

knife /naɪf/ [名詞] [複數 **knives** /naɪvz/] 刀 *I prefer to use a knife and fork.* 我更喜歡用刀叉。

knight /naɪt/ [名詞] 騎士 *In the past, knights fought for their king.* 在

過去，騎士為國王而戰。

knit /nɪt/ [動詞] [現在分詞**knitting**，過去式和過去分詞**knitted**] 編織 *She is knitting a scarf.* 她正在織一條圍巾。

knob /nɒb; 美 nɑːb/ [名詞] (門、抽屜等的)圓形把手 *The knob came off the kitchen door.* 廚房門上的圓形把手掉了。

knock /nɒk; 美 nɑːk/ [動詞] 敲 *There's someone knocking on the door.* 有人敲門。◇ *Please knock before entering.* 進來之前請先敲門。

knock sb down [又作 **knock sb over**] 撞倒某人 *She was knocked down by a taxi.* 她被一輛出租車撞倒了。

knot /nɒt; 美 nɑːt/ [名詞] (線、繩等

的)結 Can you tie a knot at the end of the rope? 你能在繩頭上打個結嗎?

know /nəʊ; 美 noʊ / [動詞] [過去式 **knew** /njuː; 美 nuː/，過去分詞 **known** /nəʊn; 美 noʊn/] **1** 知道 'Where did he go?' 'I don't know.' "他去哪裏了?" "我不知道。" ◇ Do you know his telephone number? 你知道他的電話號碼嗎? **2** 認識 I know that girl but I can't remember her name. 我認識那個女孩,但記不起她的名字了。**3** 熟悉 I don't know this part of London well. 我不大熟悉倫敦的這一地區。

know how to do sth 會做某事 Do you know how to use a computer? 你會用電腦嗎?

known /nəʊn; 美 noʊn/ **know** 的過去分詞 I've known him very long. 我認識他很久了。

L l

label /ˈleɪbl/ [名詞] 標籤 *Is there a label on the bottle?* 瓶子上有標籤嗎？

ladder /ˈlædə; 美 -ər/ [名詞] 梯子 *Henry climbed up the ladder.* 亨利爬上梯子。

lady /ˈleɪdi/ [名詞] [複數 **ladies**] [禮貌用語] 女士，夫人，小姐 *That lady is my mother's friend.* 那位女士是我母親的朋友。

laid /leɪd/ **lay** 的過去式和過去分詞 *Have you laid the table?* 你把桌子擺好了嗎？

lake /leɪk/ [名詞] 湖 *We went for a swim in the lake.* 我們到湖裏游泳去了。

lamb /læm/ [名詞] **1** 羔羊，小羊 *There were some lambs in the field.* 田裏有幾隻小羊。

2 [無複數] 羔羊肉，小羊肉 *We had roast lamb for dinner.* 我們晚餐吃烤羔羊肉。

lamp /læmp/ [名詞] 燈 *I've got a table lamp on my desk at home.* 我家裏的書桌上有一盞台燈。

land¹ /lænd/ [名詞] [無複數] 陸地 *The elephant is the largest animal on land.* 大象是陸地上最大的動物。

land² /lænd/ [動詞]（飛機）降落，着陸 *The plane landed at the airport at 10:15.* 飛機在 10 點 15 分降落在機場。 ☞ [反] **take off**（飛機）起飛

L

lane /leɪn/ [名詞] **1** (鄉間) 小路 *They walked down the lane.* 他們沿着小路走去。

2 (單行) 車道 *The road has six lanes.* 這條公路有6個車道。

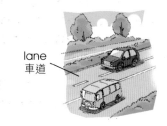

lane
車道

language /ˈlæŋgwɪdʒ/ [名詞] 語言 *How many languages can you speak?* 你會説幾門語言？

lantern /ˈlæntən; 美 -ərn/ [名詞] 提燈；燈籠 *Do you have a lantern?* 你有提燈嗎？ ☞ 燈籠為中國文化所特有，因此，指"燈籠"，一般用**Chinese lantern**。

lantern
提燈

Chinese
lantern
燈籠

lap¹ /læp/ [名詞] 大腿部 *The child sat quietly on his mother's lap.* 那個孩子靜靜地坐在母親的懷裏。

lap
大腿部

lap² /læp/ [動詞] [現在分詞 **lapping**，過去式和過去分詞 **lapped**] (動物) 舔，舔食 *The cat is lapping the milk.* 貓在舔食牛奶。

large /lɑːdʒ; 美 lɑːrdʒ/ [形容詞] 大的 *Elephants and whales are the world's two largest animals.* 大象和鯨魚是世界上最大的兩種動物。 ☞ ① [同] **big** 大的 ② [反] **small** 小的

last /lɑːst; 美 læst/ [形容詞] **1** 最後的 *Please turn to the last page of the book.* 請翻到書的最後一頁。 **2** 上一個的 *I read three books last week.* 我上週讀了三本書。

late¹ /leɪt/ [形容詞] 遲的，晚的 *Sorry I'm late.* 對不起，我遲到了。 ◇ *I was five minutes late for school this morning.* 我今天早晨上學遲到了5分鐘。 ☞ [反] **early¹** 早的

late² /leɪt/ [副詞] 遲，晚 *I got up late.* 我起牀晚了。 ☞ [反] **early²** 早

laugh /lɑːf; 美 læf/ [動詞] 大笑

Cartoons make her laugh. 卡通片逗得她大笑。 ◇ *What are you laughing at?* 你在笑甚麼？

law /lɔː/ [名詞] 法律 *It's against the law to drive without a seat belt.* 不繫安全帶駕車是違法的。

lawn /lɔːn/ [名詞] 草地，草坪 *The children were playing on the lawn.* 孩子們正在草地上玩耍。

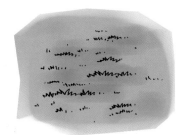

lay¹ /leɪ/ [動詞] [過去式和過去分詞 **laid** /leɪd/] 1 放，擱 *She laid the baby on the bed.* 她把寶寶放在牀上。 2 下（蛋） *The hens laid six eggs last night.* 昨晚那幾隻母雞下了6個蛋。

lay² /leɪ/ **lie** 的過去式 *Helen lay on the bed listening to music.* 海倫躺在牀上聽音樂。

layer /ˈleɪə; 美 -ər/ [名詞] 層 *This cake has got a layer of chocolate in the middle.* 這個蛋糕中間有一層巧克力。

layer 層

lazy /ˈleɪzi/ [形容詞] [比較級 **lazier**，最高級 **laziest**] 懶惰的 *Peter is so lazy. He never does any homework.* 彼得真懶，從來不做作業。

lead¹ /led/ [名詞] 鉛筆心 *The lead in my pencil has broken.* 我的鉛筆心斷了。

lead² /liːd/ [動詞] [過去式和過去分詞 **led** /led/] 1 帶領 *You lead the way, and we'll follow you.* 你帶路，我們跟着你走。 ◇ *The teacher led the students back to the classroom.* 老師把學生們帶回教室。 2 通往 *This path leads to the church.* 這條小路通往教堂。

leaf /liːf/ [名詞] [複數 **leaves** /liːvz/] 樹葉 *In autumn the leaves turn yellow.* 秋天，樹葉變黃。

leak /liːk/ [動詞] 漏 *The roof leaks when it rains.* 這個屋頂下雨時漏雨。

L

lean /liːn/ [動詞] [過去式和過去分詞 **leant** /lent/ 或 **leaned**] **1** 傾斜 Dad leaned back in his chair. 爸爸斜靠在椅背上。 **2** （使）倚，靠 Paul was leaning on a tree. 保羅倚在一棵樹上。 ◇ Can I lean my bike against the wall? 我把自行車靠在牆上行嗎？

learn /lɜːn; 美 lɜːrn/ [動詞] [過去式和過去分詞 **learnt** /lɜːnt; 美 lɜːrnt/ 或 **learned**] 學習 Helen is learning to play the piano. 海倫在學彈鋼琴。 ◇ Paul is learning French. 保羅在學法語。

least /liːst/ [副詞] 最（小程度地） Which one is the least expensive? 哪一個最便宜？ ☞ [反] **most³** 最（大程度地）

leather /ˈleðə; 美 -ər/ [名詞] [無複數] 皮革 Is your handbag real leather? 你的手提包是真皮的嗎？

leave /liːv/ [動詞] [過去式和過去分詞 **left** /left/] **1** 離開 I leave home at seven in the morning. 我早晨 7 點離開家。 ◇ When does the next train leave? 下一班火車甚麼時候開？ **2** 丟下；遺忘 Oh dear! I've left my umbrella on the bus! 糟糕！我把雨傘忘在公共汽車上了！

led /led/ **lead** 的過去式和過去分詞

He led his horse to the barn. 他把馬牽到馬棚裏。

left¹ /left/ **leave** 的過去式和過去分詞 I'm afraid I've left my homework at home. Can I give it to you tomorrow? 恐怕我把作業忘在家裏了，明天交給你行嗎？

left² /left/ [形容詞] **1** 左邊的 Do you write with your right hand or your left hand? 你用右手寫字還是左手寫字？ ☞ [反] **right¹** 右邊的 **2** 剩下的，剩餘的 There is only a small piece of cake left. 只剩下一小塊蛋糕。

left³ /left/ [副詞] 向左 Turn left at the corner. 在拐角處向左拐。 ☞ [反] **right²** 向右

left⁴ /left/ [名詞] 左邊 The school is on the left of the road. 學校在馬路的左邊。 ☞ [反] **right³** 右邊

leg /leg/ [名詞] 腿 An ant has six legs. 螞蟻有 6 條腿。

lemon /ˈlemən/ [名詞] 檸檬 Dad likes a slice of lemon in his tea. 爸爸喜歡在茶裏放一片檸檬。

lend /lend/ [動詞] [過去式和過去分詞 **lent** /lent/] 借出，借給 I can lend you £10. 我可以借給你 10 英鎊。 ◇ I've lent my bicycle to Helen. 我把

自行車借給海倫了。☞ 參見 **borrow**
"（向別人）借，借用"。

length /leŋθ/ [名詞] 長度 *The swimming pool is 20 metres in length and 10 metres in width.* 這個游泳池長 20 米，寬 10 米。

lent /lent/ **lend** 的過去式和過去分詞 *Henry lent me his bike.* 亨利把自行車借給我了。

less¹ /les/ [形容詞] [與不可數名詞連用] 更少的，較少的 *Small cars use less petrol than big cars.* 小汽車比大汽車耗油少。 ☞ [反] **more¹** 更多的，較多的

less² /les/ [代詞] 更少，較少 *You eat less than I do.* 你吃得比我少。 ☞ [反] **more²** 更多，較多

less³ /les/ [副詞] [用以構成形容詞或副詞的比較級] 更少，較少 *The red jacket is less expensive.* 這件紅夾克便宜一些。 ◇ *You've done your homework less carefully than usual.* 你的作業沒有平時做得仔細。 ☞ [反] **more³** 更多；更

lesson /ˈlesn/ [名詞] 課 *Our first lesson tomorrow is maths.* 我們明天第一節課是數學。

let /let/ [動詞] [現在分詞 **letting**，過去式和過去分詞 **let**] 讓 *Paul won't let me play on his computer.* 保羅不讓我玩他的電腦。

let's /lets/ **let us** 的縮寫 `Let's go and see what Henry is doing.'

`Okay. Let's go.' "我們去看看亨利在幹甚麼。" "好，我們走吧。"

letter /ˈletə; 美 -ər/ [名詞] **1** 信 *I'm writing a letter to my friend.* 我正在給朋友寫信。 **2** 字母 *How many letters are there in AUGUST?* AUGUST 中有幾個字母？

lettuce /ˈletɪs; 美 -əs/ [名詞] 生菜 *We made a salad with tomatoes, lettuce and eggs.* 我們用西紅柿、生菜和雞蛋拌沙拉。

level /ˈlevl/ [形容詞] 平的 *We need a level piece of ground to play football on.* 我們需要一塊平地踢足球。

library /ˈlaɪbrəri; 美 -breri/ [名詞] [複數 **libraries**] 圖書館 *Alice borrowed some books from the library.* 艾麗斯從圖書館借了幾本書。

lick /lɪk/ [動詞] 舔 *Henry licked his ice cream.* 亨利舔了舔冰淇淋。

lid /lɪd/ [名詞] 蓋子 *Where's the lid for this jar?* 這個罐子的蓋子在哪裏？

lid
蓋子

lie¹ /laɪ/ [動詞] [現在分詞 **lying**，過去式和過去分詞 **lied**] 説謊 He's lying. 他在説謊。◇ Don't lie to me! 不要對我撒謊！

lie² /laɪ/ [動詞] [現在分詞 **lying**，過去式 **lay** /leɪ/，過去分詞 **lain** /leɪn/] 躺 Henry lay down on the floor. 亨利在地板上躺下。

life /laɪf/ [名詞] 1 [無複數] 生命 Is there life on the moon? 月球上有生命嗎？2 [複數 **lives** /laɪvz/] 一生 He has lived here all his life. 他在這裏住了一輩子。

lift¹ /lɪft/ [動詞] 舉起，抬起，提起 Can you lift the other end of the table? 你能抬起桌子的另一頭嗎？

lift² /lɪft/ [名詞] 電梯 I'm afraid the lift isn't working — we'll have to take the stairs. 恐怕電梯壞了，我們得走樓梯了。 ☞ 英國英語用 **lift**，美國英語用 **elevator**。

light¹ /laɪt/ [名詞] 1 光，光線 There's more light near the window. 窗邊的光線更亮一些。2 燈 Turn off the lights when you go to bed. 上牀睡覺時要關燈。

light² /laɪt/ [形容詞] 1 輕的 You take the light bag and I'll take the heavy one. 你拿輕包，我拿重包。 ☞ [反] **heavy** 重的 2 淺色的 Helen wore a light blue dress. 海倫穿着一條淺藍色的連衣裙。 ☞ [反] **dark**¹ 深色的

light³ /laɪt/ [動詞] [過去式和過去分詞 **lit** /lɪt/ 或 **lighted**] 點燃 Paul lit the candle. 保羅點燃蠟燭。

lighthouse /'laɪthaʊs/ [名詞] 燈塔 Can you see the lighthouse out there? 你能看見那邊的燈塔嗎？

lightning /'laɪtnɪŋ/ [名詞] [無複數] 閃電 The lightning struck a tree near the school. 閃電擊中了學校附近的一棵樹。

like¹ /laɪk/ [動詞] 喜歡 Do you like ice cream? 你喜歡吃冰淇淋嗎？◇ I like swimming and horse-riding. 我喜歡游泳和騎馬。◇ Henry likes to play football after school. 亨利喜歡放學後踢足球。

like² /laɪk/ [介詞] 像 Helen is very like her mum. 海倫長得很像媽媽。◇ You should hold the brush like this. 你應該這樣拿牙刷。

line /laɪn/ [名詞] **1** 線；線條 Draw a straight line from A to B. 從A到B畫一條直線。**2** （人或物的）行，列，排 The children all stood in a line. 孩子們都排成一隊站着。🖝 表示 "行，列，排"，美國英語用 **line**，英國英語用 **queue**。

lion /'laɪən/ [名詞] 獅子 Lions are found in Africa. 獅子產於非洲。

lip /lɪp/ [名詞] 嘴唇 Your bottom lip is bleeding. 你的下唇流血了。

liquid /'lɪkwɪd/ [名詞] 液體 The bottle was full of blue liquid. 瓶子裏裝滿了藍色液體。

list /lɪst/ [名詞] 名單；清單 Put oranges on the shopping list. 在購物單上加上橙子。

listen /'lɪsn/ [動詞] 聽 Listen to me. 聽我說。 ◇ Alice is listening to the radio. 艾麗斯正在聽收音機。

lit /lɪt/ **light** 的過去式和過去分詞 He lit a cigarette. 他點了一枝香煙。

litter /'lɪtə; 美 -ər/ [名詞] [無複數] 垃圾，雜物 There was litter everywhere on the streets of the town. 那座城鎮的大街上到處都是垃圾。

little /'lɪtl/ [形容詞] **1** 小的 'Which do you want?' 'I'll take the little one.' "你要哪個？" "我要那個小的"。 ◇ My little sister is three years old. 我小妹妹3歲了。🖝 [反] **big** 大的 **2** [比較級 **less** /les/，最高級 **least** /liːst/] 很少的，不多的 She eats very little. 她吃得很少。**a little** 一些，一點 I feel a little better today. 今天我覺得好些了。◇ She knows a little French. 她懂一點法語。

live /lɪv/ [動詞] **1** 生存，活着 Is your grandmother still living? 你奶奶還活着嗎？**2** 居住 Where do you live? 你住在哪裏？

L

living room /ˈlɪvɪŋ ruːm / [名詞] 起居室，客廳 There's a sofa, two armchairs and a television in our living room. 我們的客廳裏有一個長沙發、兩個單人沙發和一台電視。

lizard /ˈlɪzəd; 美 -ərd / [名詞] 蜥蜴 A lizard is a reptile. 蜥蜴是一種爬行動物。

load /ləʊd; 美 loʊd / [名詞] 負荷物 The truck was carrying a load of sand. 那輛貨車載滿了沙子。

loaf /ləʊf; 美 loʊf / [名詞] [複數 **loaves** /ləʊvz; 美 loʊvz /] 一條麵包 Helen bought a loaf of bread. 海倫買了一條麵包。

lobster /ˈlɒbstə; 美 ˈlɑːbstər/ [名詞] 龍蝦 Last night we ate lobsters in a seafood restaurant. 昨晚我們在一家海鮮館吃了龍蝦。

lock¹ /lɒk; 美 lɑːk / [動詞] 鎖上 Did you lock the door? 你鎖門了嗎？

lock² /lɒk; 美 lɑːk / [名詞] 鎖 You can't open the lock without a key. 沒有鑰匙你打不開鎖。

log /lɒg; 美 lɔːg / [名詞] （伐下的）樹幹；原木 Put another log on the fire. 往火上再添根原木。

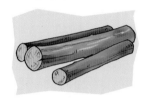

London /ˈlʌndən / [名詞] 倫敦 London is the capital of the UK. 倫敦是英國的首都。

lonely /ˈləʊnli; 美 ˈloʊn- / [形容詞] [比較級 **lonelier**，最高級 **loneliest**] 孤獨的 She often feels lonely. 她經常感到孤獨。

long¹ /lɒŋ; 美 lɔːŋ / [形容詞] [比較級 **longer** /ˈlɒŋgə; 美 ˈlɔːŋgər / ，最高級 **longest** /ˈlɒŋgɪst; 美 ˈlɔːŋgəst /] 長的 Your hair is much longer than mine. 你的頭髮比我的長多了。☞[反]**short** 短的

no longer, not any longer 不再 I can't wait any longer. 我不能再等了。◇ He no longer lives here. 他不

再住在這裏了。

long² /lɒŋ; 美 lɔːŋ / [動詞] 渴望，盼望 *I'm longing for a bicycle.* 我渴望有一輛自行車。◇ *He longed to go home.* 他盼望回家。

look¹ /lʊk/ [動詞] 看，瞧 *What are you looking at?* 你在看甚麼？◇ *Look! There's a fox!* 瞧！有隻狐狸！

look after 照料，照看 *Could you look after my watch while I'm swimming, please?* 我游泳時請你幫我照看一下手錶好嗎？

look for 尋找 `What are you doing under the desk?' `I'm looking for my pen.' "你在桌子底下做甚麼呢？" "我在找鋼筆。"

look up （在詞典、參考書等中）查尋 *Did you look up the word in the dictionary?* 你在詞典裏查那個詞了嗎？

look² /lʊk / [名詞] 看，瞧 *Have a look at this book.* 看一看這本書。

loop /luːp/ [名詞] （線、繩等繞成的）圈，環 *She made the rope into a loop to place around the cow's neck.* 她繫了一個繩圈套在牛的脖子上。

loose /luːs/ [形容詞] 1 鬆的 *My coat button is loose.* 我外套上的扣子鬆了。☞ [反] **tight** 緊的 2 （衣服）寬鬆的，肥的 *These trousers are a bit loose. Have you got a smaller size?* 這條褲子有點肥，你有小一號的嗎？

☞ [反] **tight** 緊身的，瘦的

lorry /'lɒri; 美 'lɔːri / [名詞] [複數 **lorries**] 貨車，卡車 *On the back of the lorry there was a pile of sand.* 貨車後部裝了一堆沙子。☞ 英國英語用 **lorry**，美國英語用 **truck**。

lose /luːz/ [動詞] [過去式和過去分詞 **lost** /lɒst; 美 lɔːst /] 1 丟失 *I've lost my keys.* 我把鑰匙丟了。☞ [反] **find** 找到 2 輸 *Our team lost the football match.* 我們隊輸了這場足球賽。☞ [反] **win** 贏

lost /lɒst; 美 lɔːst / **lose** 的過去式和過去分詞 *I've lost my watch. I can't find it anywhere.* 我把手錶丟了，哪裏也找不到。

lot /lɒt; 美 lɑːt / [名詞] **a lot of；lots of** 很多的，大量的 *I eat a lot of vegetables.* 我蔬菜吃得很多。◇ *She spends a lot of money on clothes.* 她花很多錢買衣服。◇ *There are lots of good books in the library.* 圖書館裏有許多好書。

L

loud /laʊd/ [形容詞] 大聲的；吵鬧的 Can you turn the television down? It's too loud. 你能把電視開小點聲嗎？太吵了。 ☞ [反] **quiet** 安靜的；輕聲的

love /lʌv/ [動詞] 1 愛 I love my mum and dad. 我愛爸爸媽媽。 2 喜歡 My mum loves music. 我媽媽喜歡音樂。 ◇ Most kids love climbing trees. 多數孩子喜歡爬樹。

lovely /ˈlʌvli/ [形容詞] [比較級 **lovelier**，最高級 **loveliest**] 漂亮的；動人的；可愛的 This is a lovely dress, but it's too small for me. 這件連衣裙很漂亮，但對我來說太小了。

low /ləʊ; 美 loʊ/ [形容詞] 1 （離地面）低的；矮的 Hang that picture a bit higher, it's much too low! 把那幅畫掛高一點，太低了！ ☞ [反] **high** 高的

2 （指低于通常的水平或數量）低的 Temperatures were very low last winter. 去年冬天氣溫很低。 ☞ [反] **high** 高的 3 低聲的 Mum said in a low voice, 'Remember to say 'Happy Birthday' to Granny.' 媽媽小聲地說，"記住對奶奶說'生日快樂'。" ☞ [反] **high** 高聲的

luck /lʌk/ [名詞] [無複數] 運氣 She wished me good luck in the exam. 她祝我考試運氣好。

lucky /ˈlʌki/ [形容詞] [比較級 **luckier**，最高級 **luckiest**] 幸運的 Who will be the lucky prizewinner? 誰將是幸運的獲獎者？ ☞ [反] **unlucky** 不幸的；倒霉的；不吉利的

luggage /ˈlʌɡɪdʒ/ [名詞] [無複數] 行李 May I carry some of your luggage for you? 我幫你拿一些行李好嗎？

lunch /lʌntʃ/ [名詞] [複數 **lunches**] 午餐，午飯 Have you had lunch yet? 你吃過午飯了嗎？ ◇ What would you like for lunch? 你午飯想吃甚麼？

lung /lʌŋ/ [名詞] 肺 Smoking is bad for your lungs. 吸煙對肺不好。

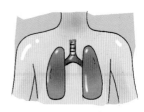

lying /ˈlaɪɪŋ/ **lie** 的現在分詞 She's lying on the sofa. 她正在沙發上躺着。

L

M m

machine /məˈʃiːn/ [名詞] 機器 *Put your dirty clothes in the washing machine.* 把你的髒衣服放到洗衣機裏。

made /meɪd/ **make** 的過去式和過去分詞 *Dad made a cup of tea.* 爸爸沏了一杯茶。

magic /ˈmædʒɪk/ [名詞] [無複數] 魔術 *The magician is doing some magic.* 魔術師在變魔術。

magician /məˈdʒɪʃn/ [名詞] 魔術師 *Mr Green is a magician.* 格林先生是一位魔術師。

magnet /ˈmægnɪt/ [名詞] 磁鐵；磁石 *The magnet picked up the needles.* 磁鐵把針吸了起來。

magnifying glass /ˈmægnɪfaɪɪŋ glɑːs; 美 ˈmægnɪfaɪɪŋ glæs/ [名詞] [複數 **magnifying glasses**] 放大鏡 *Grandma uses a magnifying glass to read the newspaper.* 奶奶用放大鏡看報紙。

mail¹ /meɪl/ [名詞] [無複數] 郵件 *Was there any mail for me this morning?* 今天上午有我的郵件嗎？ ☞ 美國英語用 **mail**，英國英語用 **post**。

mail² /meɪl/ [動詞] 郵寄 *Did you get the photo I mailed to you?* 你收到我寄給你的照片了嗎？ ☞ 美國英語用 **mail**，英國英語用 **post**。

main /meɪn/ [形容詞] [只用於名詞前] 主要的 *Maths is the main subject I am studying.* 數學是我學習的主要科目。

make /meɪk/ [動詞] [過去式和過去分詞 **made** /meɪd/] **1** 做，製造 *'What are you doing?' 'I'm making a cake.'* "你在做甚麼？""我在做蛋糕。" **2** 產生，出 *In the spelling test I made two mistakes.* 在拼寫測驗中我犯了兩個錯誤。 ◇ *Try not to make a noise. The baby is asleep.* 盡量不要出聲，寶寶在睡覺。 **3** (迫) 使 *Peter's really funny*

M

—*he always makes me laugh.* 彼得真有趣，他總是惹我發笑。**4** 等於 *Two and two make four.* 2 加 2 等於 4。

mammal /'mæml/ [名詞] 哺乳動物 *Humans and dogs are mammals; birds and fish are not.* 人和狗是哺乳動物，鳥和魚則不是。

man /mæn/ [名詞] [複數**men** /men/] 男人 *Is your teacher a man or a woman?* 你們老師是男的還是女的？

manage /'mænɪdʒ/ [動詞] [常與 **can** 或 **could** 連用] 設法做到 *I can't manage this suitcase. It's too heavy.* 我提不動這個衣箱，它太重了。

manners /'mænəs; 美 -ərz/ [名詞] [複數] 禮貌；規矩 *Some children have no manners.* 有些孩子沒有禮貌。 ◇ *It's bad manners to talk with your mouth full.* 嘴裏含着東西說話是不禮貌的。

many /'meni/ [形容詞] [與複數可數名詞連用] 許多的 *'Did I make many mistakes?' 'No, not many.'* "我犯的錯誤多嗎？" "不，不多。" ☞ ①[反] **few** 很少的 ②參見 **much**¹ "許多的"。
how many 多少 *How many girls are there in your class?* 你們班有幾個女生？

map /mæp/ [名詞] 地圖 *Can you read a map?* 你會看地圖嗎？ ◇ *I can't find Australia on the map.* 我在地圖上找不到澳大利亞。

marble /'mɑːbl; 美 'mɑːr-/ [名詞] **1** [無複數] 大理石 *The statue was made of marble.* 這座雕像是大理石的。 **2** (兒童玩的) 玻璃球 *Who wants to play marbles?* 誰想彈玻璃球？

March /mɑːtʃ; 美 mɑːrtʃ/ [名詞] 三月 *Peter's birthday is on the first of March.* 彼得的生日是 3 月 1 日。 ☞ ①參見 **August** 的示例。② **Mar** 是 **March** 的縮寫。

march /mɑːtʃ; 美 mɑːrtʃ/ [動詞] (齊步) 行走，行進 *They made us march for hours.* 他們讓我們齊步走了好幾個小時。

margin /'mɑːdʒɪn; 美 'mɑːr-/ [名詞] 頁邊空白 *The teacher wrote 'Good' in the margin.* 老師在頁邊空白處寫了"良"。

margin
頁邊空白

mark[1] /mɑːk; 美 mɑːrk / [名詞] **1** 痕跡；污點 *There's a dirty mark on this shirt.* 這件襯衣上有個污痕。**2** 成績；分數 *'What mark did you get for your English homework?' 'I got an A.'* "你的英語作業得了多少分?" "得了優。"

mark[2] /mɑːk; 美 mɑːrk / [動詞] 標示，標上…作為記號 *Helen marked her birthday on the calendar.* 海倫在日曆上標出自己的生日。

market /ˈmɑːkɪt; 美 ˈmɑːrkət / [名詞] 市場；集市 *We bought some fruit and vegetables at the market.* 我們在市場買了些水果和蔬菜。

marry /ˈmæri / [動詞] [現在分詞 **m a r r y i n g**，過去式和過去分詞 **married**] 娶；嫁；和…結婚 *She is going to marry John.* 她準備和約翰結婚。

marsh /mɑːʃ; 美 mɑːrʃ / [名詞] [複數 **marshes**] 沼澤(地帶)；濕地 *Many birds and animals live on marshes.* 很多鳥和動物生活在沼澤地帶。

mask /mɑːsk; 美 mæsk / [名詞] 面

具；面罩；口罩 *Peter wore a mask.* 彼得戴着面具。

mat /mæt / [名詞] (放在地上的) 蓆子；墊子 *Henry wiped his feet on the mat.* 亨利在墊子上蹭了蹭腳。

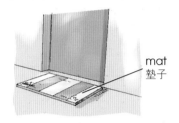

mat
墊子

match[1] /mætʃ / [名詞] [複數 **matches**] **1** 火柴 *I need a box of matches.* 我需要一盒火柴。

2 比賽 *Are you going to the football match on Sunday?* 你星期天去看足球賽嗎?

match[2] /mætʃ / [動詞] 相配 *Your jacket and trousers don't match.* 你的上衣和褲子不相配。

material /məˈtɪəriəl; 美 -ˈtɪr- / [名詞] **1** 布料 *'What material is this dress made of?' 'Cotton.'* "這件連衣裙是甚麼料子做的?" "棉布。" **2** 材料 *Stone is a very hard material.* 石頭是非常堅硬的材料。

maths /mæθs / [名詞] [無複數] 數學 *Henry is very good at maths.* 亨利很擅長數學。 ☞ **maths** 是 **mathematics** /ˌmæθəˈmætɪks / 的縮寫。

M

matter[1] /'mætə; 美 -ər/ [動詞] 有關係，要緊 'I'm really sorry I'm late.' 'That's OK—it doesn't matter.' "真對不起，我遲到了。""沒關係，不要緊。"

matter[2] /'mætə; 美 -ər/ [名詞] [單數，與**the**連用] 麻煩事，毛病 'What's the matter with you?' 'I have a headache.' "你怎麼啦？""我頭痛。"

mattress /'mætrəs/ [名詞] [複數 **mattresses**] 褥墊；牀墊 Do you like a soft mattress? 你喜歡軟牀墊嗎？

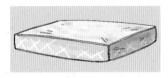

May /meɪ/ [名詞] 五月 My birthday is in May. 我的生日在5月。 ☞ 參見 **August** 的示例。

may /meɪ/ [情態動詞] [過去式**might** /maɪt/] **1** [表示可能性] 可能，也許 'Where's Helen?' 'She may be in the garden.' "海倫在哪裏？""她也許在花園裏。" **2** [表示許可] 可以 May I borrow your pen? 我可以借用你的鋼筆嗎？

maybe /'meɪbi/ [副詞] 也許，大概 Maybe Dad will call this evening. 也許爸爸今晚會打電話。◇ 'Do you think it will rain?' 'Maybe.' "你覺得會下雨嗎？""也許會。" ☞ [同] **perhaps** 也許，可能

me / 強 miː; 弱 mi/ [代詞] [**I** 的賓格] 我 Can you see me? 你能看見我嗎？ ◇ These shoes are too small for me. 這雙鞋對我來說太小了。

meal /miːl/ [名詞] 餐；飯食 We have three main meals a day—breakfast, lunch and dinner. 我們每天主要吃三頓飯——早飯、午飯和晚飯。

mean[1] /miːn/ [動詞] [過去式和過去分詞 **meant** /ment/] **1** 意思是，意味着 What does this word mean? 這個詞是甚麼意思？◇ The red light means stop. 紅燈意味着停。 **2** 想要，打算 I meant to give the book to you today, but I forgot. 我本打算今天把這本書給你的，但我忘了。

mean[2] /miːn/ [形容詞] 吝嗇的 Please lend me your calculator—don't be mean! 請把你的計算器借給我，不要吝嗇嘛！

meant /ment/ **mean**[1] 的過去式和過去分詞 I meant to remind you. 我本想提醒你。

measure /'meʒə; 美 -ər/ [動詞] 量，測量 Which line is the longest? Use your ruler to measure them. 哪條線最長？用尺子量一量。

meat /miːt/ [名詞] [無複數] 肉 'What sort of meat is this?' 'It's chicken.' "這是甚麼肉？""雞肉。" ☞ **meat** 包括 **chicken** "雞肉"，**lamb** "羔羊肉"，**mutton** "羊肉"，**beef** "牛肉"，**pork**

M

"豬肉"等。

medal /ˈmedl/ [名詞] 獎牌；獎章；勳章 Paul won a gold medal for swimming. 保羅獲得了一枚游泳金牌。

medicine /ˈmedsn/ [名詞] 藥 Have you taken your medicine this morning? 你今天早晨吃藥了嗎？

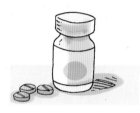

meet /miːt/ [動詞] [過去式和過去分詞**met** /met/] 1 遇見 I met my teacher in the street today. 我今天在街上遇見了我的老師。2 認識 Pleased to meet you. 很高興認識你。3 接（人）I'll come and meet you at the station. 我會來車站接你。

meeting /ˈmiːtɪŋ/ [名詞] 會議 There was a parents' meeting at the school. 學校開了個家長會。

melt /melt/ [動詞] 融化；熔化；溶化 It's dangerous to skate on the lake — the ice is starting to melt. 在湖上滑冰危險，冰已開始融化了。

member /ˈmembə; 美 -ər/ [名詞] 成員；會員 Paul is a member of the school football club. 保羅是學校足球俱樂部的會員。

memory /ˈmeməri/ [名詞] [複數 **memories**] 記憶力，記性 Alice has a good memory for names. 艾麗斯善於記住名字。

men /men/ **man** 的複數 There are eleven men in a football team. 一支足球隊有 11 人。

mend /mend/ [動詞] 修理，修補 Henry is mending his shirt. 亨利在縫補襯衫。

menu /ˈmenjuː/ [名詞] 菜單 Can I have the menu, please? 請給我看看菜單可以嗎？

merry /ˈmeri/ [形容詞] [比較級 **merrier**，最高級 **merriest**] 歡樂的，愉快的 Merry Christmas! 聖誕快樂！

mess /mes/ [名詞] [通常用作單數] 髒

M

亂,混亂 *This room is in a mess.* 這個房間亂七八糟。

message /'mesɪdʒ/ [名詞] 信息;口信 *Did you get my message?* 你收到我的信息了嗎?◇ *She's not here at the moment. Can I take a message?* 她現在不在這裏,有話要我轉告嗎?

met /met/ **meet** 的過去式和過去分詞 *Guess who I met today in the supermarket?* 猜猜我今天在超市遇見了誰?

metal /'metl/ [名詞] 金屬 *Are those buttons made of metal or plastic?* 那些鈕扣是金屬的還是塑料的?

metre /'mi:tə; 美 -ər/ [名詞] 米,公尺 *This room is five metres long.* 這個房間有5米長。 ☞ 美國英語拼寫為 **meter**。

M **mice** /maɪs/ **mouse** 的複數 *Our cat is good at catching mice.* 我們的貓擅長捉老鼠。

microphone /'maɪkrəfəʊn; 美 -foʊn/ [名詞] 擴音器,話筒,麥克風 *Can you use a microphone?* 你會用麥克風嗎?

microscope /'maɪkrəskəʊp; 美 -skoʊp/ [名詞] 顯微鏡 *The scientist looked through the microscope.* 科學家透過顯微鏡進行觀察。

midday /ˌmɪd'deɪ/ [名詞] [無複數] 正午,中午 *At midday, we go home for lunch.* 中午,我們回家吃午飯。

middle /'mɪdl/ [名詞] 中部,中間,中央 *Henry put the cake in the middle of the table.* 亨利把蛋糕放在桌子中間。

midnight /'mɪdnaɪt/ [名詞] [無複數] 半夜,午夜,子夜 *We stayed up until midnight.* 我們熬到了半夜。

might /maɪt/ **1 may** 的過去式 *Helen said she might come tomorrow.* 海倫說她明天可能會來。 **2** 也許 [表示可能性] *'Where's Peter?' 'He might be upstairs.'* "彼得在哪裏?""他也許在樓上。"

mile /maɪl/ [名詞] 英里 *We walked about half a mile.* 我們走了大約半英里。

milk[1] /mɪlk/ [名詞] [無複數] 牛奶 *Can I have a glass of milk, please?* 我可以

喝杯牛奶嗎?

milk² /mɪlk / [動詞] 擠(牛、羊等的)奶 They use a machine to milk the cows. 他們用機器擠牛奶。

million /'mɪljən / [數詞] 百萬 There are nearly six million people living in this city. 這座城市有將近600萬居民。

mind¹ /maɪnd / [名詞] 頭腦 I can see him in my mind, but I can't remember his name. 雖然他仍留在我的腦海裏,但我記不起他的名字了。

mind² /maɪnd / [動詞] [通常用於疑問句或否定句] 介意,在乎 Do you mind if I use your phone? 我用一下你的電話可以嗎?◇ 'Do you want to play tennis or watch television?' 'I don't mind.' "你想打網球還是看電視?" "我無所謂。"

mine¹ /maɪn / [代詞] [I 的物主代詞] 我的(東西) 'Isn't this yours?' 'No, that isn't mine — it's Helen's.' "這不是你的嗎?" "是的,那不是我的,那是海倫的。" ◇ Paul is a friend of mine. 保羅是我的一位朋友。

mine² /maɪn / [名詞] 礦 He works in a coal mine. 他在煤礦工作。

minus /'maɪnəs / [介詞] 減(去) 10 minus 2 is 8. 10減2等於8。

minute /'mɪnɪt; 美 -ət / [名詞] 分 [1分鐘等於60秒] It's ten minutes to eight. 現在是8點差10分。
in a minute 立刻,馬上 I'll be back in a minute. 我馬上就回來。

mirror /'mɪrə; 美 -ər / [名詞] 鏡子 Sophie looked in the mirror and brushed her hair. 索菲照着鏡子梳理頭髮。

mischievous /'mɪstʃɪvəs / [形容詞] (通常指孩子)調皮的,淘氣的 She's a mischievous little girl. 她是個淘氣的小姑娘。

miserable /'mɪzrəbl / [形容詞] 痛苦的 Oh dear, you look miserable. What's wrong? 哎呀,你看上去很痛苦,怎麼了?

Miss /mɪs / [名詞] 1 [用於姓名或姓之前對未婚女子的稱呼] 小姐 Is there a Miss Green here? 這裏有位格林小姐嗎? 2 [用於小學生對女教師的稱呼] 老師 Good morning, Miss! 老師,早上好!

miss /mɪs / [動詞] 1 未擊中;未抓住 Henry threw the ball to me, but I missed it. 亨利把球扔給我,可我沒接住。 2 趕不上,錯過 If you don't hurry, we'll miss the bus. 如果你不趕緊,我們就趕不上公共汽車了。 3 惦念 What did you miss most when you lived abroad? 你在國外生活時最惦念的是甚麼?

missing /'mɪsɪŋ / [形容詞] 找不到的;失去的 Our cat's gone missing again. 我們的貓又不見了。◇ There's

M

a page missing from this book. 這本書缺了一頁。

mist /mɪst/ [名詞] [無複數] 薄霧 There was a mist early this morning. 今天清晨有薄霧。

mistake /mɪ'steɪk/ [名詞] 錯誤 This letter's full of mistakes. 這封信錯誤百出。◇ You have made a mistake here—this 3 should be 5. 你在這裏犯了個錯誤，這個 3 應該是 5。

mix /mɪks/ [動詞] 使混合，拌和 Mix the flour and the eggs together. 把麵粉和雞蛋攪拌在一起。

mixture /'mɪkstʃə; 美 -ər/ [名詞] 混合物 Air is a mixture of gases. 空氣是多種氣體的混合物。

model /'mɒdl; 美 'mɑːdl/ [名詞] 1 模型 Peter is making a model aeroplane. 彼得在做飛機模型。 2 模特兒 Sarah wants to be a model. 莎拉想當模特兒。

model
模特兒

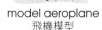

model aeroplane
飛機模型

moment /'məʊmənt; 美 'moʊ-/ [名詞] 1 瞬間；片刻 Can you wait a moment? 你等一下行嗎？ 2 [用作單數] 某一時刻 At that moment, the phone rang. 就在那時電話響了。

at the moment 此刻 We're busy at the moment. 我們此刻正在忙着。

in a moment 立刻，馬上 Just wait here. I'll be back in a moment. 就在這裏等，我馬上就回來。

Monday /'mʌndeɪ/ [名詞] 星期一 'What day is it today?' 'Monday.' "今天星期幾？" "星期一。"◇ They have piano lessons every Monday. 他們每星期一上鋼琴課。◇ We play football on Mondays. 我們每星期一踢足球。◇ We'll meet on Monday. 我們星期一見。◇ Paul was born on a Monday. 保羅是星期一出生的。 ☞ **Mon** 是 **Monday** 的縮寫。

money /'mʌni/ [名詞] [無複數] 錢，金錢 How much money have you got? 你有多少錢？

monkey /'mʌŋki/ [名詞] 猴子 Monkeys are good at climbing trees. 猴子擅長爬樹。

monster /'mɒnstə; 美 'mɑːnstər/ [名詞] 怪物 The film was about monsters. 這是一部關於怪物的電影。

M

month / mʌnθ / [名詞] 月（份）
'Which month were you born in?'
'August.'"你是幾月出生的？""8月。"

mood / muːd / [名詞] 心情，情緒
She's in a good mood today. 她今
天心情不錯。

moon / muːn / [名詞] [用作單數，與
the 連用] 月亮 The moon appeared
slowly from behind the clouds. 月亮
從雲後慢慢出現了。

more¹ / mɔː; 美 mɔːr / [形容詞] 更多
的，較多的 In my class there are
more girls than boys. 我們班女孩比
男孩多。☞ [反] **less¹** 或 **fewer** 更少
的，較少的

more² / mɔː; 美 mɔːr / [代詞] 更多，較
多 'Would you like some more of this
cake?' 'Is there any more? I'd love
some more.' "你想不想再吃點這種蛋
糕？""還有嗎？我想再吃點。"☞ [反]
less² 或 **fewer** 更少，較少

more³ / mɔː; 美 mɔːr / [副詞] [用以構
成形容詞或副詞的比較級] 更多；更 This
story book is more interesting than
that one. 這本故事書比那本有趣。◇
Please write more carefully. 請寫得
再仔細些。☞ [反] **less³** 更少，較少

morning / ˈmɔːnɪŋ; 美 ˈmɔːr- / [名詞]
早晨；上午 I usually get up at 6:30
in the morning. 我通常早晨6點30分
起牀。◇ See you tomorrow
morning. 明天早晨見。
good morning 早上好 'Good
morning, Mum.' 'Morning, Henry.' "早
上好，媽。""早上好，亨利。"☞ 在
非正式場合説"早上好"，也可以只用
Morning。

mosquito / məˈskiːtəʊ; 美 -toʊ / [名
詞] [複數 **mosquitoes**] 蚊子 I've got
two mosquito bites on my leg. 我的
腿被蚊子叮了兩口。

most¹ / məʊst; 美 moʊst / [形容詞]
1 最多的 Who has the most pencils?
誰的鉛筆最多？ **2** 大多數，大部分
Most children like animals. 大多數孩
子喜歡動物。

most² / məʊst; 美 moʊst / [代詞] **1** 最
大量，最多數 Who ate the most? 誰
吃得最多？ **2** 大多數，大部分 Most of
the children love ice cream. 大多數
孩子喜歡吃冰淇淋。

most³ / məʊst; 美 moʊst / [副詞] **1** [用
以構成形容詞或副詞的最高級] 最 This
is the most beautiful butterfly I've
ever seen. 這是我見過的最美的蝴蝶。
2 最（大程度地） What do you like
most? 你最喜歡甚麽？ ☞ [反] **least**
最（小程度地）

M

moth /mɒθ; 美 mɔ:θ/ [名詞] 蛾
Moths were flying round the lamp.
蛾在圍着燈飛舞。

mother /'mʌðə; 美 -ər/ [名詞] 母
親，媽媽 *My mother works in a bank.*
我母親在銀行工作。

motorbike /'məʊtəbaɪk; 美
'moʊtər-/ [名詞] 摩托車 *He's old
enough to ride a motorbike.* 他已經
到了騎摩托車的年齡。

motorcycle /'məʊtəˌsaɪkl; 美
'moʊtər-/ [名詞] [正式] 摩托車 *My uncle
goes to work on a motorcycle.* 我叔
叔騎摩托車去上班。

motorway /'məʊtəweɪ; 美 'moʊtər-/
[名詞] 高速公路 *We took the
motorway from London to
Birmingham.* 我們從倫敦去伯明翰走
的是高速公路。 ☞ 美國英語用
expressway 或 **freeway**。

mountain /'maʊntɪn; 美 -tn/ [名詞]
山 *Which is the highest mountain in
the world?* 哪座山是世界上最高的山？

mouse /maʊs/ [名詞] [複數 **mice**
/maɪs/] **1** 老鼠 *Some mice live in
people's houses and some mice live
out in the fields.* 有些老鼠生活在人們
的家裏，有些生活在外面的田野裏。 **2**
鼠標（器）*Do you use your right hand
or left hand to operate the mouse?*
你操作鼠標用右手還是用左手？

mouse
老鼠

mouse
鼠標

moustache /mə'stɑːʃ; 美 'mʌstæʃ/
[名詞] 小鬍子 *The man has a
moustache.* 那個人留着小鬍子。

mouth /maʊθ/ [名詞] 嘴 *Her mouth
was full of chocolate.* 她滿嘴都是巧
克力。

M

move /muːv/ [動詞] **1** 移動；搬動 *Let's move the desk into my bedroom.* 我們把書桌搬進我的卧室吧。◇ *I can't move my legs.* 我的雙腿動不了了。**2** 搬家；遷居 *We moved house last week.* 我們上星期搬家了。

movie /'muːvi/ [名詞] **1** 電影 *Shall we go and see a movie?* 我們去看電影好嗎？◇ *When I grow up, I want to be a movie star.* 我長大後想當一名電影明星。 ☞ 美國英語用 **movie**，英國英語用 **film**。 **2** the movies [複數] 電影院 *Let's go to the movies.* 我們去看電影吧。 ☞ 美國英語用 **movies**，英國英語用 **cinema**。

Mr /'mɪstə; 美 -ər/ [用在男子姓名之前] 先生 *This is Mr Brown.* 這是布朗先生。

Mrs /'mɪsɪz/ [用在已婚女子姓名之前] 夫人，太太 *This is Mrs Brown.* 這是布朗太太。

Ms /mɪz/ [用在已婚或未婚女子姓名之前] 女士 *This is Ms Smith.* 這是史密斯女士。

much¹ /mʌtʃ/ [形容詞] [與不可數名詞連用，主要用於疑問句或否定句] 許多的；大量的 *I don't have much homework tonight.* 我今晚作業不多。◇ *'Have you got much rice?' 'Yes, I have plenty.'* "你的飯夠嗎？" "夠了，我吃了很多。" ☞ 參見 **many** "許多的"。

how much 多少 *How much is it?* 這個多少錢？◇ *How much money have you got?* 你有多少錢？

much² /mʌtʃ/ [副詞] 非常，很 *Henry doesn't like apple juice very much.* 亨利不大喜歡喝蘋果汁。

mud /mʌd/ [名詞] [無複數] 泥 *After our walk in the woods, our boots were covered with mud.* 我們在樹林裏散完步後靴子上沾滿了泥。

mug /mʌg/ [名詞] (圓筒形有柄的) 大杯子 *There is a coffee mug on the table.* 桌子上有一個咖啡杯。

multiply /'mʌltɪplaɪ/ [動詞] [現在分詞 **multiplying**，過去式和過去分詞 **mutiplied**] 乘，使相乘 *If you multiply three by two, you get six.* 3 乘 2 得 6。 ☞ 參見 **times** "乘"。

mum /mʌm/ [名詞] [非正式] 媽媽 *Mum, please can I go out to play?* 媽，我可以出去玩嗎？

mummy /'mʌmi/ [名詞] [複數 **mummies**] [非正式] 媽媽 [多用於兒語] *Mummy and daddy will be back soon.* 媽媽和爸爸很快就會回來。

muscle /'mʌsl/ [名詞] 肌肉 *These exercises are good for your muscles.* 這些鍛煉有益於肌肉健康。

museum /mjuˈziːəm/ [名詞] 博物館 *Have you been to the Science Museum in London?* 你去過倫敦科

M

學博物館嗎？

mushroom /ˈmʌʃrʊm; 美 -ruːm /
[名詞] 蘑菇 *Some mushrooms are poisonous.* 有些蘑菇有毒。

music /ˈmjuːzɪk / [名詞] [無複數] 音樂 *What kind of music do you like?* 你喜歡甚麼樣的音樂？◇ *I love listening to music.* 我喜歡聽音樂。

musical /ˈmjuːzɪkl / [形容詞] 音樂的 *This shop sells musical instruments.* 這家商店出售樂器。

musical instrument /ˌmjuːzɪkl ˈɪnstrəmənt / [又作**instrument**] [名詞] 樂器 *Can you play a musical instrument?* 你會彈奏樂器嗎？

musical instruments 樂器

trumpet 小號
organ 管風琴
harmonica 口琴
piano 鋼琴
violin 小提琴
guitar 吉他

must / 強 mʌst; 弱 məst / [情態動詞] 必須 *I must go now.* 我現在必須走了。

mustn't /ˈmʌsnt / [**must not**的縮略] [情態動詞] 不得，不準 *You mustn't be late for school.* 上學不準遲到。

my /maɪ / [形容詞] [I的所有格] 我的 *Has anyone seen my keys?* 有人看見我的鑰匙嗎？◇ *My favourite colour is blue.* 我最喜歡的顏色是藍色。

myself /maɪˈself / [代詞] [I的反身代詞] 我自己 *I can look after myself.* 我能照顧自己。

mysterious /mɪˈstɪəriəs; 美 -ˈstɪr- / [形容詞] 神秘的；不可思議的 *We heard a mysterious sound.* 我們聽到一種神秘的聲音。

mystery /ˈmɪstri / [名詞] 神秘的事物；謎 *It's a mystery to me.* 這對我來說是個謎。

M

N n

nag /næg/ [動詞][現在分詞 **nagging**，過去式和過去分詞 **nagged**] 嘮叨 *My parents are always nagging me to work harder.* 我父母總是嘮叨，要我加倍用功。

nail /neɪl/ [名詞] **1** 指甲 *I like to keep my nails short.* 我喜歡把指甲留得短短的。 **2** 釘子 *Dad needs some nails to repair the chair.* 爸爸需要幾個釘子來修理椅子。

nail
指甲

nail
釘子

naked /'neɪkɪd/ [形容詞] 裸體的 *The baby was crawling around naked.* 寶寶光着身子到處爬。

name¹ /neɪm/ [名詞] 名字；姓名；名稱 *'What's your name?' 'My name's Henry.'* "你叫甚麼名字？" "我叫亨利。" ◇ *Do you know the name of this flower?* 你知道這種花的名字嗎？ ☞ 表示 "名"，用 **first name** 或 **given name**；表示 "姓"，用 **family name**，**last name** 或 **surname** /'sɜːneɪm; 美 'sɜr-/。

name² /neɪm/ [動詞] **1** 取名；命名 *They named the baby Ann.* 他們給寶寶取名叫安。 **2** 説出…的名字 *Can you name three American presidents?* 你能説出三位美國總統的名字嗎？

nap /næp/ [名詞]（白天的）小睡，瞌睡 *He always has a nap in the afternoon.* 他總會在下午睡一小覺。

napkin /'næpkɪn/ [名詞] 餐巾 *Paul wiped his mouth with a paper napkin.* 保羅用餐巾紙擦了擦嘴。

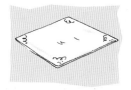

nappy /'næpi/ [名詞][複數 **nappies**] 尿布 *The mother changed the baby's nappy.* 母親給寶寶換了尿布。

narrow /'nærəʊ; 美 -oʊ/ [形容詞] 窄的，狹窄的 *The road was too narrow and the lorry had to go back.* 那條路太窄，貨車只好倒了回去。 ☞ [反] **wide**，**broad** 寬的，寬闊的

nasty /'nɑːsti; 美 'næsti/ [形容詞][比較級 **nastier**，最高級 **nastiest**] **1** 令人厭惡的 *This coffee has a nasty taste.* 這種咖啡非常難喝。 **2** 兇惡的 *Don't be so nasty to your brother.* 別對你弟弟這麼兇。

nation /'neɪʃn/ [名詞] **1** 國家 *All nations in the world should be equal.* 世界上所有國家都應該平等。 **2** 民族 *The Chinese nation is a great nation.* 中華民族是一個偉大的民族。

N

national /ˈnæʃnəl/ [形容詞] 國家的，全國性的 *Next Monday is a national holiday.* 下星期一是全國假日。

nationality /ˌnæʃəˈnæləti/ [名詞] [複數**nationalities**] 國籍 *What is your nationality?* 你是甚麼國籍？◇ *He has British nationality.* 他有英國國籍。

natural /ˈnætʃrəl/ [形容詞] [只用於名詞前] 自然的，天然的 *Butter is a natural food.* 黃油是一種天然食品。

nature /ˈneɪtʃə; 美 -ər/ [名詞] [無複數] 大自然 *The smoke from cars and trucks is very harmful to nature.* 小汽車和卡車排出來的煙對大自然非常有害。

naughty /ˈnɔːti/ [形容詞] [比較級 **naughtier**，最高級 **naughtiest**] [尤用於英國英語] (指孩子) 調皮的，淘氣的 *He's the naughtiest child in the class.* 他是班上最調皮的孩子。

near¹ /nɪə; 美 nɪr/ [形容詞] 近的 *Let's walk to the shop. It's quite near.* 我們走着去商店吧，離這裏很近。◇ *Where's the nearest bank?* 最近的銀行在哪裏？ 🖙 [反] **far²** 遠的

near² /nɪə; 美 nɪr/ [副詞] 在附近 *A bomb exploded somewhere near.* 附近有顆炸彈爆炸了。

near³ /nɪə; 美 nɪr/ [介詞] 接近 *Do you live near here?* 你住的地方離這裏近嗎？

nearly /ˈnɪəli; 美 ˈnɪrli/ [副詞] 幾乎，差不多，將近 *It's nearly six o'clock.* 快

6點了。◇ *The little boy nearly fell into the river.* 那個小男孩差點掉進河裏。

neat /niːt/ [形容詞] 整潔的；整齊的 *Keep your room neat and tidy.* 要保持房間整潔。

neck /nek/ [名詞] 脖子 *Helen wore a scarf round her neck.* 海倫脖子上圍着一條圍巾。

necklace /ˈnekləs/ [名詞] [無複數] 項鏈 *She was wearing a beautiful necklace.* 她戴着一條漂亮的項鏈。
🖙 參見 **jewellery** "珠寶"。

need¹ /niːd/ [動詞] 1 需要 *You don't need your coat — it's not cold.* 你不需要穿大衣，天氣不冷。 2 必須 *We don't need to get up early.* 我們不必早起。◇ *I need to go to the library to return the books.* 我得去圖書館還書。

need² /niːd/ [情態動詞] [通常用於疑問句或否定句] 必須 *Need I pay now?* 我是不是得現在付錢？ ◇ *You needn't apologize.* 你不必道歉。

needle /ˈniːdl/ [名詞] 針 *Have you*

got a needle and thread? 你有針線嗎？

needn't /'niːdnt/ **need not**的縮寫 We needn't get up early tomorrow. 我們明天不必早起。

neighbour /'neɪbə; 美 -ər/ [名詞] 鄰居 All our friends and neighbours are coming to the party. 我們所有的朋友和鄰居都會來參加聚會。☞美國英語拼寫為 **neighbor**。

neither[1] /'naɪðə; 美 'niːðər/ [形容詞]（兩者）都不的 Neither answer is correct. 兩個答案都不對。

neither[2] /'naɪðə; 美 'niːðər/ [代詞]（兩者）都不 'Would you like tea or coffee?' 'Neither, thank you. I'm not thirsty.' "你想喝茶還是喝咖啡？""都不想喝，謝謝。我不渴。" ◇ Neither of the children liked the film. 兩個孩子都不喜歡那部電影。

neither[3] /'naɪðə; 美 'niːðər/ [副詞] 也不 'I don't like fish.' 'Neither do I.' "我不喜歡吃魚。""我也不喜歡。" **neither...nor** 既不…也不… Neither Paul nor I went to the party. 保羅和我都沒去參加聚會。◇ He can neither swim nor ride a bicycle. 他既不會游泳，也不會騎自行車。

nephew /'nefjuː/ [名詞] 侄子；外甥 My dad's brother Jack is my uncle and my brother and I are Uncle Jack's nephews. 我爸爸的弟弟傑克是我的叔叔，我和我弟弟是傑克叔叔的侄子。

nervous /'nɜːvəs; 美 'nɜːr-/ [形容詞]

緊張的 People are usually nervous when they take exams. 人們考試時通常會感到緊張。

nest /nest/ [名詞] 鳥巢，鳥窩 The young birds are still in their nest. 小鳥仍在鳥巢裏。

net /net/ [名詞] 網 They catch fish in nets. 他們用網捕魚。

never /'nevə; 美 -ər/ [副詞] 從未；永不 I've never been abroad. 我從未出過國。◇ You never help me. 你從來不幫我。

new /njuː; 美 nuː/ [形容詞] 新的 'Give me the box, please.' 'Which one? The new one or the old one?' "請把盒子給我。""哪一個？新的還是舊的？"☞ [反] **old** 舊的

news /njuːz; 美 nuːz/ [名詞] [無複數] 消息；新聞 Henry's just told me an interesting piece of news. 亨利剛告訴我一條有趣的新聞。◇ That's great news. 那是個好消息。

N

newspaper /'njuːzˌpeɪpə; 美 'nuːzˌpeɪpər/ [名詞] 報紙 *I read about it in the newspaper.* 我在報紙上看到了有關報道。 ☞ [同] **paper** 報紙

new year /ˌnjuː 'jɪə; 美 ˌnuː 'jɪr/ [又作 **New Year**] [名詞] [用作單數] 新年，元旦 *Happy New Year!* 新年快樂！◇ *I'll see you in the new year.* 我們新年見。 ☞ 在西方人眼中，**New Year** 指公曆或陽曆新年；在中國人眼中，"新年"既指公曆或陽曆新年，也指中國農曆或陰曆新年。指"中國農曆或陰曆新年"，一般用 **Chinese New Year**。

next¹ /nekst/ [形容詞] 下一個的 *Turn to the next page.* 翻到下一頁。◇ *See you next week!* 下週見！

next² /nekst/ [副詞] 然後；後來 *I'll do my English homework first, and next my maths.* 我先做英語作業，然後再做數學作業。

next to /'nekst tə/ [介詞] 緊挨着；在…旁邊 *Henry sat next to Peter on the sofa.* 亨利挨着彼得坐在沙發上。

nice /naɪs/ [形容詞] **1** 令人愉快的，美好的 *Nice to meet you!* 很高興認識你！◇ *Did you have a nice time?* 你玩得開心嗎？◇ *It's such a nice day,* *why not go for a swim?* 今天天氣這麼好，為甚麼不去游泳呢？**2** 好心的，友善的 *She's a nice girl.* 她是個好姑娘。

nickname /'nɪkneɪm/ [名詞] 綽號 *John's nickname is 'Tiny' because he is very small.* 約翰的綽號叫"小不點"，因為他個子矮小。

niece /niːs/ [名詞] 侄女；外甥女 *My dad's sister Kelly is my aunt and my sister and I are Aunt Kelly's nieces.* 我爸爸的妹妹凱莉是我的姑姑，我和我妹妹是凱莉姑姑的侄女。

night /naɪt/ [名詞] **1** 夜，夜晚 *The baby cried all night.* 寶寶哭了一整夜。**2** 晚上 *Let's go out on Saturday night.* 我們星期六晚上出去吧。

good night 晚安 *Good night. See you tomorrow.* 晚安，明天見。 ☞ 在非正式場合說"晚安"，也可以只用 **Night**，如：*Night! Sleep well.*（晚安！睡個好覺。）

last night 昨晚 *I went to bed early last night.* 我昨晚很早就上牀睡覺了。

nightmare /'naɪtmeə; 美 -mer/ [名詞] 惡夢 *I had a nightmare last night.* 我昨晚做了一個惡夢。

nine /naɪn/ [數詞] 九 *Three times three is nine.* 3 乘 3 得 9。 ☞ 參見 **five** 的示例。

nineteen /ˌnaɪn'tiːn/ [數詞] 十九 *Ten and nine make nineteen.* 10 加 9 等於 19。 ☞ 參見 **five** 的示例。

ninety /'naɪnti/ [數詞] 九十 *Nine times ten is ninety.* 9 乘 10 得 90。

☞ 參見 **fifty** 的示例。

ninth /naɪnθ/ [數詞] 第九 *Today is the ninth of August.* 今天是 8 月 9 日。☞ 參見 **fifth** 的示例。

no¹ /nəʊ; 美 noʊ/ [形容詞] **1** 沒有 *I have no money.* 我沒有錢。**2** 不准，禁止 *No smoking.* 禁止吸煙。◇ *No parking.* 禁止停車。

NO SMOKING　　NO PARKING
禁止吸煙　　　　禁止停車

no² /nəʊ; 美 noʊ/ [感歎詞] [用以表示否定的回答] 不，不是 *Just say yes or no.* 只需說是或不是。◇ *'Would you like something to eat?' 'No, thank you.'* "你想不想吃點東西？" "不，謝謝。" ☞ [反] **yes** [用以表示肯定的回答] 是，是的

nobody /'nəʊbədi; 美 'noʊ-/ [代詞] 沒有人 *There was nobody in the house.* 房子裏沒有人。☞ = **no one**

nod /nɒd; 美 nɑːd/ [動詞] [現在分詞 **nodding**，過去式和過去分詞 **nodded**] 點頭 *He nodded when I asked if he liked the film.* 當我問他是否喜歡這部電影時，他點了點頭。

noise /nɔɪz/ [名詞] 聲音；喧鬧聲 *Don't make a noise. The baby's asleep.* 別出聲，寶寶在睡覺。

noisy /'nɔɪzi/ [形容詞] [比較級 **noisier**，最高級 **noisiest**] 吵鬧的 *Don't be so noisy! The baby's asleep.* 別這麼吵鬧！寶寶在睡覺。

none /nʌn/ [代詞] 一個也沒有；毫無 *'How many mistakes did you make?' 'None.'* "你出了幾個錯？" "一個也沒有。" ◇ *None of the children know the answer.* 沒有一個孩子知道答案。

nonsense /'nɒnsns; 美 'nɑːnsens/ [名詞] [無複數] 胡說；廢話 *You're talking nonsense.* 你胡說八道。

noodle /'nuːdl/ [名詞] 麵條 *Have some more noodles.* 再吃點麵條吧。

noon /nuːn/ [名詞] [無複數] 中午，正午 *They arrived at noon.* 他們是中午到的。

no one /'nəʊ wʌn; 美 'noʊ wʌn/ [又作 **nobody**] [代詞] 沒有人 *No one was at home.* 沒有人在家。

normal /'nɔːml; 美 'nɔːr-/ [形容詞] 正常的；平常的 *Her temperature is normal.* 她的體溫正常。

north /nɔːθ; 美 nɔːrθ/ [名詞] [用作單數，常與 **the** 連用] 北，北方 *They live in the north.* 他們住在北方。◇ *Which way is north?* 哪個方向是北？

nose /nəʊz; 美 noʊz/ [名詞] 鼻子 *His nose is bleeding.* 他的鼻子在流血。

not /nɒt; 美 nɑːt / [副詞] 不;沒有 *It's red, not pink.* 那是紅色的，不是粉紅色的。◇ *Henry is not here today. He's ill.* 亨利今天沒有來，他病了。

note /nəʊt; 美 noʊt / [名詞] **1** 筆記，記錄 *Can I borrow your notes?* 我可以借一下你的筆記嗎？◇ *Please make a note of my new address.* 請把我的新地址記下來。**2** 便條 *If Paul's not at home we'll leave a note for him.* 如果保羅不在家，我們就給他留個便條。**3** 紙幣 *I changed a five-dollar note for five one-dollar notes.* 我把1張5元的紙幣換成了5張1元的紙幣。

notebook /ˈnəʊtbʊk; 美 ˈnoʊt- / [名詞] **1** 筆記本 *'Open your notebooks and write down what I tell you,' said the teacher.* "打開你們的筆記本，記下我對你們說的話，"老師說。**2** [又作 **notebook computer**] 筆記本電腦 *Do you have a notebook computer?* 你有筆記本電腦嗎？

notebook
筆記本

notebook
筆記本電腦

nothing /ˈnʌθɪŋ / [代詞] 甚麼也沒有 *There is nothing in this box — it's empty.* 這個箱子裏面甚麼也沒有，是空的。

notice /ˈnəʊtɪs; 美 ˈnoʊtəs / [動詞] 注意到;看到 *I noticed that the door was open.* 我注意到門是開着的。◇ *Sorry, I didn't notice you.* 對不起，我沒有看見你。

November /nəʊˈvembə; 美 noʊˈvembər / [名詞] 十一月 *He's going to Germany in November.* 他打算11月去德國。☞ ① 參見 **August** 的示例。② **Nov** 是 **November** 的縮寫。

now /naʊ / [副詞] 現在 *We can't go for a walk now — it's raining.* 我們現在不能去散步，下雨了。

number /ˈnʌmbə; 美 -ər / [名詞] **1** 數，數字 *Choose a number between ten and twenty.* 在10與20之間選一個數字。**2** 號碼 *What's your phone number?* 你的電話號碼是多少？

nurse /nɜːs; 美 nɜːrs / [名詞] 護士 *She wants to be a nurse when she grows up.* 她長大後想當護士。

nursery /ˈnɜːsəri; 美 ˈnɜːr- / [名詞] [複數 **nurseries**] 托兒所 *Does your son go to nursery?* 你兒子上托兒所了嗎？

nursery school /ˈnɜːsəri skuːl; 美 ˈnɜːr- / [名詞] 幼兒園 *My little brother goes to nursery school.* 我弟弟上幼兒園。

nut /nʌt/ [名詞] 堅果（如胡桃、栗子等）*Do you like nuts?* 你喜歡吃堅果嗎？

N

O o

oar /ɔː; 美 ɔːr/ [名詞] 槳 *He pulled hard on the oars.* 他拼命地划槳。

obey /əˈbeɪ; 美 oʊ-/ [動詞] 服從；聽從 *You should obey your teacher.* 你應該聽老師的話。

object /ˈɒbdʒekt; 美 ˈɑːb-/ [名詞] 實物，物體 *What is that big red object over there?* 那邊那個紅色的大東西是甚麼？

observe /əbˈzɜːv; 美 -ˈzɜːrv/ [動詞] 觀察 *Children can learn to do things by observing other people.* 孩子們能通過觀察別人學着做事情。

obtain /əbˈteɪn/ [動詞] [正式] 獲得，得到 *I haven't been able to obtain the book that you wanted.* 我一直沒能買到你想要的那本書。

obvious /ˈɒbviəs; 美 ˈɑːb-/ [形容詞] 顯然的；明顯的 *It is obvious that he is wrong.* 顯然他錯了。

ocean /ˈəʊʃn; 美 ˈoʊ-/ [名詞] 海洋，大海 *Our house is right beside the ocean.* 我們家就在海邊。

o'clock /əˈklɒk; 美 əˈklɑːk/ [副詞] …點鐘 *'What time is it?' 'It's four o'clock.'* "現在幾點？""4點。" ☞ **o'clock** 只用於完整的一個小時，又如 **three o'clock**。但說"3點半"，要用 **half past three**。

October /ɒkˈtəʊbə; 美 ɑːkˈtoʊbər/ [名詞] 十月 *Tomorrow is the first of October.* 明天是10月1日。☞ ① 參見 **August** 的示例。② **Oct** 是 **October** 的縮寫。

odd /ɒd; 美 ɑːd/ [形容詞] **1** 奇怪的，古怪的 *Her father is an odd man.* 她父親是個古怪的人。**2** 奇數的，單數的 *One, three, five and seven are all odd numbers.* 1，3，5，7都是奇數。☞ [反] **even** 偶數的，雙數的

of / 強 ɒv; 美 ʌv; 弱 əv/ [介詞] **1** （屬於）…的 *He's a friend of mine.* 他是我的一位朋友。**2** （關於）…的 *I've never heard of it.* 我從來沒有聽說過這件事。**3** [表示數量] *I ate two pieces of chocolate.* 我吃了兩塊巧克力。**4** [表示種類] *I like all kinds of music.* 我喜歡各種各樣的音樂。**5** [表示包含某物] *This bag of rice is very heavy.* 這袋大米很沉。**6** [表示日期] *My birthday is on the sixteenth of May.* 我的生日是5月16日。

off¹ /ɒf; 美 ɔːf/ [副詞] **1** 離開 *I called him but he ran off.* 我喊他，可他跑開

了。**2** 脫掉 *Take off your shoes.* 把鞋脫掉。**3**（機器、電燈等）不運轉的；關上的 *Turn off the light.* 關燈。◇ *The TV is off.* 電視是關着的。 ☞[反]**on¹**（機器、電燈等）運轉着的；開着的

off² /ɒf; 美 ɔːf / [介詞] 從…離開；從…向下 *Henry fell off his bicycle.* 亨利從自行車上摔了下來。◇ *We get off the bus at the next stop.* 我們在下一站下車。

offer /'ɒfə; 美 'ɔːfər / [動詞] **1** 提供 *Henry offered his seat on the bus to an old lady.* 亨利在公共汽車上把自己的座位讓給了一位老太太。**2** 表示願意（做某事）*Our neighbour offered to drive us to school.* 我們的鄰居主動提出開車送我們上學。

office /'ɒfɪs; 美 'ɑːfəs / [名詞] 辦公室 *My mother's office is on the second floor.* 我母親的辦公室在二層。

often /'ɒfn; 美 'ɔːfn / [副詞] 經常 *We often go swimming at the weekend.* 我們經常週末去游泳。
how often 每隔多久 [用於詢問某事發生的次數] *How often do you wash your hair?* 你每隔多久洗一次頭？

oh /əʊ; 美 oʊ / [感歎詞] [表示驚訝、恐懼等] 啊，哎呀 *Is that for me? Oh,* you're so kind! 那是給我的嗎？哎呀，你真好！◇ *Oh no! I've forgotten to do my homework.* 哎呀！我忘了做作業。◇ *Oh dear! It's raining.* 哎呀！下雨了。

oil /ɔɪl / [名詞] [無複數] **1**（動物或植物）油 *My parents cook everything in vegetable oil.* 我父母燒甚麼菜都用菜子油。**2**（用作燃料等的）油 *Put some oil in the car.* 給汽車加點油。

OK¹ /ˌəʊ'keɪ; 美 ˌoʊ- / [又作**okay**] [形容詞] [非正式]（身體狀況）好的 *'How's your mother?' 'She's OK.'* "你母親好嗎？" "她很好。"

OK² /ˌəʊ'keɪ; 美 ˌoʊ- / [感歎詞] [非正式] 行，好，可以 *'Shall we go for a walk?' 'OK.'* "我們去散步好嗎？" "好。"

old /əʊld; 美 oʊld / [形容詞] **1** 老的；年老的 *Old people sometimes find it difficult to hear.* 老年人有時聽力有困難。 ☞[反]**young** 年幼的；年輕的 **2** …歲的 *'How old are you?' 'I'm ten.'* "你幾歲了？" "我10歲了。" **3** 舊的 *They sold my old bicycle and bought me a new one.* 他們把我的舊自行車賣掉，給我買了輛新的。☞[反]**new** 新的

on¹ /ɒn; 美 ɑːn / [副詞] **1** 向前；（繼續）下去 *Go on!* 往前走！（或：說下去！）**2** 穿上；戴上 *Put your coat on.* 穿上外套。◇ *I didn't have my glasses on.* 我沒戴眼鏡。**3**（機器、電燈等）運轉着的；開着的 *The washing machine's still on.* 洗衣機還在轉呢。◇ *Do you want the TV on?* 你想讓電視開着嗎？☞[反]**off¹**（機器、電燈等）不運轉的；關上的

on² /ɒn; 美 ɑːn/ [介詞] **1** 在⋯上 *Your pen is on your desk.* 你的鋼筆在你的書桌上。◇ *We sat on the grass.* 我們坐在草地上。 **2** 在⋯的時候 [用於表示日期或星期幾] *Her birthday is on 15th March.* 她的生日是在3月15日。◇ *I'll see you on Saturday.* 我們星期六見。 **3** 關於 *Henry loves reading books on animals.* 亨利喜歡看關於動物的書。 ☞ [同] **about¹** 關於

once /wʌns/ [副詞] **1** 一次 *I've only been there once.* 我只去過那裏一次。◇ *They go there once a week.* 他們每週去那裏一次。 **2** 曾經；從前 *This book was famous once, but nobody reads it today.* 這本書從前很出名，但現在沒人讀了。
at once 立刻，馬上 *Come here at once!* 立刻到這裏來！ ☞ [同] **immediately** 立即，馬上
once upon a time 從前 [用於兒童故事的開頭] *Once upon a time there was a beautiful princess...* 從前有個美麗的公主⋯

one¹ /wʌn/ [數詞] 一 *I have one brother and two sisters.* 我有一個弟弟兩個妹妹。

one² /wʌn/ [代詞] 一個 *'Give me the glass, please.' 'Which one? The full one or the empty one?'* "請把玻璃杯給我。""哪一個？滿的那一個還是空的那一個？"

one another /ˌwʌn əˈnʌðə; 美 -ər/ [代詞] 彼此，相互 *They all shook hands with one another.* 他們都彼此握手。 ☞ 參見 **each other** "彼此，相互"。

onion /ˈʌnjən/ [名詞] 洋葱 *Do you like onions?* 你喜歡吃洋葱嗎？

only¹ /ˈəʊnli; 美 ˈoʊn-/ [形容詞] [只用於名詞前] 惟一的，僅有的 *She is the only girl in her family.* 她是家裏惟一的女孩。

only² /ˈəʊnli; 美 ˈoʊn-/ [副詞] 只有；僅僅；才 *She only likes pop music.* 她只喜歡流行音樂。◇ *There are only a few biscuits left.* 只剩下幾塊餅乾了。

open¹ /ˈəʊpən; 美 ˈoʊ-/ [形容詞] **1** 開着的 *Don't leave the door open.* 不要讓門開着。◇ *The windows are open.* 窗子都開着。 ☞ [反] **closed** 關着的 **2** 開門的；營業的 *When are the shops open?* 商店甚麼時候開門？◇ *Is the school open yet?* 學校開學了嗎？ ☞ [反] **closed** 關門的；停止營業的

open² /ˈəʊpən; 美 ˈoʊ-/ [動詞] **1** 開；打開；張開；睜開 *At that moment the door opened.* 就在那時門開了。 ◇ *Open your mouth.* 張開（你的）嘴。 ☞ [反] **close¹**，**shut** 關上；閉上；合上 **2** 開門；營業 *The shop opens at nine o'clock.* 商店9點開門。 ☞ [反] **close¹**，**shut** 關門；停止營業

operation /ˌɒpəˈreɪʃn; 美 ˌɑːp-/ [名詞] 手術 *She needs an operation on her stomach.* 她的胃部需要動手術。

opposite[1] /ˈɒpəzɪt; 美 ˈɑːp-/ [形容詞] 對面的 *I saw Henry on the opposite side of the road.* 我看見亨利在馬路的對面。

opposite[2] /ˈɒpəzɪt; 美 ˈɑːp-/ [名詞] 反義詞 *Good and bad are opposites.* 好和壞是反義詞。◇ *What is the opposite of heavy?* 重的反義詞是甚麼？

opposite[3] /ˈɒpəzɪt; 美 ˈɑːp-/ [介詞] 在…對面 *The bank is opposite the supermarket.* 銀行在超市對面。

or /ɔː; 美 ɔːr/ [連詞] 1 [表示選擇] 或，或者；還是 *You can have lamb, beef or fish.* 你可以吃羔羊肉、牛肉或魚肉。◇ *Are you coming or not?* 你來還是不來？◇ *Do you want to go to a restaurant or would you prefer to eat at home?* 你想去餐館吃還是寧願在家裏吃？ 2 [用於否定句] 也不 *My little sister can't read or write.* 我的小妹妹不會看書寫字。

orange[1] /ˈɒrɪndʒ; 美 ˈɔːr-/ [名詞] 橙子；橘子 *Oranges are my favourite fruit.* 橙子是我最喜歡吃的水果。◇ *Who would like some orange juice?* 誰想喝橙汁？

orange[2] /ˈɒrɪndʒ; 美 ˈɔːr-/ [形容詞] 橙色的 *Helen is wearing an orange dress.* 海倫穿着一件橙色連衣裙。

orchestra /ˈɔːkɪstrə; 美 ˈɔːr-/ [名詞] 管弦樂隊 *Paul plays the violin in our school orchestra.* 保羅在我們校管弦樂隊拉小提琴。

order[1] /ˈɔːdə; 美 ˈɔːrdər/ [名詞] [用作單數] 次序，順序 *The words in a dictionary are in alphabetical order.* 詞典中的詞是按字母順序排列的。

order[2] /ˈɔːdə; 美 ˈɔːrdər/ [動詞] 1 命令 *I'm not asking you to do your homework. I'm ordering you!* 我不是在請求你做作業，我是在命令你！ 2 點（飯菜等） *I ordered a hamburger and Peter ordered a pizza.* 我點了一個漢堡包，彼得點了一個薄餅。

ordinary /ˈɔːdnri; 美 ˈɔːrdneri/ [形容詞] 普通的，平常的 *I thought they were very ordinary people.* 我覺得他們都是非常普通的人。

organ /ˈɔːgən; 美 ˈɔːr-/ [名詞] 1 器官 *The disease spread to her other organs.* 疾病擴散到了她的其他器官。 2 管風琴 *Who can play the organ?*

誰會彈管風琴？

organize / 'ɔːgənaɪz; 美 'ɔːr- / [又作 **organise**] [動詞] 組織；安排 *Our teacher has organized a trip to the zoo.* 我們老師已經組織過一次動物園之旅。

ostrich / 'ɒstrɪtʃ; 美 'ɑː- / [名詞] [複數 **ostriches**] 鴕鳥 *The ostrich cannot fly, but it can run very fast.* 鴕鳥不會飛，但跑得很快。

other¹ / 'ʌðə; 美 'ʌðər / [形容詞] **1** 另外的，其他的 *I don't like any other kind of music — only pop music.* 我不喜歡其他音樂，只喜歡流行音樂。 **2** （兩個中）另一的 *I've lost the other glove!* 我把另一隻手套弄丟了！

other² / 'ʌðə; 美 'ʌðər / [代詞] 另外的人（或物），其他的人（或物） *Why don't you and play in the garden with the others?* 你為甚麼不跟其他人一起去花園裏玩？

ought / ɔːt / [情態動詞] [與 **to** 連用] 應該 *You ought to work harder at school.* 你在學校應該更加用功。

our / 'aʊə; 美 'aʊr / [形容詞] [**we** 的所有格] 我們的 *We all like our teacher; she's very friendly.* 我們都喜歡我們的老師，她非常友好。

ours / 'aʊəz; 美 'aʊrz / [代詞] [**we** 的物主代詞] 我們的（東西）*His house is bigger than ours.* 他的房子比我們的大。

ourselves / aʊə'selvz; 美 aʊr- / [代詞] [**we** 的反身代詞] 我們自己 *We could see ourselves in the mirror.* 我們可以在鏡子裏看到自己。◇ *We did it ourselves, without anyone's help.* 我們是自己幹的，沒有別人幫忙。

out / aʊt / [副詞] **1** 出去 *Oh look — the sun's come out.* 瞧，太陽出來了。 ☞ [反] **in¹** 進入 **2** 不在家 *My mother's out — would you like to leave a message?* 我母親不在家，你要留口信嗎？ ☞ [反] **in¹** 在家

outdoors / ˌaʊt'dɔːz; 美 -'dɔːrz / [副詞] 在室外，在戶外 *We're not allowed to play outdoors when it's raining.* 下雨時我們不準在戶外玩。 ☞ [反] **indoors** 在室內，在屋裏

outing / 'aʊtɪŋ / [名詞] （尤指一羣人的）短途旅遊，遠足 *We're going for an outing tomorrow.* 我們明天去遠足。

outside¹ / ˌaʊt'saɪd / [副詞] 在外面 *Please wait outside for a few*

minutes. 請在外面等幾分鐘。 ☞ [反]
inside² 在裏面

outside² /ˌaʊt'saɪd/ [介詞] 在⋯外面
*Leave your empty bottles outside
your door.* 把空瓶放在門外。 ☞ [反]
inside¹ 在⋯裏面

oval /'əʊvl; 美 'oʊ-/ [形容詞] 卵形
的;橢圓形的 *She has an oval face.*
她長着一副瓜子臉。

oven /'ʌvn/ [名詞] 烤箱;烤爐 *Take
the cake out of the oven.* 把蛋糕從
烤箱裏取出來。

over¹ /'əʊvə; 美 'oʊvər/ [副詞] **1**
(越)過 *I went over and asked her
name.* 我走過去問她的名字。 **2** (倒)
下 *I slipped and fell over.* 我滑了一跤
摔倒了。 **3** 結束 *I'm glad the exams
are over.* 我很高興,考試結束了。

over² /'əʊvə; 美 'oʊvər/ [介詞] **1** 在⋯
上面 *She put a blanket over the
sleeping child.* 她在睡着的孩子身上蓋
了一條毯子。 ☞ [反] **under** 在⋯下
面 **2** 越過 *Henry climbed over the
wall.* 亨利爬過那堵墙。 **3** (在數目、
程度方面)超過,仕⋯以上 *He's over
sixty.* 他六十多歲了。 ☞ [反] **under**

少於,低於

overtake /ˌəʊvə'teɪk; 美 ˌoʊvər-/
[動詞] [過去式 **overtook** /ˌəʊvə'tʊk; 美
ˌoʊvər-/ ,過去分詞 **overtaken**
/ˌəʊvə'teɪkən; 美 ˌoʊvər-/] 超過 *A police
car overtook us.* 一輛警車超過了我們。

overseas /ˌəʊvə'siːz; 美 ˌoʊvər-/ [副
詞] 在海外,在國外 *My dad is working
overseas.* 我爸爸在國外工作。

owe /əʊ; 美 oʊ/ [動詞] 欠 *How much
do I owe you?* 我欠你多少錢?

owl /aʊl/ [名詞] 貓頭鷹 *An owl can
see in the dark.* 貓頭鷹在黑暗中能看
見東西。

own /əʊn; 美 oʊn/ [形容詞] 自己的 *I
have my own bedroom.* 我有自己的
卧室。

on your own 1 單獨地,獨自地 *I
don't want to go to the cinema on
my own.* 我不想獨自去看電影。 **2** 獨
立地,無援地 *Did you write this story
on your own?* 你是自己寫的這個故事
嗎?

P p

pack /pæk/ [動詞] 把…打包（或裝箱等）；收拾行李 *Have you packed your toothbrush?* 你把牙刷裝進行李包了嗎？◇ *She went upstairs to pack.* 她上樓收拾行李去了。

package /ˈpækɪdʒ/ [名詞] 包裹 *There's a large package for you on the table.* 桌子上有你一個大包裹。☞ 美國英語通常用 **package**，英國英語通常用 **parcel**。

packet /ˈpækɪt; 美 -ət/ [名詞] 小包；小盒；小袋 *May I open this packet of sweets?* 我可以打開這袋糖果嗎？

paddle /ˈpædl/ [動詞] 涉水，蹚水 *The children paddled in the sea.* 孩子們在海邊蹚着水。☞ **paddle** 用於英國英語，美國英語用 **wade**。

padlock¹ /ˈpædlɒk; 美 -lɑːk/ [名詞] 掛鎖，扣鎖 *Henry has a padlock on his bicycle.* 亨利的自行車上有一把掛鎖。

padlock² /ˈpædlɒk; 美 -lɑːk/ [動詞] 用掛鎖（或扣鎖）把…鎖上 *I padlocked my bicycle to a post.* 我用掛鎖把自行車鎖在一根柱子上。

page /peɪdʒ/ [名詞] 頁 *Turn to page 12.* 翻到第 12 頁。◇ *The answers are on page 36.* 答案在第 36 頁。

paid /peɪd/ **pay** 的過去式和過去分詞 *I paid £10 for the book.* 這本書我花了 10 英鎊。

pain /peɪn/ [名詞] 疼痛 *I've got a bad pain in my leg.* 我的腿痛得厲害。☞ 參見 **ache¹** "疼痛"。

painful /ˈpeɪnfl/ [形容詞] 疼痛的 *Is your back still painful?* 你的背還痛嗎？

paint¹ /peɪnt/ [名詞] 油漆；塗料 *Dad bought a tin of blue paint.* 爸爸買了一罐藍漆。

paint² /peɪnt/ [動詞] **1** 油漆 *He painted the door red.* 他把門漆成了紅色。

2 （用顏料）畫 *She loves painting the sea.* 她喜歡畫海。

paintbrush /ˈpeɪntbrʌʃ/ [名詞] [複數 **paintbrushes**] 畫筆；漆刷 *Do you have a paintbrush?* 你有畫筆嗎？

painter /ˈpeɪntə; 美 -ər/ [名詞] **1** 油漆工 *The painters were painting the windows.* 那幾個油漆工正在油漆窗戶。 **2** 畫家 *Who's your favourite painter?* 你最喜愛的畫家是誰？

painting /ˈpeɪntɪŋ/ [名詞] 油畫 *Do you like this painting?* 你喜歡這幅油畫嗎？

pair /peə; 美 per/ [名詞] **1** （由兩件一起使用的相同的物品組成的）一對，一雙 *I've got a new pair of shoes.* 我買了一雙新鞋。 **2**（由兩個連在一起的部分組成的）一條，一把，一副 *I'd like to buy this pair of trousers.* 我想買這條褲子。

palace /ˈpæləs/ [名詞] 皇宮，宮殿 *The Queen of England lives in the Buckingham Palace.* 英國女王住在白金漢宮。

pale /peɪl/ [形容詞] （指人或臉色等)蒼白的 *You look a bit pale — are you feeling OK?* 你的臉色有點蒼白，你覺得還好嗎？

palm /pɑːm; 美 pɑːlm/ [名詞] **1** 手掌；掌心 *He put the insect on the palm of his hand.* 他把昆蟲放在手掌心上。 **2** [又作 **palm tree**] 棕櫚樹 *A row of palms grew near the edge of the beach.* 海灘邊上長着一排棕櫚樹。

pan /pæn/ [名詞] （平底）鍋 *Be careful! That pan is very hot!* 小心！那口鍋很熱！

pancake /ˈpænkeɪk/ [名詞] 薄煎

餅 *Henry likes pancakes for breakfast.* 亨利早餐喜歡吃薄煎餅。

panda /ˈpændə/ [名詞]（大）熊貓 *The panda is a rare animal.* 熊貓是稀有動物。

panic /ˈpænɪk/ [動詞] [現在分詞 **panicking**，過去式和過去分詞 **panicked**] 恐慌，驚慌 *Stay calm and don't panic.* 保持鎮靜，不要驚慌。

pants /pænts/ [名詞] [複數] **1** （男子穿的）內褲 *Where are my clean pants?* 我的乾淨內褲在哪裏？ **2** 褲子，長褲 *I need to buy a new pair of pants.* 我需要買一條新褲子。☞ **pants** 在英國英語中指內褲，在美國英語中指長褲（= **trousers**）。

paper /ˈpeɪpə; 美 -ər/ [名詞] **1** [無複數] 紙 *She wrote her name and address on a piece of paper.* 她把姓名和地址寫在一張紙上。 **2** 報紙 *Where's today's paper?* 今天的報紙在哪裏？ ☞ = **newspaper**

parcel /ˈpɑːsl; 美 ˈpɑːr-/ [名詞] 包裹 *I wonder what's inside the parcel.* 我想知道包裹裏面有甚麼。☞ 英國英語通常用 **parcel**，美國英語通常用 **package**。

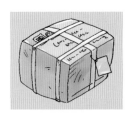

pardon¹ /ˈpɑːdn; 美 ˈpɑːrdn/ [感嘆詞] [口語] 對不起，請原諒 [用升調説，表示沒聽清楚對方的話，請他重複一遍] *Pardon? Could you say that again?* 對不起，你再説一遍好嗎？ ☞ [同] **sorry²** 抱歉，對不起

pardon² /ˈpɑːdn; 美 ˈpɑːrdn/ [名詞] 原諒，寬恕

I beg your pardon [口語，正式] 對不起，請原諒 *Oh, I beg your pardon, I didn't realize this was your chair.* 哎呀，對不起，我不知道這是你的椅子。

parent /ˈpeərənt; 美 ˈper-/ [名詞] [通常用作複數] 父親；母親 *My parents live in London.* 我父母住在倫敦。 ☞ 指"父母"，要用 **parents**。

park¹ /pɑːk; 美 pɑːrk/ [名詞] 公園 *Let's go to the park to fly our kites.* 我們去公園放風箏吧。

park² /pɑːk; 美 pɑːrk/ [動詞] 停放（車輛）；停車 *You can't park there.*

你不能在那裏停車。

parrot /ˈpærət/ [名詞] 鸚鵡 *The parrot imitates everything we say to it.* 我們説甚麼這隻鸚鵡就模仿甚麼。

part /pɑːt; 美 pɑːrt/ [名詞] **1** 部分 *Part of the building was destroyed in the fire.* 那棟樓的一部分被大火燒毀了。 **2**（機器等的）零件,部件 *I need some new parts for my bicycle.* 我的自行車需要換一些新零件。 **3**（戲劇、電影等中的）角色 *He played the part of a policeman in the play.* 他在劇中扮演警察這個角色。
take part (in sth) 參加（某事） *Would you like to take part in the school concert?* 你想參加學校音樂會嗎?

particular /pəˈtɪkjʊlə; 美 pərˈtɪkjələr/ [形容詞] [只用於名詞前] 特別的,特殊的 *You need to pay particular attention to your spelling.* 你必須特別注意你的拼寫。

partner /ˈpɑːtnə; 美 ˈpɑːrtnər/ [名詞] 夥伴;舞伴 *Tell your partner what you can see in the picture.* 告訴你的夥伴你在畫中看見的東西。

party /ˈpɑːti; 美 ˈpɑːrti/ [名詞] [複數 **parties**] 聚會;宴會 *I'm sorry I can't come to your party.* 很抱歉,我不能來參加你的聚會了。

pass /pɑːs; 美 pæs/ [動詞] **1** 經過 *We pass Henry's house on the way to school.* 我們上學經過亨利家。 **2**（尤指用手）遞,傳給 *Could you pass me that book, please?* 請你把那本書遞給我好嗎? **3** 通過（考試）;及格 *Henry passed all his examinations.* 亨利所有的考試都及格了。 ☞ [反] **fail** 沒有通過（考試）;不及格

passage /ˈpæsɪdʒ/ [名詞] 通道;走廊 *The toilets are at the end of the passage on the left.* 廁所在左邊走廊的盡頭。 ☞ [同] **corridor** 走廊

passenger /ˈpæsɪndʒə; 美 -ər/ [名詞] 乘客 *There were nine passengers in the bus.* 公共汽車上有9位乘客。

passport /ˈpɑːspɔːt; 美 ˈpæspɔːrt/ [名詞] 護照 *You have to show your passport when you enter or leave a country.* 你出入一個國家時必須出示護照。

past¹ /pɑːst; 美 pæst/ [形容詞]（指時間）過去的 *The time for discussion is past.* 討論的時間過去了。

past² /pɑːst; 美 pæst/ [名詞] [無複數] 以前;過去 *In the past, a lot of people couldn't read or write.* 從前很多人都不識字。

past³ /pɑːst; 美 pæst/ [介詞] **1**（指時間）超過,在…之後 *It's just past four o'clock.* 剛過4點。 ◇ *It's half past four.* 4點半了。 **2** 經過 *Dad drove past me without seeing me.* 爸爸開車從我身旁經過,但沒有看見我。

past⁴ /pɑːst; 美 pæst/ [副詞] 經過
Dad drove past without stopping.
爸爸開車經過，但沒有停下來。

paste /peɪst/ [名詞] [無複數] 糨糊
*You can make your own paste from
flour and water.* 你可以用麵粉和水自
己做糨糊。

pat /pæt/ [動詞] [現在分詞**patting**，
過去式和過去分詞**patted**]（用手）輕
拍 *Henry patted the dog.* 亨利輕輕
地拍了拍狗。

patch /pætʃ/ [名詞] [複數**patches**]
補丁 *Paul has patches on his jeans.*
保羅的牛仔褲上有幾處補丁。

patch
補丁

path /pɑːθ; 美 pæθ/ [名詞] 小路，小
道，小徑 *We walked along the path
through the woods.* 我們沿着小路步
行穿過了樹林。

patient¹ /'peɪʃnt/ [形容詞] 耐心的
*She's very patient with young
children.* 她對小孩子非常有耐心。

[反] **impatient** 不耐煩的

patient² /'peɪʃnt/ [名詞] 病人 *The
dentist examined the patient's
teeth.* 牙醫檢查了病人的牙齒。

pattern /'pætn; 美 -tərn/ [名詞] 圖
案 *The dress has a pattern of flowers
on it.* 這件連衣裙上有印花圖案。

pause /pɔːz/ [動詞] 停頓，暫停 *He
paused for a moment.* 他停了片刻。

pavement /'peɪvmənt/ [名詞] 人
行道 *Keep on the pavement when
you are walking down the street.* 你
在大街上走時，要走在人行道上。
英國英語用 **pavement**，美國英語用
sidewalk。

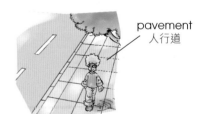

pavement
人行道

paw /pɔː/ [名詞]（狗、貓等的）腳
爪 *A dog has four paws.* 狗有 4 爪。

pay /peɪ/ [動詞] [過去式和過去分詞
paid /peɪd/] 付錢；付給 *You pay
over there.* 你去那邊付錢。 ◇ *How
much did you pay for this book?* 這

本書你花了多少錢？

pea /piː/ [名詞] 豌豆 Mum put some peas in the soup. 媽媽在湯裏放了些豌豆

peace /piːs/ [名詞] [無複數] **1** 和平 Everyone was tired of the war and was longing for peace. 人人都厭倦戰爭，渴望和平。☞[反]**war** 戰爭 **2** 平靜，寧靜 I love the peace of this village. 我喜歡這個村莊的寧靜。

peaceful /'piːsfl/ [形容詞] 平靜的，安靜的 The countryside is very peaceful. 鄉村很寧靜。

peach /piːtʃ/ [名詞] [複數 **peaches**] 桃子 Peter ate a peach. 彼得吃了一個桃子。

peacock /'piːkɒk; 美 -kɑːk/ [名詞] 孔雀 The peacock has a beautiful tail. 孔雀的尾巴很美麗。

peak /piːk/ [名詞] 山頂；山峯 Henry climbed to the peak. 亨利登上了山頂。

peanut /'piːnʌt/ [名詞] 花生 They were eating peanuts. 他們在吃花生。

pear /peə; 美 per/ [名詞] 梨 Mum bought some pears at the market. 媽媽在市場買了一些梨。

pebble /'pebl/ [名詞] 卵石 Henry found some smooth pebbles near the river. 亨利在河邊發現了一些光滑的卵石。

peculiar /pɪ'kjuːliə; 美 -'kjuːljər/ [形容詞] 奇怪的 There's a very peculiar smell in here. 這裏有一股很奇怪的味道。

pedal /'pedl/ [名詞] （自行車的）踏板，腳蹬 My feet slipped off the pedals and I nearly crashed into a tree. 我的腳在腳蹬上滑了一下，差點撞在一棵樹上。

pedestrian /pə'destriən/ [名詞] 行人 The pavements were full of pedestrians. 人行道上擠滿了行人。

pedestrian crossing /pə-ˌdestriən 'krɒsɪŋ; 美 pəˌdestriən 'krɔːsɪŋ/ [名詞] 人行橫道 The cars stopped at the pedestrian crossing. 汽車在人行

橫道前停了下來。

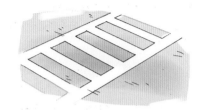

peel¹ /piːl/ [動詞] 削掉（或剝掉）…的皮 *Could you peel the potatoes, please?* 請你把土豆皮削掉好嗎？

peel² /piːl/ [名詞] [無複數]（水果或蔬菜的）皮 *Apples have red or green peel.* 蘋果的皮有紅色的，也有綠色的。

peep /piːp/ [動詞] 偷看；窺視 *I peeped through the window to see if he was there.* 我透過窗戶向外窺視，看他是否在那裏。

peg /peg/ [名詞] **1**（掛衣帽的）掛鈎 *You can put your hat on the peg there.* 你可以把帽子掛在那邊的掛鈎上。 **2**（晾衣服的）衣夾 *Here are some pegs. Could you please go and hang out the clothes?* 這兒有幾個衣夾，請你去把衣服晾起來好嗎？

peg 掛鈎 　peg 衣夾

pen /pen/ [名詞]（用墨水的）筆；鋼筆 *I need a pen and some paper.* 我需要一枝筆和一些紙。

pencil /ˈpensl/ [名詞] 鉛筆 *If you write in pencil, you can rub out what*

you have written. 如果用鉛筆寫，可以把寫的東西擦掉。

penguin /ˈpeŋgwɪn/ [名詞] 企鵝 *Penguins cannot fly but use their wings for swimming.* 企鵝不會飛，但會用翅膀游泳。

penny /ˈpeni/ [名詞] [複數 **pence** 或 **pennies**] 便士（1英鎊等於100便士）*I found a penny on the floor.* 我在地板上發現了一便士。

people /ˈpiːpl/ [名詞] [**person**的複數] 人；人們 *Lots of people were waiting in the rain for the bus.* 許多人正在雨裏等公共汽車。

pepper /ˈpepə; 美 -ər/ [名詞] **1** [無複數] 胡椒粉 *The soup needs a little more salt and pepper.* 這湯需要再加點鹽和胡椒粉。 **2** 柿子椒 *I bought some green peppers for the salad.* 我買了一些柿子椒做沙拉。

per /強 pɜː; 美 pɜːr; 弱 pə; 美 pər/ [介詞] 每，每一 *Rooms cost £50 per person per night.* 房費每人每夜50英鎊。

per cent /pə 'sent; 美 pər 'sent / [名詞] 百分之一 Sixty per cent of the pupils are boys. 60%的小學生是男生。☞ 美國英語通常合寫為 **percent**。

perch /pɜːtʃ; 美 pɜːrtʃ / [動詞] （指鳥類在樹枝上）棲息，暫歇 Birds perched on the branch. 鳥在樹枝上棲息。

perfect /'pɜːfɪkt; 美 'pɜːr- / [形容詞] 完美的；極好的 She speaks perfect English (=Her English is perfect). 她的英語完美無缺。

perform /pə'fɔːm; 美 pər'fɔːrm / [動詞] 表演；演戲 At the end of the term our class performed a play in front of all the parents. 我們班學期末在全體家長面前演了一齣戲。◇ Do you enjoy performing on stage? 你喜歡舞台表演嗎？

performance /pə'fɔːməns; 美 pər'fɔːr- / [名詞] 演出；表演 What time does the performance start? 演出甚麼時候開始？

perfume /'pɜːfjuːm; 美 'pɜːrfjuːm / [名詞] [無複數] 香水 Are you wearing perfume? 你噴香水了嗎？

perhaps /pə'hæps; 美 pər- / [副詞] 也許，可能 Perhaps he's forgotten. 也許他忘了。☞ [同] **maybe** 也許，大概

period /'pɪəriəd; 美 'pɪr- / [名詞] 一段時間 She will be in Australia for a period of six weeks. 她要在澳大利亞待6個星期。

permission /pə'mɪʃn; 美 pər- / [名詞] [無複數] 允許，許可，准許 Who gave you permission to leave early? 誰允許你早走的？

permit /pə'mɪt; 美 pər- / [動詞] [現在分詞 **permitting**，過去式和過去分詞 **permitted**] 允許，許可，准許 Smoking is not permitted in the hospital. 醫院裏不准吸煙。

person /'pɜːsn; 美 'pɜːr- / [名詞] [複數 **people**] 人 She's a very kind person. 她是一個非常善良的人。

persuade /pə'sweɪd; 美 pər- / [動詞] 說服，勸服 Try to persuade him to come. 盡量說服他來。

pest /pest / [名詞] **1** 害蟲 Insects which eat crops are pests. 吃莊稼的昆蟲是害蟲。 **2** [非正式] 討厭的人，害人精 That child is such a pest! 那個孩子真討厭！

pet /pet / [名詞] 寵物 Do you have any pets? 你養寵物了嗎？

petrol /'petrəl / [名詞] [無複數] 汽油 My father had to stop to fill the car up with petrol. 我父親不得不停下車加

滿油。

phone¹ /fəʊn; 美 foʊn/ [名詞] [非正式]
電話 *The phone is ringing — could you
answer it?* 電話響了，你去接一下好嗎？
◇ *What's your phone number?* 你
的電話號碼是多少？ ☞ = **telephone**

phone² /fəʊn; 美 foʊn/ [動詞]
（給⋯）打電話 *Did anyone phone
while I was out?* 我不在家時有人打電
話來嗎？ ◇ *I phoned Henry last night.*
我昨晚給亨利打了個電話。

photo /'fəʊtəʊ; 美 'foʊtoʊ/ [名詞] [複
數 **photos**] [非正式] 相片，照片 *I took
a photo of the beach.* 我照了一張海
灘的照片。 ☞ = **photograph**

photograph /'fəʊtəɡrɑːf; 美
'foʊtəɡræf/ [又作 **photo**] [名詞] 相片，
照片 *She's taking photographs of
the children.* 她在給孩子們照相。

piano /pɪ'ænəʊ; 美 -oʊ/ [名詞] [複數
pianos] 鋼琴 *Mum is teaching me to
play the piano.* 媽媽在教我彈鋼琴。

pick /pɪk/ [動詞] **1** 挑選，選擇 *The
child picked the biggest sweet.* 那
個孩子挑了一塊最大的糖。 **2** 採，摘
（花朵、水果等） *Don't pick those
apples — they're not ripe yet.* 別摘
那些蘋果，還沒熟呢。

pick up 撿起，拾起 *Pick up your toys
and put them in the cupboard.* 把
你的玩具撿起來放在櫥櫃裏。

picnic /'pɪknɪk/ [名詞] 野餐 *We
had a picnic on the beach.* 我們在
海灘上吃了一頓野餐。

picture /'pɪktʃə; 美 -ər/ [名詞] **1** 畫，
圖畫 *Who painted the picture on the
wall?* 牆上那幅畫是誰畫的？ **2** 相片，
照片 *That's a nice picture of Alice.*
那是艾麗斯的一張可愛的照片。

pie /paɪ/ [名詞] （尤指肉或果子）餡
餅，派 *Have another slice of pie.* 再
吃一塊餡餅吧。

piece /piːs/ [名詞] 片，塊，件，張
*Would you like another piece of
cake?* 你想再吃塊蛋糕嗎？ ◇ *I need a
new piece of paper.* 我需要一張新紙。

pig /pɪg/ [名詞] 豬 *The farmer was
feeding the pigs.* 那位農民正在餵豬。

pigeon /ˈpɪdʒən/ [名詞] 鴿子 We fed the pigeons in the park. 我們在公園裏喂鴿子。

pile /paɪl/ [名詞] 一堆 There was a pile of books on the table. 桌子上有一堆書。

pill /pɪl/ [名詞] 藥丸；藥片 Take one pill, three times a day after meals. 每天吃三次藥，飯後服用，每次吃一片。

pillow /ˈpɪləʊ; 美 -oʊ/ [名詞] 枕頭 I'll be asleep as soon as my head hits the pillow. 我頭一挨着枕頭就能睡着。

pilot /ˈpaɪlət/ [名詞] 飛行員 The pilot landed the plane safely at the airport. 飛行員把飛機安全地降落在機場。

pin /pɪn/ [名詞] 大頭針 He fixed the card to his jacket with a pin. 他用大頭針把卡片別在夾克上。

pinch /pɪntʃ/ [動詞] 捏，掐 He pinched my brother and made him cry. 他把我弟弟捏哭了。

pineapple /ˈpaɪnæpl/ [名詞] 菠蘿 Can I have another slice of pineapple? 我可以再吃一塊菠蘿嗎？

pink¹ /pɪŋk/ [形容詞] 粉紅色的 What are these little pink flowers called? 這些粉紅色的小花叫甚麼花？

pink² /pɪŋk/ [名詞] 粉紅色 Alice was dressed in pink. 艾麗斯穿着粉紅色的衣服。

pipe /paɪp/ [名詞] 管子 There is something blocking the water pipe. 有東西把水管堵住了。

pirate /ˈpaɪərət; 美 ˈpaɪrət/ [名詞] 海盜 The pirates attacked the ship. 海盜襲擊了那艘船。

pit /pɪt/ [名詞] 坑 They dug a pit to bury the rubbish. 他們挖了一個坑埋垃圾。

pitch /pɪtʃ/ [名詞] [複數 **pitches**] （板球、足球等的）球場 The school has a football pitch. 那所學校有個足球場。

pity /'pɪti/ [名詞] [無複數] 同情，憐憫 I felt great pity for people with nowhere to live. 我很同情那些無家可歸的人。

it's a pity, what a pity 真可惜，很遺憾 It's a pity you can't come to the party. 你不能來參加聚會，真可惜。◇ What a pity you can't come and see us! 你不能來看我們，真是遺憾！

pizza /'piːtsə/ [名詞] 薄餅 Do you like pizza? 你喜歡吃薄餅嗎？

place¹ /pleɪs/ [名詞] 地方，地點 That's a good place for a picnic. 那是一個野餐的好地方。

take place 發生，舉行 The next match will take place on Saturday afternoon. 下一場比賽將於星期六下午舉行。

place² /pleɪs/ [動詞] 放置，安放 Helen placed a book on the table. 海倫把一本書放在桌子上。

plain /pleɪn/ [形容詞] **1** 清楚的，明白的 It's plain that he doesn't agree. 他顯然不同意。 **2** 簡單的，樸素的 Mum wears plain clothes for work. 媽媽穿着樸素的衣服上班。

plan¹ /plæn/ [名詞] 計劃 Have you made any plans for the weekend? 你這個週末訂計劃了嗎？

plan² /plæn/ [動詞] [現在分詞 **p l a n n i n g**，過去式和過去分詞 **planned**] 計劃，打算 We're planning to go to Australia for our holidays. 我們打算去澳大利亞度假。

plane /pleɪn/ [名詞] 飛機 It's time to get on the plane. 到上飛機的時間了。◇ I love travelling by plane. 我喜歡坐飛機旅行。☞ = **aeroplane**

planet /'plænɪt/ [名詞] 行星 The Earth is one of the planets. 地球是行星之一。

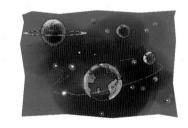

plant¹ /plɑːnt; 美 plænt/ [名詞] 植物 Don't forget to water the plants. 別忘了給植物澆水。

plant² /plɑːnt; 美 plænt / [動詞] 種植 We planted an apple tree in the yard. 我們在院子裏種了一棵蘋果樹。

plastic /'plæstɪk / [名詞] 塑料 These toys are made of plastic. 這些玩具是塑料的。

plate /pleɪt / [名詞] 盤子，碟子 Put the plates on the dining table. 把盤子放在餐桌上。

platform /'plætfɔːm; 美 -fɔːrm / [名詞] **1** （火車站的）站台 There are a lot of people waiting on the platform. 有很多人在站台上等車。 **2** 講台；舞台 The teacher stood on a platform at the front of the classroom. 老師站在教室前面的講台上。

play¹ /pleɪ / [動詞] **1** 玩耍，玩 Do you want to play with my car? 你想玩我的小汽車嗎？ **2** 打 (球)，踢(球)，下(棋) After lunch we played badminton in the garden. 午飯後我們在花園裏打羽毛球。◇ Do you know how to play chess? 你會下棋嗎？ **3** 演奏，彈奏，吹奏 I'm learning how to play the piano. 我在學彈鋼琴。 **4** 放（唱片、磁帶等）Dad often plays CDs while he drives. 爸爸開車時經常放激光唱片。 **5** 扮演（某人）Who does he play in the film? 他在這部電影裏扮演誰？

play² /pleɪ / [名詞] 戲劇 We went to see a play last night. 昨晚我們去看了一齣戲。

player /'pleɪə; 美 -ər/ [名詞] 運動員，選手，隊員 She's an excellent tennis player. 她是一名出色的網球手。

playground /'pleɪɡraʊnd / [名詞] 操場；遊樂場 Peter fell over in the school playground and hurt his knee. 彼得在學校操場上摔了一跤，把膝蓋摔傷了。

pleasant /'pleznt / [形容詞] 令人愉快的 The weather here is very pleasant. 這裏天氣宜人。 ☞ [反] **unpleasant** 令人不愉快的

please¹ /pliːz / [感嘆詞] **1** [表示有禮貌地請求對方] 請 What's the time, please? 請問現在幾點鐘了？ ◇ Please come in. 請進來。 **2** [表示客氣地接受對方的東西或邀請] 好，謝謝 'Would you like some more soup?' 'Yes, please.' "再來點湯好嗎？" "好，謝謝。"

please² /pliːz / [動詞] 使高興；使滿意 You can't please everybody. 你不可能讓所有的人都滿意。

pleased /pliːzd / [形容詞] 高興的；滿意的 I'm really pleased that you're feeling better. 我真的很高興你身體好些了。

plenty /'plenti / [代詞] 充足，大量

When we go to the park, we always take plenty of water with us. 我們去公園時總是帶着充足的水。◇ 'Is there any milk left?' 'Yes, plenty.' "有牛奶剩下嗎?""有,有很多。"

plug /plʌg/ [名詞] **1** 插頭 The television is not working because the plug has been pulled out of the wall. 電視不亮了,因為插頭從牆上拔出來了。 **2** (塞浴缸、洗臉池等的)塞子 Where is the bath plug? 浴缸的塞子在哪裏?

plug
插頭

plug
塞子

plum /plʌm/ [名詞] 李子,梅子 These plums are very good to eat. 這些李子很好吃。

plus /plʌs/ [介詞] 加,加上 Three plus five equals eight. 3加5等於8。

pocket /'pɒkɪt; 美 'pɑːkət/ [名詞] 衣袋,口袋 I put my hands in my pockets. 我把手放在口袋裏。

pocket money /'pɒkɪt ˌmʌni; 美 'pɑːkət ˌmʌni/ [名詞] [無複數] (家長給孩子的) 零花錢 What are you going to buy with your pocket money? 你打算用零花錢買甚麼?

poem /'pəʊɪm; 美 'poʊəm/ [名詞] 詩 There are two poems on this page of the book. 在書的這一頁上有兩首詩。

point¹ /pɔɪnt/ [名詞] **1** (物體的)尖 The point of this knife is very sharp. 這把刀的刀尖很鋒利。 **2** (比賽中的)分 Henry needs two more points to win the match. 亨利再得兩分就能贏得這場比賽。

point² /pɔɪnt/ [動詞] 指,指向 'That's where my mother works,' she said, pointing to the bank. "那是我母親工作的地方,"她指着銀行說。

poisonous /'pɔɪzənəs/ [形容詞] 有毒的 The leaves of this plant are poisonous. 這種植物的葉子有毒。

polar bear /ˌpəʊlə ˈbeə; 美 ˌpoʊlər ˈber/ [名詞] 北極熊 *The polar bear is a large white bear that lives near the North Pole.* 北極熊是一種生活在北極附近的大白熊。

pole /pəʊl; 美 poʊl/ [名詞] **1** 桿,柱 *Henry put a flag on the pole.* 亨利在桿上掛起一面旗子。

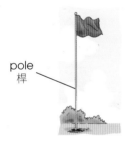

pole
桿

2 (地球的南北兩端) 極 *It's very cold at the North Pole.* 北極非常寒冷。

police /pəˈliːs/ [名詞] [常用作 **the police**][複數] 警察機關,警方 *Quick! Call the police!* 快!報警!

policeman /pəˈliːsmən/ [名詞] [複數 **policemen** /pəˈliːsmən/] (男) 警察 *I told the policeman everything I had seen.* 我把自己看到的一切都告訴了那名警察。

policewoman /pəˈliːsˌwʊmən/ [名詞] [複數 **policewomen** /pəˈliːsˌwɪmɪn/] (女) 警察 *The thief was taken away by two policewomen.* 那個小偷被兩名女警察帶走了。

polish /ˈpɒlɪʃ; 美 ˈpɑː-/ [動詞] 擦亮 *Your shoes need polishing.* 你的鞋需要擦了。

polite /pəˈlaɪt/ [形容詞] 有禮貌的 *A polite child always says 'thank you'.* 有禮貌的孩子總會說"謝謝你"。

pollution /pəˈluːʃn/ [名詞] [無複數] 污染 *We must prevent further pollution.* 我們必須防止進一步污染。

pond /pɒnd; 美 pɑːnd/ [名詞] (尤指人造的) 池塘 *There are lots of fish in the pond.* 池塘裏有很多魚。

pool /puːl/ [名詞] 游泳池 *I hate swimming in an indoor pool.* 我不喜歡在室內游泳池游泳。 ☞ **= swimming pool**

poor /pɔː; 美 pʊr/ [形容詞] 1 貧窮的 *The old man was very poor.* 那個老人很窮。 ☞ [反] **rich** 富有的 2 不好的，差的 *His writing is poor.* 他的字寫得不好。

pop music /'pɒp ˌmjuːzɪk; 美 'pɑːp ˌmjuːzɪk/ [名詞] 流行音樂 *He likes pop music.* 他喜歡流行音樂。

popular /'pɒpjʊlə; 美 'pɑːpjələr/ [形容詞] 流行的；受大眾喜愛的 *Henry is very popular at school.* 亨利在學校很受歡迎。

pork /pɔːk; 美 pɔːrk/ [名詞] 豬肉 *Do you like pork?* 你喜歡吃豬肉嗎？

porridge /'pɒrɪdʒ; 美 'pɔː-/ [名詞] [無複數] 粥 *Peter does not like porridge.* 彼得不喜歡喝粥。

port /pɔːt; 美 pɔːrt/ [名詞] 港口，海港 *The ferry sailed into the port.* 那艘渡輪駛進了港口。 ☞ [同] **harbour** 港口，海港

position /pə'zɪʃn/ [名詞] 1 位置 *Are you happy with the position of the chairs?* 你對椅子擺放的位置滿意嗎？ 2 （某人的）姿勢 *You should lie in a comfortable position.* 你應該舒舒服服地躺着。

possible /'pɒsəbl; 美 'pɑː-/ [形容詞] 可能的 *Is it possible to get to the city by train?* 能坐火車到那個城市去嗎？ ☞ [反] **impossible** 不可能的

post¹ /pəʊst; 美 poʊst/ [名詞] [無複數] 郵件 *Is there any post for me today?* 今天有我的郵件嗎？ ☞ 英國英語用 **post**，美國英語用 **mail**。

post² /pəʊst; 美 poʊst/ [動詞] 郵寄 *Could you post this letter for me, please?* 請你替我寄這封信好嗎？ ☞ 英國英語用 **post**，美國英語用 **mail**。

postbox /'pəʊstbɒks; 美 'poʊstbɑːks/ [名詞] [複數 **postboxes**] 郵筒，郵箱 *Henry dropped the letter into the postbox.* 亨利把信投進了郵筒。

postcard /'pəʊstkɑːd; 美 'poʊstkɑːrd/ [名詞] 明信片 *Helen sent me a postcard from France.* 海倫從法國給我寄來一張明信片。

poster /'pəʊstə; 美 'poʊstər/ [名詞] 招貼；海報 *There is a new poster about Harry Potter in our school.* 我們學校貼了一張有關哈利‧波特的新海報。

postman /'pəʊstmən; 美 'poʊst-/ [名詞] [複數 **postmen** /'pəʊstmən; 美 'poʊst-/] 郵遞員 *Our postman usually brings the post before eight o'clock in the morning.* 我們的郵遞員通常在早晨 8 點以前把郵件送來。

post office /'pəʊst ˌɒfɪs; 美 'poʊst ˌɑːfəs/ [名詞] 郵局 *Our post office sells pens, postcards, writing paper and stamps.* 我們郵局出售鋼筆、明信片、信紙和郵票。

pot /pɒt; 美 pɑːt/ [名詞] **1** (煮飯用的) 鍋 *There was a big pot of soup on the stove.* 爐子上有一大鍋湯。**2** 罐，壺，盆 *He sat down and ordered a pot of tea.* 他坐下點了一壺茶。

potato /pə'teɪtəʊ; 美 -oʊ/ [名詞] [複數 **potatoes**] 馬鈴薯，土豆 *Have you peeled the potatoes yet?* 你削完土豆皮了嗎？

pottery /'pɒtəri; 美 'pɑː-/ [名詞] [無複數] 陶器 *This shop sells beautiful pottery.* 這家商店出售精美的陶器。

pound /paʊnd/ [名詞] **1** 英鎊 [英國貨幣單位，符號為£] *These shoes cost me twenty pounds.* 這雙鞋花了我 20 英鎊。**2** 磅 [重量單位] *These apples cost 40p a pound.* 這些蘋果 40 便士一磅。

pour /pɔː; 美 pɔːr/ [動詞] 倒（液體）*He poured me a glass of orange juice.* 他給我倒了一杯橙汁。

powder /'paʊdə; 美 -ər/ [名詞] 粉，粉末 *I often wash my clothes with washing powder.* 我常用洗衣粉洗衣服。

power /'paʊə; 美 'paʊr/ [名詞] [無複數] **1** 力量；能力 *After the accident she lost the power of speech.* 那次事故之後她失去了說話的能力。**2** 動力，電力 *The television and the computer both use electrical* *power.* 電視和電腦都使用電力。

practice /'præktɪs/ [名詞] 練習 *Speaking a foreign language takes lots of practice.* 說外語需要大量練習。

practise /'præktɪs/ [動詞] 練習 *You will never play the piano well if you don't practise.* 你如果不練習就永遠彈不好鋼琴。☞ 用作動詞時，美國英語拼寫為 **practice**。

praise /preɪz/ [動詞] 稱讚，讚揚，表揚 *The teacher praised my work.* 老師表揚了我的作業。

pray /preɪ/ [動詞] 祈禱；祈求 *Let us pray for peace.* 讓我們為和平祈禱吧。

precious /'preʃəs/ [形容詞] 貴重的；寶貴的 *Gold and silver are precious metals.* 金和銀是貴重金屬。◇ *You're wasting precious time!* 你在浪費寶貴的時間！

prefer /prɪ'fɜː; 美 -'fɜːr/ [動詞] [現在分詞 **preferring**，過去式和過去分詞 **preferred**] 寧願(選擇)，更喜歡 *I prefer English to maths.* 我喜歡英語勝過數學。◇ *Do you prefer reading or watching television?* 你更喜歡看書還是看電視？

prepare /prɪ'peə; 美 -'per/ [動詞] 準備 *The whole class is working hard preparing for the exams.* 全班都在用功準備考試。

present¹ /'preznt/ [形容詞] **1** [不用於名詞前] 在場的，出席的 *There were 200 people present at the meeting.* 有200人出席了會議。☞ [反] **absent** 不在的，缺席的 **2** [只用於名詞前] 現在的，目前的 *Our present head teacher is much younger than our last one.* 我們現在的校長比上一任校長年輕多了。

present² /'preznt/ [名詞] 禮物，贈品 *Dad gave me a birthday present.* 爸爸送給我一件生日禮物。☞ [同] **gift** 禮物

at present 現在 *I'm a bit busy at present—I'll phone you later.* 我現在有點忙，過一會給你打電話。

president /'prezɪdənt/ [名詞] 總統 *The first American president was George Washington.* 美國第一任總統是喬治‧華盛頓。

press /pres/ [動詞] 按 *Which button do you press to start recording?* 開始錄音按哪個鈕？

pretend /prɪ'tend/ [動詞] 假裝，裝作 *Henry pretended to be asleep.* 亨利假裝睡着了。

pretty /'prɪti/ [形容詞] [比較級 **prettier**，最高級 **prettiest**] 漂亮的，好看的 *His younger sister is very pretty.* 他妹妹長得很漂亮。

prevent /prɪ'vent/ [動詞] 防止；阻止 *This fence is to prevent the* animals getting out. 這道圍欄是防止動物跑出去的。

price /praɪs/ [名詞] 價格，價錢 What's the price of this bike? 這輛自行車的價錢是多少？

prick /prɪk/ [動詞] 刺（破），扎（穿） I pricked my finger on a thorn. 我的手指被刺扎破了。

prince /prɪns/ [名詞] 王子 Sleeping Beauty was rescued by a handsome prince. 睡美人被一位英俊的王子救了。

princess /ˌprɪnˈses; 美 ˈprɪnsəs/ [名詞] [複數 **princesses**] 公主 Do you know

the fairy story about the princess and the pea? 你知道豌豆公主的童話故事嗎？

print /prɪnt/ [動詞] 印刷 How much did it cost to print the posters? 印刷這些海報花了多少錢？

printer /ˈprɪntə; 美 -ər/ [名詞] 打印機 Press this button to make the printer work. 按這個按鈕打印。

prison /ˈprɪzn/ [名詞] 監獄，牢房 He was in prison for five years. 他坐了 5 年牢。

private /ˈpraɪvət/ [形容詞] 私人的 That is a private garden. 那是個私人花園。

prize /praɪz/ [名詞] 獎品，獎賞 I won first prize in the competition. 我在比賽中獲得了一等獎。

probably /ˈprɒbəbli; 美 ˈprɑː-/ [副詞] 大概，很可能 I'm going to the library — I'll probably be back in an hour. 我去圖書館，大概一小時後回來。

problem /ˈprɒbləm; 美 ˈprɑː-/ [名詞] 問題；難題 This is a very serious problem. 這是個非常嚴重的問題。◇ I can't do this maths problem. 我不會做這道數學題。

no problem [口語] 沒問題 'Can I

bring a friend?' 'Sure, no problem.'
"我可以帶朋友來嗎？""當然，沒問題。"

produce /prə'djuːs; 美 -'duːs/ [動詞] 生產，製造 This factory produces 5,000 cars a week. 這家工廠每星期生產5,000輛小汽車。

program /'prəʊgræm; 美 'proʊ-/ [名詞]（電腦的）程序 He wrote a program for a game. 他編寫了一個遊戲程序。

programme /'prəʊgræm; 美 'proʊ-/ [名詞]（電視或廣播的）節目 What's your favourite television programme? 你最喜歡甚麼電視節目？ ☞ 美國英語用 **program**。

progress /'prəʊgres; 美 'prɑːgrəs/ [名詞] [無複數] 進步，進展 You have made good progress with your English. 你的英語取得了很大的進步。

promise¹ /'prɒmɪs; 美 'prɑːməs/ [動詞] 允諾，答應 She promised to give me the book back tomorrow. 她答應明天把書還給我。

promise² /'prɒmɪs; 美 'prɑːməs/ [名詞] 許諾，諾言 If you make a promise, you should keep it. 你如果許了諾言，就應該信守諾言。

pronounce /prə'naʊns/ [動詞] 發…的音 How do you pronounce your name? 你的名字怎麼唸？

pronunciation /prə,nʌnsi'eɪʃn/ [名詞] 發音 Is that the correct pronunciation? 那個發音對嗎？

proper /'prɒpə; 美 'prɑːpər/ [形容詞] [只用於名詞前] 適當的，合適的；正確的 If you're going skiing you must have the proper clothes. 如果你去滑雪，必須穿上合適的衣服。

protect /prə'tekt/ [動詞] 保護 We are doing our best to protect the environment from pollution. 我們正在盡最大努力保護環境不受污染。

proud /praʊd/ [形容詞] 自豪的，引以為榮的 He is proud of his daughter's ability to speak four languages. 他為女兒能講四種語言而引以為榮。

provide /prə'vaɪd/ [動詞] 提供 The school provides lunch for pupils. 學校為學生提供午餐。

public /'pʌblɪk/ [形容詞] [只用於名詞前] 公共的，公用的 Where's the nearest public telephone? 最近的公用電話在哪裏？

pull /pʊl/ [動詞] 拉，拖 You pull the table and I'll push. 你拉桌子，我推。 ☞ [反] **push** 推

push   pull
推   拉

pump /pʌmp/ [名詞] 泵；抽水機；打氣筒 *A bicycle pump puts air into the tyres.* 自行車打氣筒能把氣打到輪胎裏去。

pump 打氣筒   pump 抽水機

punch /pʌntʃ/ [動詞]（用拳）猛擊 *He punched John on the nose.* 他用拳猛擊約翰的鼻子。

punish /'pʌnɪʃ/ [動詞] 懲罰，處罰 *My parents used to punish me by not letting me watch TV.* 我父母過去常常不讓我看電視，以此來懲罰我。

pupil /'pjuːpl/ [名詞] 小學生 *How many pupils are there in your class?* 你們班有多少名學生？

puppy /'pʌpi/ [名詞] [複數 **puppies**] 小狗 *The dog had two puppies.* 那條狗生了兩條小狗。

purple¹ /'pɜːpl; 美 'pɜːr-/ [形容詞] 紫色的 *Helen is wearing a purple skirt.* 海倫穿着一條紫色的裙子。

purple² /'pɜːpl; 美 'pɜːr-/ [名詞] 紫色 *Purple is one of my favourite colours.* 紫色是我最喜歡的顏色之一。

purpose /'pɜːpəs; 美 'pɜːr-/ [名詞] 目的，意圖 *The teacher told the students the purpose of the exercise.* 老師告訴學生們做這個練習的目的。
on purpose 故意地 *She did not break the cup on purpose.* 她不是故意打破杯子的。

purse /pɜːs; 美 pɜːrs/ [名詞] 錢包 *I had very little money in my purse.* 我錢包裏的錢很少。

push /pʊʃ/ [動詞] 推 *They had to push the car to the nearest petrol station.* 他們不得不把小汽車推到最近的加油站。◇ *Alice pushed the door open.* 艾麗斯推開門。☞ [反] **pull** 拉

put /pʊt/ [動詞] [現在分詞 **putting**，過去式和過去分詞 **put**] 放 *Put the books on the shelf, please.* 請把書放在書架上。◇ *Where did I put my keys?* 我把鑰匙放在哪裏了？
put on 穿上 *He put on his coat and went out.* 他穿上外套出去了。☞ [反] **take off** 脫下
put out 撲滅 *The firemen soon put out the fire.* 消防隊員們很快撲滅了大火。

puzzle¹ /'pʌzl/ [名詞]（測驗智力的）遊戲 *Can you do this jigsaw*

puzzle? 你會拼這個拼圖嗎？◇ *Henry does a crossword puzzle every day.* 亨利每天都做縱橫填字遊戲。

puzzle² /ˈpʌzl/ [動詞] 使迷惑，使為難 *English spelling really puzzles me.* 英語拼寫真讓我傷腦筋。

pyjamas /pəˈdʒɑːməz/ [名詞] [複數] 睡衣 *Your pyjamas are under your*

pillow. 你的睡衣在你的枕頭底下。

P

Q q

quantity /'kwɒntəti; 美 'kwɑ:n-/ [名詞] [複數 **quantities**] 量，數量 *Paul ate a small quantity of rice.* 保羅吃了少量米飯。

quarrel¹ /'kwɒrəl; 美 'kwɑ:-/ [名詞] 爭吵，吵架 *They had a quarrel about money.* 他們因錢的問題吵了一架。

quarrel² /'kwɒrəl; 美 'kwɑ:-/ [動詞] [現在分詞 **quarrelling**，過去式和過去分詞 **quarrelled**] 爭吵，吵架 *They're always quarrelling.* 他們總是爭吵不休。

quarter /'kwɔ:tə; 美 'kwɔ:rtər/ [名詞] 四分之一 *She cut the cake into four quarters.* 她把蛋糕切成了4份。

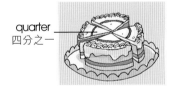

quarter
四分之一

queen /kwi:n/ [名詞] 女王 *Queen Elizabeth is the queen of the UK.* 伊麗莎白女王是英國女王。

question /'kwestʃən/ [名詞] 問題 *Who can answer the question?* 誰能回答這個問題？◇ *What's the answer to Question 5?* 第5道題的答案是甚麼？

queue /kju:/ [名詞]（人或物的）行，列，排 *There was a long queue outside the cinema.* 電影院門外排着長隊。 ☞ 英國英語用 **queue**，美國英語用 **line**。

quick /kwɪk/ [形容詞] 快的，迅速的 *Taxis are quicker than buses.* 出租車比公共汽車快。

quickly /'kwɪkli/ [副詞] 快，迅速地 *Henry runs away very quickly.* 亨利迅速跑掉了。

quiet /'kwaɪət/ [形容詞] 安靜的；輕聲的 *Please be quiet. I've got a headache.* 請安靜，我頭疼。 ☞ [反] **loud** 大聲的；吵鬧的

quietly /'kwaɪətli/ [副詞] 靜靜地，靜悄悄地 *You'll have to play quietly while the baby is asleep.* 寶寶睡覺時，你必須靜靜地玩。

quilt /kwɪlt/ [名詞] 被子 *Henry has a quilt on his bed in winter.* 冬天亨利的牀上放着被子。

quilt
被子

quite /kwaɪt/ [副詞] **1** 相當，頗 *The film's quite good.* 這部電影相當不錯。◇ *It's quite a good film.* 這是一部相當不錯的電影。**2** 完全，十分，非常 *I quite agree—you're quite right.* 我完全同意，你非常對。

quiz /kwɪz/ [名詞] [複數 **quizzes**] 問答比賽 *Alice won the spelling quiz.* 艾麗斯在拼寫比賽中獲勝。

Q

R r

rabbit /ˈræbɪt; 美 -ət/ [名詞] 兔子 *Peter has a pet rabbit.* 彼得養了一隻寵物兔子。

race /reɪs/ [名詞] （人、馬、車等的）速度比賽 *Who won the 100-metre race?* 誰贏了100米賽跑？◇ *Henry came first in this race.* 亨利賽跑得了第一。

racket /ˈrækɪt; 美 -ət/ [名詞] （網球、羽毛球等的）球拍 *Do you have a tennis racket?* 你有網球拍嗎？

radio /ˈreɪdɪəʊ; 美 -oʊ/ [名詞] [複數 **radios**] 收音機 *Turn on the radio. It's time for the news.* 打開收音機，到聽新聞的時間了。

rag /ræg/ [名詞] 破布，抹布 *Clean the lamp with a rag.* 用抹布把燈擦一擦。

raid /reɪd/ [動詞] 襲擊，突襲 *They raided the village.* 他們襲擊了那個村莊。

rail /reɪl/ [名詞] **1** （樓梯的）扶手 *The steps are slippery, so hold on to the rail.* 台階很滑，所以要扶着扶手。

2 [通常用作複數] 鐵軌 *Don't walk on the rails.* 不要在鐵軌上走。

railroad /ˈreɪlrəʊd; 美 -oʊd/ [名詞] [美國英語] **= railway**

railway /ˈreɪlweɪ/ [名詞] 鐵路，鐵道 *You mustn't walk across the railway.* 不得橫穿鐵路。　☞ 英國英語用 **railway**，美國英語用 **railroad**。

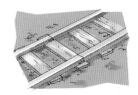

railway station /'reɪlweɪ ˌsteɪʃn/ [名詞] 火車站 *We went to meet my grandmother at the railway station.* 我們去火車站接我外婆了。☞ = **station (1)**

rain¹ /reɪn/ [名詞] [無複數] 雨 *You'll get wet if you go out in the rain.* 如果下雨出去，你會淋濕的。

rain² /reɪn/ [動詞] 下雨 *Oh no! It's raining again.* 哎呀！又下雨了。

rainy /'reɪni/ [形容詞] 下雨的；多雨的 *On rainy days I have to stay indoors.* 下雨時我不得不待在屋裏。

rainbow /'reɪnbəʊ; 美 -boʊ/ [名詞] 彩虹 *Look! There's a rainbow!* 瞧！有一道彩虹！

raincoat /'reɪnkəʊt; 美 -koʊt/ [名詞] 雨衣 *Have you brought your raincoat?* 你帶雨衣了嗎？

raise /reɪz/ [動詞] 舉起，抬起 *If you have a question, raise your hand.* 有問題的請舉手。

ran /ræn/ **run**的過去式 *Henry ran to the shop for some milk.* 亨利跑到商店買了些牛奶。

rang /ræŋ/ **ring**的過去式 *Mum rang the school to say I was ill.* 媽媽給學校打電話說我病了。

rare /reə; 美 rer/ [形容詞] 稀有的，罕見的 *This kind of bird is becoming very rare.* 這種鳥變得越來越稀少了。

rat /ræt/ [名詞] （大）老鼠 *Rats sometimes spread disease.* 老鼠有時會傳播疾病。

rather /'rɑːðə; 美 'ræðər/ [副詞] 很，相當 *It's rather cold today.* 今天天氣相當冷。

would rather 寧願，寧可 *I don't want to go tomorrow. I'd rather go today.* 我不想明天去，我寧願今天去。

raw /rɔː/ [形容詞] 生的；未煮過的 *Raw vegetables are good for your teeth.* 生吃蔬菜對牙齒有益。

reach /riːtʃ/ [動詞] **1** 到達，抵達 *They reached London on Saturday.* 他們星期六抵達倫敦。☞ [同] **arrive**，**get** 到達 **2** 伸（手）去拿 *Henry reached out his hand and caught the ball.* 亨利伸手接住球。

read /riːd/ [動詞] 讀，閱讀 *Do you enjoy reading?* 你喜歡看書嗎？ ◇ *My father likes to read the newspaper before dinner.* 我爸爸喜歡在飯前看報。

ready /'redi/ [形容詞] 準備好的 *Are you ready to go shopping with me?* 你準備跟我一起去購物嗎？ ◇ *Go and wash your hands. The dinner's ready.* 去洗手，飯好了。

real /'rɪəl; 美 riːl/ [形容詞] **1** 真的，真實的，真正的 *Is Joe Brown his real name?* 喬·布朗是他的真實姓名嗎？ ◇ *Tell me the real reason.* 告訴我真正的原因。 **2** 天然的，真的 *My schoolbag is real leather, not plastic.* 我的書包是真皮的，不是塑料的。

really /'rɪəli; 美 'riːli/ [副詞] **1** 事實上；真正地 *You're not really sleeping — you're just pretending.* 你不是真的在睡覺，你只是在裝睡。 **2** 非常 *I'm really hungry.* 我餓極了。 **3** [表示興趣、驚訝、懷疑等] 真的？ *'We're going to America for our holidays!' 'Really?'* "我們要去美國度假了！" "真的？"

reason /'riːzn/ [名詞] 原因，理由 *What's your reason for being so late?* 你遲到這麼長時間的原因是甚麼？ ◇ *He said he couldn't come but he didn't give a reason.* 他說他不能來，但沒說明原因。

receive /rɪ'siːv/ [動詞] 收到，接到 *How many birthday cards did you receive?* 你收到多少張生日賀卡？

recent /'riːsnt/ [形容詞] 最近的，近來的 *This is a recent photograph of my daughter.* 這是我女兒最近的一張照片。

recently /'riːsntli/ [副詞] 最近，近來 *Have you seen Paul recently?* 你最近見過保羅嗎？

recite /rɪ'saɪt/ [動詞] 背誦 *Alice recited a poem in class.* 艾麗斯在班上背誦了一首詩。

recognize /'rekəgnaɪz/ [又作**recognise**] [動詞] 認出 *I recognized him but I couldn't remember his name.* 我認出了他，但記不起他的名字了。

record /rɪ'kɔːd; 美 -'kɔːrd/ [動詞] 錄音；錄像 *Quiet, please! We're recording.* 請安靜！我們在錄音。

recorder /rɪ'kɔːdə; 美 -'kɔːrdər/ [名詞] 錄音機 *Henry has a cassette recorder.* 亨利有一台盒式錄音機。

R

recover /rɪˈkʌvə; 美 -ər/ [動詞] 康復，痊癒 *Have you recovered from your cold yet?* 你感冒好了嗎？

rectangle /ˈrektæŋgl/ [名詞] 長方形，矩形 *Do you know how to draw a rectangle?* 你會畫長方形嗎？

red¹ /red/ [形容詞] [比較級 **redder**，最高級 **reddest**] 紅色的 *Helen wore a red dress.* 海倫穿着一件紅色連衣裙。

red² /red/ [名詞] 紅色 *'What's your favourite colour?' 'Red.'* "你最喜歡甚麼顏色？" "紅色。"

referee /ˌrefəˈriː/ [名詞] 裁判 *Just at that moment the referee blew his whistle.* 就在那個時候裁判吹哨了。

reflection /rɪˈflekʃn/ [名詞] （鏡中或水中的）映像，倒影 *We looked at our reflections in the lake.* 我們看着自己在湖中的倒影。

refrigerator /rɪˈfrɪdʒəreɪtə; 美 -ər/ [名詞] [正式] 冰箱 *Put the milk in the refrigerator.* 把牛奶放在冰箱裏。

☞ = **fridge**

refuse /rɪˈfjuːz/ [動詞] 拒絕 *I asked my brother to help me with my homework but he refused.* 我請哥哥幫我做作業，但他拒絕了。◇ *She refused to eat vegetables.* 她拒絕吃蔬菜。

region /ˈriːdʒən/ [名詞] 地區 *We don't get very much snow in this region.* 我們這個地區不大下雪。

register /ˈredʒɪstə; 美 -ər/ [名詞] 名單，名冊 *The teacher calls the register first thing in the morning.* 老師早晨第一件事是點名。

regular /ˈregjʊlə; 美 -jələr/ [形容詞] 有規律的；定期的 *Regular exercise is good for you.* 有規律的鍛煉有益於健康。

regularly /ˈregjʊləli; 美 -jələrli/ [副詞] 經常地；定期地 *Alice eats fruit regularly.* 艾麗斯經常吃水果。

regulation /ˌregjuˈleɪʃn; 美 -jə-/ [名詞] 規則；條例 *All pupils must obey school regulations.* 所有學生都要遵守校規。

relative /ˈrelətɪv/ [名詞] 親戚 *We'll be visiting relatives at Christmas.* 我們聖誕節要看望親戚。

relax /rɪˈlæks/ [動詞] 休息，放鬆 *Don't worry about it — just try to relax.* 別擔心，盡量放鬆。

remain /rɪˈmeɪn/ [動詞] 1 逗留，留下 *I decided to remain at home.* 我

決定留在家裏。**2** 保持不變，仍然是 *Children can't remain quiet for long.* 兒童不可能長時間保持安靜。

remember /rɪ'membə; 美 -ər/ [動詞] 記得；記住 *I can't remember his phone number.* 我不記得他的電話號碼了。 ◇ *Remember to bring your swimming things tomorrow!* 記住明天把你游泳的東西帶來！ ☞ [反] **forget** 忘記

remind /rɪ'maɪnd/ [動詞] 提醒 *Remind me to write to my uncle.* 提醒我給我叔叔寫信。

remove /rɪ'muːv/ [動詞] **1** 移開；拿走 *Will you remove your books from my desk?* 把你的書從我的桌子上拿走好嗎？**2** 脫掉；摘下 *He removed his hat and sat down.* 他摘下帽子坐了下來。

rent /rent/ [動詞] 租用 *I'd like to rent a room.* 我想租一間房。

repair /rɪ'peə; 美 -'per/ [動詞] 修理 *Can you repair my bike?* 你給我修修自行車行嗎？

repeat /rɪ'piːt/ [動詞] 重複 *Could you repeat it please?* 請你重複一遍好嗎？

replace /rɪ'pleɪs/ [動詞] **1** 更換，替換 *His watch broke so he replaced it with a new one.* 他的手錶壞了，所以他換了一塊新的。 **2** 把⋯放回原處 *He replaced the book on the shelf.* 他把書放回到書架上。

reply¹ /rɪ'plaɪ/ [動詞] [現在分詞 **replying**，過去式和過去分詞 **replied**] 答復；回答 *Peter didn't reply to my question.* 彼得沒有答復我的問題。

reply² /rɪ'plaɪ/ [名詞] [複數 **replies**] 答復；回答 *Peter made no reply.* 彼得沒有答復。

reptile /'reptaɪl; 美 -tl/ [名詞] 爬行動物 *Do all reptiles lay eggs?* 所有爬行動物都下蛋嗎？

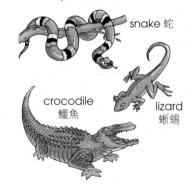

reptiles 爬行動物
snake 蛇
crocodile 鱷魚
lizard 蜥蜴

require /rɪ'kwaɪə; 美 -'kwaɪr/ [動詞] 需要 *These plants require a lot of light.* 這些植物需要充足的光線。

rescue /'reskjuː/ [動詞] 營救，救出 *They rescued the boy from the river.* 他們把那個男孩從河裏救了上來。

respect¹ /rɪ'spekt/ [名詞] 尊敬，敬

R

R

重 *Henry has great respect for the teacher.* 亨利非常尊敬老師。

respect² /rɪ'spekt/ [動詞] 尊敬，敬重 *Students should respect their teacher.* 學生應該尊敬老師。

responsible /rɪ'spɒnsəbl; 美 rɪ'spɑːn-/ [形容詞] [不用於名詞前] 負責的 *Who is responsible for watering the flowers this week?* 這個星期誰負責澆花？

rest¹ /rest/ [動詞] 休息 *I rested for an hour before I went out.* 我休息了一小時才出門。

rest² /rest/ [名詞] **1** 休息 *We all need sleep and rest.* 我們都需要睡覺和休息。**2** [用作單數，與**the**連用，後跟單數或複數動詞] 其餘的人（或物）*Have you seen the rest of the children?* 你看見其餘的孩子了嗎？

restaurant /'restərɒnt; 美 -rənt/ [名詞] 飯館，餐館 *We ate at the Chinese restaurant.* 我們在那家中餐館吃的飯。

result /rɪ'zʌlt/ [名詞] 結果；成績 *What was the result of your examination —*

did you pass or fail? 你的考試成績怎麼樣，及格了還是沒及格？

return /rɪ'tɜːn; 美 -'tɜːrn/ [動詞] **1** 返回，回來 *When did you return from France?* 你甚麼時候從法國回來的？ **2** 還，歸還 *Could you return the book I lent you?* 你能否把我借給你的書還給我？

rhinoceros /raɪ'nɒsərəs; 美 -'nɑ-/ [名詞] [複數**rhinoceroses**] 犀牛 *The rhinoceros is an African or Asian animal.* 犀牛是一種產於非洲或亞洲的動物。

rhyme /raɪm/ [動詞] 押韻 'Tail' rhymes with 'mail'. tail和mail押韻。

rhythm /'rɪðəm/ [名詞] 節奏 *People can dance to all sorts of rhythms.* 人們能伴隨着各種各樣的節奏跳舞。

ribbon /'rɪbən/ [名詞] 絲帶，緞帶 *Alice wore a red ribbon in her hair.* 艾麗斯頭髮上繫着一條紅絲帶。

ribbon
絲帶

rice /raɪs/ [名詞] [無複數] 大米；米

飯 *Would you like boiled rice or fried rice?* 你想吃煮飯還是炒飯？

rich /rɪtʃ/ [形容詞] 富有的 *She's one of the richest people in the world.* 她是世界上最富有的人之一。 ☞[反] **poor** 貧窮的

riddle /ˈrɪdl/ [名詞] 謎語 *Do you know the answer to the riddle?* 你知道謎底嗎？

ride¹ /raɪd/ [動詞][過去式**rode** /rəʊd; 美 roʊd/，過去分詞**ridden** /ˈrɪdn/] 騎（馬、自行車等）*Henry loves riding his horse.* 亨利喜歡騎馬。◇ *When did you learn to ride a bicycle?* 你甚麼時候學會騎自行車的？

ride² /raɪd/ [名詞] 騎馬；騎車 *We went for a ride on our bikes.* 我們去騎自行車了。

right¹ /raɪt/ [形容詞] 1 正確的，對的 *The right answer is 12.* 正確答案是12。☞①[同] **correct¹** 正確的，對的②[反] **wrong** 錯誤的 2 右邊的 *I write with my right hand.* 我用右手寫字。☞[反] **left²** 左邊的

right² /raɪt/ [副詞] 1 正確地 *You guessed right.* 你猜對了。2 向右 *Turn right at the next traffic lights.* 在下一個紅綠燈向右拐。☞[反] **left³** 向左

right³ /raɪt/ [名詞] 右邊 *My house is on the right of the road.* 我家在馬路的右邊。☞[反] **left⁴** 左邊

ring¹ /rɪŋ/ [名詞] 1 戒指 *She's wearing a diamond ring.* 她戴着一枚鑽戒。2 圓圈 *The children sat in a ring.* 孩子們圍坐成一圈。

ring² /rɪŋ/ [動詞][過去式**rang** /ræŋ/，過去分詞**rung** /rʌŋ/] 1（給…）打電話 *What time will you ring tomorrow?* 你明天幾點打電話？2（鈴、電話等）響 *We were just going out when the telephone rang.* 我們正準備出去，電話響了。3 按（門鈴）*He rang the bell but no one came to the door.* 他按了門鈴，但沒有人來開門。

ripe /raɪp/ [形容詞]（水果、穀物等）成熟的 *This apple is not ripe yet — you can't eat it.* 這個蘋果還沒熟，你不能吃。

rise /raɪz/ [動詞][過去式**rose** /rəʊz; 美 roʊz/，過去分詞**risen** /ˈrɪzn/] 升起 *The sun rises in the east and sets in the west.* 太陽從東方升起，在西方落下。☞[反] **set¹** 落下

risk /rɪsk/ [名詞] 危險，風險 *Don't take any risks when you go swimming.* 游泳時不要冒險。

river /ˈrɪvə; 美 -ər/ [名詞] 河，江 *The*

longest river in Asia is the Yangtze. 亞洲最長的河流是長江。

road /rəʊd; 美 roʊd / [名詞] 路，道路，公路 It's safer to cross this road by the pedestrian crossing. 過這條馬路時走人行橫道更安全。

roar /rɔː; 美 rɔːr / [動詞]（獅、虎等）吼叫，咆哮 The lion opened its huge mouth and roared. 那頭獅子張開大嘴吼叫起來。

roast /rəʊst; 美 roʊst / [形容詞] 烘烤的 Henry likes roast duck. 亨利喜歡吃烤鴨。

rob /rɒb; 美 rɑːb / [動詞] [現在分詞 **robbing**，過去式和過去分詞 **robbed**] 搶劫，盜竊 The men robbed the bank. 那幾個人搶劫了銀行。

robber /'rɒbə; 美 'rɑːbər / [名詞] 搶劫者，強盜，盜賊 The robbers were sent to prison for robbing a bank. 那幾個搶劫犯因搶劫銀行而入獄。

robot /'rəʊbɒt; 美 'roʊbɑːt / [名詞]

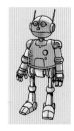

機器人 Most of the work in the factory is now done by robots. 現在工廠裏大部分工作由機器人來做。

rock¹ /rɒk; 美 rɑːk / [名詞] 大石塊 We sat on a large rock. 我們坐在一塊巨石上。

rock² /rɒk; 美 rɑːk / [動詞] 搖擺 I rocked the baby to sleep. 我把寶寶搖睡了。

rocket /'rɒkɪt; 美 'rɑːkət / [名詞] 火箭 In future we may be able to fly to the moon in a rocket. 將來我們也許能坐火箭上月球。

rode /rəʊd; 美 roʊd / **ride** 的過去式 Paul jumped on his bike and rode off. 保羅跳上自行車騎走了。

roll¹ /rəʊl; 美 roʊl / [名詞] 一卷 I only had one roll of film left. 我只剩下一卷膠卷。

roll² /rəʊl; 美 roʊl / [動詞] 滾動 The pencil rolled off the table. 那枝鉛筆從桌子上滾了下來。

roll up 捲起 Roll the paper up — don't fold it. 把紙捲起來，不要摺。

roof /ruːf / [名詞] [複數 **roofs**] 屋頂

The house has a flat roof. 這棟房子的屋頂是平的。

room /ruːm/ [名詞] 房間 *His mother opened the door and came into the room.* 他媽媽打開門進了房間。

root /ruːt/ [名詞] （植物的）根 *Plants take in water through their roots.* 植物通過根吸收水分。

rope /rəup; 美 roup/ [名詞] 繩子 *They tied up the boat with rope.* 他們用繩子把船拴好。

rose¹ /rəuz; 美 rouz/ **rise**的過去式 *The sun rose at five o'clock.* 太陽5點升起。

rose² /rəuz; 美 rouz/ [名詞] 玫瑰（花）*My father bought some red roses for my mother.* 我父親給我母親買了幾朵紅玫瑰。

rough /rʌf/ [形容詞] 1 （表面）粗糙的 *I have rough skin on my hands.* 我的手皮膚粗糙。 [反] **smooth** 平滑的，光滑的 2 粗魯的，粗野的，粗暴的 *He's a rough child.* 他是個粗野的孩子。

round¹ /raund/ [形容詞] 圓的 *CDs are round.* 鐳射唱片是圓的。 ◇ *This is a round table.* 這張桌子是圓的。

round² /raund/ [副詞] 朝另一方向（通常指反方向）*Turn your chair round.* 把你的椅子轉過來。 ◇ *You're going the wrong way — you need to turn round and go back.* 你走錯路了，應該轉身往回走。

round³ /raund/ [介詞] 圍繞，環繞 *We sat round the table.* 我們圍着桌子坐着。

row¹ /rəu; 美 rou/ [名詞] （人或物的）（一）排，（一）行 *There are six desks in each row.* 每一排有6張書桌。 ◇ *Let's sit in the back row.* 我們坐在後排吧。

row² /rəu; 美 rou/ [動詞] 划（船）*We often go rowing on the lake.* 我們常去湖裏划船。

royal /ˈrɔɪəl/ [形容詞] 國王的，女王的，王室的 *The royal family live in a palace.* 王室成員住在王宮裏。

rub /rʌb/ [動詞] [現在分詞**rubbing**，過去式和過去分詞**rubbed**] 擦；搓 *I rubbed my hands together to keep them warm.* 我來回搓着手取暖。

R

rub out（用橡皮或布）擦掉 *I rubbed the word out and wrote it again.* 我把字擦掉，又寫了一個。

rubber /ˈrʌbə; 美 -ər/ [名詞] **1** [無複數] 橡膠 *Do you know that tyres are made of rubber?* 你知道輪胎是橡膠做的嗎？ **2** 橡皮；黑板擦 *If you need a rubber, there's one in my pencil box.* 如果你需要橡皮，我的鉛筆盒裏有一塊。 ☞ **rubber (2)** 用於英國英語，美國英語通常用**eraser**。

rubbish /ˈrʌbɪʃ/ [名詞] [無複數] 垃圾，廢物 *Could you put this rubbish outside in the dustbin?* 你把這些垃圾扔進外面的垃圾箱裏好嗎？

rude /ruːd/ [形容詞] 粗魯的，無禮的 *Don't be so rude to your father.* 不要對你父親這麼無禮。

rug /rʌg/ [名詞] 小地毯 *The cat was asleep on the rug.* 貓在地毯上睡着了。

rugby /ˈrʌgbi/ [名詞] [無複數]（英式）橄欖球（運動）*Do you play rugby?* 你玩橄欖球嗎？

rugby ball
橄欖球

rugby
（英式）橄欖球

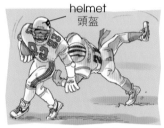

helmet
頭盔

American football
美式足球，美式橄欖球

ruin /ˈruːɪn/ [動詞] 毀壞 *The storm ruined the crops.* 暴風雨毀壞了莊稼。

rule¹ /ruːl/ [名詞] 規則 *You must always obey the school rules.* 你必須時刻遵守校規。

rule² /ruːl/ [動詞] 統治 *Queen Victoria ruled England for 64 years.* 維多利亞女王統治了英國64年。

ruler /ˈruːlə; 美 -ər/ [名詞] **1** 統治者 *The queen is the ruler of the country.* 女王是這個國家的統治者。 **2** 尺，直尺 *Do you have a ruler?* 你有尺子嗎？

run /rʌn/ [動詞] [現在分詞**running**，過去式**ran** /ræn/，過去分詞**run**] **1** 跑 *How fast can you run?* 你能跑多快？

running off the roof. 水正從屋頂上流下來。

rung /rʌŋ/ **ring**的過去分詞 *Have you rung the restaurant to book a table yet?* 你給餐館打電話訂餐桌了嗎?

rush /rʌʃ/ [動詞] 衝,奔 *She rushed to the phone.* 她衝向電話。

2 (指水、液體等) 流 *The water was*

S s

sack /sæk/ [名詞] 口袋，麻袋 *Dad bought a sack of rice.* 爸爸買了一袋大米。

sad /sæd/ [形容詞] [比較級**sadder**，最高級**saddest**] 悲哀的，傷心的，難過的 *Peter was sad because the holiday was nearly over.* 彼得覺得不開心，因為假期快結束了。☞ [反]**happy** 高興的，快樂的

saddle /'sædl/ [名詞]（馬的）鞍子；（自行車的）車座 *The man put a saddle on the horse.* 那個男人把馬鞍裝在馬背上。

saddle 鞍子 saddle 車座

safe /seɪf/ [形容詞] 安全的 *Don't sit on that chair. It isn't safe.* 不要坐那把椅子，不安全。☞ [反]**dangerous** 危險的

safely /'seɪfli/ [副詞] 安全地 *The plane landed safely.* 飛機安全着陸了。

said /sed/ **say** 的過去式和過去分詞 *He said he wanted to see you.* 他說他想見你。

sail[1] /seɪl/ [動詞]（坐船）航行 *They sail for America next week.* 他們下週坐船去美國。

sail[2] /seɪl/ [名詞] 帆 *Does that boat have sails?* 那艘船有帆嗎？

sail 帆

salad /'sæləd/ [名詞] 色拉，沙拉 *For dessert we had fruit salad and ice cream.* 我們甜食吃的是水果沙拉和冰淇淋。

sale /seɪl/ [名詞] 賣，出售 *He made a lot of money from the sale of his house.* 他賣了自己的房子，賺了不少錢。

for sale 待售 *Are these books for sale?* 這些書賣嗎？

salt /sɔːlt/ [名詞] [無複數] 鹽 *The chicken soup needs a bit more salt.* 雞湯需要再放點兒鹽。

same[1] /seɪm/ [形容詞] [與**the**連用] 相同的，同一的 *My sister and I go to the same school.* 我和妹妹上同一所學校。☞ [反]**different** 不同的

same² /seɪm/ [代詞] [與**the**連用] 同樣的事物 *Your pen is the same as mine.* 你的筆和我的一樣。

sand /sænd/ [名詞] [無複數] 沙，沙子 *The children were playing in the sand.* 孩子們正在沙灘上玩。

sandwich /'sænwɪdʒ/ [名詞] [複數 **sandwiches**] 三明治 *These sandwiches are delicious.* 這些三明治很好吃。

sang /sæŋ/ **sing** 的過去式 *They sang three songs at the concert.* 他們在音樂會上唱了 3 首歌。

sank /sæŋk/ **sink** 的過去式 *The stone sank to the bottom of the pond.* 石頭沉到了池塘底。

sat /sæt/ **sit** 的過去式和過去分詞 *Henry sat down on the floor.* 亨利在地板上坐下來。

satellite /'sætəlaɪt/ [名詞] **1** 衛星 *The moon is a satellite of the earth.* 月亮是地球的衛星。**2** 人造衛星 *Do you have satellite television?* 你有衛星電視嗎？

satisfy /'sætɪsfaɪ/ [動詞] [現在分詞

satisfying，過去式和過去分詞 **satisfied**] 使滿意 *Henry works hard because he wants to satisfy his mother.* 亨利非常用功，因為他想讓母親感到滿意。

Saturday /'sætədeɪ; 美 -ər-/ [名詞] 星期六 *It's Saturday tomorrow.* 明天是星期六。☞ ① 參見**Monday**的示例。② **Sat** 是 **Saturday** 的縮寫。

sauce /sɔːs/ [名詞] 調味汁；醬 *I like tomato sauce with my chips.* 我喜歡吃薯條蘸番茄醬。

saucer /'sɔːsə; 美 -ər/ [名詞] 茶碟 *There are three cups but only two saucers.* 有三個茶杯，但只有兩個茶碟。

sausage /'spsɪdʒ; 美 'sɔː-/ [名詞] 香腸 *I have sausages and eggs for breakfast.* 我早餐吃香腸和雞蛋。

save /seɪv/ [動詞] **1** 救，挽救 *The doctor saved his life.* 醫生救了他的命。

2 保留，留下 Save some of the cake for tomorrow. 留點蛋糕明天吃。

saw¹ /sɔː/ **see** 的過去式 I saw Henry this morning but he didn't see me. 我今天早晨看見亨利了，但他沒看見我。

saw² /sɔː/ [名詞] 鋸 He cut the wood with a saw. 他用鋸把木頭鋸開。

say /seɪ/ [動詞] [過去式和過去分詞 **said** /sed/] 說 What did he say to you? 他對你說甚麼啦？◇ He said he was going home. 他說他要回家。

scales /skeɪlz/ [名詞] [複數] 天平；磅秤 I weighed myself on the scales. 我在磅秤上稱了稱體重。

scar /skɑː; 美 skɑːr/ [名詞] 傷痕，傷疤 He has some scars on his leg. 他的腿上有幾處傷疤。

scare /skeə; 美 sker/ [動詞] 嚇，使恐懼，使害怕 That noise scared me! 那響聲把我嚇壞了！

scared /skeəd; 美 skerd/ [形容詞] 受到驚嚇的，感到害怕的 Are you scared of snakes? 你怕蛇嗎？

scarf /skɑːf; 美 skɑːrf/ [名詞] [複數 **scarfs** 或 **scarves** /skɑːvz; 美 skɑːrvz/] 圍巾，頭巾 You need a warm scarf if you visit Britain in the winter. 如果你冬天訪問英國，需要帶一條暖和的圍巾。

scatter /'skætə; 美 -ər/ [動詞] 撒；撒播 We scattered the seeds in the garden. 我們把種子撒在園子裏。

school /skuːl/ [名詞] 學校 Which school does your sister go to? 你妹妹上哪所學校？

science /'saɪəns/ [名詞] [無複數] 科學；理科 Henry is good at science. 亨利擅長科學。

scientist /'saɪəntɪst; 美 -əst/ [名詞] 科學家 Newton was one of the greatest scientists in the world. 牛頓是世界上最偉大的科學家之一。

scissors /'sɪzəz; 美 -ərz/ [名詞] [複數] 剪刀 Be careful with these scissors — they're very sharp. 小心這把剪刀，很鋒利。

scold /skəʊld; 美 skoʊld/ [動詞] 責罵，訓斥 Don't scold the child. It's not *his fault.* 不要訓斥孩子，這不是他的錯。

score[1] /skɔ:; 美 skɔ:r/ [名詞] 分數；比分 *What's your score?* 你得了多少分？

score[2] /skɔ:; 美 skɔ:r/ [動詞] 得（分） *Each correct answer scores five points.* 每個正確答案得5分。◇ *Henry scored the highest marks in the exam.* 亨利在這次考試中得了最高分。

scrape /skreɪp/ [動詞] **1** 刮掉，擦掉 *Scrape all the mud off your shoes before you come in.* 把你鞋子上的泥都刮掉然後再進來。 **2** 擦傷，刮壞 *Henry fell and scraped his knee.* 亨利摔了一跤，擦傷了膝蓋。

scratch /skrætʃ/ [動詞] **1** 抓傷，划破 *The cat scratched me!* 貓把我抓傷了！**2** 撓，搔 *Could you scratch my back for me?* 你給我撓撓背行嗎？

scream /skri:m/ [動詞] 尖叫 *Peter screamed when he saw the rat.* 彼得看見那隻老鼠時尖叫了起來。

screen /skri:n/ [名詞]（電視、電腦等的）屏幕；熒光屏 *Henry pressed the wrong key and the screen went blank.* 亨利按錯了鍵，屏幕變成一片空白。

screen
屏幕

screw /skru:/ [名詞] 螺絲（釘） *This screw is loose.* 這個螺絲鬆了。

scrub /skrʌb/ [動詞] [現在分詞 **scrubbing**，過去式和過去分詞 **scrubbed**] 擦洗 *Mum scrubbed the floor.* 媽媽擦洗了地板。

sea /si:/ [名詞] [無複數，常與**the**連用] 海，海洋 *Let's go for a swim in the sea.* 我們去海裏游泳吧。

seafood /'si:fu:d/ [名詞] [無複數] 海味，海鮮 *You can eat seafood in this restaurant.* 你可以在這家餐館吃海鮮。

seagull /'si:gʌl/ [名詞] 海鷗 *There are lots of seagulls near the fishing boats.* 漁船附近聚集了許多海鷗。

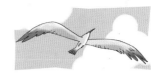

seal[1] /si:l/ [名詞] 海豹 *I saw some seals at the zoo.* 我在動物園裏看見了幾隻海豹。

seal[2] /si:l/ [動詞] 封 *Henry sealed the envelope.* 亨利把信封封上了。

S

search /sɜːtʃ; 美 sɜːrtʃ/ [動詞] 尋找，搜尋 *They are still searching for the missing child.* 他們仍在尋找那個失蹤的孩子。

seaside /'siːsaɪd/ [名詞] [用作單數，常與 **the** 連用] 海邊，海濱 *Let's go to the seaside.* 我們去海邊吧。

season /'siːzn/ [名詞] 季 (節) *Summer is the hottest season.* 夏天是最熱的季節。

seat /siːt/ [名詞] 座位 *The teacher told us all to go back to our seats.* 老師讓我們都回到自己的座位上。

second¹ /'sekənd/ [數詞] 第二 *Tuesday is the second day of the week.* 星期二是一個星期的第二天。◇ *I came second in the race.* 我在賽跑中得了第二名。

second² /'sekənd/ [名詞] **1** 秒 *There are 60 seconds in one minute.* 1 分鐘有 60 秒。**2** 一會；片刻 *Wait a second!* 等一會！

secret¹ /'siːkrət/ [名詞] 祕密 *You mustn't tell anyone — it's a secret.* 你不要告訴任何人，這是一個祕密。◇

Can you keep a secret? 你能保密嗎？

secret² /'siːkrət/ [形容詞] 祕密的 *They made a secret plan.* 他們制訂了一個祕密計劃。

see /siː/ [動詞] [過去式 **saw** /sɔː/，過去分詞 **seen** /siːn/] **1** 看見，看到 *It's too dark in here — I can't see anything.* 這裏太暗，我甚麼也看不見。**2** 觀看 (電影等) *What film shall we go and see?* 我們去看甚麼電影？**3** 理解，領會 *Do you see what I mean?* 你懂我的意思嗎？**4** 會見；看望 *You should go and see a doctor.* 你應該去看醫生。

seed /siːd/ [名詞] 種 (子)；籽 *Where did you plant the seeds?* 你把種子種在哪裏了？

seem /siːm/ [動詞] 似乎，好像 *She seems tired.* 她好像累了。◇ *He seems a nice man.* 他像是個不錯的人。

seen /siːn/ **see** 的過去分詞 *Have you seen Alice this morning?* 你今天上午看見艾麗斯了嗎？

seesaw /'siːsɔː/ [名詞] 蹺蹺板 *The children were playing on the seesaw.* 孩子們正在玩蹺蹺板。

seldom /'seldəm/ [副詞] 不常，很

少 *He seldom goes out.* 他很少出去。

selfish /'selfɪʃ/ [形容詞] 自私的 *Mark is a selfish boy and won't let anyone play with his computer games.* 馬克是個自私的男孩，他不讓任何人玩他的電腦遊戲。

sell /sel/ [動詞] [過去式和過去分詞 **sold** /səʊld; 美 soʊld/] 賣 *Does that shop sell ice cream?* 那個商店賣冰淇淋嗎？ ▷ [反] **buy** 買

send /send/ [動詞] [過去式和過去分詞 **sent** /sent/] 發送；寄 *Do you know how to send emails?* 你會發電子郵件嗎？ ◇ *Don't forget to send me a postcard.* 別忘了給我寄一張明信片。

sense /sens/ [名詞] **1** 感官；官能(指視覺、聽覺、嗅覺、味覺和觸覺) *Dogs have a good sense of smell.* 狗的嗅覺很靈敏。**2** 意思；意義 *This word has four senses.* 這個詞有四個意思。

sensible /'sensəbl/ [形容詞] 明智的；合理的 *It's sensible to stay at home when you have a bad cold.* 得了重感冒待在家裏是明智的。

sent /sent/ **send** 的過去式和過去分詞 *I sent Peter a postcard.* 我給彼得寄了一張明信片。

sentence /'sentəns/ [名詞] 句子 *A sentence should end with a full stop, a question mark or an exclamation mark.* 句子應該用句號、問號或感歎號結尾。

separate¹ /'sepərət/ [形容詞] 分開

的 *Cut the cake into six separate pieces.* 把蛋糕切成 6 塊。

separate² /'sepəreɪt/ [動詞] 把…分開 *The teacher separated the pupils into three groups.* 老師把學生分成了三組。

September /sep'tembə; 美 -ər/ [名詞] 九月 *She was born in September.* 她是 9 月出生的。 ▷ ① 參見 **August** 的示例。② **Sep** 是 **September** 的縮寫。

series /'sɪəriːz; 美 'sɪr-/ [名詞] [複數 **series**] 連續，系列 *Have you been watching the series about dinosaurs?* 你一直在看恐龍系列片嗎？

serious /'sɪəriəs; 美 'sɪr-/ [形容詞] **1** 嚴重的 *Pollution is a very serious problem.* 污染是一個非常嚴重的問題。**2** 嚴肅的；認真的 *John is a serious child.* 約翰是個嚴肅的孩子。

serve /sɜːv; 美 sɜːrv/ [動詞] **1** (為…)服務；(為…)服役 *He served in the army for ten years.* 他在軍隊服了 10 年役。 **2** 為…端上(或擺出)食物(或飲料等)；端上，擺出(食物或飲料等) *I'm going to serve the soup now.* 我現在就把湯端上來。

set¹ /set/ [動詞] [現在分詞 **setting**，

S

過去式和過去分詞 **set**] **1** 放 *She set the flowers on the table.* 她把花放在桌子上。 **2**（日、月等）落下 *The sun sets early in winter.* 冬天日落早。 ☞ [反] **rise** 升起

set² /set/ [名詞] **1**（一）套；（一）組 *I have a set of American stamps.* 我有一套美國郵票。**2** 電視機；收音機 *They have two television sets in the house.* 他們家裏有兩台電視機。

seven /'sevn/ [數詞] 七 *Three and four are seven.* 3 加 4 等於 7。 ☞ 參見 **five** 的示例。

seventeen /ˌsevn'ti:n/ [數詞] 十七 *Ten and seven make seventeen.* 10 加 7 等於 17。 ☞ 參見 **five** 的示例。

seventh /'sevnθ/ [數詞] 第七 *Today is the seventh of July.* 今天是 7 月 7 日。 ☞ 參見 **fifth** 的示例。

seventy /'sevnti/ [數詞] 七十 *Ten times seven is seventy.* 10 乘 7 得 70。 ☞ 參見 **fifty** 的示例。

several /'sevrəl/ [形容詞] 幾個的，數個的 *Several pupils got full marks in the exam.* 有幾個學生在這次考試中得了滿分。

sew /səʊ; 美 soʊ/ [動詞] [過去式

sewed，過去分詞 **sewn** /səʊn; 美 soʊn/ 或 **sewed**] 縫，縫製，縫補 *Granny has sewn some clothes for my doll.* 奶奶給我的洋娃娃縫了幾件衣服。

shade /ʃeɪd/ [名詞] [無複數] 蔭；陰涼處 *Let's sit in the shade and keep cool.* 我們坐在陰涼處乘乘涼吧。

shadow /'ʃædəʊ; 美 -oʊ/ [名詞] 陰影；影子 *The dog is chasing its own shadow.* 狗在追自己的影子。

shadow
影子

shake /ʃeɪk/ [動詞] [過去式 **shook** /ʃʊk/，過去分詞 **shaken** /'ʃeɪkən/] 搖，搖動 *Shake the bottle before you open it.* 把瓶子搖一搖再打開。
shake hands (with sb)（與某人）握手 [表示問候或道別等] *The two men shook hands.* 那兩個男人握了握手。
shake your head 搖頭 [表示不同意] *'Are you coming?' I asked. Paul shook his head.* "你來嗎?"我問道。保羅搖了搖頭。

shall /強 ʃæl; 弱 ʃəl/ [情態動詞] **1** [舊

式用法] 將要，會 *This time next week I shall be in London.* 下個星期的這個時候我就在倫敦了。 **2** [表示提議或建議等] ⋯好嗎？ *Shall I help you carry that box?* 我幫你提那個箱子好嗎？

shallow /ˈʃæləʊ; 美 -oʊ/ [形容詞] 淺的 *The sea is shallow here.* 這裏的海水淺。 ☞ [反] **deep** 深的

shampoo /ʃæmˈpuː/ [名詞] 洗髮劑，洗髮液，洗髮膏 *I wash my hair with shampoo.* 我用洗髮膏洗頭。

shape /ʃeɪp/ [名詞] 形狀 *What shape is an orange, round or oval?* 橙子是甚麼形狀的，圓的還是橢圓的？

shapes 形狀

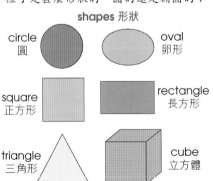

circle
圓

oval
卵形

square
正方形

rectangle
長方形

triangle
三角形

cube
立方體

share /ʃeə; 美 ʃer/ [動詞] **1** 均分；分享 *We shared the cake between us.* 我們倆人把蛋糕分了。 **2** 共有；共用 *The twins share a bedroom.* 這對雙胞胎共用一間臥室。

shark /ʃɑːk; 美 ʃɑːrk/ [名詞] 鯊魚 *Most sharks live in the sea, but some sharks live in rivers, too.* 大多數鯊魚生活在海裏，但也有一些鯊魚生活在河裏。

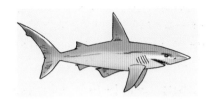

sharp /ʃɑːp; 美 ʃɑːrp/ [形容詞] 鋒利的，銳利的；尖的 *Be careful, Peter—that knife's very sharp.* 小心，彼得——那把刀很鋒利。◇ *I need a ruler and a sharp pencil.* 我需要一把尺子和一枝削尖的鉛筆。 ☞ [反] **blunt** 鈍的

sharpen /ˈʃɑːpən; 美 ˈʃɑːr-/ [動詞] (把⋯) 削尖 *Helen helped me to sharpen all my pencils.* 海倫幫我把所有的鉛筆都削尖了。

sharpener /ˈʃɑːpnə; 美 ˈʃɑːrpnər/ [名詞] 鉛筆刀 *I can't find my pencil sharpener.* 我找不着我的鉛筆刀了。

shave /ʃeɪv/ [動詞] 剃鬚；刮鬍子；刮臉 *My dad shaves every morning.* 我爸爸每天早晨都刮鬍子。

she / 強 ʃiː; 弱 ʃi / [代詞] [主格] 她 *Who does she look like?* 她長得像誰？

sheep / ʃiːp / [名詞] [複數**sheep**] 綿羊 *There was a sheep in the field.* 地裏有一隻綿羊。

sheet / ʃiːt / [名詞] **1** 被單，牀單 *I change the sheets on my bed every week.* 我每週都換牀單。 **2** 一張（紙）*Give me a sheet of paper, please.* 請給我一張紙。

shelf / ʃelf / [名詞] [複數**shelves** / ʃelvz /]（牆上的）架子 *He took a cup from the shelf.* 他從架子上取下一個杯子。

shell / ʃel / [名詞] 殼；貝殼 *Where shall I put the empty shells?* 這些空殼放哪裏？◇ *The crab has a hard shell.* 螃蟹長有硬殼。

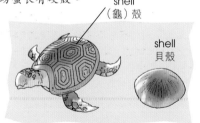

shell
（龜）殼

shell
貝殼

she'll / 強 ʃiːl; 弱 ʃil / **she will** 的縮寫 *She'll be back in a minute.* 她馬上就回來。

shelter / 'ʃeltə; 美 -ər / [名詞] 隱蔽處，躲避處，避難所 *He waited in the bus shelter for the next bus.* 他在候車亭裏等下一班公共汽車。

she's / 強 ʃiːz; 弱 ʃiz / **1 she is** 的縮寫 *She's very tall.* 她個子很高。 **2 she has** 的縮寫 *She's got a new car.* 她有一輛新車。

shine / ʃaɪn / [動詞] [過去式和過去分詞 **shone** / ʃɒn; 美 ʃoʊn /] 照耀；發光 *The sun is shining today.* 今天陽光燦爛。

ship / ʃɪp / [名詞] 船，輪船 *Do you love travelling by ship?* 你喜歡坐船旅行嗎？

shirt / ʃɜːt; 美 ʃɜːrt / [名詞]（男式）襯衫 *Remember to put on a clean shirt.* 別忘了穿上一件乾淨襯衫。

shiver / 'ʃɪvə; 美 -ər / [動詞] 顫抖，哆嗦 *The cold wind made us shiver.* 寒風凍得我們直打哆嗦。

shoe /ʃuː/ [名詞] 鞋 *What size are your shoes?* 你的鞋是多大號的？◇ *Where's my other shoe?* 我的另一隻鞋在哪裏？

shone /ʃɒn; 美 ʃoʊn/ **shine** 的過去式和過去分詞 *The sea shone in the light of the moon.* 大海在月光下閃閃發光。

shook /ʃʊk/ **shake** 的過去式和過去分詞 *When they met, the two men shook hands.* 那兩名男子見面時握了握手。

shoot /ʃuːt/ [動詞] [過去式和過去分詞 **shot** /ʃɒt; 美 ʃɑːt/] 1 開(槍)；射(箭) *Don't shoot!* 不要開槍！◇ *He shot an arrow at the target, but missed it.* 他朝靶子射了一箭，但沒射中。

2 用槍射擊 *The policeman was shot in the arm.* 警察的胳膊中了一槍。 3 射門；投籃 *Henry shot and scored.* 亨利射門得分。

shop /ʃɒp; 美 ʃɑːp/ [名詞] 商店；店鋪 *Please go to the shop and buy some milk.* 請到商店裏買些牛奶。
☞ 英國英語用 **shop**，美國英語用 **store**。

shopping /ˈʃɒpɪŋ; 美 ˈʃɑː-/ [名詞] [無複數] 1 買東西，購物 *We usually go shopping on Saturday afternoon.* 我們通常星期六下午去購物。 2 買的東西 *Put the shopping on the table.* 把買的東西放在桌子上。

shore /ʃɔː; 美 ʃɔːr/ [名詞] (海、河、湖的)岸，濱 *We searched along the sea shore for shells.* 我們沿着海岸尋找貝殼。

short /ʃɔːt; 美 ʃɔːrt/ [形容詞] 1 短的 *The film was quite short. It was over in less than an hour.* 那部電影相當短，不到一小時就結束了。 ☞ [反] **long** 長的 2 矮的 *Peter is a lot shorter than you.* 彼得比你矮多了。 ☞ [反] **tall** 高的

shorts /ʃɔːts; 美 ʃɔːrts/ [名詞] [複數] 短褲 *She was wearing a red T-shirt and a pair of white shorts.* 她穿着一件紅 T 恤衫和一條白短褲。

shorts
短褲

shot /ʃɒt; 美 ʃɑːt/ **shoot** 的過去式和過去分詞 *He was shot in the back.*

S

他的背中了一槍。

should /強 ʃʊd; 弱 ʃəd/ [情態動詞] 應該 *You should finish your homework before you go out and play.* 你應該做完作業再出去玩。

shoulder /'ʃəʊldə; 美 'ʃoʊldər/ [名詞] 肩,肩膀 *He carried the child on his shoulders.* 他把孩子馱在肩上。

shout /ʃaʊt/ [動詞] 喊,喊叫,大叫 *I can hear you — there's no need to shout.* 我能聽見你,沒必要喊叫。

show¹ /ʃəʊ; 美 ʃoʊ/ [動詞] [過去式 **showed**,過去分詞 **shown** /ʃəʊn; 美 ʃoʊn/ 或 **showed**] **1** 給…看,出示,展示 *Show me the picture you drew.* 給我看看你畫的畫。**2** 示範,解釋,說明 *Can you show me how to use your camera?* 你能給我示範一下怎樣使用你的相機嗎?

show² /ʃəʊ; 美 ʃoʊ/ [名詞] 演出;表演;節目 *What television shows do you usually watch?* 你通常看甚麼電視節目?

shower /'ʃaʊə; 美 'ʃaʊr/ [名詞] **1** (淋浴用的)噴頭,淋浴器 *Press this button to turn the shower on.* 按這個按鈕把噴頭打開。◇ *Is there anybody in the shower?* 有人在洗淋浴嗎?**2** 淋浴 *He's having a shower.* 他在洗淋浴。

3 陣雨 *We may have some showers today.* 今天可能有陣雨。

shown /ʃəʊn; 美 ʃoʊn/ **show** 的過去分詞 *Have you shown her the photos?* 你給她看過這些照片嗎?

shrink /ʃrɪŋk/ [動詞] [過去式 **shrank** /ʃræŋk/ 或 **shrunk** /ʃrʌŋk/,過去分詞 **shrunk**] 收縮,縮水 *Henry's T-shirt shrank when he washed it.* 亨利的 T 恤衫一洗就縮水了。

shut /ʃʌt/ [動詞] [現在分詞 **shutting**,過去式和過去分詞 **shut**] **1** 關上;閉上;合上 *Can you shut the door, please?* 請把門關上好嗎?◇ *Shut your books, please.* 請把書本合上。☞ ① [同] **close¹** 關上;閉上;合上 ② [反] **open²** 開;打開;張開;睜開 **2** 關門;停止營業 *The shops shut at six o'clock today.* 商店今天6點關門。☞ ① [同] **close¹** 關門;停止營業 ② [反] **open²** 開門;營業

shy /ʃaɪ/ [形容詞] 害羞的,腼腆的 *The child was shy and hid behind his mother.* 這孩子害羞,躲在了母親身後。

sick /sɪk/ [形容詞] 生病的 *Her mother's very sick.* 她母親病得很重。☞ 參見 **ill** "生病的"。

feel sick 噁心的,作嘔的 *I felt sick*

when the ship started to move. 輪船一開，我就覺得要嘔吐了。

side /saɪd/ [名詞] **1** （物體的）面 *A cube has six sides.* 立方體有6個面。 **2** 邊 *Henry is sitting at my right side and Peter is on my left side.* 亨利坐在我的右邊，彼得坐在我的左邊。 **3** （比賽的）隊 *My side won again!* 我們隊又贏了！

sidewalk /'saɪdwɔːk/ [名詞] [美國英語] = **pavement**

sigh /saɪ/ [動詞] 歎息，歎氣 *'I'll wait,' he said with a sigh.* "我等，"他歎了口氣説。

sight /saɪt/ [名詞] **1** [無複數] 視力；視覺 *She has very good sight.* 她的視力很好。 ◇ *He lost his sight in a car accident.* 他在一次車禍中失明了。 **2** [用作複數] 名勝；風景 *We're going to Paris for the weekend to see the sights.* 我們打算週末去巴黎觀光。

sign[1] /saɪn/ [名詞] 標誌；標記；指示牌 *The sign said 'No Smoking'.* 指示牌上寫着"禁止吸煙"。

sign[2] /saɪn/ [動詞] 簽（名）；簽（字）；在…上簽名（或簽字） *Sign here, please.* 請在這裏簽字。 ◇ *Sign your name here, please.* 請在這裏簽名。 ◇ *Have you signed the letter?* 你在信上簽字了嗎？

signal /'sɪɡnəl/ [名詞] 信號 *Don't start until I give the signal.* 等我發出信號再開始。

silent /'saɪlənt/ [形容詞] **1** 沉默的 *Henry was silent for a moment.* 亨利沉默了片刻。 **2** 無聲的，寂靜的 *The streets were silent at night.* 夜裏街道上一片寂靜。

silk /sɪlk/ [名詞] [無複數] 絲；絲綢 *Is your scarf made of silk?* 你的圍巾是絲的嗎？

silly /'sɪli/ [形容詞] [比較級 **sillier**，最高級 **silliest**] 愚蠢的；傻的 *What a silly question!* 多麼傻的問題！ ◇ *Don't be so silly!* 別這麼傻了！

silver /'sɪlvə; 美 -ər/ [名詞] [無複數] 銀 *Is your chain silver?* 你的項鏈是銀的嗎？ ◇ *Her ring is made of silver.* 她的戒指是銀的。

similar /'sɪmələ; 美 -ər/ [形容詞] 相似的，類似的 *Our dresses are similar.* 我們的連衣裙很相似。 ◇ *His interests are similar to mine.* 他的興趣和我的相似。

simple /'sɪmpl/ [形容詞] 簡單的 *It's a simple question — do you want to come or not?* 這個問題很簡單，你想來還是不想來？

S

since /sɪns/ [介詞] 自從…以來 *He has lived in London since 2000.* 他自2000年以來就住在倫敦。

sing /sɪŋ/ [動詞] [過去式 **sang** /sæŋ/, 過去分詞 **sung** /sʌŋ/] 唱；唱歌 *Alice likes to sing and dance.* 艾麗斯喜歡唱歌跳舞。◇ *She's going to sing a song at the school concert.* 她要在學校音樂會上唱一首歌。

singer /'sɪŋə; 美 -ər/ [名詞] 歌唱家，歌手 *Who's your favourite singer?* 你最喜愛的歌手是誰?

single /'sɪŋgl/ [形容詞] **1** [只用於名詞前] 單一的，單個的 *She didn't say a single word.* 她一句話都沒說。**2** 單人的 *I sleep in a single bed.* 我睡單人牀。**3** 單身的，獨身的 *Are you married or single?* 你是已婚還是單身? **4** 單程的 *How much is a single ticket to London, please?* 請問, 到倫敦的單程票多少錢一張?

sink¹ /sɪŋk/ [動詞] [過去式 **sank** /sæŋk/, 過去分詞 **sunk** /sʌŋk/] 下沉, 沉沒 *The ship is sinking.* 船在下沉。

sink² /sɪŋk/ [名詞] (厨房的) 洗滌槽 *Put the dishes in the sink.* 把碟子放在洗滌槽裏。

sink
洗滌槽

sip /sɪp/ [動詞] [現在分詞 **sipping**, 過去式和過去分詞 **sipped**] 小口地喝；抿 *He sipped the hot tea.* 他抿着熱茶。

sir / 強 sɜː; 美 sɜːr; 弱 sə; 美 sər/ [名詞] [用作單數] [對男士的尊稱] 先生；[英國小學生對男教師的稱呼] 老師 *'Good morning, children.' 'Good morning, sir.'* "同學們, 早上好。""老師, 早上好。"

sister /'sɪstə; 美 -ər/ [名詞] 姐；妹 *I've got one brother and two sisters.* 我有一個弟弟兩個妹妹。

sit /sɪt/ [動詞] [現在分詞 **sitting**, 過去式和過去分詞 **sat** /sæt/] 坐 *Come and sit next to me.* 來坐在我旁邊。
sit down 坐下 *Would you like to sit down?* 你坐下好嗎?

six /sɪks/ [數詞] 六 *Three and three make six.* 3加3等於6。☞ 參見 **five** 的示例。

sixteen /ˌsɪks'tiːn/ [數詞] 十六 *Ten and six make sixteen.* 10加6等於16。☞ 參見 **five** 的示例。

sixth /sɪksθ/ [數詞] 第六 *Today is the sixth of May.* 今天是5月6日。☞ 參見 **fifth** 的示例。

sixty /'sɪksti/ [數詞] 六十 *Ten times six is sixty.* 10乘6得60。☞ 參見 **fifty** 的示例。

S

size /saɪz/ [名詞] **1** 大小；尺寸 *His room is the same size as mine.* 他的房間跟我的一樣大。**2** (服裝、鞋等)號，碼 *'What size shoes do you take?' 'Size 36.'* "你穿多大號的鞋？" "36 號。"

skate¹ /skeɪt/ [名詞] 滑冰鞋 *Do you have skates?* 你有滑冰鞋嗎？

skate² /skeɪt/ [動詞] 滑冰，溜冰 *Can you skate?* 你會滑冰嗎？

skate
滑冰鞋

skeleton /'skelɪtn/ [名詞] (人體或動物的) 骨骼，骨架 *The human skeleton consists of 206 bones.* 人體骨骼由 206 塊骨頭組成。

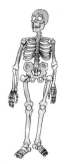

sketch /sketʃ/ [動詞] 畫…的素描，畫…的速寫 *I sketched the house.* 我畫了一幅那棟房子的素描。

ski¹ /skiː/ [名詞] 滑雪板 *She put on her skis.* 她穿上滑雪板。

ski² /skiː/ [動詞] [現在分詞 **skiing**，過去式和過去分詞 **skied**] 滑雪 *How well do you ski?* 你滑雪滑得怎麼樣？

skid /skɪd/ [動詞] [現在分詞 **skidding**，過去式和過去分詞 **skidded**] 打滑 *The car skidded on the ice.* 汽車在冰上打滑。

skill /skɪl/ [名詞] 技能；技巧；技術 *Listening, speaking, reading and writing are four different skills.* 聽、說、讀、寫是四種不同的技能。

skin /skɪn/ [名詞] **1** (人或動物的) 皮；皮膚 *She has pale skin.* 她皮膚白皙。**2** (水果或蔬菜的) 皮 *Peter slipped on a banana skin.* 彼得踩在香蕉皮上滑倒了。

skip /skɪp/ [動詞] [現在分詞 **skipping**，過去式和過去分詞 **skipped**] **1** 蹦蹦跳跳地走 *A little girl came skipping along the road.* 一個小女孩沿着馬路蹦蹦跳跳地走來。**2** 跳繩 *The girls were skipping in the playground.* 女孩子們正在操場上跳繩。☞ 在美國英語中，說 "跳繩" 用 **jump rope**。

skirt /skɜːt; 美 skɜːrt/ [名詞] 裙子 *She wore a white blouse and a blue skirt.* 她穿着白襯衫藍裙子。

sky /skaɪ/ [名詞] [複數 **skies**，通常用作單數] 天；天空 *There wasn't a cloud in the sky.* 天上沒有雲彩。

slap /slæp/ [動詞] [現在分詞 **slapping**，過去式和過去分詞 **slapped**] 用巴掌打，拍打 *He slapped me in the face.* 他打了我一個耳光。

sleep[1] /sliːp/ [動詞] [過去式和過去分詞 **slept** /slept/] 睡；睡覺 *Did you sleep well?* 你睡得好嗎？◇ *The baby's sleeping.* 寶寶在睡覺。

sleep[2] /sliːp/ [名詞] 睡覺，睡眠 *Did you have a good sleep?* 你睡得好嗎？ **go to sleep** 入睡 *Henry went to sleep when he closed his eyes.* 亨利一閉上眼睛就睡着了。

sleepy /ˈsliːpi/ [形容詞] 睏倦的；欲睡的 *You look sleepy — it's time for bed.* 你好像睏了，該上牀睡覺了。

sleeve /sliːv/ [名詞] 袖子 *Dad's wearing a shirt with short sleeves.* 爸爸穿着一件短袖襯衫。

slept /slept/ **sleep** 的過去式和過去分詞 *Have you ever slept in a tent?* 你在帳篷裏睡過嗎？

slice /slaɪs/ [名詞] 一片（食物） *Cut the bread in thin slices.* 把麵包切成薄片。

slide[1] /slaɪd/ [動詞] [過去式和過去分詞 **slid** /slɪd/] （使）滑動 *The children were sliding on the ice.* 孩子們正在冰上滑。

slide[2] /slaɪd/ [名詞] 滑梯 *My dad has put up a small slide in our garden.* 我爸爸在我們家的花園裏搭建了一個小滑梯。

slim /slɪm/ [形容詞] 苗條的，細長的 *Our English teacher is tall and slim.* 我們英語老師身材高挑。

slip /slɪp/ [動詞] [現在分詞 **slipping**，

過去式和過去分詞 **slipped**] 滑；滑倒 I slipped and fell downstairs. 我滑了一跤，從樓梯上摔了下來。

slipper /'slɪpə; 美 -ər/ [名詞] 拖鞋，便鞋 Where are my slippers? 我的拖鞋在哪裏？

slippery /'slɪpəri/ [形容詞] （指表面或物體）滑的，滑溜的 Be careful — the floor is very slippery. 小心，地板很滑。

slope /sləup; 美 sloup/ [名詞] 斜坡 This slope is too steep. 這個斜坡太陡了。

slope 斜坡   slope 斜坡

slot /slɒt; 美 slɑːt/ [名詞] （機器或工具上的）狹長口；投幣口；投信口 Put

slot 投幣口

the coins in this slot. 把硬幣放入這個投幣口。

slow /sləu; 美 slou/ [形容詞] 1 慢的 Trains are slower than planes. 火車比飛機慢。 ☞ [反] **fast¹**快的 2 [用於名詞後] （鐘錶）走得慢的 My watch is five minutes slow. 我的錶慢了 5 分鐘。 ☞ [反] **fast¹**（鐘錶）走得快的

slowly /'sləuli; 美 'slouli/ [副詞] 慢 He speaks very slowly. 他說話很慢。 ☞ [反] **fast²**快

small /smɔːl/ [形容詞] 小的 Our house is quite small. 我們的房子很小。 ◇ Would you like a small apple or a big one? 你想吃個小蘋果還是大蘋果？ ☞ [反] **big**, **large** 大的

smash /smæʃ/ [動詞] 打碎 I dropped the cup and it smashed. 我把杯子掉在地上摔碎了。

smell¹ /smel/ [動詞] [過去式和過去分詞 **smelt** /smelt/ 或 **smelled**] 1 聞到，嗅出 Come and smell these flowers. 來聞聞這些花。 2 有…的氣味，發出…的氣味 This fish smells bad. 這條魚有臭味了。◇ The flowers smell sweet. 這些花聞起來很香。

smell² /smel/ [名詞] 氣味 I hate the smell of cigarettes. 我討厭煙味。

S

smile /smaɪl/ [動詞] 微笑 *Alice is always smiling.* 艾麗斯總是在微笑。

smoke¹ /sməʊk; 美 smoʊk/ [名詞] [無複數] 煙 *The kitchen was full of smoke.* 廚房裏到處都是煙。

smoke² /sməʊk; 美 smoʊk/ [動詞] 抽煙 *Do you smoke?* 你吸煙嗎？◇ *Smoking is bad for your health.* 吸煙有害健康。

smooth /smuːð/ [形容詞] 平滑的，光滑的 *Your skin feels so smooth.* 你的皮膚摸起來真光滑。 ☞ [反] **rough** 粗糙的

snack /snæk/ [名詞] 小吃；快餐 *I had a snack on the train.* 我在火車上吃了點小吃。

snail /sneɪl/ [名詞] 蝸牛 *Snails move very slowly.* 蝸牛爬得很慢。

snake /sneɪk/ [名詞] 蛇 *Some snakes are poisonous.* 有些蛇有毒。

snap /snæp/ [動詞] [現在分詞 **snapping**，過去式和過去分詞 **snapped**] 啪的一聲折斷 *Suddenly, the rope snapped.* 突然繩子啪的一聲斷了。

snatch /snætʃ/ [動詞] 搶；攫取；奪取 *He snatched the book from my hands.* 他從我手裏把書搶走了。

sneeze /sniːz/ [動詞] 打噴嚏 *I've been sneezing all morning.* 我整個早晨都在打噴嚏。

sniff /snɪf/ [動詞] 聞，嗅 *I sniffed the milk to see if it was fresh.* 我聞了聞牛奶看是否新鮮。

snore /snɔː; 美 snɔːr/ [動詞] 打鼾，打呼嚕 *Dad sometimes snores when he falls asleep.* 爸爸睡着了有時打呼嚕。

snow¹ /snəʊ; 美 snoʊ/ [名詞] [無複數] 雪 *The ground was covered with snow.* 地上積滿了雪。

snow² /snəʊ; 美 snoʊ / [動詞] 下雪
Look, it's snowing! 瞧，下雪了！

so¹ /səʊ; 美 soʊ / [副詞] **1** 這麼，那麼，如此 *Why is Peter so angry?* 彼得為甚麼這麼生氣？ **2** 非常，很 *Thank you so much for the flowers.* 非常感謝你的花。**3** 也 'I like English.' 'So do I.' "我喜歡英語。""我也喜歡。"

so² /səʊ; 美 soʊ / [連詞] 因此，所以 *We missed the bus so we had to walk home.* 我們沒趕上公共汽車，所以不得不走回家。

soak /səʊk; 美 soʊk / [動詞] 浸濕，浸透 *Your shirt is soaking.* 你的襯衫浸濕了。

soap /səʊp; 美 soʊp / [名詞] [無複數] 肥皂 *There's a new bar of soap in the bathroom.* 浴室裏有一塊新肥皂。

sock /sɒk; 美 sɑːk / [名詞] 短襪 *Where are my socks?* 我的襪子在哪裏？

sofa /'səʊfə; 美 'soʊ- / [名詞] (長) 沙發 *Alice was sitting on the sofa watching television.* 艾麗斯正坐在沙發上看電視。

soft /sɒft; 美 sɔːft / [形容詞] **1** 軟的，柔軟的 *This pillow is soft.* 這個枕頭很軟。

☞ [反] **hard¹** 硬的，堅硬的 **2** (聲音) 低沉的，輕柔的 '*I'm sorry,' she said in a soft voice.* "對不起，"她輕聲説。

soil /sɔɪl / [名詞] [無複數] 土壤，泥土 *Dad put some soil in a flower pot.* 爸爸把一些泥土放進花盆裏。

sold /səʊld; 美 soʊld / **sell** 的過去式和過去分詞 *He sold his old car and bought a new one.* 他把舊車賣掉，買了一輛新的。

soldier /'səʊldʒə; 美 'soʊldʒər / [名詞] 士兵；軍人 *My brother is a soldier.* 我哥哥是一個軍人。

solid /'sɒlɪd; 美 'sɑːləd / [形容詞] **1** 固體的 *Water becomes solid when it freezes.* 水冰凍時凝結成固體。**2** 實心的 *Henry is playing with a solid rubber ball.* 亨利在玩一個實心橡皮球。

some¹ / 強 sʌm; 弱 səm / [形容詞] [用於不可數名詞或複數可數名詞前] 一些；若干 *Would you like some water?* 你想喝水嗎？ ◇ *Some birds cannot fly.* 有些鳥不會飛。 ☞ 參見 **any** "一些"。

some² / 強 sʌm; 弱 səm / [代詞] 一些；若干 *Some of the pupils go home* *for lunch.* 有些學生回家吃午飯。

somebody /ˈsʌmbədi/ [代詞] 某人；有人 *There's somebody at the door.* 門口有人。 ☞ **= someone**

someone /ˈsʌmwʌn/ [又作 **somebody**] [代詞] 某人；有人 *Someone has broken the window.* 有人把窗户打破了。

something /ˈsʌmθɪŋ/ [代詞] 某事；某物 *Would you like something to eat?* 你想吃東西嗎？

sometimes /ˈsʌmtaɪmz/ [副詞] 有時 *Sometimes after school I go to a friend's house.* 有時放學後我去朋友家。

somewhere /ˈsʌmweə; 美 -wer/ [副詞] 在某處；到某處 `Where's the football?' `It's somewhere in the garden.'* "足球在哪裏？""在花園的某個地方。"

son /sʌn/ [名詞] 兒子 *They have two sons and a daughter.* 他們有兩個兒子一個女兒。

song /sɒŋ; 美 sɔːŋ/ [名詞] 歌（曲）*We learnt a new song in the music lesson today.* 我們今天在音樂課上學了一首新歌。

soon /suːn/ [副詞] 不久 *Wait here for me. I'll be back soon.* 在這裏等我，我不久就回來。

sore /sɔː; 美 sɔːr/ [形容詞] （指身體的某個部位）痛的，疼痛的 *Mum says her back is sore.* 媽媽説她背疼。◇ *Peter has a sore throat.* 彼得嗓子痛。

sorry[1] /ˈsɒri; 美 ˈsɑːri/ [形容詞] [比較級 **sorrier**，最高級 **sorriest**] **1** [用於道歉] 抱歉的，對不起的 *I'm sorry, I forgot.* 對不起，我忘了。**2** 難過的 *I'm sorry to hear that your mother is ill.* 聽説你媽媽病了，我很難過。

sorry[2] /ˈsɒri; 美 ˈsɑːri/ [感歎詞] **1** [用於道歉] 抱歉，對不起 *Sorry I'm late.* 對不起，我来晚了。**2** [表示沒聽清楚對方的話，請對方再説一遍] 抱歉（你説甚麼），對不起（請再説一遍）*Sorry? What did you say?* 對不起，你説甚麼？ ☞ [同] **pardon**[1] 對不起，請原諒

sort /sɔːt; 美 sɔːrt/ [名詞] 種類 *What sort of music do you like?* 你喜歡甚麼樣的音樂？

sound /saʊnd/ [名詞] 聲音 *Ssh — don't make a sound!* 嘘，別出聲！

soup /suːp/ [名詞] 湯 *Be careful. The soup is very hot.* 小心，湯很燙。

sour /ˈsaʊə; 美 ˈsaʊr/ [形容詞] **1** 酸的，有酸味的 *Lemons taste sour.* 檸檬的味道是酸的。**2** （牛奶）酸臭的，餿的 *This milk has gone sour.* 這牛奶酸了。

south /saʊθ/ [名詞] [用作單數，常與 **the** 連用] 南，南方 *My parents are on holiday in the south of England.* 我父母正在英格蘭南部度假。

sow /səʊ; 美 soʊ/ [動詞] [過去式

sowed，過去分詞**sown** /səʊn; 美 soʊn/
或 **sowed**] 播（種）；把（種子）埋在
（地裏、土裏等）*We sow beans in
spring.* 我們春天種豆莢。

space /speɪs/ [名詞] **1** 空間；空位
*There's space for two more people
on the bus.* 公共汽車上還可以再坐兩
個人。◇ *He couldn't find a parking
space.* 他找不到停車位。**2** [無複數] 太
空 *The astronauts will spend two
weeks in space.* 宇航員們要在太空飛
行兩個星期。

spaceship /'speɪsʃɪp/ [名詞] 宇宙
飛船，太空船 *They travelled to the
moon in a spaceship.* 他們乘坐宇宙
飛船飛向月球。

spade /speɪd/ [名詞] 鏟，鐵鍬 *The
children were digging in the sand with
their spades.* 孩子們在用鐵鍬挖沙子。

speak /spiːk/ [動詞] [過去式**spoke**
/spəʊk; 美 spoʊk/，過去分詞 **spoken**
/'spəʊkən; 美 'spoʊ-/] **1** 説話，講話
Please speak more slowly. 請再慢點

兒説。◇ *Hello, this is Henry. May I
speak to Helen, please?* 你好，我是
亨利。請問，可以請海倫接電話嗎？**2**
説，講（某種語言）*Do you speak
Chinese?* 你説漢語嗎？

special /'speʃl/ [形容詞] 特殊的，特
別的 *What are your special interests?*
你有甚麼特殊愛好？◇ *He's my special
friend.* 他是我特殊的朋友。

speed /spiːd/ [名詞] 速度 *We
travelled at great speed.* 我們快速
趕路。

spell /spel/ [動詞] [過去式和過去分
詞 **spelled** 或 **spelt** /spelt/] 拼寫 *How
do you spell your name?* 你的名字
怎麼拼？

spend /spend/ [動詞] [過去式和過去
分詞 **spent** /spent/] **1** 用（錢）；花（錢）
*How much money do you spend
each week?* 你每個星期花多少錢？**2**
消磨（時間）；度過（時間）*We spent
the weekend in London.* 我們在倫敦
度過了週末。

spider /'spaɪdə; 美 -ər/ [名詞] 蜘蛛
`How many legs do spiders have?'
`Eight legs.' "蜘蛛有幾條腿？" "8 條
腿。"

spill /spɪl/ [動詞] [過去式和過去分詞
spilt /spɪlt/ 或 **spilled**]（使）溢出；

S

（使）灑出 *The milk spilled all over the floor.* 牛奶灑了一地。

spin /spɪn/ [動詞] [現在分詞 **spinning**，過去式和過去分詞 **spun** /spʌn/]（使）旋轉 *The dancer spun round and round on the ice.* 那個舞蹈演員在冰上轉來轉去。

spit /spɪt/ [動詞] [現在分詞 **spitting**，過去式和過去分詞 **spat** /spæt/] 吐；吐唾沫；吐痰 *The child spat out her food.* 孩子把食物吐出來了。◇ *Don't spit on the floor.* 不要往地板上吐痰。

splash /splæʃ/ [動詞] 濺，潑；濺濕 *Don't splash your dress.* 不要把你的衣服濺濕了。

split /splɪt/ [動詞] [現在分詞 **splitting**，

split
裂開

過去式和過去分詞 **split**] 裂開 *My T-shirt has split.* 我的 T 恤衫裂開了。

spoil /spɔɪl/ [動詞] [過去式和過去分詞 **spoilt** /spɔɪlt/ 或 **spoiled**] 損壞；糟蹋；破壞 *My brother spoilt my favourite book.* 我弟弟把我最喜愛的一本書弄壞了。

spoke /spəʊk; 美 spoʊk/ **speak** 的過去式 *I spoke to him about this yesterday.* 我昨天跟他講過此事。

spoon /spuːn/ [名詞] 匙，勺，調羹 *The child eats with a spoon.* 這孩子用勺吃飯。

sport /spɔːt; 美 spɔːrt/ [名詞] 運動 *What is your favourite sport?* 你最喜歡甚麼運動？◇ *He's good at sport.* 他擅長運動。

spot[1] /spɒt; 美 spɑːt/ [名詞] **1** 點；斑點 *Do tigers have spots?* 老虎身上有斑點嗎？ **2** 地方，地點 *This is a good spot for a picnic.* 這是一個野餐的好地方。

spot[2] /spɒt; 美 spɑːt/ [動詞] [現在分詞 **spotting**，過去式和過去分詞 **spotted**]（突然）看見，發現 *I spotted Henry in the crowd.* 我在人羣中看見了亨利。

sprang /spræŋ/ **spring**[2] 的過去式 *The cat sprang at the bird.* 貓跳起來向鳥兒撲去。

spray /spreɪ/ [動詞] 噴 *She sprayed some perfume on her wrist.* 她往手腕上噴了點香水。◇ *He sprayed the* *flowers with water.* 他給花噴水。

spread /spred/ [動詞] [過去式和過去分詞**spread**] **1** 傳播；蔓延 *The forest fire quickly spread towards the houses.* 森林大火迅速向房屋蔓延。 **2** 展開；鋪開；攤開 *Spread out the map on the table.* 把地圖攤開放在桌子上。◇ *The bird spread its wings.* 那隻鳥展開了雙翅。 **3** 塗；敷 *I spread butter on the bread.* 我把黃油塗在麵包上。

spring¹ /sprɪŋ/ [名詞] 春天，春季 *I love spring flowers.* 我喜歡春天的花。

spring² /sprɪŋ/ [動詞] [過去式 **sprang** /spræŋ/，過去分詞 **sprung** /sprʌŋ/] 跳，躍 *Peter sprang out of bed.* 彼得從牀上一躍而起。

spun /spʌn/ **spin** 的過去式和過去分詞 *Henry spun a coin on the table.* 亨利在桌子上旋轉一個硬幣。

square¹ /skweər; 美 skwer/ [形容詞] 正方形的；方的 *Is the table round or square?* 那張桌子是圓的還是方的？

square² /skweər; 美 skwer/ [名詞] **1** 正方形 *Do you know how to draw a square?* 你會畫正方形嗎？ **2** 廣場 *There is a fountain in the middle of the square.* 廣場中央有一個噴水池。

squash /ˈskwɒʃ; 美 skwɑːʃ/ [動詞] 壓扁；擠扁 *Peter squashed the bananas.* 彼得把香蕉壓扁了。

squeeze /skwiːz/ [動詞] 擠；壓；榨 *I squeezed an orange.* 我榨了一個橙子。

squirrel /ˈskwɪrəl; 美 ˈskwɜːrəl/ [名詞] 松鼠 *The squirrel ran up the tree.* 松鼠很快爬到樹上。

stadium /ˈsteɪdiəm/ [名詞]（有看台的）體育場，運動場 *We went to the stadium to watch a football match last night.* 我們昨晚去體育場看了一場足球賽。

staff /stɑːf; 美 stæf/ [名詞] [無複數] 全體職工 *The staff of the school are* very friendly. 這所學校的教職員工都很友好。

stage /steɪdʒ/ [名詞] 舞台 *The actors were performing on the stage.* 演員們正在舞台上演出。

stain /steɪn/ [名詞] 污跡，污點 *There's a stain on this shirt.* 這件襯衫上有一塊污跡。

stain
污跡

stairs /steəz; 美 sterz/ [名詞] [複數] 樓梯 *Henry ran up the stairs.* 亨利跑上樓梯。

stalk /stɔːk/ [名詞]（植物的）莖，秆，柄，梗 *Cut the stalks before putting the flowers in water.* 把莖剪一剪再把花放進水裏。

stamp¹ /stæmp/ [名詞] 郵票 *My hobby is collecting foreign stamps.* 我的愛好是收集外國郵票。

stamp² /stæmp/ [動詞] 跺腳；踩踏 *Don't stamp on the spider.* 不要踩着蜘蛛。

stand /stænd/ [動詞] [過去式和過去分詞 **stood** /stʊd/] 站，立 *Don't just stand there — do something!* 別只是站在那裏，做點甚麼！
stand up 起立，站起來 *We stood up when the teacher came in.* 老師進來時我們起立。

star /stɑː; 美 stɑːr/ [名詞] **1** 星星 *The stars seem much brighter in the country than in the city.* 在鄉下看星星似乎比在城裏要明亮得多。**2** 明星 *She wants to be a film star.* 她想當一名電影明星。

stare /steə; 美 ster/ [動詞] 盯，凝視 *Don't stare at me!* 別盯着我！◇ *He was staring out of the window.* 他凝視着窗外。

start /stɑːt; 美 stɑːrt/ [動詞] 開始 *What time does the film start?* 電影幾點開演？◇ *Suddenly Peter started to cry.* 突然彼得哭了起來。

starve /stɑːv; 美 stɑːrv/ [動詞] 餓死；挨餓 *He got lost in the desert and starved to death.* 他在沙漠中迷了路，餓死了。

station /'steɪʃn/ [名詞] **1** [又作 **railway station**] 火車站 *I'm getting off at the next station.* 我下一站下車。**2** [指總站] 汽車站 *I'll meet you at the bus station.* 我在汽車站接你。☞ 參見 **stop**² "公共汽車站"。

statue /'stætʃuː/ [名詞] 雕像，塑像

There is a statue of a famous man in the square. 廣場上有一個著名人物的塑像。

stay /steɪ/ [動詞] **1** 待，逗留 *Stay here until I come back.* 在這裏待着，等我回來。 **2** 暫住 *Which hotel are you staying at?* 你住在哪個賓館？

steady /'stedi/ [形容詞] [比較級 **steadier**，最高級 **steadiest**] 穩固的，穩定的 *This desk isn't very steady — one of its legs is loose.* 這張書桌不太穩，有條腿鬆了。

steal /stiːl/ [動詞] [過去式 **stole** /stəʊl; 美 stoʊl/，過去分詞 **stolen** /'stəʊlən; 美 'stoʊ-/] 偷，竊取 *My bag has been stolen!* 我的包被偷了。

steam /stiːm/ [名詞] [無複數] 蒸汽，水蒸氣 *The bathroom was full of steam.* 浴室裏滿是水蒸氣。

steel /stiːl/ [名詞] [無複數] 鋼 *These knives and forks are steel.* 這些刀叉是鋼的。

steep /stiːp/ [形容詞] （指山、街道等）陡的，陡峭的 *I can't ride my bike here — it's too steep.* 我在這裏騎不了自行車，路太陡了。

steer /stɪə; 美 stɪr/ [動詞] 駕駛（車、船、飛機等） *He steered the boat into the harbour.* 他把船駛進了海港。

stem /stem/ [名詞] （樹木的）幹；（花草的）莖 *These flowers have nice long stems.* 這些花的莖長得又長又好看。

stem
莖

step¹ /step/ [名詞] **1** （腳）步；腳步聲 *He took a step towards the door.* 他向門口邁了一步。◇ *I heard steps outside.* 我聽見外面有腳步聲。 **2** 台階 *He was sitting on the top step.* 他坐在最上面的一級台階上。

step² /step/ [動詞] [現在分詞 **stepping**，過去式和過去分詞

stepped] 行走；踏 *You stepped on my foot!* 你踩着我的腳了！

stick[1] /stɪk/ [名詞] **1** 木棍，木棒 *We collected dry sticks to start a fire.* 我們找了些乾木棍生火。 **2** 手杖，拐杖 *The old man had to walk with a stick.* 那位老人不得不拄着拐杖走路。

stick
拐杖

stick[2] /stɪk/ [動詞] [過去式和過去分詞 **stuck** /stʌk/] **1** 粘住，粘貼 *I stuck a picture on the wall.* 我在牆上貼了一幅畫。 **2** 把…刺入 *The nurse stuck a needle into my arm.* 護士把針扎進了我的胳膊。

stiff /stɪf/ [形容詞]（指材料、紙張等）硬的，不易彎曲的 *The cards were made of stiff paper.* 這些卡片是用硬紙做的。

still[1] /stɪl/ [副詞] 還，仍然 *Do you still live here?* 你還住在這裏嗎？ ◇ *Mum, I'm still hungry!* 媽媽，我還餓！

still[2] /stɪl/ [形容詞]（指人）不動的 *Keep still while I comb your hair.* 我給你梳頭時不要動。

sting /stɪŋ/ [動詞] [過去式和過去分詞 **stung** /stʌŋ/] 刺，螫，叮 *The bee stung me on the leg.* 蜜蜂螫了我的腿一下。

stink /stɪŋk/ [動詞] [過去式 **stank** /stæŋk/ 或 **stunk** /stʌŋk/，過去分詞 **stunk**] 發臭味 *It stinks in here — open a window!* 這裏有臭味，打開一扇窗戶！

stir /stɜː; 美 stɜːr/ [動詞] [現在分詞 **stirring**，過去式和過去分詞 **stirred**] 攪拌，攪動 *He stirred his coffee with a spoon.* 他用勺子攪了攪咖啡。

stole /stəʊl; 美 stoʊl/ **steal** 的過去式 *He stole all her money.* 他把她所有的錢都偷走了。

stolen /ˈstəʊlən; 美 ˈstoʊ-/ **steal** 的過去分詞 *His camera has been stolen.* 他的相機被偷了。

stomach /ˈstʌmək/ [名詞] 胃；肚子，腹部 *It's not a good idea to drink on an empty stomach.* 空腹喝酒不好。

stomach ache /ˈstʌmək eɪk/ [名詞] 胃痛；肚子痛 *I've got a stomach ache.* 我肚子痛。

stone /stəʊn; 美 stoʊn/ [名詞] 石頭；石子；石塊 *The house was built of stone.* 那棟房子是用石頭蓋的。◇ *He picked up a stone and threw it into the sea.* 他撿起一塊石子把它扔進海裏。

stood /stʊd/ **stand**的過去式和過去分詞 *We stood and waited for the bus.* 我們站着等公共汽車。

stool /stuːl/ [名詞] 凳子 *The children were sitting on stools.* 孩子們坐在凳子上。 ☞ 參見 **chair** "椅子"。

stop[1] /stɒp; 美 staːp/ [動詞] [現在分詞 **stopping**，過去式和過去分詞 **stopped**] 停止 *The rain has stopped.* 雨停了。

stop[2] /stɒp; 美 staːp/ [名詞] 公共汽車站 *We get off at the next stop.* 我們下一站下車。 ☞ 參見 **station** "汽車站"。

store[1] /stɔː; 美 stɔːr/ [名詞] 商店；店鋪 *There's a furniture store near here.* 離這裏不遠有一家傢具店。 ☞ 美國英語用 **store**，英國英語用 **shop**。

store[2] /stɔː; 美 stɔːr/ [動詞] 儲藏，儲存 *I store all my old books in this room.* 我把所有的舊書都儲藏在這個房間。

storm /stɔːm; 美 stɔːrm/ [名詞] 暴風雨

I think there's going to be a storm. 我看暴風雨要來了。

story /'stɔːri/ [名詞] [複數 **stories**] 故事 *Do you like stories? I want to tell you a true story.* 你喜歡聽故事嗎？我想給你講一個真實的故事。

stove /stəʊv; 美 stoʊv/ [名詞] 爐子 *She heated some milk on the stove.* 她在爐子上熱了一些牛奶。

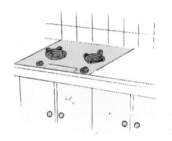

straight[1] /streɪt/ [形容詞] 直的，筆直的 *Can you draw a straight line?* 你會畫直線嗎？

straight[2] /streɪt/ [副詞] **1** 直地，筆直地 *Go straight ahead until you come to the traffic lights.* 一直往前走，走到紅綠燈。 **2** 直接地；馬上 *Come straight home after school.* 放學後直接回家。

strange /streɪndʒ/ [形容詞] 奇怪的 *There's a strange smell in the kitchen. What is it?* 廚房裏有股怪味兒，是甚麼味兒？

stranger /'streɪndʒə; 美 -ər/ [名詞] 陌生人 *Don't talk to strangers when you're on your own.* 你獨自一個人時不要跟陌生人說話。

S

strap /stræp/ [名詞] 帶子 *Mum bought a new watch strap.* 媽媽買了一條新錶帶。

watch strap
錶帶

street
街道

straw /strɔː/ [名詞] **1** [無複數] 稻草；麥秸 *This hat was made of straw.* 這頂帽子是用稻草編織的。**2** 吸管 *Peter drank the orange juice through a straw.* 彼得用吸管吸橙汁喝。

strength /streŋθ/ [名詞] [無複數] 力量，力氣 *I haven't the strength to lift this box.* 我沒有力氣舉起這個箱子。

stretch /stretʃ/ [動詞] **1** 拉長；撐大 *Don't pull my sweater— you'll stretch it.* 別拽我的毛衣，你會把它拽大的。**2** 伸展 *Stretch your arm above your head.* 把你的胳膊舉過頭。

straw
吸管

strawberry /'strɔːbəri; 美 'strɔːˌberi/ [名詞] [複數 **strawberries**] 草莓 *Would you like some strawberries?* 你想吃草莓嗎？

strict /strɪkt/ [形容詞] 嚴格的；嚴厲的 *Some parents are very strict with their children.* 有些家長對孩子非常嚴格。

strike /straɪk/ [動詞] [過去式和過去分詞 **struck** /strʌk/] **1** 打，擊 *He was struck on the head by a stone.* 他的頭被一塊石子擊中了。**2** （時鐘）敲響 *The clock was striking six when I got up.* 我起牀時時鐘在敲6點。

stream /striːm/ [名詞] 小河，小溪 *Are there any fish in this stream?* 這條小河裏有魚嗎？

street /striːt/ [名詞] 大街，街道 *I'm not allowed to play in the street.* 不允許我在街道上玩。

string /strɪŋ/ [名詞] **1** [無複數] 細繩 *The parcel was tied with string.* 這個

包裹是用繩子捆好的。

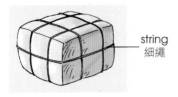

string
細繩

2 (樂器的)弦 *A guitar has six strings.* 吉他有6根弦。

stripe /straɪp/ [名詞] 條紋 *Zebras have black and white stripes.* 斑馬的身上長有黑白條紋。

stroke /strəʊk; 美 stroʊk/ [動詞] 撫摸 *The cat loves being stroked.* 貓喜歡被人撫摸。

strong /strɒŋ; 美 strɔːŋ/ [形容詞] **1** 強壯的，健壯的 *He's a strong swimmer.* 他是個游泳健將。 [反] **weak** 弱的，虛弱的 **2** (指物)結實的 *The bed isn't strong enough to jump on.* 這張牀不夠結實，不能在上面跳。 **3** (味)濃的 *These flowers have a strong smell.* 這些花的香味很濃。

struck /strʌk/ **strike** 的過去式和過去分詞 *The clock struck nine.* 時鐘敲了9點。

struggle /ˈstrʌgl/ [動詞] 掙扎，努力 (做某事) *He was struggling to learn English.* 他正在努力學英語。

stuck /stʌk/ **stick**的過去式和過去分詞 *I stuck a stamp on the envelope.* 我在信封上貼了一張郵票。

student /ˈstjuːdnt; 美 ˈstuː-/ [名詞] 學生 *Henry is a good student.* 亨利是個好學生。

study /ˈstʌdi/ [動詞] [現在分詞 **studying**，過去式和過去分詞 **studied**] 學習 *The students are studying English.* 學生們在學英語。◇ *Do you enjoy studying English?* 你喜歡學英語嗎？

stuff /stʌf/ [動詞] 把…裝進，把…塞進 *He stuffed the letter into his pocket.* 他把信塞進了口袋。

stung /stʌŋ/ **sting** 的過去式和過去分詞 *I've been stung on the finger by a wasp.* 我的手指被黃蜂蜇了一下。

stupid /ˈstjuːpɪd; 美 ˈstuːpəd/ [形容詞] 笨的，愚蠢的 *I'm so stupid! I've left my pencil box at home.* 我真笨！我把鉛筆盒忘在家裏了。◇ *I made a stupid mistake.* 我犯了一個愚蠢的錯誤。

subject /ˈsʌbdʒekt/ [名詞] 學科，科目 *'What's your favourite subject?' 'It's art.'* "你最喜歡甚麼

S

科目？""藝術。"

submarine /'sʌbməriːn/ [名詞] 潛（水）艇 *The submarine ran into the fishing net.* 潛艇撞在了漁網上。

subtract /səb'trækt/ [動詞] 減去 *If you subtract three from ten, you get seven.* 10 減 3 等於 7。

$$10-3=7$$

subway /'sʌbweɪ/ [名詞] **1** 地下通道 *Use the subway to cross the road.* 過馬路請走地下通道。

2 地鐵 *Do you take the subway to work?* 你坐地鐵上班嗎？☞ 指 "地

鐵"，美國英語用 **subway**，英國英語用 **underground**。

succeed /sək'siːd/ [動詞] 成功 *If you try hard, you'll succeed.* 如果你盡力，你會成功。◇ *Did you succeed in passing your exam?* 你考試及格了嗎？☞ [反] **fail** 失敗

successful /sək'sesfl/ [形容詞] 成功的 *He's a successful teacher.* 他是一位成功的教師。

such /sʌtʃ/ [形容詞] 這樣的，如此的 *That was such a good film I'd like to see it again.* 那部電影棒極了，我想再看一遍。

suck /sʌk/ [動詞] 吸，吮 *The baby was sucking milk from its mother.* 寶寶在吮母親的奶。

sudden /'sʌdn/ [形容詞] 突然的 *Henry gave a sudden laugh.* 亨利突然大笑起來。

suddenly /'sʌdnli/ [副詞] 突然 *Suddenly, everybody started shouting.* 突然，大家都喊叫起來。

sugar /'ʃʊgə; 美 -ər/ [名詞] [無複數] 食糖 *Do you take sugar in your coffee?* 你的咖啡裏加糖嗎？

suggest /sə'dʒest; 美 səg'dʒest/ [動

詞] 建議 *Henry suggested (that) we go out for a walk.* 亨利建議我們出去散散步。

suit /suːt/ [名詞] 套服，套裝 *He always wears a suit and tie to work.* 他總是穿西服戴領帶上班。

suitable /ˈsuːtəbl/ [形容詞] 適合的，合適的 *This toy isn't suitable for young children.* 這個玩具不適合小孩子們玩。

suitcase /ˈsuːtkeɪs/ [名詞] （旅行用的）衣箱 *The suitcase was so heavy that I couldn't lift it.* 衣箱太重，我提不動。

sum /sʌm/ [名詞] 算術題 *I did all my sums right.* 我把所有的算術題都做對了。

summer /ˈsʌmə; 美 -ər/ [名詞] 夏天，夏季 *Are you going on holiday this summer?* 你今年夏天去度假嗎？

sun /sʌn/ [名詞] [用作單數，與 **the** 連用] 太陽 *The sun was just rising.* 太

陽剛剛升起。

Sunday /ˈsʌndeɪ/ [名詞] 星期天，星期日 *What are you doing on Sunday?* 你星期天做甚麼？ ① 參見 **Monday** 的示例。② **Sun** 是 **Sunday** 的縮寫。

sunflower /ˈsʌnˌflaʊə; 美 -ˌflaʊər/ [名詞] 向日葵 *He planted some sunflowers in the garden.* 他在花園裏種了些向日葵。

sung /sʌŋ/ **sing** 的過去分詞 *We haven't sung this song, so listen to it carefully.* 我們沒唱過這首歌，所以要仔細聽。

sunglasses /ˈsʌnˌɡlɑːsɪz; 美 -ˌɡlæsəz/ [名詞] [複數] 太陽鏡，墨鏡 *She was wearing sunglasses.* 她戴着太陽鏡。

sunlight /ˈsʌnlaɪt/ [名詞] [無複數] 陽光 *Plants need sunlight.* 植物需要陽光。

sunny /ˈsʌni/ [形容詞] [比較級 **sunnier**，最高級 **sunniest**] 陽光充足的，陽光明媚的 *It was sunny yesterday.* 昨天陽光明媚。

sunrise /ˈsʌnraɪz/ [名詞] 日出 *We*

get up at sunrise. 我們日出時起牀。

sunset /ˈsʌnset/ [名詞] 日落 *The park closes at sunset.* 公園在日落時關門。

sunshine /ˈsʌnʃaɪn/ [名詞] [無複數] 陽光 *Let's play in the sunshine.* 咱們在陽光裏玩吧。

supermarket /ˈsuːpəˌmɑːkɪt; 美 -ərˌmɑːrkət/ [名詞] 超級市場，超市 *We buy everything at the supermarket.* 我們每樣東西都在超市買。

supper /ˈsʌpə; 美 -ər/ [名詞] 晚餐，晚飯 *It's time for supper.* 到吃晚飯的時間了。

support /səˈpɔːt; 美 -ˈpɔːrt/ [動詞] **1** 支持 *Which football team do you support?* 你支持哪一支足球隊？ **2** 支撐 *That cardboard box won't support your weight.* 那個硬紙箱撐不起你的體重。

suppose /səˈpəʊz; 美 -ˈpoʊz/ [動詞] 猜想；以為 *Who do you suppose will win?* 你認為誰會贏？

sure¹ /ʃɔː; 美 ʃʊr/ [形容詞] [不用於名詞前] **1** 確信的；有把握的 *Are you sure you locked the door?* 你肯定把門鎖上了嗎？ **2** 一定的，必定的 *If you*

work hard you are sure to pass the exam. 你如果用功就一定能及格。

sure² /ʃɔː; 美 ʃʊr/ [副詞] 當然 *'Can I have a look at your newspaper?' 'Sure.'* "我可以看一下你的報紙嗎？" "當然可以。" ☞ [同] **certainly** 當然

surface /ˈsɜːfɪs; 美 ˈsɜːrfəs/ [名詞] （物體的）表面 *Don't scratch the surface of the table.* 別把桌面劃了。

surname /ˈsɜːneɪm; 美 ˈsɜːr-/ [名詞] 姓，姓氏 *What's your cousin's surname?* 你表兄姓甚麼？ ☞ 參見 **name** "名字；姓名"。

surprise¹ /səˈpraɪz; 美 sər-/ [名詞] 意想不到的事物，驚奇 *I have a surprise for you!* 我要給你一個驚奇！

surprise² /səˈpraɪz; 美 sər-/ [動詞] 使驚奇 *His answer surprised me.* 他的回答讓我感到驚奇。

surround /səˈraʊnd/ [動詞] 環繞；圍繞；圍住 *The garden is surrounded by a high wall.* 花園四周有一道高高的圍牆。

swallow /ˈswɒləʊ; 美 ˈswɑːloʊ/ [動詞] 吞下；嚥下 *Don't chew the pills. Just swallow them.* 別嚼藥片，直接嚥下去。

swam /swæm/ **swim** 的過去式 *He swam across the river.* 他游過了河。

swan /swɒn; 美 swɑːn/ [名詞] 天鵝 *Most swans are white but there are black ones in Australia.* 大多數天鵝是白的，但在澳大利亞有黑天鵝。

swap /swɒp; 美 swɑːp/ [動詞] [現在分詞 **swapping**，過去式和過去分詞 **swapped**] 交換 *Can I swap seats with you?* 我可以跟你換一下座位嗎？

sweat¹ /swet/ [名詞] [無複數] 汗（水）*My shirt was wet with sweat.* 我的襯衫被汗水浸濕了。

sweat² /swet/ [動詞] 流汗，出汗 *I always sweat a lot when I exercise.* 我鍛煉時總出很多汗。

sweater /'swetə; 美 -ər/ [名詞]（套頭）毛衣 *Alice was wearing a pink sweater.* 艾麗斯穿着一件粉紅色的毛衣。 ☞ **jumper** 用於英國英語，**sweater** 既可用於英國英語，也可用於美國英語。

sweatshirt /'swetʃɜːt; 美 -ʃɜːrt/ [名詞]（圓領長袖）運動衫 *He was dressed*

in a sweatshirt and jeans. 他穿着一件圓領運動衫和一條牛仔褲。

sweep /swiːp/ [動詞] [過去式和過去分詞 **swept** /swept/] 掃（地）；打掃（房間）*Could you sweep the floor?* 你掃一下地行嗎？

sweet¹ /swiːt/ [形容詞] 甜（味）的 *I don't like this cake. It's too sweet.* 我不喜歡吃這種蛋糕，太甜了。☞[反] **bitter** 苦（味）的

sweet² /swiːt/ [名詞] [通常用作複數 **sweets**] 糖果 *Sweets are bad for your teeth.* 糖果對牙齒不好。 ☞ **sweet** "糖果" 用於英國英語，美國英語用 **candy**。

swept /swept/ **sweep** 的過去式和過去分詞 *I swept the floor.* 我掃了掃地。

swim¹ /swɪm/ [動詞] [現在分詞 **swimming**，過去式 **swam** /swæm/，過去分詞 **swum** /swʌm/] 游泳 *How far can you swim?* 你能游多遠？◇ *Let's go swimming this afternoon.* 我們今天下午去游泳吧。

swim² /swɪm/ [名詞] 游泳 *Let's go for a swim.* 咱們去游泳吧。

swimmer /'swɪmə; 美 -ər/ [名詞] 游泳的人 *Henry is a good swimmer.* 亨利是一名游泳健將。

swimming pool /ˈswɪmɪŋ puːl/ [又作 **pool**] [名詞] 游泳池 *Does the school have a swimming pool?* 學校有游泳池嗎?

swing[1] /swɪŋ/ [動詞] [過去式和過去分詞 **swung** /swʌŋ/] 搖擺,擺動,晃動 *Peter was swinging his schoolbag.* 彼得把書包晃來晃去。

swing[2] /swɪŋ/ [名詞] 鞦韆 *Let's go and play on the swing.* 咱們去盪鞦韆吧。

switch[1] /swɪtʃ/ [名詞] [複數 **switches**] 開關,電閘 *My torch doesn't work. I think the switch is broken.* 我的手電筒不亮了,我看是開關壞了。

switch[2] /swɪtʃ/ [動詞]
switch off 關掉(電燈、電視等) *Could you switch off the television?* 你把電視關上好嗎? ☞ ① [同] **turn off** 關掉 ② [反] **switch on**,**turn on** 打開
switch on 打開(電燈、電視等) *Could you switch on the light?* 你把燈打開好嗎? ☞ ① [同] **turn on** 打開 ② [反] **switch off**,**turn off** 關掉

sword /sɔːd; 美 sɔːrd/ [名詞] 劍 *Peter has a plastic sword.* 彼得有一把塑料劍。

swum /swʌm/ **swim** 的過去分詞 *Have you ever swum in the sea?* 你在海裏游過泳嗎?

swung /swʌŋ/ **swing** 的過去式和過去分詞 *The door swung in the wind.* 門隨風晃動。

T t

table /'teɪbl/ [名詞] 桌子 *I put the plates on the table.* 我把盤子放在桌子上。

table tennis /'teɪbl ˌtenɪs/ [名詞] [無複數] 乒乓球（運動） *Henry and Peter are playing table tennis.* 亨利和彼得在打乒乓球。 ☞ 在口語中，也可以使用 **ping-pong** /'pɪŋ pɒŋ; 美 -pɑːŋ/。

tablet /'tæblət/ [名詞] 藥片 *The doctor gave Henry some tablets.* 醫生給了亨利一些藥片。

tadpole /'tædpəʊl; 美 -poʊl/ [名詞] 蝌蚪 *Tadpoles grow into frogs.* 蝌蚪長成青蛙。

tail /teɪl/ [名詞] 尾巴 *A monkey has a long tail.* 猴子長着長長的尾巴。

tail
尾巴

take /teɪk/ [動詞] [過去式 **took** /tʊk/，過去分詞 **taken** /'teɪkən/] **1** 拿；取；帶 *Don't forget to take your bag!* 別忘了拿包！**2** 把（某人）帶往（某處）*Mum is taking me to the dentist's tomorrow.* 媽媽明天帶我去牙科診所。**3** 拿走；取走；帶走 *Who has taken my pen?* 誰把我的鋼筆拿走了？**4** 乘，坐（交通工具）*We take the bus to school.* 我們乘公共汽車上學。**5** 吃；喝 *If you do not take the medicine, you will not get better.* 如果你不吃藥，病就不會好。**6** 穿 *What size shoes do you take?* 你穿多大號的鞋？
take off 1 脱下，脱掉 *Take off your dirty shirt.* 脱下你的髒襯衫。 ☞ [反] **put on** 穿上 **2**（飛機）起飛 *The plane took off at 8.* 飛機 8 點起飛了。 ☞ [反] **land**[2]（飛機）降落，着陸

tale /teɪl/ [名詞]（虛構的）故事，童話 *Mum told me the tale of Three Little Pigs.* 媽媽給我講了《三隻小豬》的故事。

talk¹ /tɔːk/ [動詞] 説話；談話 *Can I talk to you for a minute?* 我可以跟你説會兒話嗎？◇ *They were talking about their holiday.* 他們在談論假期的事。

talk² /tɔːk/ [名詞] 交談；談話 *The teacher had a talk with Peter.* 老師跟彼得談了一次話。

tall /tɔːl/ [形容詞] 高的 *How tall are you?* 你多高？◇ *The giraffe is the world's tallest animal.* 長頸鹿是世界上最高的動物。 ☞ [反] **short** 矮的

tame /teɪm/ [形容詞] （指動物）馴服的 *We saw a tame monkey at the circus.* 我們看見馬戲團有隻馴服的猴子。 ☞ [反] **wild** 野生的

tank /tæŋk/ [名詞] （盛水或油的）箱 *My father filled up the petrol tank at the petrol station.* 我爸爸在加油站給油箱加滿了油。

tap¹ /tæp/ [動詞] [現在分詞 **tapping**，過去式和過去分詞**tapped**] 輕拍，輕敲 *He tapped me on the shoulder.* 他輕輕地拍了拍我的肩膀。

tap² /tæp/ [名詞] （水、煤氣等的）開關，龍頭 *Don't forget to turn the tap off.* 別忘了關水龍頭。

tape /teɪp/ [名詞] 磁帶；錄像帶 *Alice is listening to a tape.* 艾麗斯在聽一盒磁帶。

target /ˈtɑːɡɪt; 美 ˈtɑːrɡət/ [名詞] 目標；靶子 *Our target is to finish the work by Friday.* 我們的目標是週五以前完成這項工作。

taste¹ /teɪst/ [名詞] 味道 *I don't like the taste of lemons. They're too sour.* 我不喜歡檸檬的味道，太酸了。

taste² /teɪst/ [動詞] 1 嘗，品嘗 *Can I taste your drink?* 我能嘗一口你的飲料嗎？ 2 有…味道 *This drink tastes sweet.* 這飲料有甜味。

tasty /ˈteɪsti/ [形容詞] [比較級 **tastier**，最高級 **tastiest**] 美味的，可口的 *This pizza is really tasty.* 這個薄餅真好吃。

taught /tɔːt/ **teach** 的過去式和過去分詞 *My mother taught me to play the piano.* 我母親教我彈鋼琴。

taxi /ˈtæksi/ [名詞] 出租車 *I came by taxi.* 我是坐出租車來的。

tea /tiː/ [名詞] [無複數] 茶 *Would you prefer tea or coffee?* 你更喜歡喝茶還是喝咖啡?

teach /tiːtʃ/ [動詞] [過去式和過去分詞 **taught** /tɔːt/] 教 *Who teaches you English?* 誰教你英語? ◇ *My father is teaching me how to swim.* 我父親在教我游泳。

teacher /'tiːtʃə; 美 -ər/ [名詞] 教師,老師 *Miss Brown is my English teacher.* 布朗小姐是我的英語老師。

☞ **teacher** 指教師職業,不能用於稱呼。例如,不能説 "**Good morning, teacher.**" 或 "**Teacher Smith**"。可以説 "**Good morning, sir.**"(\"老師,早上好。\")(對男老師稱呼)或 "**Good morning, Miss.**"(\"老師,早上好。\")(對女老師稱呼);可以説 "**Mr Smith**"(對男老師史密斯稱呼),"**Mrs Smith**"(對已婚女老師史密斯夫人稱呼)或 "**Miss Smith**"(對未婚女老師史密斯稱呼)。

team /tiːm/ [名詞] 隊 *Henry plays in the school football team.* 亨利在校足球隊踢球。

tear¹ /tɪə; 美 tɪr/ [名詞] [通常用作複數 **tears**] 眼淚 *I dried my tears on my handkerchief.* 我用手帕擦乾眼淚。

tear² /teə; 美 ter/ [動詞] [過去式 **tore** /tɔː; 美 tɔːr/ ,過去分詞 **torn** /tɔːn; 美 tɔːrn/] 撕開;撕裂;撕破;划破 *He tore the piece of paper in half.* 他把那張紙撕成了兩半。 ◇ *I tore my shirt on a nail.* 我的襯衫被釘子划破了。

tease /tiːz/ [動詞] 逗,取笑,戲弄 *People often tease me because I'm short.* 因為我矮,大家常逗我。

teddy bear /'tedi beə; 美 'tedi ber/ [英國英語又作 **teddy**,複數 **teddies**] [名詞] 玩具熊 *Alice never goes to bed without her teddy bear.* 艾麗斯沒有玩具熊從不上牀睡覺。

teenager /'ti:neɪdʒə; 美 -ər/ [名詞]
(13-19歲的）青少年 *This book is for
teenagers.* 這本書是為青少年寫的。

teeth /ti:θ/ **tooth**的複數 *Remember
to clean your teeth before you go to
bed.* 別忘了睡覺前刷牙。

telephone¹ /'telɪfəʊn; 美 -əfoʊn/
[又作 **phone**] [名詞] 電話 *Can I use
your telephone?* 我可以用一下你的電
話嗎？ ◇ *Will you answer the
telephone?* 你接一下電話好嗎？

telephone² /'telɪfəʊn; 美 -əfoʊn/
[又作 **phone**] [動詞] （給…）打電話
*Did anyone telephone me while I
was out?* 我不在家時有人給我打電話
嗎？ ☞ 在英國英語中，**telephone**
比 **phone**，**call** 正式。

telephone number /'telɪfəʊn
ˌnʌmbə; 美 'teləfoʊn ˌnʌmbər/ [又作
phone number] [名詞] 電話號碼 *Do
you know Henry's telephone
number?* 你知道亨利的電話號碼嗎？

telescope /'telɪskəʊp; 美 -əskoʊp/
[名詞] 望遠鏡 *He looked at the stars
through a telescope.* 他用望遠鏡看
星星。

television /'telɪˌvɪʒn; 美 -ə-/ [名詞]
電視 *Don't sit too close to the
television.* 不要坐得離電視太近。 ◇
Turn the television on. 打開電視。

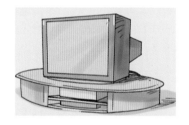

tell /tel/ [動詞] [過去式和過去分詞
told /təʊld; 美 toʊld/] **1** 告訴；講述，
說 *Can you tell me where you live?*
你能告訴我你住哪兒嗎？◇ *Mum told
me a story about a baby elephant.*
媽媽給我講了一個小象的故事。 **2** 吩
咐，命令 *The teacher told Peter to
be quiet.* 老師讓彼得安靜。

temper /'tempə; 美 -ər/ [名詞] 心
情，情緒 *He's in a very good temper
today.* 他今天心情非常好。
lose one's temper 發脾氣 *She lost
her temper with the naughty child.*
她對那個頑皮的孩子發起脾氣來。

temperature /'tempərətʃə; 美 -ər/ [名
詞] 溫度；氣溫 *What's the temperature
today?* 今天氣溫是多少？

have a temperature 發燒 *Does he have a temperature?* 他發燒嗎？

ten /ten/ [數詞] 十 *Two times five is ten.* 2 乘 5 得 10。 ☞ 參見 **five** 的示例。

tennis /'tenɪs/ [名詞] [無複數] 網球（運動）*Can you play tennis?* 你會打網球嗎？◇ *Let's have a game of tennis.* 我們打一場網球吧。

tent /tent/ [名詞] 帳篷 *Have you ever slept in a tent?* 你在帳篷裏睡過嗎？

tenth /tenθ/ [數詞] 第十 *Today is my tenth birthday.* 今天是我的 10 歲生日。 ☞ 參見 **fifth** 的示例。

term /tɜːm; 美 tɜːrm/ [名詞] （學校的）學期 *How many terms are there in a year?* 一年有幾個學期？

terrible /'terəbl/ [形容詞] 很糟的，極差的 *Your spelling is terrible.* 你的拼寫差極了。◇ *I have a terrible headache.* 我的頭痛得很厲害。

test¹ /test/ [名詞] 測試，測驗 *We're having a maths test tomorrow.* 我們明天進行數學測驗。

test² /test/ [動詞] 測試，測驗 *The teacher tested us on our homework.* 老師對我們的作業進行了測試。

than /強 ðæn; 弱 ðən/ [連詞] [用於形容詞、副詞的比較級之後] 比 *Henry can run faster than I can, but I can swim faster than him.* 亨利跑得比我快，但我游得比他快。

thank /θæŋk/ [動詞] 謝謝，感謝 *Thank you for my birthday present.* 謝謝你送給我的生日禮物。

thank you, thanks 謝謝你，謝謝 *'Do you want another piece of cake?' 'No, thank you.'* "你要不要再吃一塊蛋糕？""不，謝謝。"

that¹ /ðæt/ [形容詞] [複數 **those** /ðəuz; 美 ðouz/] **1** [指離説話人較遠的一個人或事物] 那，那個 *I like this book but I don't like that one.* 我喜歡這本書但不喜歡那本書。 **2** [指已提到過的人或事物] 那，那個 *Did you bring that photograph?* 你帶來那張照片了嗎？

that² /ðæt/ [代詞] [複數 **those** /ðəuz; 美 ðouz/] **1** [指離説話人較遠的一個人或事物] 那，那個 *'What's that?' 'It's a book.'* "那是甚麼？""那是一本書。" **2** [指已提到過的人或事物] 那，那個 *That was the hardest exam so far.* 那是迄今為止最難的考試。

that³ /強 ðæt; 弱 ðət/ [連詞] [用以連接

句子的兩個部分] *He said that he is a friend of yours.* 他說他是你的一位朋友。

the / 強 ði:; 弱 ði; ðə/ [定冠詞] **1** [指已提到或能體會到的人或事物] *No one could answer the question.* 沒人能回答這個問題。◇ *The milk is in the fridge.* 牛奶在冰箱裏。**2** [用於單數名詞前，泛指類別] *The dolphin is an intelligent animal.* 海豚是一種聰明的動物。◇ *Can you play the piano?* 你會彈鋼琴嗎？

theatre /'θɪətə; 美 'θiːətər/ [名詞] 劇院 *How often do you go to the theatre?* 你多長時間去看一次戲？☞ 美國英語拼寫為 **theater**。

their /ðeə; 美 ðer/ [形容詞] [**they** 的所有格] 他（她、它）們的 *What is their phone number?* 他們的電話號碼是多少？

theirs /ðeəz; 美 ðerz/ [代詞] [**they** 的物主代詞] 他（她、它）們的（東西）*Our house is bigger than theirs.* 我們的房子比他們的大。

them / 強 ðem; 弱 ðəm/ [代詞] [**they** 的賓格] 他（她、它）們 *I saw them in the park.* 我在公園裏看見了他們。

themselves /ðəm'selvz/ [代詞] [**they** 的反身代詞] 他們自己，她們自己；它們本身 *They bought themselves a new car.* 他們為自己買了一輛新車。

then /ðen/ [副詞] **1** 當時；那時 *He lived in a village then, but now he lives in a town.* 那時候他住在鄉村，但現在住在城裏。**2** 然後；接着；於是 *We watched a film and then went for a meal.* 我們看了場電影，然後去吃飯。

there / 強 ðeə; 美 ðer; 弱 ðə; 美 ðər/ [副詞] **1** 在那裏；往那裏 *Don't put the box there — put it here.* 別把箱子放那裏，放這裏。**2** [與動詞 **be** 連用，表示"有"] *How much money is there on the table?* 桌子上有多少錢？◇ *There are thirty students in my class.* 我們班有 30 名學生。

there's / 強 ðeəz; 美 ðerz; 弱 ðəz; 美 ðərz/ **there is** 的縮寫 *There's a man at the door.* 門口有個男的。

thermometer /θə'mɒmɪtə; 美 θər'mɑːmətər/ [名詞] 溫度計；體溫計 *The doctor put a thermometer in my mouth to take my temperature.* 醫生把體溫計放進我的嘴裏來測量我的體溫。

these /ðiːz/ **this²** 的複數 *These are my books and those are yours.* 這些書是我的，那些是你的。

they /ðeɪ/ [代詞] [主格] 他（她、它）

們 'Where are Henry and Peter?'
'They are in the garden.' "亨利和
彼得在哪裏？""他們在花園裏。"

they'd /ðeɪd/ **1 they had** 的縮寫
Their mum said they'd gone out. 他
們的媽媽説他們出去了。**2 they would**
的縮寫 *They said they'd love to
come.* 他們説他們很想來。

they'll /ðeɪl/ **they will** 的縮寫 *They'll
arrive tomorrow.* 他們明天到。

they're /ðeə; 美 ðer/ **they are** 的縮
寫 *They're playing football.* 他們正
在踢足球。

they've /ðeɪv/ **they have** 的縮寫
They've gone shopping. 他們去購物
了。

thick /θɪk/ [形容詞] **1** （指物體）厚
的；粗的 *This book is very thick.* 這本
書很厚。 ☞ [反] **thin** 薄的；細的

2 （指液體）濃的，稠的 *This soup is
too thick.* 這湯太濃了。

thief /θiːf/ [名詞] [複數 **thieves** /θiːvz/]
小偷，賊 *A thief stole his car.* 小偷把
他的車偷走了。

thigh /θaɪ/ [名詞] 大腿，股 *The
longest bone in your body is your
thigh bone.* 人體最長的骨頭是大腿骨。

thin /θɪn/ [形容詞] [比較級 **thinner**，
最高級 **thinnest**] **1** （指物體）薄的；細
的 *This string is too thin. I need a
thicker piece.* 這繩子太細了，我需要
一根粗一點的。 ☞ [反] **thick** 厚的；
粗的 **2** （指人）瘦的 *He's tall and thin.*
他又高又瘦。 ☞ [反] **fat** 胖的

thing /θɪŋ/ [名詞] **1** 物，東西 *What's
that thing on the table?* 桌子上的那
個東西是甚麼？ **2** 事，事情 *That was
a difficult thing to do.* 那件事很難做。

think /θɪŋk/ [動詞] [過去式和過去分
詞 **thought** /θɔːt/] **1** 想，思考 *Think
before you answer the question.* 這
個問題要先想一想再回答。 ◇ *What
are you thinking about?* 你在想甚麼？
2 認為，以為 *I think it's going to rain.*
我看要下雨了。 ◇ *What do you think
of the film?* 你認為這部電影怎麼樣？

third /θɜːd; 美 θɜːrd/ [數詞] 第三
*Henry came first, Peter was second
and I was third.* 亨利是第一名，彼得
是第二名，我是第三名。 ☞ 參見 **fifth**
的示例。

thirsty /ˈθɜːsti; 美 ˈθɜːr-/ [形容詞] [比
較級 **thirstier**，最高級 **thirstiest**] 渴的 *Is
there anything to drink? I'm so

thirsty! 有喝的東西嗎？我渴死了！

thirteen /ˌθɜːˈtiːn; 美 ˌθɜːr-/ [數詞] 十三 *Ten and three make thirteen.* 10 加 3 等於 13。☞ 參見 **five** 的示例。

thirty /ˈθɜːti; 美 ˈθɜːrti/ [數詞] 三十 *Ten times three is thirty.* 10 乘 3 得 30。☞ 參見 **fifty** 的示例。

this¹ /ðɪs/ [形容詞] [複數 **these** /ðiːz/] 這，這個 *This little girl can't find her mother.* 這個小女孩找不到她母親了。

this² /ðɪs/ [代詞] [複數 **these** /ðiːz/] 這，這個 *What's this — is it salt or sugar?* 這是甚麼，是鹽還是糖？

thorn /θɔːn; 美 θɔːrn/ [名詞] （植物的）刺 *Rose bushes have thorns.* 玫瑰叢有很多刺。

thorn
刺

those /ðəʊz; 美 ðoʊz/ **that²** 的複數 *Do you know those boys over there?* 你認識那邊的那幾個男孩嗎？

though /ðəʊ; 美 ðoʊ/ [連詞] 儘管，雖然 *Though he was poor, he was happy.* 雖然他窮，但很快樂。

thought¹ /θɔːt/ **think** 的過去式和過去分詞 *Henry thought he was going to be late.* 亨利以為自己要遲到了。

thought² /θɔːt/ [名詞] 想法，見解

Do you have any thoughts about what we should do? 關於我們應該做甚麼你有想法嗎？

thousand /ˈθaʊznd/ [數詞] **1** 千 *There are two thousand students in our school.* 我們學校有 2,000 名學生。 **2** [用作複數 **thousands**] 成千上萬，許許多多 *There were thousands of people there.* 那裏有許許多多的人。

thread¹ /θred/ [名詞] 線 *Mend it with a needle and thread.* 用針線補一補。

thread² /θred/ [動詞] 穿線於 *I can't thread this needle.* 這個針我穿不上線。

three /θriː/ [數詞] 三 *One and two are three.* 1 加 2 等於 3。☞ 參見 **five** 的示例。

threw /θruː/ **throw** 的過去式 *Henry picked up a stone and threw it into the river.* 亨利撿起一塊石子把它扔進河裏。

throat /θrəʊt; 美 θroʊt/ [名詞] 咽喉，喉嚨 *I have a sore throat.* 我喉嚨痛。

throne /θrəʊn; 美 θroʊn/ [名詞] （國王、女王等的）寶座 *The queen's throne was made of gold.* 女王的寶座是金的。

through /θruː/ [介詞]（指空間）穿過，通過 We drove through the tunnel. 我們開車穿過隧道。

throw /θrəʊ; 美 θroʊ/ [動詞] [過去式 **threw** /θruː/，過去分詞 **thrown** /θrəʊn; 美 θroʊn/] 扔，拋 People still throw their rubbish everywhere. 人們仍然到處扔垃圾。

thumb /θʌm/ [名詞]（大）拇指 Peter sometimes sucks his thumb. 彼得有時吸大拇指。

thunder /'θʌndə; 美 -ər/ [名詞] 雷；雷聲 Some people are scared of thunder. 有些人怕雷聲。

Thursday /'θɜːzdeɪ; 美 'θɜːrz-/ [名詞] 星期四 It's Thursday tomorrow. 明天是星期四。 ① 參見 **Monday** 的示例。 ② **Thur** 或 **Thurs** 是 **Thursday** 的縮寫。

tick[1] /tɪk/ [名詞] [表示正確或已完成使用的] 鈎號（√） Put a tick after each correct answer. 在每個正確答案後面打上鈎。

tick[2] /tɪk/ [動詞] 給…打鈎號 The teacher ticked all my correct answers. 老師給我的正確答案全打了鈎。

ticket /'tɪkɪt; 美 -ət/ [名詞] 票 How much is a bus ticket to London? 去倫敦的公共汽車票多少錢一張？

tickle /'tɪkl/ [動詞] 使覺得癢 He tickled my feet. 他撓得我的腳癢。

tidy[1] /'taɪdi/ [形容詞] [比較級 **tidier**，最高級 **tidiest**] 整潔的，整齊的 I like to keep my bedroom tidy. 我喜歡保持臥室整潔。 [反] **untidy** 不整潔的，凌亂的

tidy[2] /'taɪdi/ [動詞] 收拾，整理 Go upstairs and tidy your bedroom! 上樓把你的臥室收拾一下！

tie[1] /taɪ/ [名詞] 領帶 Dad always wears a tie to go to work. 爸爸總是戴着領帶去上班。

tie² /taɪ/ [動詞] [現在分詞 **tying**，過去式和過去分詞 **tied**] (用繩、帶等) 繫；拴；紮；捆 *Paul tied the boat to a tree.* 保羅把船繫在一棵樹上。

tiger /'taɪgə; 美 -ər/ [名詞] 老虎 *I saw some lions and tigers at the zoo.* 我看見動物園有幾隻獅子和老虎。

tight /taɪt/ [形容詞] **1** 緊的 *The lid is too tight.* 這蓋子太緊了。 ☞[反] **loose** 鬆的 **2** (衣服、鞋、襪等) 緊身的，瘦的 *These shoes are too tight.* 這雙鞋太緊了。 ☞[反] **loose** 寬鬆的，肥的

time /taɪm/ [名詞] [無複數] **1** (一段) 時間 *I haven't seen you for a long time.* 我好久沒見你了。 **2** 時候，時刻 *What's the time (=What time is it)?* 現在幾點了？
have a good time 過得快樂，過得愉快 *Did you have a good time on your holiday?* 你假期過得愉快嗎？
in time 及時 *We were just in time for the bus.* 我們正好趕上公共汽車。
on time 按時，準時 *Most of the students finished their homework on time.* 大部分學生按時完成了作業。

timid /'tɪmɪd/ [形容詞] 膽小的，膽怯的 *Mice are very timid animals.* 老鼠是非常膽小的動物。

times /taɪmz/ [介詞] 乘 *Three times three is nine.* 3 乘 3 得 9。 ☞ 參見 **multiply** "乘，使相乘"。

$$3 \times 3 = 9$$

tin /tɪn/ [名詞] 罐頭，聽 *Let's open a tin of peaches.* 咱們開一個桃罐頭吧。 ☞ 英國英語通常用 **tin**，美國英語通常用 **can**。

tiny /'taɪni/ [形容詞] [比較級 **tinier**，最高級 **tiniest**] 很小的，極小的 *Ants are tiny insects.* 螞蟻是很小的昆蟲。

tip /tɪp/ [名詞] (某物的) 尖，尖端 *The tip of my pen bent.* 我的鋼筆尖彎了。

tip
尖

tired /'taɪəd; 美 'taɪrd/ [形容詞] 疲勞的，累的 *If you're tired, you should go to bed early.* 如果你累了，你應該早點上牀睡覺。
be tired of 厭煩，厭倦 *I'm tired of this game. Let's play something else.* 這個遊戲我玩膩了，咱們玩點別的吧。

tissue /'tɪʃuː/ [名詞] 紙巾 *Mum bought two boxes of tissues.* 媽媽買了兩盒紙巾。

title /'taɪtl/ [名詞] (書、電影、電視節目等的) 名稱；標題；題目 *Do you still remember the title of the book?* 你還記得那本書的書名嗎？

to¹ / 強 tuː; 弱 tʊ; tə / [介詞] **1** [表示方向] 向，朝 *Alice always walks to school.* 艾麗斯總是步行上學。**2**[表示動作的對象]對，於 *Be kind to animals.* 要善待動物。**3** [表示關聯、關係] 對於，關於 *Where's the key to the front door?* 前門的鑰匙在哪裏？**4**[指時間]在⋯之前；直到 *It's ten to six.* 現在差10分鐘6點。◇ *We go to school from Monday to Friday.* 我們星期一到星期五上學。

to² / 強 tuː; 弱 tʊ; tə / [用於動詞前，構成不定式] *I want to go home.* 我想回家。◇ *Don't forget to lock the door.* 別忘了鎖門。

toast /təʊst; 美 toʊst / [名詞] [無複數] 烤麵包（片），吐司 *I like toast for breakfast.* 我早餐喜歡吃烤麵包。

today¹ / təˈdeɪ / [副詞] 今天 *It's Monday today.* 今天是星期一。

today² /təˈdeɪ / [名詞] 今天 *Today is Monday.* 今天是星期一。

toe /təʊ; 美 toʊ / [名詞] 腳趾 *These shoes are too small. I can't move my toes.* 這雙鞋太小了，我的腳指頭動不了。

toe
腳趾

together /təˈɡeðə; 美 -ər / [副詞] 共同，一起 *Sometimes my dad and I go fishing together.* 有時我和爸爸一起去釣魚。

toilet /ˈtɔɪlət / [名詞] 廁所，洗手間 *Mum, I want to go to the toilet.* 媽，我想去洗手間。

told /təʊld; 美 toʊld / **tell** 的過去式和過去分詞 *The doctor told her to eat lots of fruit.* 醫生讓她多吃水果。

tomato /təˈmɑːtəʊ; 美 -ˈmeɪtoʊ / [名詞] [複數 **tomatoes**] 番茄，西紅柿 *Do you like tomato juice?* 你喜歡番茄汁嗎？

tomorrow¹ /təˈmɒrəʊ; 美 -ˈmɑːroʊ / [副詞] 明天 *Let's go swimming tomorrow.* 我們明天去游泳吧。

tomorrow² /təˈmɒrəʊ; 美 -ˈmɑːroʊ / [名詞] 明天 *Tomorrow is Tuesday.* 明天是星期二。

tongue /tʌŋ / [名詞] 舌頭 *It's rude to put out your tongue.* 伸舌頭是不

禮貌的。

tonight¹ /tə'naɪt/ [副詞] 今晚 *What're you doing tonight?* 你今晚做甚麼？

tonight² /tə'naɪt/ [名詞] 今晚 *Tonight will be cloudy.* 今晚多雲。

too /tuː/ [副詞] **1** 也 *I like bananas, but I like oranges too.* 我喜歡吃香蕉，但我也喜歡吃橙子。 ☞ 參見 **also** "也，還"。 **2** 太，過於 *This shirt is too small for me.* 這件襯衫太小了，我穿不下。

took /tʊk/ **take** 的過去式 *It took me ten minutes to walk home.* 我走到家用了 10 分鐘。

tool /tuːl/ [名詞] 工具 *Hammers and saws are tools.* 錘子和鋸都是工具。

tooth /tuːθ/ [名詞] [複數 **teeth** /tiːθ/] 牙齒 *She's got beautiful teeth.* 她的牙齒很美。

toothache /'tuːθeɪk/ [名詞] 牙疼 *I've got a toothache.* 我牙疼。

toothbrush /'tuːθbrʌʃ/ [名詞] [複數 **toothbrushes**] 牙刷 *Where's my toothbrush?* 我的牙刷在哪裏？

toothpaste /'tuːθpeɪst/ [名詞] [無複數] 牙膏 *I don't like the taste of this toothpaste.* 我不喜歡這種牙膏的味道。

top /tɒp; 美 tɑːp/ [名詞] **1** 頂，頂部 *Henry climbed to the top of the hill.* 亨利爬到山頂。 **2** 蓋子 *Where's the top of this bottle?* 這個瓶子的蓋子在哪裏？

topic /'tɒpɪk; 美 'tɑː-/ [名詞] 題目；話題；主題 *I want to speak for two minutes on the topic of homework.* 我想就家庭作業這個話題講兩分鐘。

torch /tɔːtʃ; 美 tɔːrtʃ/ [名詞] 手電筒 *Alice has got a small torch.* 艾麗斯有個小手電筒。 ☞ 美國英語通常用 **flash light**。

tore /tɔː; 美 tɔːr/ **tear** 的過去式 *I tore my jeans on a nail.* 我的牛仔褲被釘子刮破了。

tortoise /'tɔːtəs; 美 'tɔːr-/ [名詞] 龜，烏龜；陸龜 *Tortoises move very slowly.* 烏龜爬得很慢。

total¹ /'təʊtl; 美 'toʊ-/ [形容詞] 總的，全部的 *What's the total number of students in this school?* 這所學校一共有多少學生？

total[2] /'təʊtl; 美 'toʊ-/ [名詞] 總數 When you add three and five and eight the total is sixteen. 3 加 5 加 8 總數是 16。

touch /tʌtʃ/ [動詞]（尤指用手）觸摸，碰 Don't touch that bowl — it's very hot. 別摸那個碗，燙得很。

tough /tʌf/ [形容詞] **1** 堅韌的；結實的 These shoes are very tough. 這雙鞋很結實。 **2** 堅強的，能吃苦的 Henry's very tough. 亨利很堅強。

towards /tə'wɔːdz; 美 tɔːrdz/ [介詞] 向，朝 Look towards the camera and smile. 看着相機笑一笑。

towel /'taʊəl/ [名詞] 毛巾 Remember to bring a towel. 別忘了帶一條毛巾來。

tower /'taʊə; 美 -ər/ [名詞] 塔；塔樓 We visited the Eiffel Tower. 我們參觀了埃菲爾鐵塔。

town /taʊn/ [名詞] 城鎮，市鎮 A town is bigger than a village but smaller than a city. 城鎮比鄉村大，但比城市小。

toy /tɔɪ/ [名詞] 玩具 I like Helen. She lets me play with her toys. 我喜歡海倫，她讓我玩她的玩具。

toy car
玩具汽車

track /træk/ [名詞] **1** 小道，小徑 We walked along a track through the woods. 我們沿着小道步行穿過樹林。 **2** 足跡，痕跡 We saw his tracks in the snow. 我們看見雪地上有他的足跡。

T

tractor /'træktə; 美 -ər/ [名詞] 拖拉機 The farmer has a tractor. 那位農民有一輛拖拉機。

traffic /'træfɪk/ [名詞][無複數]（路上的）車輛 There is a lot of traffic in the streets today. 今天街道上車輛很多。

traffic lights /ˈtræfɪk laɪts/ [名詞] [複數] 交通信號燈，紅綠燈 *Turn left at the traffic lights.* 在紅綠燈向左拐。

train /treɪn/ [名詞] 火車 *We get off the train at the next station.* 我們下一站下火車。

transparent /trænsˈpærənt/ [形容詞] 透明的 *Glass is transparent.* 玻璃是透明的。

transport /ˈtrænspɔːt; 美 -ɔːrt/ [名詞] [無複數] 交通工具 *I travel to school by public transport.* 我乘坐公共交通工具上學。

trap /træp/ [動詞] [現在分詞 **trapping**，過去式和過去分詞 **trapped**] (用捕捉器) 捕捉 (動物) *The farmer trapped the rats.* 那位農民用老鼠夾捕住老鼠。

travel¹ /ˈtrævl/ [動詞] [現在分詞 **travelling**，過去式和過去分詞 **travelled**] 從一處到另一處；旅行 *How do you travel to school — do you walk or take the bus?* 你怎樣去上學，你走路還是坐公共汽車？

travel² /ˈtrævl/ [名詞] [無複數] 旅行 *She loves travel.* 她喜歡旅行。

tray /treɪ/ [名詞] 托盤 *She put the glasses on a tray.* 她把玻璃杯放在托盤上。

tray
托盤

treasure /ˈtreʒə; 美 -ər/ [名詞] [無複數] 金銀財寶 *The treasure had been hidden in a cave by pirates.* 那些金銀財寶被海盜藏在洞裏了。

treat /triːt/ [動詞] **1** 對待 *He treats me very well.* 他對我很好。**2** 醫治，治療 *The doctor was treating a patient.* 醫生在給一位病人治病。

tree /triː/ [名詞] 樹 *We sat under a tree to keep cool.* 我們坐在樹下乘涼。

triangle /'traɪæŋgl/ [名詞] 三角形 *Do you know how to draw a triangle?* 你會畫三角形嗎？

trick /trɪk/ [名詞] 詭計 *He didn't really lose his wallet — that's just a trick.* 他並沒有真的丟錢包，那只是一個詭計。 **play a trick on sb** 捉弄某人，戲弄某人 *Peter played a trick on me and hid my schoolbag.* 彼得捉弄我，把我的書包藏了起來。

tricycle /'traɪsɪkl/ [名詞] 三輪車 *Small children usually ride a tricycle before learning to ride a bike.* 小孩子們在學騎自行車以前通常騎三輪車。

tried /traɪd/ **try** 的過去式和過去分詞 *He tried to climb the tree, but he could not.* 他試圖爬樹，但沒能爬上去。

trip¹ /trɪp/ [名詞] （尤指短途的）旅行；出行 *Did you enjoy your trip to France?* 你的法國之行愉快嗎？

trip² /trɪp/ [動詞] [現在分詞 **tripping**，過去式和過去分詞 **tripped**] 絆倒 *Be careful! Don't trip over that box.* 小心！別被那個箱子絆倒。

trouble /'trʌbl/ [名詞] **1** 困難 *Did you have any trouble finding my house?* 你找到我家有困難嗎？ **2** 問題 *I'd like to go to the party, but the trouble is my parents won't let me.* 我想去參加聚會，但問題是我父母不讓我去。 **3** 麻煩 *I'm sorry to put you to so much trouble.* 給你添這麼多麻煩真對不起。

trousers /'traʊzəz; 美 -ərz/ [名詞] [複數] 褲子，長褲 *Go and put on a clean pair of trousers.* 去穿一條乾淨褲子。

truck /trʌk/ [名詞] 貨車，卡車 *My uncle drives a truck.* 我叔叔開卡車。 ☞ 美國英語用 **truck**，英國英語用 **lorry**。

true /truː/ [形容詞] 真的，真實的；正確的 *Is it true that some birds cannot fly?* 有些鳥不會飛，這是真的嗎？ ◇ *It's a true story.* 這是一個真實的故事。

trumpet /'trʌmpɪt; 美 -tə/ [名詞] 喇

叭;小號 *Can you play the trumpet?*
你會吹小號嗎?

trunk /trʌŋk/ [名詞] **1** 樹幹 *The tree has a thick trunk.* 這棵樹的樹幹很粗。**2** (象的)鼻子 *The elephant sucked water with its trunk.* 大象用鼻子吸水。

trust /trʌst/ [動詞] 信任,信賴 *Don't trust him — he never tells the truth.* 別相信他,他從來不說實話。

truth /truːθ/ [名詞] [用作單數] 真相;事實 *You should tell the truth.* 你應該說實話。

try /traɪ/ [動詞] [現在分詞 **trying**,過去式和過去分詞 **tried**] **1** 試圖;努力 *I tried to open the door, but it was locked.* 我試圖開門,可門鎖着呢。◇ *Please try not to be late.* 請盡量不要遲到。**2** 試,嘗試 *Let me try.* 讓我試一試。◇ *Have you tried this chocolate?* 你嘗過這種巧克力嗎?

try on 試穿 *Can I try these shoes on, please?* 請問,我可以試一下這雙鞋嗎?

T-shirt /'tiːʃɜːt; 美 -ʃɜːrt/ [名詞] 短袖汗衫;T恤衫 *Henry is wearing a green T-shirt.* 亨利穿着一件綠T恤衫。

tube /tjuːb; 美 tuːb/ [名詞] **1** 管子 *He used a tube to remove the water.* 他用一根管子排水。

2 (裝牙膏等的)軟管 *I bought a new tube of toothpaste.* 我買了一管新牙膏。

Tuesday /'tjuːzdi; 美 'tuːz-/ [名詞] 星期二 *Today is Tuesday.* 今天是星期二。① 參見**Monday**的示例。② **Tue** 或 **Tues** 是 **Tuesday** 的縮寫。

tune /tjuːn; 美 tuːn/ [名詞] 調子,曲調 *That song has a happy tune.* 那首歌調子歡快。

tunnel /'tʌnl/ [名詞] 隧道 *The train went through a long tunnel.* 那列火車穿過一條長長的隧道。

tunnel
隧道

turkey /'tɜːki; 美 'tɜːrki / [名詞] 火雞 *We usually have turkey at Christmas.* 我們通常在聖誕節吃火雞。☞ 在英國人們通常在聖誕節吃火雞，在美國通常在感恩節（**Thanksgiving**）吃火雞。

turn[1] /tɜːn; 美 tɜːrn / [動詞] **1** （使）轉動；（使）旋轉 *The wheels were turning.* 輪子都在轉動。◇ *I turned the handle and opened the door.* 我轉了一下把手，把門打開。 **2** 翻，翻轉 *Turn to page 36.* 翻到36頁。 **3** （使）轉向；轉彎 *Turn right at the traffic lights.* 在紅綠燈向右拐。 **4** 變成 *His hair has turned grey.* 他的頭髮白了。

turn off 關掉（電燈、電視等） *Do you want me to turn off the television?* 你要我關掉電視嗎？☞ ①[同]**switch off** 關掉 ②[反]**turn on**，**switch on** 打開

turn on 打開（電燈、電視等） *Turn on the light, please.* 請開燈。☞ ①[同]**switch on** 打開 ②[反]**turn off**，**switch off** 關掉

turn[2] /tɜːn; 美 tɜːrn / [名詞] [通常用作單數]（輪流的）一次機會 *Whose turn is it?* 輪到誰了？◇ *It's my turn to play.* 輪到我玩了。

in turn 依次，輪流 *We used the computer in turn.* 我們輪流使用這台電腦。

take turns 依次，輪流 *We took turns to use the computer.* 我們輪流使用這台電腦。

TV /ˌtiː 'viː/ [名詞] 電視 *We're watching TV.* 我們在看電視。☞ **TV** 是 **television** 的縮寫。

twelfth /twelfθ/ [數詞] 第十二 *It's her twelfth birthday today.* 今天是她的12歲生日。 ☞ 參見 **fifth** 的示例。

twelve /twelv/ [數詞] 十二 *Four times three is twelve.* 4乘3得12。 ☞ 參見 **five** 的示例。

twenty /'twenti/ [數詞] 二十 *Five times four is twenty.* 5乘4得20。 ☞ 參見 **fifty** 的示例。

twice /twaɪs/ [副詞] 兩次；兩倍 *I have a piano lesson twice a week.* 我每週上兩次鋼琴課。

twin /twɪn/ [名詞] 孿生兒，雙胞胎 *These two boys are twins. They're very alike.* 這兩個男孩是雙胞胎，他們倆長得很像。

T

twinkle /'twɪŋkl/ [動詞] 閃爍，閃耀
The stars twinkled in the sky. 星星在
空中閃爍。

twist /twɪst/ [動詞] **1** 盤繞，纏繞
Twist the wire to form a circle. 把電
線盤成一個圈。 **2** 轉動，擰 *Twist the
lid to open it.* 把蓋子擰開。

3 扭傷（腳踝） *I twisted my ankle
when I fell downstairs.* 我從樓梯摔下
時把腳踝扭傷了。

two /tuː/ [數詞] 二 *One and one are
two.* 1 加 1 等於 2。 ☞ 參見 **five** 的
示例。

type¹ /taɪp/ [名詞] 類型；種類
*Which type of ice cream would you
like — chocolate or strawberry?* 你
想吃哪一種冰淇淋，巧克力的還是草莓
的？◇ *I like all types of fruit.* 我喜歡
吃各種各樣的水果。

type² /taɪp/ [動詞]（用電腦鍵盤）打
（字）*Can you type?* 你會打字嗎？◇
Can you type your name? 你會打你
的名字嗎？

tyre /'taɪə; 美 'taɪr/ [名詞] 輪胎 *My
bike's got a flat tyre.* 我的自行車輪
胎癟了。

U u

ugly /ˈʌgli/ [形容詞] [比較級**uglier**，最高級**ugliest**] 醜陋的，難看的 *He was wearing an ugly jacket.* 他穿着一件難看的夾克。

umbrella /ʌmˈbrelə/ [名詞] 雨傘 *Bring an umbrella in case it rains.* 帶把雨傘，以防下雨。

unable /ʌnˈeɪbl/ [形容詞] **be unable to** [用作情態動詞] 不能，不會 *She is unable to swim.* 她不會游泳。 ☞ 表示"不能，不會"，也可以使用**can't**或**cannot**。

uncle /ˈʌŋkl/ [名詞] 伯父；叔父；舅父；姑父；姨夫 *One of my uncles is a doctor.* 我的一位叔叔是醫生。

uncomfortable /ʌnˈkʌmftəbl/ [形容詞] 不舒適的，不舒服的 *This bed is very uncomfortable.* 這張牀很不舒適。 ☞ [反] **comfortable** 舒適的，舒服的

under /ˈʌndə; 美 -ər/ [介詞] **1** 在…下面，在…底下 *'Where's the dog?' 'It's under the table.'* "狗在哪裏?" "在桌子底下。" ☞ [反] **over²** 在…以上

2 (在數目、年齡等方面)少於，低於 *The meal was cheap — under $30.* 這頓飯便宜，不到30美元。◇ *Most children under five don't go to school.* 大部分5歲以下的孩子不上學。 ☞ [反] **over²** 超過，在…以上

underground¹ /ˌʌndəˈgraʊnd; 美 -ər-/ [副詞] 在地下 *They're putting the telephone lines underground.* 他們正在把電話線埋在地下。

underground² /ˈʌndəgraʊnd; 美 -ər-/ [名詞] [用作單數] 地鐵 *We went there by underground.* 我們乘地鐵去的那裏。 ☞ 指"地鐵"，英國英語用**underground**，美國英語用**subway**。

underline /ˌʌndəˈlaɪn; 美 -ər-/ [動詞] 在…的下面畫線 *This sentence is underlined.* 本句下面畫了線。

underneath /ˌʌndəˈniːθ; 美 -ər-/ [介詞] 在…下面，在…底下 *The dog is sitting underneath the table.* 狗正在桌子底下蹲着呢。 ☞ 參見**under** "在…下面，在…底下"。

understand /ˌʌndə'stænd; 美 -ər/
[動詞] [過去式和過去分詞 **understood**
/ˌʌndə'stʊd; 美 -ər-/] 懂；理解；明白
She doesn't understand English. 她
不懂英語。◇ *'Do you understand?'*
'No, can you explain that again?'
"你明白了嗎？""沒有，你再解釋一下
行嗎？"

understood /ˌʌndə'stʊd; 美 -ər-/
understand 的過去式和過去分詞 *I*
only understood a few words. 我只
懂幾個詞。

underwear /'ʌndəweə; 美 -ərwer/
[名詞] [無複數] 內衣 *Put these pants*
in your underwear drawer. 把這條
內褲放在你的內衣抽屜裏。

undo /ʌn'duː/ [動詞] [過去式 **undid**
/ʌn'dɪd/，過去分詞 **undone** /ʌn'dʌn/]
解開，鬆開 *Henry undid his belt and*
took his jeans off. 亨利解開皮帶，脫
下牛仔褲。

undress /ʌn'dres/ [動詞] 脫衣服
You can undress in here. 你可以在這
裏脫衣服。

unexpected /ˌʌnɪk'spektɪd/ [形
容詞] 想不到的；出人意料的 *We had*
an unexpected visit from my
grandparents. 我的祖父母出乎意料地
來看我們。

unfair /ˌʌn'feə; 美 -'fer/ [形容詞] 不
公平的，不公正的 *It's unfair to give*
sweets to him and not to me. 給他
糖而不給我是不公平的。☞ [反] **fair**
公平的，公正的

unhappy /ʌn'hæpi/ [形容詞] [比
較級 **unhappier**，最高級 **unhappiest**]
不高興的，不快樂的 *Peter was*
unhappy because he had failed his
maths exam. 彼得不高興，因為他數
學考試沒及格。☞ [反] **happy** 高興
的，快樂的

uniform /'juːnɪfɔːm; 美 -fɔːrm/ [名詞]
制服 *Peter was still wearing his school*
uniform. 彼得仍穿着校服。

unit /'juːnɪt/ [名詞] (計數或計量的)單
位 *The pound is the unit of money in*
Britain. 英鎊是英國的貨幣單位。

United Kingdom /juˌnaɪtɪd
'kɪŋdəm; 美 -əd/ [名詞] [用作單數，與
the 連用] 聯合王國(大不列顛及北愛爾
蘭聯合王國的簡稱)，英國 *She is going*
to study in the United Kingdom. 她打
算去英國留學。☞ ① 縮寫為 **UK**。②
參見 **Great Britain** "大不列顛，英國"。

United Nations /juˌnaɪtɪd ˈneɪʃnz; 美 -əd/ [名詞] [用作單數，與the連用] 聯合國 *When was the United Nations established?* 聯合國是甚麼時候成立的？ 🔊 縮寫為**UN**。

United States (of America) /juˌnaɪtɪd ˈsteɪts (əv əˈmerɪkə); 美 -əd/ [名詞] [用作單數，與**the**連用] 美利堅合眾國，美國 *The United States is the richest country in the world.* 美國是世界上最富的國家。🔊 ① 縮寫為**US**或**USA**。② 參見**America**"美國"。

universe /ˈjuːnɪvɜːs; 美 -vɜːrs/ [名詞] [用作單數，與**the**連用] 宇宙 *The earth is one of the planets in the universe.* 地球是宇宙中的一顆行星。

university /ˌjuːnɪˈvɜːsəti; 美 -ɜːr-/ [名詞] [複數**universities**] 大學 *Which university did you go to?* 你上的是哪所大學？

unkind /ˌʌnˈkaɪnd/ [形容詞] 不仁慈的；刻薄的；殘忍的 *I don't know why he's always so unkind to me.* 我不知道他為甚麼總是對我這麼刻薄。🔊 [反] **kind** 和藹的；仁慈的

unlucky /ʌnˈlʌki/ [形容詞] [比較級 **unluckier**，最高級**unluckiest**] 不幸的；倒霉的；不吉利的 *Some people think that the number 13 is unlucky.* 有些人認為13這個數字不吉利。🔊 [反] **lucky** 幸運的

unpleasant /ʌnˈpleznt/ [形容詞] 令人不愉快的 *What's that unpleasant smell?* 那種難聞的氣味是甚麼？ 🔊 [反] **pleasant** 令人愉快的

untidy /ʌnˈtaɪdi/ [形容詞] [比較級 **untidier**，最高級**untidiest**] 不整潔的，凌亂的 *This bedroom is very untidy.* 這間卧室太不整潔。🔊 [反] **tidy** 整潔的，整齊的

until /ənˈtɪl/ [連詞] 直到…(為止) *We stayed on the beach until it got dark.* 我們在海灘上一直待到天黑。

unusual /ʌnˈjuːʒuəl/ [形容詞] 不平常的，異常的 *It's unusual for Henry to be late.* 亨利遲到很不尋常。🔊 [反] **usual** 通常的，平常的

up¹ /ʌp/ [副詞] **1** 向上 *Put your hand up if you know the answer.* 知道答案的請舉手。🔊 [反] **down¹** 向下 **2** 趨向(直立)姿勢；起來；起牀 *Stand up, please.* 請站起來。◇ *Is he up yet?* 他起牀了嗎？

up² /ʌp/ [介詞] 向(高處) *The monkey climbed up a tree.* 猴子爬上了一棵樹。🔊 [反] **down²** 向(低處)

upon /əˈpɒn; 美 əˈpɑːn/ [介詞] [正式] 在…上 *Mum laid a cloth upon the table.* 媽媽在桌子上鋪了一塊布。

upright /ˈʌpraɪt/ [副詞] 垂直地，直立地 *Keep the bottle upright.* 把瓶子豎直。

upset /ˌʌpˈset/ [形容詞] 心裏難過的，悶悶不樂的 *Peter was very upset when he failed the exam.* 彼得考試沒及格，他心裏很難過。

upside down /ˌʌpsaɪd ˈdaʊn/ [副詞] 顛倒着;倒掛着 *The picture is upside down.* 這幅畫掛倒了。

upstairs /ˌʌpˈsteəz; 美 -ˈsterz/ [副詞] 樓上 *"Where's Henry?" "He's upstairs."* "亨利在哪裏?" "他在樓上。" ☞ [反] **downstairs** 樓下

urgent /ˈɜːdʒənt; 美 ˈɜːr-/ [形容詞] 緊急的,急迫的 *It is not urgent—I'll tell you about it later.* 這事不急,我以後再告訴你吧。

us /強 ʌs; 弱 əs/ [代詞] [**we**的賓格] 我們 *The teacher told us to be quiet.* 老師讓我們安靜。

use /juːz/ [動詞] 用;使用 *Do you want to use chopsticks or a knife and fork?* 你想用筷子還是想用刀叉?

used /juːst/ [形容詞] [作表語,與**to**連用]習慣於…的 *I'm not used to getting up so early.* 我不習慣起得這麼早。

used to /句末或元音前ˈjuːst tu; 輔音前ˈjuːst tə/ [情態動詞] 過去通常 *When I was small, I used to sleep in my parents' bedroom.* 我小時候通常睡在父母的卧室裏。

useful /ˈjuːsfl/ [形容詞] 有用的;有益的 *You can get a lot of useful information from the Internet.* 你可以從互聯網上獲取大量有用的信息。☞ [反] **useless** 無用的;無益的

useless /ˈjuːsləs/ [形容詞] 無用的;無益的 *A pen is useless without ink.* 鋼筆沒有墨水沒用。☞ [反] **useful** 有用的;有益的

usual /ˈjuːʒuəl/ [形容詞] 通常的,平常的 *I ate more than usual.* 我比平常吃得多。◇ *He sat in his usual seat at the back.* 他坐在後面平常坐的座位上。☞ [反] **unusual** 不平常的,異常的

usually /ˈjuːʒuəli/ [副詞] 通常 *I usually get up at half past six.* 我通常6點半起牀。

V v

vacuum cleaner /ˈvækjuəm ˌkliːnə; 美 -ər/ [名詞] (真空)吸塵器 *Mum cleaned the floor with a vacuum cleaner.* 媽媽用吸塵器把地板吸乾淨。

valley /ˈvæli/ [名詞] 山谷，峽谷 *There is a village in the valley.* 山谷中有一個村莊。

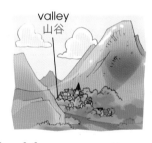

valley
山谷

valuable /ˈvæljʊəbl; 美 -jə-/ [形容詞] **1** 值錢的；貴重的 *Is this painting valuable?* 這幅畫值錢嗎？ **2** 寶貴的；有價值的；極有用的 *Your help has been very valuable.* 你的幫助一直十分有用。

value /ˈvæljuː/ [名詞] 價值 *What is the value of this painting?* 這幅畫值多少錢？

van /væn/ [名詞] (小型)貨車 *The van driver got out and opened the back door of his van.* 司機下車把貨車的後門打開。 ☞ **van**比**lorry**小，有篷蓋。

vanish /ˈvænɪʃ/ [動詞] 突然不見，消失 *Their son vanished six weeks ago.* 他們的兒子6個星期前不見了。

variety /vəˈraɪəti/ [名詞] [複數 **varieties**] **1** [用作單數] 種種 *These shirts come in a variety of colours.* 這些襯衫有多種顏色。 **2** 種類 *This variety of apple is very sweet.* 這種蘋果很甜。

various /ˈveəriəs; 美 ˈveriəs/ [形容詞] 各種各樣的 *There are various colours to choose from — which do you like best?* 有多種顏色可供選擇，你最喜歡哪一種？

vase /vɑːz; 美 veɪz/ [名詞] 花瓶 *She put the roses into a glass vase.* 她把玫瑰放進了一個玻璃花瓶。

vegetables 蔬菜

aubergine
[英國英語] 茄子
eggplant
[美國英語] 茄子

cabbage
洋白菜

leek
韭葱

tomato
西紅柿

carrot
胡蘿蔔

cucumber
黃瓜

peas
豌豆

pepper
柿子椒

lettuce
生菜

mushrooms
蘑菇

cauliflower
花椰菜

potatoes
土豆

onion
洋葱

vegetable /ˈvedʒtəbl/ [名詞] 蔬菜
We eat lots of fruit and vegetables.
我們吃大量的水果和蔬菜。

vehicle /ˈviːɪkl; 美 ˈviːəkl/ [名詞] 運
載工具；車輛 *You can also call a*
bicycle or tricycle a vehicle. 你也可
以把自行車或三輪車叫做運載工具。

very /ˈveri/ [副詞] 很，非常 *It's very*
hot in this room. 這個房間裏很熱。◇
Thank you very much. 非常感謝。

vehicles 運載工具

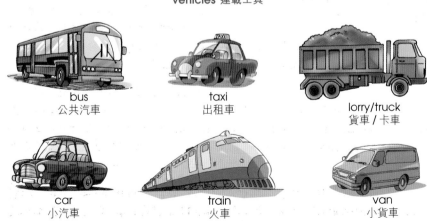

bus
公共汽車

taxi
出租車

lorry/truck
貨車 / 卡車

car
小汽車

train
火車

van
小貨車

vest /vest/ [名詞] 內衣，汗衫 *Paul is wearing a cotton vest.* 保羅穿着一件棉汗衫。

學校學小提琴。

vet /vet/ [名詞] 獸醫 *We took the dog to the vet.* 我們帶狗去就醫。

video /'vɪdɪəu; 美 -ou/ [名詞] [複數 **videos**] 錄像帶 *We're going to watch some videos tonight.* 我們今晚打算看幾盤錄像帶。

view /vjuː/ [名詞] **1** 意見，看法，觀點 *What are your views on animal rights?* 你對動物權有甚麼看法？ **2** [用作單數] 視綫，視力 *Sit down — you're blocking my view.* 坐下，你擋住我的視綫了。 **3** 景色 *There are great views from the mountain.* 從山上看景色壯觀。

village /'vɪlɪdʒ/ [名詞] 鄉村，村莊 *In some villages there's no school.* 有些村莊沒有學校。

vinegar /'vɪnɪgə; 美 -ər/ [名詞] [無複數] 醋 *Pass the vinegar, please.* 請把醋遞過來。

violent /'vaɪələnt/ [形容詞] 猛烈的，激烈的 *A lot of trees were blown down in violent storm.* 許多樹在狂風暴雨中被颳倒了。

violin /ˌvaɪə'lɪn/ [名詞] 小提琴 *I'm learning the violin at school.* 我正在

visit¹ /'vɪzɪt; 美 -ət/ [動詞] 訪問；探望；參觀；遊覽 *We're visiting my aunt this evening.* 我們今晚要去看望我姑姑。

visit² /'vɪzɪt; 美 -ət/ [名詞] 訪問；探望；參觀；遊覽 *Did you enjoy your visit to the zoo?* 你在動物園玩得高興嗎？

visitor /'vɪzɪtə; 美 -ətər/ [名詞] 訪問者；來賓；遊客；參觀者 *Beijing has millions of visitors each year.* 北京每年有千百萬遊客。

vitamin /'vɪtəmɪn; 美 'vaɪ-/ [名詞] 維生素，維他命 *Oranges contain vitamin C.* 橙子含有維生素C。

voice /vɔɪs/ [名詞] 嗓音；(説話、唱歌的)聲音 *I could hear voices in the next room.* 我能聽見隔壁房間的聲音。 ◇ *She spoke in a loud voice.* 她大聲地説。

volcano /vɒl'keɪnəu; 美 vɑ-l'keɪnou/ [名詞] [複數 **volcanoes**] 火山 *Smoke and flames were pouring from the volcano.* 煙和火焰正在從火山中噴出。

volume /'vɒljuːm; 美 'vɑːljəm/ [名詞] **1** [無複數] 體積；容積；容量 *What's* the volume of this box? 這個箱子的體積是多少？**2** [用作單數] 音量 *The television's too loud — turn the volume down.* 電視聲音太大，請把音量開小一點。

vote /vəʊt; 美 voʊt/ [動詞] 選舉；投票；表決 *Did you vote for her or against her?* 你投票支持她還是反對她？

vowel /ˈvaʊəl/ [名詞] 元音字母 *There are five vowel letters in the English alphabet.* 英語字母表中有5個元音字母。 ☞ 英語中以 **a、e、i、o、u** 表示元音字母。

voyage /ˈvɔɪɪdʒ/ [名詞]（一般指長途乘船的）旅行；航行 *I'd love to go on a voyage round the world.* 我很想去環球旅行。

V

W w

wade /weɪd/ [動詞] 涉水，蹚水 *We had to wade across the river.* 我們不得不蹚水過河。　☞ 美國英語用 **wade**，英國英語用 **paddle**。

waist /weɪst/ [名詞] 腰，腰部 *Henry fastened a belt around his waist.* 亨利繫上了腰帶。

wait /weɪt/ [動詞] 等，等候，等待 *We can't wait any longer.* 我們再也不能等了。◇ *She was waiting for the bus.* 她正在等公共汽車。

waiter /ˈweɪtə; 美 -ɪr/ [名詞] （男）侍者，（男）服務員 *Waiter, could you bring us some water?* 服務員，給我們來點水好嗎？

waitress /ˈweɪtrəs/ [名詞] [複數 **waitresses**] （女）侍者，（女）服務員

The waitress gave us each a menu and asked if we'd like something to drink. 女服務員給我們每人一份菜單，問我們是否要點喝的。

wake /weɪk/ [動詞] [過去式 **woke** /wəʊk; 美 wouk/，過去分詞 **woken** /ˈwəʊkən; 美 ˈwou-/] **1** 醒，醒來 *What time did you wake up this morning?* 你今天早晨幾點鐘醒的？ **2** 喚醒，弄醒 *Mum usually wakes me up at 6:30.* 媽媽通常 6 點半叫醒我。◇ *Don't wake the baby.* 別把寶寶吵醒了。　☞ **wake up** 比 **wake** 常用。

walk[1] /wɔːk/ [動詞] 走，步行；散步 *We usually walk to school.* 我們通常走着上學。

walk[2] /wɔːk/ [名詞] 步行；散步 *Shall we go for a walk this afternoon?* 我

們今天下午去散散步好嗎？

wall /wɔːl/ [名詞] 牆 *There was a wall around the park.* 公園四周有一道圍牆。

wallet /ˈwɒlɪt; 美 ˈwɑːlət/ [名詞] （男用）錢包 *Dad took some money out of his wallet.* 爸爸從錢包裏拿出一些錢。

wallpaper /ˈwɔːlˌpeɪpə; 美 -ər/ [名詞] [無複數] 牆紙，壁紙 *He put some wallpaper on the wall of his bedroom.* 他在臥室的牆上貼了些壁紙。

wander /ˈwɒndə; 美 ˈwɑːndər/ [動詞] 漫遊；閒逛；徘徊 *The children wandered about in the woods.* 孩子們在樹林裏閒逛。

want /wɒnt; 美 wɑːnt/ [動詞] 要，想要 *What do you want for your birthday?* 你過生日想要甚麼？ ◇ *They want to go to the park.* 他們想去公園。

war /wɔː; 美 wɔːr/ [名詞] 戰爭 *Many people died in the war.* 很多人在戰爭中死去了。

wardrobe /ˈwɔːdrəʊb; 美 ˈwɔːrdroʊb/ [名詞] 衣櫃，衣櫥 *Hang your school uniform up in the wardrobe.* 把你的校服掛在衣櫃裏。

warm¹ /wɔːm; 美 wɔːrm/ [形容詞] 溫暖的，暖和的 *It's warm today.* 今天天氣暖和。 ☞ [反] **cool** 涼的，涼爽的

warm² /wɔːm; 美 wɔːrm/ [動詞] 使溫暖，使暖和，使暖熱 *Mum was warming some milk for the baby.* 媽媽正在為寶寶加熱牛奶。

warn /wɔːn; 美 wɔːrn/ [動詞] 警告；提醒 *Mum warned me to be careful when I crossed the road.* 媽媽提醒我過馬路時要小心。

was /強 wɒz; 美 wʌz; 弱 wəz/ *I was late for school yesterday.* 我昨天上學遲到了。 ☞ 參見 **be¹**。

wash /wɒʃ; 美 wɑːʃ/ [動詞] 洗 *Have you washed your hands?* 你洗手了嗎？

washing machine /ˈwɒʃɪŋ məˌʃiːn; 美 ˈwɑː-/ [名詞] 洗衣機 *Mum put some clothes in the washing machine.* 媽媽把衣服放進了洗衣機。

wasn't /'wɒznt; 美 'wʌznt / **was not** 的 縮寫 *I phoned Henry but he wasn't at home.* 我給亨利打電話，可他不在家。

wasp /wɒsp; 美 wɑːsp / [名詞] 黃蜂 *A wasp stung me.* 一隻黃蜂把我螫了 一下。

waste /weɪst / [動詞] 浪費 *Don't waste water.* 不要浪費水。

watch[1] /wɒtʃ; 美 wɑːtʃ / [動詞] 觀 看，注視 *Do you often watch television?* 你經常看電視嗎？

watch[2] /wɒtʃ; 美 wɑːtʃ / [名詞] [複 數 **watches**] 手錶 *My watch is a bit slow.* 我的手錶有點慢了。

water[1] /'wɔːtə; 美 -ər / [名詞] [無複 數] 水 *I poured two glasses of water.* 我倒了兩杯水。

water[2] /'wɔːtə; 美 -ər / [動詞] 給…澆 水（或灌水）*Have you watered the flowers?* 你澆花了嗎？

waterfall /'wɔːtəfɔːl; 美 -ər- / [名詞] 瀑布 *We walked through the forest to see the waterfall.* 我們步行穿過森 林去看瀑布。

wave[1] /weɪv / [名詞] 浪，波浪 *Huge waves were breaking on the shore.* 巨浪拍打在岸上。

wave[2] /weɪv / [動詞] 揮手 *Henry waved goodbye to them.* 亨利向他 們揮手告別。

 W

wax /wæks / [名詞] [無複數] 蠟 *Candles are made of wax.* 蠟燭是 用蠟做的。

way /weɪ / [名詞] **1** 方法；方式 *One of the best ways to learn a language is to* read. 學習語言的最好方法之一就是閱讀。 **2** [通常用作單數] 路線 Is this the way to the station? 這是去車站的路嗎？

by the way 順便說一下，附帶說說 By the way, I saw Peter yesterday. 順便說一句，我昨天看見彼得了。

lose one's way 迷路 If you lose your way, phone me. 如果你迷了路，就給我打電話。

on the way 在…的路上 Dad bought a newspaper on his way home. 爸爸在回家的路上買了一份報紙。◇ On the way to the supermarket I met Henry. 在去超市的路上我遇見了亨利。

we /強 wiː; 弱 wi/ [代詞] [主格] 我們 We're going to the cinema. 我們要去看電影。

weak /wiːk/ [形容詞] 弱的，虛弱的 He told the doctor that he felt very weak. 他告訴醫生他覺得很虛弱。
☞ [反] **strong** 強壯的，健壯的

weapon /'wepən/ [名詞] 武器 Long ago, armies used bows and arrows as weapons. 很久以前，軍隊用弓箭作武器。

wear /weə; 美 wer/ [動詞] [過去式 **wore** /wɔː; 美 wɔːr/，過去分詞 **worn** /wɔːn; 美 wɔːrn/] 穿着；戴着 Helen is wearing a yellow blouse. 海倫穿着一件黃襯衫。

weather /'weðə; 美 -ər/ [名詞] [無複數] 天氣 What's the weather like in your country? 你們國家的天氣怎麼樣？

web /web/ [名詞] （蜘蛛的）網 Lots of spiders make webs to catch food. 許多蜘蛛織網來獵取食物。

we'd /強 wiːd; 弱 wid/ **1 we had** 的縮寫 We'd already eaten. 我們已經吃過了。**2 we would** 的縮寫 We'd like some water, please. 請給我們來點水。

wedding /'wedɪŋ/ [名詞] 婚禮 He's going to his brother's wedding tomorrow. 他明天去參加他哥哥的婚禮。

Wednesday /'wenzdeɪ/ [名詞] 星期三 It's Henry's birthday on Wednesday. 星期三是亨利的生日。
☞ ① 參見 **Monday** 的示例。② **Wed** 是 **Wednesday** 的縮寫。

weed /wiːd/ [名詞] 野草，雜草 Our garden is full of weeds. 我們的花園裏雜草叢生。

week /wiːk/ [名詞] 星期，週 Last

week I read two books. 上週我看了兩本書。

weekend /ˌwiːk'end/ [名詞] 週末 'What do you do at the weekend, Peter?' 'I go to the park.' "你週末做甚麼，彼得？""我去公園。" 英國英語用 **at the weekend**，美國英語用 **on the weekend**。

weigh /weɪ/ [動詞] **1** 稱…的重量（或體重） Have you ever weighed yourself? 你稱過體重嗎？**2** 重量（或體重）是 How much do you weigh? 你的體重是多少？

weight /weɪt/ [名詞] [無複數] 重量；體重 What's the weight of this parcel? 這個包裹有多重？◇ What is your weight? 你的體重是多少？

welcome[1] /'welkəm/ [動詞] 歡迎 Everyone came to the door to welcome us. 大家都到門口來歡迎我們。

welcome[2] /'welkəm/ [形容詞] 受歡迎的 You're always welcome here. 歡迎你隨時光臨。
you're welcome [口語] [用作答謝的客套話] 不用謝，別客氣 'Thanks for your help.' 'You're welcome.' "謝謝你的幫助。""不用謝。"

well[1] /wel/ [副詞] [比較級 **better**，最高級 **best**] 好 Did you sleep well? 你睡得好嗎？◇ Henry plays football well. 亨利足球踢得好。

well done! [口語] 幹得好！ You passed your exam! Well done! 你考試及格了！太好啦！

well[2] /wel/ [形容詞] [比較級 **better**，最高級 **best**] [不用於名詞前] 健康的 'How are you today?' 'I'm very well, thank you.' "你今天好嗎？""很好，謝謝你。"

well[3] /wel/ [名詞] 井 Some people have to fetch water from the well. 有些人不得不從井裏打水。

we'll / 強 wiːl; 弱 wil/ **we will** 的縮寫 We'll be late. 我們要遲到了。

well-known /ˌwel 'nəʊn; 美 -'noʊn/ [形容詞] 有名的，出名的 She is a well-known writer. 她是一位有名的作家。

went /went/ **go** 的過去式 We went to the beach yesterday. 我們昨天去了海灘。

were / 強 wɜː; 美 wɜːr; 弱 wə; 美 wər/ They were very happy. 他們非常快樂。 參見 **be**[1]。

we're /wɪə; 美 wɪr/ **we are** 的縮寫 We're in the same class. 我們在同一

W

個班。

weren't /wɜːnt; 美 wɜːrnt/ **were not** 的縮寫 *We weren't at school yesterday.* 我們昨天沒有上學。

west /west/ [名詞] [用作單數，常與 **the** 連用] 西，西方 *Which way is west?* 哪個方向是西？

wet /wet/ [形容詞] [比較級 **wetter**，最高級 **wettest**] 濕的，潮的 *My hair's still wet.* 我的頭髮還沒乾。 ☞ [反] **dry** 乾的

we've / 強 wiːv; 弱 wiv/ **we have** 的縮寫 *We've missed the train!* 我們沒趕上火車！

whale /weɪl/ [名詞] 鯨魚 *A whale looks like a fish, but it is actually a mammal.* 鯨魚長得像魚，但實際上是哺乳動物。

what /wɒt; 美 wʌt/ [疑問代詞] 甚麼 *What's this?* 這是甚麼？ ◇ *What are you doing?* 你在做甚麼？ ◇ *What kind of music do you like?* 你喜歡甚麼樣的音樂？

what's /wɒts; 美 wʌts/ **what is** 的縮寫 *What's your name?* 你叫甚麼名字？

wheat /wiːt/ [名詞] [無複數] 小麥

We drove past fields of wheat. 我們開車經過一片片麥地。

wheel /wiːl/ [名詞] 輪，車輪 *A car has four wheels.* 轎車有 4 個輪子。

wheelchair /ˈwiːltʃeə; 美 -tʃer/ [名詞] 輪椅 *He'll be in a wheelchair for the rest of his life.* 他要在輪椅上度過餘生。

when¹ /wen/ [疑問副詞] 甚麼時候 *When is your birthday?* 你的生日是甚麼時候？

when² /wen/ [連詞] 當⋯的時候 *Be careful when you cross the road.* 過馬路時要小心。

where /weə; 美 wer/ [疑問副詞] 在哪裏 *Where do you live?* 你住在哪裏？ ◇ *Where are you going?* 你去哪裏？

whether /ˈweðə; 美 -ər/ [連詞] 是否 *I don't know whether he'll come or not.* 我不知道他是否來。

which¹ /wɪtʃ/ [疑問代詞] 哪一個；

哪一些 Which is your bicycle? 哪一輛是你的自行車？

which[2] /wɪtʃ/ [疑問形容詞] 哪個；哪些 Which book do you like best? 你最喜歡哪本書？

while[1] /waɪl/ [連詞] 當⋯的時候，在⋯時 They arrived while we were having dinner. 我們正吃晚飯的時候，他們到了。

while[2] /waɪl/ [名詞] [用作單數] 一段時間，（尤指）一會 After a while she fell asleep. 過了一會，她睡着了。

whisper /ˈwɪspə; 美 -ər/ [動詞] 低語，低聲說話，耳語 You don't have to whisper — no one can hear us. 你不必小聲說，沒人能聽見我們。

whistle[1] /ˈwɪsl/ [名詞] 哨子 The teacher blew his whistle to start the race. 老師吹響了哨子，賽跑開始。

whistle[2] /ˈwɪsl/ [動詞] 吹口哨 Dad often whistles while he's shaving. 爸爸經常一邊刮鬍子一邊吹口哨。

white[1] /waɪt/ [形容詞] 白色的 She was wearing a white blouse. 她穿着一件白襯衫。

white[2] /waɪt/ [名詞] 白色 She was dressed in white. 她穿着白色的衣服。

who /huː/ 1 [疑問代詞] 誰 Who gave you that book? 誰給你的那本書？ 2 [關係代詞] [用以指提到的人] That's the boy who broke my ruler. 那個就是弄斷我尺子的男孩。

who'd /huːd/ 1 who had 的縮寫 Henry was the only one who'd seen the film. 亨利是惟一看過這部電影的人。2 who would 的縮寫 Who'd like to come? 誰想來？

whole[1] /həʊl; 美 hoʊl/ [形容詞] 全部的，整體的 He ate the whole packet of sweets. 他把整袋糖都吃了。

whole[2] /həʊl; 美 hoʊl/ [名詞] 全部，整體 Two halves make a whole. 兩個一半構成一個整體。

who'll /huːl/ who will 的縮寫 Who'll be there tomorrow? 明天誰在那裏？

whom /huːm/ [**who** 的賓格] 1 [疑問代詞] 誰 Whom did you see? 你看見誰了？ 2 [關係代詞] [用以指提到的人] That's the man whom I saw this morning. 那個就是我今天早上見到的人。 ☞ 在口語中常用 **who** 代替 **whom**，如：Who did you speak to? （你跟誰說話？）

who's /huːz/ 1 who is 的縮寫 Who's that boy? 那個男孩是誰？ 2 who has 的縮寫 Who's taken my pen? 誰拿了我的鋼筆？

whose / huːz / [疑問代詞] 誰的
Whose book is this? 這是誰的書？

why / waɪ / [疑問副詞] 為甚麼 *Why is she crying?* 她為甚麼哭了？ ◇ *No one knows why.* 沒有人知道為甚麼。

wicked /'wɪkɪd/ [形容詞] 壞的，邪惡的 *He is a wicked man.* 他是個壞蛋。

wide / waɪd / [形容詞] **1** 寬的，寬闊的 *This road is very wide.* 這條馬路很寬。 ☞ [反] **narrow** 窄的，狹窄的 **2** 寬度為…的，…寬的 *The table is one metre wide.* 這張桌子有 1 米寬。

width /wɪdθ/ [名詞] 寬度 *What's the width of the table?* 這張桌子有多寬？

wife / waɪf / [名詞] [複數 **wives** / waɪvz/] 妻子 *He loves his wife very much.* 他非常愛他的妻子。

wig / wɪg / [名詞] 假髮 *Some bald people wear wigs.* 有些禿頂的人戴假髮。

wig
假髮

wild / waɪld / [形容詞] (指動植物) 野生的 *The woods are full of wild flowers.* 樹林裏到處都是野花。

will / wɪl / [情態動詞] **1** [表示將來] 將要，會 *It will probably rain tomorrow.* 明天可能會下雨。 **2** [表示意願、請求等] 願；…行嗎 *Will you open the window, please?* 請你把窗戶打開好嗎？

willing /'wɪlɪŋ/ [形容詞] 願意的，心甘情願的 *Are you willing to help?* 你願意幫忙嗎？

win / wɪn / [動詞] [現在分詞 **winning**，過去式和過去分詞 **won** / wʌn /] 贏，獲勝 *Paul is good at chess. He always wins.* 保羅擅長國際象棋，他總是贏。

wind¹ / wɪnd / [名詞] 風 *The wind blew her hat off.* 風把她的帽子颳走了。

wind² / waɪnd / [動詞] [過去式和過去分詞 **wound** / waʊnd /] **1** 彎曲前進，蜿蜒 *The path winds through the woods.* 小路彎彎曲曲地穿過樹林。

2 纏繞 *She wound the rope around her arm.* 她把繩子纏在手臂上。

window /'wɪndəʊ; 美 -oʊ / [名詞] 窗，窗戶 *Open the window. It's hot in here.* 打開窗戶，這裏很熱。

windy /'wɪndi/ [形容詞] 有風的，風大的 *Tomorrow will be windy.* 明天有風。

wine / waɪn / [名詞] [無複數] 葡萄酒

W

Dad bought two bottles of wine. 爸爸買了兩瓶葡萄酒。

wing /wɪŋ/ [名詞] **1** 翅膀 *Some insects have one pair of wings and some have two pairs.* 有些昆蟲有一對翅膀，有些有兩對。 **2** 機翼 *I had a seat next to the wing.* 我的座位靠近機翼。

wink /wɪŋk/ [動詞] 眨眼 *Henry winked at me.* 亨利衝着我眨了眨眼。

winner /'wɪnə; 美 -ər/ [名詞] 獲勝者；優勝者 *Who was the winner of the competition?* 誰是比賽的獲勝者？

winter /'wɪntə; 美 -ər/ [名詞] 冬天，冬季 *In winter, many trees have no leaves on them.* 冬天許多樹上都沒有樹葉。

wipe /waɪp/ [動詞] 擦；擦淨；擦乾

She wiped the table. 她把桌子擦乾淨。◇ *Stop crying and wipe your eyes.* 別哭了，把眼淚擦乾。

wire /'waɪə; 美 'waɪr/ [名詞] 電線 *Twist those two wires together.* 把那兩根電線擰在一起。

wise /waɪz/ [形容詞] 聰明的，有智慧的 *He was a wise old man.* 他是一位有智慧的老人。

wish[1] /wɪʃ/ [動詞] **1** 但願 *I wish I could fly.* 但願我能飛。 **2** [正式] 想要，希望 *I wish to see him.* 我想見他。 **3** 祝，祝願 *I wished her a happy birthday.* 我祝她生日快樂。

W

wish[2] /wɪʃ/ [名詞] [複數**wishes**] **1** 願望；希望 *Doctors should respect the patient's wishes.* 醫生應該尊重病人的意願。 **2** 祝願，好意 *Please give my best wishes to your parents.* 請代我向你父母問好。◇ *Best wishes* 祝好 [信末結束語，通常以逗號結尾]

with /wɪð; 美 wɪθ/ [介詞] **1** 和…在一起，跟…在一起 *He lives with his parents.* 他跟父母住在一起。 **2** 具有，帶有 *Henry came back with a letter* *in his hand.* 亨利手裏拿着一封信回來了。**3** 用 *He opened the door with his key.* 他用鑰匙把門打開。

within /wɪð'ɪn/ [介詞] **1** [指時間] 在…之內 *I'll be back within an hour.* 我一小時以內回來。**2** 在…裏面，在…內部 *Please stay within the school ground.* 請待在學校操場裏邊。

without /wɪð'aʊt/ [介詞] 沒有 *You can't see the film without a ticket.* 沒有票看不了這場電影。

woke /wəʊk; 美 woʊk/ **wake** 的過去式 *Mum woke me up at seven o'clock.* 媽媽 7 點鐘把我叫醒了。

woken /'wəʊkən; 美 'woʊ-/ **wake** 的過去分詞 *The noise has woken the baby.* 噪音把寶寶吵醒了。

wolf /wʊlf/ [名詞] [複數 **wolves** / wʊlvz/] 狼 *Did you see a wolf at the zoo?* 你在動物園裏看見狼了嗎？

woman /'wʊmən/ [名詞] [複數 **women** /'wɪmɪn/] 婦女 *Most of the teachers at my school are women.* 我們學校大部分教師是女的。

won /wʌn/ **win** 的過去式和過去分詞 *Who won the football match?* 誰贏了足球比賽？

wonder /'wʌndə; 美 -ər/ [動詞] 想知道 *I wonder why John is always late for school.* 我想知道為甚麼約翰總是上學遲到。

won't /wəʊnt; 美 woʊnt/ **will not** 的縮寫 *I won't be late for school.* 我上學不會遲到。

wood /wʊd/ [名詞] **1** [無複數] 木材，木頭 *This furniture is made of wood.* 這件傢具是木製的。 **2** [常作複數] 樹林 *Last Friday, we went for a walk in the woods.* 上週五我們到樹林裏去散步了。

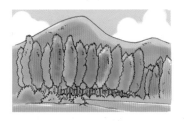

wooden /'wʊdn/ [形容詞] 木製的 *This is a wooden chair.* 這是一把木椅子。

wool /wʊl/ [名詞] [無複數] 羊毛 *Is the suit made of wool?* 那套衣服是羊毛的嗎？

word /wɜːd; 美 wɜːrd/ [名詞] 詞，單詞；字 *What does this word mean?* 這個詞是甚麼意思？

wore /wɔː; 美 wɔːr/ **wear** 的過去式

W

He wore glasses. 他戴着眼鏡。

work¹ /wɜːk; 美 wɜːrk/ [動詞] **1** 工作；幹活，勞動 He works in a bookshop. 他在書店工作。 **2**（機器等）運轉 Does this light work? 這盞燈能用嗎？

work² /wɜːk; 美 wɜːrk/ [名詞] [無複數] **1** 工作；勞動 His work is teaching. 他的工作是教書。 **2** 作業 The teacher marked our work. 老師批改了我們的作業。

worker /'wɜːkə; 美 'wɜːrkər/ [名詞] 工人 There are more than 200 workers in the factory. 這家工廠有 200 多名工人。

world /wɜːld; 美 wɜːrld/ [名詞] [用作單數，與 **the** 連用] 世界 Which is the longest river in the world? 哪條河是世界上最長的河？

worm /wɜːm; 美 wɜːrm/ [名詞]（細長的）蠕蟲；蚯蚓 Birds eat worms and insects. 鳥吃蠕蟲和昆蟲。

worn /wɔːn; 美 wɔːrn/ **wear** 的過去分詞 Have you worn your new coat yet? 你穿過你的新外套了嗎？

worry /'wʌri; 美 'wɜːri/ [動詞] [現在分詞 **worrying**，過去式和過去分詞 **worried**] 擔憂，擔心 Don't worry. We have plenty of time. 別擔心，我們有

的是時間。◇ He's always worrying about his weight. 他總是擔心自己的體重。

worse /wɜːs; 美 wɜːrs/ [形容詞] [**bad** 的比較級] 更壞的，更差的，更糟的 This film is much worse than the one we saw last week. 這部電影比我們上週看的那部差多了。

worst /wɜːst; 美 wɜːrst/ [形容詞] [**bad** 的最高級] 最壞的，最差的 He's the worst student in the class. 他是班上最差的學生。

worth /wɜːθ; 美 wɜːrθ/ [形容詞] 值…錢 How much is this ring worth? 這枚戒指值多少錢？

would / 強 wʊd; 弱 wəd/ **1** will 的過去式 Henry said he would play football on Saturday. 亨利說他星期六要踢球。 **2** [表示禮貌地請求] …好嗎 Would you pass me the salt, please? 請把鹽遞給我好嗎？ **3** [與 **like** 或 **love** 連用，以詢問或表達想要的東西] Would you like to come with us? 你想不想跟我們一塊兒去？◇ I'd love a piece of cake. 我想要一塊蛋糕。

wouldn't /'wʊdnt/ **would not** 的縮寫 I knew he wouldn't come. 我知道他不會來。

wound¹ /wuːnd/ [名詞]（尤指武器造成的）傷；傷口 The wound healed slowly. 傷口慢慢癒合了。

wound
傷口

W

wound² /wuːnd/ [動詞] 使受傷 *Many people were wounded when the bomb exploded.* 炸彈爆炸時許多人受了傷。

wound³ /waʊnd/ **wind²** 的過去式和過去分詞 *Henry wound the rope round the post.* 亨利把繩子纏在柱子上。

wrap /ræp/ [動詞] [現在分詞 **wrapping**，過去式和過去分詞 **wrapped**] 包，裹 *I wrapped up the present in paper.* 我用紙把禮物包起來。

wrinkle /ˈrɪŋkl/ [名詞] 皺紋 *The old man's face was covered with wrinkles.* 那位老人滿臉都是皺紋。

wrist /rɪst/ [名詞] 手腕 *Do you wear your watch on your left wrist or your right wrist?* 你的手錶是戴在左手腕上還是右手腕上？

write /raɪt/ [動詞] [過去式 **wrote** /rəʊt; 美 roʊt/，過去分詞 **written** /ˈrɪtn/] 1 寫（書、文章、詩等）；寫字 *He wrote some very famous books.* 他寫了幾本非常有名的書。◇ *The child is not yet able to write.* 這孩子還不會寫字。2 寫（信）*I've written a letter to my uncle (=I've written my uncle a letter).* 我給叔叔寫了一封信。◇ *Have you written to him?* 你給他寫信了嗎？

writer /ˈraɪtə; 美 -ər/ [名詞] 作家 *Who's your favourite writer?* 你最喜愛的作家是誰？

written /ˈrɪtn/ **write** 的過去分詞 *The article is very well written.* 這篇文章寫得很好。

wrong /rɒŋ; 美 rɔːŋ/ [形容詞] 1 錯誤的 *I got the wrong answer.* 我的答案錯了。◇ *You've got the wrong number.* 你把號碼弄錯了。 ☞ [反] **right¹**，**correct¹** 正確的，對的 2 [不用於名詞前] 不正常的，有毛病的 *What's wrong with the television? There's sound but no picture.* 電視出甚麼毛病了？有聲音卻沒畫面。 3 不對的 *Cheating is wrong.* 作弊是不對的。◇ *It's wrong to tell lies.* 撒謊是不對的。

wrote /rəʊt; 美 roʊt/ **write** 的過去式 *The teacher wrote the answers on the blackboard.* 老師把答案寫在了黑板上。

W

Xx

Xmas /ˈkrɪsməs/ [名詞] [非正式，書面用語] 聖誕節 *A merry Xmas to all our readers!* 敬祝各位讀者聖誕快樂！

X-ray /ˈeksreɪ/ [名詞] X 光片 *The X-ray showed that his hand was not broken.* X 光片顯示他的手沒有骨折。

Yy

yacht /jɒt; 美 jɑːt/ [名詞] 帆船；快艇；遊艇 *There were some yachts in the harbour.* 海港裏有幾艘遊艇。

yacht
帆船

yard /jɑːd; 美 jɑːrd/ [名詞] **1** 院子，庭院 *The children were playing in the school yard.* 孩子們正在學校院子裏玩。 **2** 碼 [長度單位，1碼等于3英尺] *This room is four yards wide.* 這間房間有4碼寬。

yawn¹ /jɔːn/ [動詞] 打哈欠 *You've been yawning all morning. Didn't you sleep last night?* 你整個早晨都在打哈欠，難道昨晚沒睡覺嗎？

yawn² /jɔːn/ [名詞] 哈欠 *'I'm going to bed,' he said with a yawn.* "我睡覺去了，"他邊說邊打了個哈欠。

year /jɪə; 美 jɪr/ [名詞] **1** 年 *There are twelve months in a year.* 1年有12個月。 **2** 年齡，年歲，年紀 *She is ten years old.* 她10歲。

yell /jel/ [動詞] 叫喊，大叫 *'Come back!' he yelled.* "回來！"他大聲叫道。

yellow¹ /'jeləʊ; 美 -oʊ/ [形容詞] 黃色的 *Alice picked some yellow flowers.* 艾麗斯摘了一些黃色的花。

yellow² /'jeləʊ; 美 -oʊ/ [名詞] 黃色 *Helen was dressed in yellow.* 海倫穿着黃色的衣服。

yes /jes/ [感歎詞] [用以表示肯定的回答] 是，是的 *'Are you ready?' 'Yes, I am.'* "你準備好了嗎？""是的，準備好了。" ⇨ [反] **no²** [用以表示否定的回答] 不，不是

yesterday¹ /'jestədi; 美 -ər-/ [副詞] 昨天 *It was very hot yesterday.* 昨天很熱。

yesterday² /'jestədi; 美 -ər-/ [名詞] 昨天 *Yesterday was Friday and* *tomorrow will be Sunday.* 昨天是星期五，明天是星期日。

yet /jet/ [副詞] **1** [用於否定句] 還 *Henry hasn't come yet.* 亨利還沒有來。 **2** [用於疑問句] 已經 *Has Henry come yet?* 亨利來了嗎？

yoghurt /ˈjɒgət; 美 ˈjougərt/ [又作 **yogurt**] [名詞] [無複數] 酸乳酪 *I usually have yoghurt for my breakfast.* 我早餐通常吃酸乳酪。

you / 強 juː; 弱 ju/ [代詞] [單數、複數、主格、賓格形式均同] 你；你們 *Can you swim?* 你會游泳嗎？ ◇ *Thank you for your help.* 謝謝你的幫助。

you'd / 強 juːd; 弱 jud/ **1 you had** 的縮寫 *I thought you'd finished your work.* 我以為你已經做完了作業。 **2 you would** 的縮寫 *You said you'd like this book.* 你說你喜歡這本書。

you'll / 強 juːl; 弱 jul/ **you will** 的縮

寫 *I hope you'll enjoy your trip.* 希望你旅途愉快。

young /jʌŋ/ [形容詞] [比較級 **younger** /ˈjʌŋgə; 美 -ər/，最高級 **youngest** /ˈjʌŋgɪst/] 年幼的；年輕的 *My brother is two years younger than me.* 我弟弟比我小兩歲。 ☞ [反] **old** 老的；年老的

your / 強 jɔː; 美 jʊr; 弱 jə; 美 jər/ [形容詞] [**you** 的所有格] 你的；你們的 *Have you finished your homework yet?* 你做完作業了嗎？

you're / 強 jɔː; 美 jʊr; 弱 jə; 美 jər/ **you are** 的縮寫 *You're late again!* 你又遲到了！

yours /jɔːz; 美 jʊrz/ [代詞] [**you** 的物主代詞] 你（們）的（東西） *Is this book yours?* 這本書是你的嗎？

yourself /jɔːˈself; 美 jʊr-/ [代詞] [**you** 的反身代詞] 你自己 *Look at yourself in the mirror.* 你照照鏡子。 ◇ *Why are you playing by yourself?* 你為甚麼獨自一個人玩？

you've / 強 juːv; 弱 juv/ **you have** 的縮寫 *You've forgotten your coat.* 你忘記拿外套了。

Z z

zebra /ˈzebrə; 美 ˈziː-/ [名詞] 斑馬 *Did you see a zebra at the zoo?* 你在動物園裏看見斑馬了嗎？

zero /ˈzɪərəu; 美 ˈzɪrou/ [名詞] [複數 **zeros** 或 **zeroes**] 零 *He counted backwards from ten to zero.* 他從 10 倒數到 0。

zigzag /ˈzɪgzæg/ [名詞] Z字形，之字形 *Peter walked in a zigzag.* 彼得 Z 字形地走路。

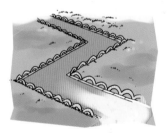

zip /zɪp/ [名詞] 拉鏈 *The zip on my pencil case has broken.* 我鉛筆盒上的拉鏈壞了。

zoo /zuː/ [名詞] 動物園 *We're going to the zoo tomorrow.* 我們明天去動物園。

Z

Appendices

附　錄

Appendix 1　附錄一

Numbers　數字

	cardinal numbers 基數			ordinal numbers 序數	
1	one	一	1st	first	第一
2	two	二	2nd	second	第二
3	three	三	3rd	third	第三
4	four	四	4th	fourth	第四
5	five	五	5th	fifth	第五
6	six	六	6th	sixth	第六
7	seven	七	7th	seventh	第七
8	eight	八	8th	eighth	第八
9	nine	九	9th	ninth	第九
10	ten	十	10th	tenth	第十
11	eleven	十一	11th	eleventh	第十一
12	twelve	十二	12th	twelfth	第十二
13	thirteen	十三	13th	thirteenth	第十三
14	fourteen	十四	14th	fourteenth	第十四
15	fifteen	十五	15th	fifteenth	第十五
16	sixteen	十六	16th	sixteenth	第十六
17	seventeen	十七	17th	seventeenth	第十七
18	eighteen	十八	18th	eighteenth	第十八
19	nineteen	十九	19th	nineteenth	第十九
20	twenty	二十	20th	twentieth	第二十
30	thirty	三十	30th	thirtieth	第三十
40	forty	四十	40th	fortieth	第四十
50	fifty	五十	50th	fiftieth	第五十
60	sixty	六十	60th	sixtieth	第六十
70	seventy	七十	70th	seventieth	第七十
80	eighty	八十	80th	eightieth	第八十
90	ninety	九十	90th	ninetieth	第九十
100	one hundred	一百	100th	hundredth	第一百
1,000	one thousand	一千	1,000th	thousandth	第一千
1,000,000	one million	一百萬	1,000,000th	millionth	第一百萬

Appendix 2　附錄二

Time　時間

What time is it?
What's the time?
現在幾點？

It's six.
六點。

It's half past six.
六點半。

It's five past six.
六點過五分。

It's a quarter past six.
六點過一刻。

It's five to six.
六點差五分。

It's a quarter to six.
六點差一刻。

Days of the week 星期

Monday 星期一
Tuesday 星期二
Wednesday 星期三
Thursday 星期四
Friday 星期五
Saturday 星期六
Sunday 星期日

What day is today? 今天是星期幾？
Today is Monday. 今天是星期一。

Months of the year 月份

January 一月	July 七月
February 二月	August 八月
March 三月	September 九月
April 四月	October 十月
May 五月	November 十一月
June 六月	December 十二月

What's the date today? 今天是幾號？
It's the first of June. 今天是 6 月 1 日。

Seasons 季節

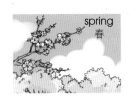

spring
春

summer
夏

autumn
秋

winter
冬

Appendix 3　附錄三

Common English names　常見英語人名

Men 男子名

Adam /'ædəm/ 亞當

Alan /'ælən/ 艾倫

Albert /'ælbət; 美 -ərt/ 艾伯特

Alex /'ælɪks/ 亞歷克斯(Alexander 的暱稱)

Alexander /ˌælɪg'zɑːndə; 美 -'zændər/
　亞歷山大

Alfred /'ælfrɪd/ 艾爾弗雷德

Andrew /'ændʒuː/ 安德魯

Anthony /'æntəni/ 安東尼

Ben /ben/ 本(Benjamin 的暱稱)

Benjamin /'bendʒəmɪn/ 本傑明

Bill /bɪl/ 比爾(William 的暱稱)

Bob /bɒb; 美 bɑːb/ 鮑勃(Robert 的暱稱)

Charles /tʃɑːlz; 美 tʃɑːrlz/ 查爾斯

Christopher /'krɪstəfə; 美 -ər/
　克里斯托弗

Daniel /'dænjəl/ 丹尼爾

David /'deɪvɪd/ 戴維

Dennis /'denɪs/ 丹尼斯

Edward /'edwəd; 美 -wərd/ 愛德華

Frank /fræŋk/ 弗蘭克

Fred /fred/ 弗雷德

Geoffrey /'dʒefri/ 傑弗里

George /dʒɔːdʒ; 美 dʒɔːrdʒ/ 喬治

Gilbert /'gɪlbət; 美 -ərt/ 吉爾伯特

Harry /'hæri/ 哈里

Henry /'henri/ 亨利

Ian /'iːən/ 伊恩

Jack /'dʒæk/ 傑克(John 的暱稱)

James /dʒeɪmz/ 詹姆斯

Jim /dʒɪm/ 吉姆(James 的暱稱)

Jimmy /'dʒɪmi/ 吉米(James 的暱稱)

Joe /dʒəʊ; 美 dʒoʊ/ 喬(Joseph 的暱稱)

John /dʒɒn; 美 dʒɑːn/ 約翰

Joseph /'dʒəʊzɪf; 美 'dʒoʊzəf/ 約瑟夫

Kevin /'kevɪn/ 凱文

Mark /mɑːk; 美 mɑːrk/ 馬克

Martin /'mɑːtɪn; 美 'mɑːrtn/ 馬丁

Matthew /'mæθjuː/ 馬修

Michael /'maɪkl/ 邁克爾

Mike /maɪk/ 邁克(Michael 的暱稱)

Patrick /'pætrɪk/ 帕特里克

Paul /pɔːl/ 保羅

Peter /'piːtə; 美 -ər/ 彼得

Philip /'fɪlɪp/ 菲利普

Richard /'rɪtʃəd; 美 -ərd/ 理查德

Robert /'rɒbət; 美 'rɑːbərt/ 羅伯特

Robin /'rɒbɪn; 美 'rɑːbən/ 羅賓

Sam /sæm/ 薩姆(Samuel 的暱稱)

Samuel /'sæmjuəl/ 塞繆爾

Simon /'saɪmən/ 西蒙

Thomas /'tɒməs; 美 'tɑːməs/ 托馬斯

Tom /tɒm; 美 tɑːm/ 湯姆(Thomas 的暱稱)

William /'wɪljəm/ 威廉

Women 女子名

Alice /'ælɪs/ 艾麗斯

Alison /'ælɪsən/ 艾莉森

Amanda /ə'mændə/ 阿曼達

Amy /'eɪmi/ 埃米

Ann /æn/ 安

Bridget /'brɪdʒɪt/ 布麗奇特

Carol /'kærəl/ 卡羅爾

Caroline /'kærəlaɪn/ 卡羅琳

Catherine /'kæθərɪn/ 凱瑟琳

Clare /kleə; 美 kler/ 克萊爾

Deborah /'debərə/ 德博拉

Diana /daɪˈænə/ 黛安娜

Elizabeth /ɪˈlɪzəbəθ/ 伊麗莎白

Emily /ˈeməli/ 埃米莉

Emma /ˈemə/ 埃瑪

Helen /ˈhelən/ 海倫

Jane /dʒeɪn/ 簡

Jennifer /ˈdʒenɪfə; 美 -ər/ 珍妮弗

Jenny /ˈdʒeni/ 珍妮（Jennifer 的暱稱）

Joanne /dʒəʊˈæn; 美 dʒoʊ-/ 喬安妮

Julie /ˈdʒuːli/ 朱莉

Karen /ˈkærən/ 卡倫

Laura /ˈlɔːrə/ 勞拉

Linda /ˈlɪndə/ 琳達

Lucy /ˈluːsi/ 露西

Maggie /ˈmægi/ 瑪吉（Margaret 的暱稱）

Margaret /ˈmɑːgrət; 美 ˈmɑːrg-/ 瑪格麗特

Mary /ˈmeəri; 美 ˈmeri/ 瑪麗

Ruth /ruːθ/ 露絲

Sally /ˈsæli/ 薩莉（Sarah 的暱稱）

Sarah /ˈseərə; 美 ˈserə/ 薩拉

Sophie /ˈsəʊfi; 美 ˈsoʊfi/ 索菲

Sue /suː/ 蘇（Susan 的暱稱）

Susan /ˈsuːzn/ 蘇珊

Tracy /ˈtreɪsi/ 特蕾西

Victoria /vɪkˈtɔːriə/ 維多利亞

Virginia /vəˈdʒɪniə; 美 vərˈdʒɪnjə/
　弗吉尼亞

Wendy /ˈwendi/ 溫迪

Appendix 4　附錄四

Irregular verbs　不規則動詞

infinitive 不定式	present participle 現在分詞	past tense 過去式	past participle 過去分詞
be	being	was/were	been
beat	beating	beat	beaten
become	becoming	became	become
begin	beginning	began	begun
bend	bending	bent	bent
bite	biting	bit	bitten
bleed	bleeding	bled	bled
blow	blowing	blew	blown
break	breaking	broke	broken
bring	bringing	brought	brought
build	building	built	built
burn	burning	burnt 或 burned	burnt 或 burned
burst	bursting	burst	burst
buy	buying	bought	bought
catch	catching	caught	caught
choose	choosing	chose	chosen
come	coming	came	come
cost	costing	cost	cost
creep	creeping	crept	crept
cut	cutting	cut	cut
die	dying	died	died
dig	digging	dug	dug
do	doing	did	done
draw	drawing	drew	drawn
dream	dreaming	dreamt 或 dreamed	dreamt 或 dreamed
drink	drinking	drank	drunk
drive	driving	drove	driven
eat	eating	ate	eaten
fall	falling	fell	fallen
feed	feeding	fed	fed

infinitive 不 定 式	present participle 現 在 分 詞	past tense 過 去 式	past participle 過 去 分 詞
feel	feeling	felt	felt
fight	fighting	fought	fought
find	finding	found	found
fly	flying	flew	flown
forget	forgetting	forgot	forgotten
forgive	forgiving	forgave	forgiven
freeze	freezing	froze	frozen
get	getting	got	got
give	giving	gave	given.
go	going	went	gone
grow	growing	grew	grown
hang	hanging	hung	hung
have	having	had	had
hear	hearing	heard	heard
hide	hiding	hid	hidden
hit	hitting	hit	hit
hold	holding	held	held
hurt	hurting	hurt	hurt
keep	keeping	kept	kept
kneel	kneeling	knelt 或 kneeled	knelt 或 kneeled
know	knowing	knew	known
lay	laying	laid	laid
lead	leading	ted	led
lean	leaning	leant 或 leaned	leant 或 leaned
learn	learning	learnt 或 loarnod	learnt 或 learned
leave	leaving	left	left
lend	lending	lent	lent
let	letting	let	let
lie	lying	lay	lain
light	lighting	lit 或 lighted	lit 或 lighted
lose	losing	lost	lost

infinitive 不定式	present participle 現在分詞	past tense 過去式	past participle 過去分詞
make	making	made	made
mean	meaning	meant	meant
meet	meeting	met	met
overtake	overtaking	overtook	overtaken
pay	paying	paid	paid
put	putting	put	put
read	reading	read	read
ride	riding	rode	ridden
ring	ringing	rang	rung
rise	rising	rose	risen
run	running	ran	run
say	saying	said	said
see	seeing	saw	seen
sell	selling	sold	sold
send	sending	sent	sent
set	setting	set	set
sew	sewing	sewed	sewn 或 sewed
shake	shaking	shook	shaken
shine	shining	shone	shone
shoot	shooting	shot	shot
show	showing	showed	shown 或 showed
shrink	shrinking	shrank 或 shrunk	shrunk
shut	shutting	shut	shut
sing	singing	sang	sung
sink	sinking	sank	sunk
sit	sitting	sat	sat
sleep	sleeping	slept	slept
slide	sliding	slid	slid
smell	smelling	smelt 或 smelled	smelt 或 smelled
sow	sowing	sowed	sown 或 sowed
speak	speaking	spoke	spoken

infinitive 不定式	present participle 現在分詞	past tense 過去式	past participle 過去分詞
spell	spelling	spelt 或 spelled	spelt 或 spelled
spend	spending	spent	spent
spill	spilling	spilt 或 spilled	spilt 或 spilled
spin	spinning	spun	spun
split	splitting	split	split
spoil	spoiling	spoilt 或 spoiled	spoilt 或 spoiled
spring	springing	sprang	sprung
stand	standing	stood	stood
steal	stealing	stole	stolen
stick	sticking	stuck	stuck
sting	stinging	stung	stung
stink	stinking	stank 或 stunk	stunk
strike	striking	struck	struck
sweep	sweeping	swept	swept
swim	swimming	swam	swum
swing	swinging	swung	swung
take	taking	took	taken
teach	teaching	taught	taught
tear	tearing	tore	torn
tell	telling	told	told
think	thinking	thought	thought
throw	throwing	threw	thrown
understand	understanding	understood	understood
undo	undoing	undid	undone
wake	waking	woke	woken
wear	wearing	wore	worn
win	winning	won	won
wind	winding	wound	wound
write	writing	wrote	written

English alphabet and phonics　英語字母表及讀音法

Aa　　　　**B**b　　　　**C**c　　　　**D**d

cake　　　banana　　　cat　　　　dog
蛋糕　　　香蕉　　　　貓　　　　狗

Jj　　　　**K**k　　　　**L**l　　　　**M**m

jacket　　　kite　　　　lion　　　monkey
夾克　　　風箏　　　　獅子　　　猴子

Ss　　　　**T**t　　　　**U**u　　　　**V**v

sun　　　　tiger　　　uniform　　violin
太陽　　　老虎　　　制服　　　小提琴

E e   F f   G g   H h   I i

elephant
大象

flower
花

goose
鵝

horse
馬

ice cream
冰淇淋

N n   O o   P p   Q q   R r

nest
鳥巢

notebook
筆記本

pig
豬

quilt
被子

rabbit
兔子

W w   X x   Y y   Z z

watch
手錶

X-ray
X 光片

yoghurt
酸乳酪

zebra
斑馬